The Forgotten Daughter

Mary Wood was born in Maidstone, Kent, and brought up in Claybrooke, Leicestershire. Born one of fifteen children to a middle-class mother and an East End barrow boy, Mary's family were poor but rich in love. This encouraged her to develop a natural empathy with the less fortunate and a fascination with social history. In 1989 Mary was inspired to pen her first novel and she is now a full-time novelist.

Mary welcomes interaction with readers and invites you to subscribe to her website where you can contact her, receive regular newsletters and follow links to meet her on Facebook and Twitter: www.authormarywood.com

The Forgotten Daughter

Mary Wood

First published 2018 by Pan Books
an imprint of Pan Macmillan
20 New Wharf Road, London N1 9RR
Associated companies throughout the world
www.panmacmillan.com

ISBN 978-1-5098-5052-5

1 3 5 7 9 8 6 4 2

A CIP catalogue record for this book is available from the British Library.

Typeset in ITC Galliard Std by Palimpsest Book Production Ltd, Falkirk, Stirlingshire
Printed and bound by CPI Group (UK) Ltd, Croydon, CR0 4YY

In memory of two special ladies in my life: my niece Eileen Rigley and my long-term friend, Eve Wheatley. You both provided me with wonderful support, and your love enriched my life. Always in my heart. Never forgotten. Loved and cherished.

PART ONE
London, 1899–14

~

Flora and Pru

An Unwanted Child

Chapter One

A noise woke Flora from her sleep and she sat up and listened. Through the connecting door linking her room and her nanny's she heard giggling and voices, and a sound she knew well – a loud squeaking, which she loved to hear when she played one of her favourite games of jumping as high as she could on Nanny Pru's squidgy old bed.

'Naw, you mustn't.'

'Shush, Pru, just relax . . .'

Daddy? Why would Daddy be in Nanny Pru's bedroom? Flora crept out of bed towards the door.

The man's voice came again, louder this time. 'You're beautiful, Pru.'

It is Daddy! Fear shuddered through Flora, splintering the safe world that Nanny provided for her, and plunging her into the terror of what her mummy would do, if she found out that Daddy was in Nanny Pru's bedroom. Was Daddy hurting Nanny?

Nanny was saying his name over and over again, and she didn't sound cross. She was making moaning noises and was giggling.

The cold of the linoleum beneath Flora's small feet seeped into her, chilling her body. The warmth of her bed called to her, but climbing back in wasn't as easy as slipping out had been. She caught her already-bruised ribs on the iron bedstead and let out a pain-filled cry.

The noises from the next room stopped for a moment.

'Oh God, we've woken her!'

'She'll be all right. Don't stop me now, Pru, don't—'

Flora covered her ears at the sound of her daddy's gasping moan. Her stomach churned. She was going to be sick . . . Choking on her vomit, she registered the connecting door opening. The flicker of candlelight danced on her walls.

'Eeh, Flora, lass, what's to do? It's alreet – Nanny's here.'

There was something different about Nanny Pru. In the candlelight, her face shone. Beads of sweat glistened on her forehead and arms, and her hair clung to her head in damp, tight curls.

Feeling unsure and ill at ease, Flora cowered away. The nanny she loved had turned into a monster. A wicked monster, of the kind her mummy said would one day find her and eat her up. A scream rasped her throat, as terror gripped her. Kicking out, she tried to ward off the monster. 'Don't eat me . . . Nooo!'

'No, no, my child.' Her daddy's voice came to her. Soft, loving. 'There, there now. Everything's all right.'

The sound of her father's voice made Flora feel safe once more. She calmed and opened her eyes; the monster had gone, and Nanny Pru was back.

Daddy stood up from where he'd been sitting on her bed and tied his dressing gown. 'Nanny will take care of you – no need to worry. And no need to tell Mummy anything, eh? Promise Daddy?'

Flora nodded her head.

'Eeh, me little lass, I'm sorry I scared you.'

Nanny grabbed the towel off the washstand next to the bed and gently wiped Flora's mouth with it, before placing it over the nasty-smelling vomit. With this done, she held Flora and stroked her hair.

'Look, while we're here, George, I reckon as you should see sommat.'

Hearing Nanny call her daddy by his name made everything feel right again. It put together the nice worlds Flora shared with each of them. Unlike when she was with her mummy, because then she felt fear and knew Mummy didn't love her. But shyness came over Flora as Nanny went to lift her nightdress, and she tried to resist.

'Come on, Flora, let Nanny show your daddy. I should have told him what you go through, but I thought as it would make things worse for you with your mummy. I've tried to protect you, me little lass, but your daddy should knaw what goes on.'

'Good God! You mean? No. Her own mother? I'll—'

'You'll what?'

Flora cringed and clung on to Nanny as fear knotted her tummy. Mummy stood in the doorway, her beautiful face screwed up into an evil expression, her voice shaking with anger.

'Inflict another brat on me, as you beg my forgiveness for being unfaithful again?'

Her daddy's fury compounded Flora's fear. 'You wicked woman. How could you take your jealous hatred and spite out on our child?'

'You are to blame! You're to blame for it all. The affair you had . . . It – it kills me every day. Over and over I suffer that agony, and now you go to this lowlife northern slut – and in my own home – while I sleep in our bed. You are my husband, remember.' Her voice rose. 'Am I expected to put up with this? You creeping from my bed to go to the paid hand! You're disgusting.'

Daddy ushered Mummy out of the room. Nanny Pru stood staring after them, before slumping down onto the bed. 'I'm sorry, me little lass. I'm so sorry.' A tear plopped onto her face, and Flora's world became unsafe once more.

'Nanny, w – will Daddy hurt Mummy?'

'No, don't worry. Eeh, lass, let's get you cleaned up and off to sleep. You're not to blame for any of this. It's unfair what you go through – and you only a wee bairn. Me heart aches for you, and now I'll more than likely have to leave you. I won't want to, Flora – I loves the heart of you – but I've done a bad thing, so I won't be given a choice.'

'But Daddy loves you, Nanny Pru. He'll take care of you and let you stay.'

'Eeh, little one, it don't work like that. Though I were daft enough to think it did.'

Flora put her arms around Nanny Pru; she loved snuggling into her soft, rounded, squidgy body, and she loved her pretty round face, her blue eyes and the two dimples that appeared when she smiled. 'Don't cry, Nanny Pru, I'll come with you, and then Daddy can visit us. I don't want to stay here.'

'That's not possible, lass.' Nanny Pru's tear-filled eyes looked into Flora's own. Once more her hand stroked Flora's hair. 'Eeh, you're a bonny child. You have your mummy's beauty and her silky brown hair, and your daddy's big brown eyes, with that same twinkle in them that melts hearts. But you're not like your mummy; she's vindictive and she has a temper. Nor are you like your daddy, who breaks hearts. And, naw, he doesn't love me – only what he can get from me. And it sounds as though I'm not the first, either. I reckon as he's broken your mummy's heart, which is probably why she's like she is.'

None of this made any sense to Flora. 'How do you break a heart, Nanny? I have a pain in mine when Mummy is cross with me, but I don't think it breaks. Will Daddy break it?'

'Naw, I reckon as your daddy will allus protect you. Now, let's get you settled. I need a good wash meself an' all. I'll see to you first, then I'll get meself sorted. And then, if you're still not settled, I'll lie with you. How does that sound?'

'I feel safe when you lie with me.'

But despite her words, Flora didn't feel safe. Even after her bath, when Nanny put her back into her clean bed, which had been warmed with a bedpan, she didn't feel safe. And as she waited for Nanny to come and lie with her, she wondered if Nanny would ever do so again, because she had said she was leaving; and her daddy now seemed a different person from the daddy she'd always known.

He was someone who broke hearts, and who hurt Mummy by going to Nanny Pru's room and making her giggle. And Mummy had said he'd done these things before. And Flora was sure he'd hurt Nanny Pru, too.

A few days later Flora stood outside the door of the drawing room, the only room in their lovely big house in London's Cromwell Road that she didn't like. Dimly lit and furnished in ruby-reds with a dark-blue carpet, it always smelt musty, and of stale smoke from Daddy's cigar. Mummy spent most of her time in this room, with the curtains half-closed and all the windows shut. She complained of having a headache, and often had traces of tears on her cheeks and red, swollen eyes.

Flora was glad that the room was out of bounds and that she was only allowed in there with Nanny each evening to say goodnight to her parents – a time she always dreaded. If Daddy was there, she would get a cold peck on the cheek from her mummy and some critical remark. Daddy would give her a quick hug, almost as if he was saying sorry, rather than it being a loving gesture. But it was when Daddy was out that Flora most dreaded the nightly ritual. Then Mummy would dismiss Nanny and, within minutes, would become very angry. Her words – like those spoken the night Daddy had visited Nanny – didn't make sense, but Flora felt she was somehow being blamed for something bad in Daddy.

Mummy's slaps would sting her face and legs, but none of that hurt as much as when Mummy had flung her across the room, screaming that everything bad had been marked by Flora's birth – all the deceit and the lies. 'He thought he could wipe it all out by coming to me, but I was a fool to let him. And *you* were the result. YOU! I couldn't have been saddled with a more vile apology than you!'

Her painful grip on Flora's arm had increased and Mummy had lifted her into the air, almost wrenching her arm from its socket, before throwing her as if she was nothing more than a bag of rubbish. She'd come crashing down onto the small table next to Mummy's chair. Her breath had left her body, and pain had seared through her. When she'd been able to draw air into her lungs, her scream had brought Nanny rushing back through the door and yelling at Mummy, 'What have you done? By God, she's just a wee bairn.'

Mummy had sat back down in her chair. Her expression had made the feeling shudder through Flora that everything in her world had changed. Mummy had spoken as if dismissing her daughter forever. 'Take her out of my sight!'

Since then she'd not been taken to say goodnight to Mummy. And now something of what Nanny had said, about being parted from Nanny, began to take on true meaning as her parents' voices came to her. And the knowledge that she was unwanted and unloved ground a pain into her heart so deep that she was sure it was breaking.

'Flora is so unruly, George. We have to do something. Why she can't be like Harold and Francis, I don't know. That incident in church this morning – I have never been so embarrassed!'

Her father's reply shocked Flora, for he wasn't cross with Mummy. Not like he usually was, if Mummy complained about her. 'My dear, surely something must have caused her to cry out like that, during the sanctifying of the bread?'

'Oh, she probably saw a spider or something; she has no control. She cannot even keep quiet when it is important to do so. It was humiliating in the extreme. She has to go to that boarding school I told you about. I can't cope with her any longer.'

Indignation got Flora standing to her full height. *No, that's not fair.* Harold, her older brother by three years, had been teasing her all morning and then, when the whole congregation was meant to fall silent, he'd pulled one of her plaits so hard that she couldn't help squealing. Mummy had seen it happen and had smiled. *Why is she not saying so?* Flora waited for Daddy to refuse to send her away, but once more his voice held a soothing quality, and what he said caused a tear to plop onto Flora's cheek.

'But to send her away to school is a bit drastic. She's so young. Maybe if she goes to my sister's for six months? I'll pay half the tuition fees they are already paying for their son. That will be a big incentive to them to say yes, as they are struggling as it is.'

'No, I want Flora somewhere that she has to stay – and the sooner, the better. If she plays up with your sister in the way she does with me, then she will soon be sent back here. That won't do. I want to know that won't happen. A school will cope better with her.'

'That's a terrible thing to say. She's our daughter! Our own little girl. Why are—'

'She's your conscience-soother, you mean.'

'Grace!'

'Don't deny it. When I found out about your long-running affair, and your bastard son, born before our own sons, I wanted a divorce. But no, you got round me. You said it was over and would never happen again. I allowed you back into my bed, but I caught you out once more. Flora reminds me of that, every time I look at her. She is a lie – your lie, something you thought would make me believe you!'

Daddy didn't reply. Flora was shocked. Somehow she'd wronged Mummy, but she couldn't understand how.

'We will never be happy again, with Flora around. Besides, we have to do something to tame her, or God knows how she will turn out. I'm not going to be budged on this, George. You don't have to put up with her as much as I do. If you didn't work such long hours, you would see more of your children and would know what a devil Flora is!'

Her father's voice rose. 'Don't start that again, Grace. It takes a lot of work to run the haberdashery shops and, what with having half the responsibility for the Roford mill in Blackburn, since my father died, I'm very busy. I can't avoid being away from home. Besides which, the opening of our tenth shop is taking all my time.'

'Oh? So, where were you when I called into the new shop the other evening?'

Flora's tummy tensed. Daddy was losing this argument with Mummy, and that meant they would send her away for certain.

'I – I didn't know you called. You didn't mention that you would. Was it Thursday? I – I was probably in a meeting. Yes, that was it, I had a meeting with a supplier.'

'At five in the evening? I thought I would surprise you and that we could go out to dinner, but no doubt you had someone else you preferred to go to dinner with.'

Her father's sigh was audible. 'I told you, Grace, that is over. I—'

'Oh? *That* may be over, but you soon crept into another's bed. Thursday was that slut Nanny's day off!'

'Grace, please . . . I – I didn't meet her. I told you, she made a play for me. I know I'm weak. I admit it. I need you. I need you to get strong again and to have me back. I can't lie on one side of the bed while you lie on the other. I have needs, Grace. These others are a substitute, but a very poor one. With you strong and well, darling, and taking care of me, I would never stray. You've always used our relationship as a bargaining tool. You're doing it now. Refusing me last night, because you had something you needed me to agree to first – asking me to send away my own daughter – is cruel! You're cruel, Grace, cruel!'

11

Mummy's sobs hurt Flora. She wanted to burst in and tell Mummy that she loved her and would be a good girl from now on. But most of all she wanted Daddy to say no to sending her away to school. She held her breath.

'Look, darling, we can compromise. Don't cry. I do love you. If we send Flora away to school, it must be to one that is musically inclined. Flora shows the talent that I was denied.'

'Talent! My God, her incessant banging on the piano drives me insane.'

Flora's pain deepened. Even her music – her wonderful music that she made up herself – didn't make Mummy happy, when Flora so wanted it to.

'What are you up to, Flora? Listening means you'll hear no good of yourself. Hey, are you crying?' Francis, her brother, made her jump as he came up behind her.

'Mummy wants to send me away.'

'What? No, she won't, she's just angry at you for that noise you made.'

He pulled a face and made her smile. Older than her by two years, Francis always saw the funny side of life. He never seemed to care about anything.

'Come on, I've built a fort in the garden. You can be the soldiers, and I'll be the Red Indians attacking you. You can name one of yours Harold and let me hit him with an arrow, to get your own back for him pulling your hair.'

A sound came from within Flora that wasn't a sob, and yet wasn't a laugh. It echoed around the vast hallway.

Mummy's voice rose in triumph. 'There, see what I mean!'

Francis took Flora's hand and pulled her away. 'Come on. The parents are having a row, that's all. Nothing new about that. Mummy's cross with you, but she'll calm down.'

Wanting to believe this, Flora latched on to the way Francis saw everything, and ran off with him. Excitement at the prospect of the game ahead saw her wiping her eyes as the anguish left her. Everything would be all right. Daddy would make it so.

Chapter Two

Resting her head in her hands, Pru felt her stomach rumbling. The cries from her young son, Freddy, born just nine months after she left the Rofords' employ and now fourteen months old, tore at her heart.

The front door, leading straight into the combined kitchen and sitting room of her one-up, one-down terraced house in Stepney, opened. The stench of the many piddle-pots that had been emptied into the gutter outside mingled with the smell of the smoked-salmon factory and brought bile to her throat. She could never understand why people were too lazy to empty their pots into the shared lav in the yard.

'I've brought you the remains of our dinner, Prudence. I – I hope you don't mind.'

Pru looked into the lovely face of Rifka, whose straight coal-black hair framed her face. Her smile spoke of the kindness she'd once told Pru that her namesake in the Bible – the mother of Jacob – was known for.

A lot of the folk who lived in these parts were Jews, but Pru's near-neighbours were immigrants of various origins, and it was some of these, although lovely gentle people, who had the filthy habits that caused the constant stench of the street.

'It's a chickpea stew, and I've brought you a challah loaf, too. I made it myself.'

Tears pricked Pru's eyes. 'Thank you' was all she could manage to say.

'Let me help you. I'll lay the table while you heat the stew.'

'Eeh, I wish I could, lass, but I have nothing to light the stove with.'

'Oh, Pru, I'm sorry. I – I see that you have your house up for sale. Are things that bad?'

'Aye, they are, lass. All me money's gone, and I can't get a job, as I've no one to look after Freddy. And me Parish Relief is a pittance. They say I don't qualify for more, with me owning me own house. So I have no choice but to sell it.'

She looked around the room. Nothing about it reflected her poverty. George Roford had paid her off with a generous sum, which would have bought her a much better house in a different area, but she'd purchased this small terraced house and had furnished it like a palace, and had kept the rest of the money for a rainy day. That day had soon come, when she'd discovered that she was pregnant with George's child. Unable to earn enough to keep herself, let alone a child, she'd been too proud to tell him, so she'd lived on the residue of the money, hoping that it would last until her child went to school and she could go out to work.

'Will you go back to the North?'

'Naw. I only had me dad up there. No other relatives that I know of. He was of Irish descent and was always looking

15

to better himself. He worked as a clerk and brought me down to London, where he'd secured a job. I were only twelve. He died a couple of years after we arrived, and I worked as a nanny from the age of fourteen.' The lie that Pru had so often spoken now rolled off her tongue: 'I were married young, but me husband was killed in an accident, just afore I knew as I were pregnant. I bought this house out of the insurance payment and lived on what was left, but that's all gone . . . Look, I were wondering, do you reckon your mam would buy a few of me pieces of furniture? I'll be sad to see them go, but selling a few pieces is all I can do for now.'

'You could marry again, Pru. You're still young and you've a pretty face, and men would go for that figure of yours. I'm surprised you haven't had offers. My brother's always saying that if you were Jewish, he'd marry you tomorrow.'

Pru smiled, but the smile hid the aching knowledge that what Rifka said was true. Men did want her, but only for one thing. And aye, Rifka's brother, Abe, was one of them. He didn't care that she wasn't Jewish when he came knocking, declaring his love and his intention to take care of her, if she played ball. But Pru had vowed she'd never allow a man to treat her like that again – she'd travelled that road once, and look where it had got her.

Abe's and Rifka's father owned the successful cobbler's at the end of the street, and they lived around the corner in one of the large semi-detached three-storey houses. But Pru had long known that Abe had his fingers in other pies. He was never short of money, and had far more than his family could provide him with. Often he would beg Pru to go for a ride with him into the country in his red car. But Pru knew better than to put herself in such a compromising position.

But she didn't voice all this in her answer. 'I'm not much of a catch, having a young 'un, Rifka. I'll be reet, once me house sells. There's plenty of immigrants looking for these properties – not to mention landlords.'

'I'll miss you, Prudence, and I'm sorry for your plight. I'll pop back home and get our Eilam to bring you a barrowful of wood and coal from our shed.'

'Naw, you mustn't do that. We can eat the stew cold.'

Without heeding this, Rifka left.

Breaking a noggin off the delicious-looking plaited loaf, Pru lifted Freddy and gave it to him. His crying had stopped when Rifka entered, but his face showed signs of his snot being wiped with his tears on the back of his hand.

Taking Freddy to the sink, Pru wet the corner of her pinny and, ignoring his loud protests, cleaned him up, before holding him close. 'Eat your bread, me little lad. Things'll get better. I promise.'

Freddy had just gone off to sleep when a loud banging on her door made Pru jump. 'Eeh, there's no need to break me door down . . .' About to say 'Eilam', Pru was stopped in her tracks by the sight of a postman standing there with a letter. Only bills ever arrived on her doorstep, never letters.

Eilam followed close on the postman's heels. 'Where do you want this, Pru? Oh, and me ma said to tell you that she's not a charity, so don't expect this again. It was our Rifka that persuaded her. Now she's been sent to her room, for promising you stuff. Ma says she wants her dish back as well, and that our Rifka had no right bringing the leftovers to you, as she could have made a pie with them for tomorrow. Oh, and your offer of some of your bits for sale: Ma said you can send her something now, as payment for the stew and the fuel.'

'Eeh, lad, get in off the street and keep your voice down. I'd send you back with this and not accept it, but I'm desperate, for me lad's sake. Tell your mam I'm sorry, and give me love to Rifka and tell her that I'll understand if she don't want to visit again. Now, fill the coal-scuttle with the coal, and lay the logs on the hearth.'

Looking around, Pru's eyes rested on the nursing chair. She loved that chair and had had good use out of it, when seeing to Freddy, but it was a fine piece, intricately carved, and might attract Mrs Manning to want to buy more of her furniture.

'Here, load this on your barrow for your mam, there's a good lad. And if I had a penny, I'd give it to thee.'

'That don't matter. Look, I'll tell you what: when my parents are out, I'll bring you something, if Rifka can't. We'll work together, as we're sorry for your plight, Missus.'

Shutting the door on Eilam, Pru smiled. Then she shook her head at how many different personalities there were in the Manning family. From Abe to his mother, to Rifka and Eilam and even their father, they were all different in nature, although Eilam, a cheeky minx who would throw a stone at you if you weren't looking, showed signs of developing Rifka's kind nature.

It was an hour later, with the fire banked down with slack to keep it burning longer, that Pru sat down and took the letter out of the pocket in her pinny. Her curiosity rose, as she didn't recognize the writing on the envelope. Then her heart lifted with hope as she looked at the childlike scrawl of the letter inside. Flora? Oh, let it be from Flora!

Pru had written many times to Flora at the school she had accompanied her to, but had never received an answer.

Dear Nanny Pru,

Thank you for your letters. I love receiving them. I haven't been allowed to reply, as I am only allowed to write letters to Mummy and Daddy. But today my friend, Millicent, and I have been given extra free time for being good.

Millicent is my best friend. She is three years older than me. She is a monitor and it is her job to look after the new starters. She looked after me when I arrived, and still does, even though she doesn't have to any longer. She knows all about you, and how you cared for me because Mummy doesn't love me. She is very clever. She plays the violin, and we write music and musical plays together.

I hope you can understand my letter. Now that I'm seven, I am learning joined-up writing . . .

'Eeh, lass, I knaw, I knaw . . .'

And I have started to learn languages too, as Daddy said I must. If I become a famous pianist, I will have to travel to concerts all over Europe. I love these lessons, and my tutor says I am a very good learner. Then he said that I might be a ling-something, only I can't spell it. I like French best, it sounds nicer than German does . . .

Millicent doesn't board, so she sneaked this paper in for me and, as she can mimic her mummy's writing, as she did on the envelope of this letter, she is going to take

19

it and put it in the pile of letters that are always waiting to be posted at her home. I hope you receive it, and we are not found out.

I so want to see you, Nanny Pru. I miss you very much. And now Millicent has an idea. She says that she can write to my daddy, using her mother's writing paper and in her mother's handwriting, and will ask if I can stay for one week of my holiday. She says her parents are going away for a few weeks, and she will be at home with her nanny and the servants, so she can go to her daddy's office in the evening and check the post, and pick out Daddy's reply and let me know what he says. I have given her one of Daddy's letters so that she knows the handwriting. If the answer is yes, then I can come to stay with you, and no one will know. Don't you think that Millicent is so clever to come up with this plan?

I am to go to Aunt Amelia's, from when I break up on 17th July until 4th August, when I can go home for a week and then back to Aunt Amelia's until I return to school. Daddy says that Mummy will be away the week I am home. This means that she still doesn't love me, Nanny Pru. So please say yes, please, please, Nanny Pru.

If you do, you will need to pick me up on the 17th, and then help me get to Aunt Amelia's a week later. Please, Nanny Pru.

If I can't write again, Millicent will write to you and make the arrangements with you.

I love you, Nanny Pru. Please write soon.

Yours, Flora x

The tears, which Pru had stemmed, flowed freely. How could she bring the child here? Even if she could afford to fetch Flora, and keep her and deliver her to her aunt's? It was impossible. *Oh, but I so want to. Eeh, me poor Flora, unloved and looked upon as a reminder of her father's sins.*

Freddy stirred at that moment. Pru lifted him. 'By, lad, you're a reminder of that same man's sins, but I love you, and allus will. We'll find a way – we will. There's two months afore Flora would come to visit. I'll sort sommat by then. I'll tell her "yes", shall I? You'd like that, wouldn't you? You'd like to meet your half-sister.'

Freddy gurgled, then stretched his hand out towards the stew.

'Aye, lad. There's enough there for three days for thee, and with the bread an' all, you'll be reet.'

Her own stomach churned in protest at this, but she ignored it. She could manage on water. In three days' time the Parish Relief would give her another handout and she would spend it on a sack of tatties and a few bones from the butcher, and that would keep them going for a while.

Freddy was sleeping soundly when, later that night, the one candle Pru had left fluttered and died, casting her into darkness. Dare she light the gas mantle? She knew there was just enough in the meter to sustain it for a while, but what if Freddy woke in the night? He'd be terrified if she couldn't illuminate the room.

The flicker of a flame in the grate penetrated the blackness and gave some comfort. Putting down her copy of *Little Women*, a book she'd read over and over again but never tired of, she felt the loss of the only thing that could transport her to a world where she didn't feel the pain of her

21

loneliness and hunger. At least, in reading the book, she hadn't got to the part where Beth dies. That would have opened a floodgate that she'd never be able to stop.

Her mantel clock struck the hour of nine. Sighing, Pru stood up. *Best go to bed and try to sleep; the morning will bring its own troubles.* Tomorrow she would go to the second-hand shop and ask Mr Gorth, the owner, to come and look at her bits and pieces and give her a price. She'd laid them all out earlier. A washbasin and jug, made of bone china and beautifully painted with a paisley blue-and-white pattern. A pile of pristine white, hand-embroidered antimacassars, and a tray and some tablecloths. Her good thick winter curtains, which were made of velvet and a deep blue. She'd only recently taken them down and laundered them, replacing them with her summer yellow cotton curtains. Then there was a vase. It, too, was bone china. Pru loved the willow pattern adorning it, showing scenes from China. *Why did I buy such expensive things? Eeh, lass, you got too far above your station.* George had done that to her. His declaration of love for her – his need of her – had made her think she was as good as the next person.

Pru decided not to go down that road of thought. She'd been a fool, and now she was paying for it. She'd have to get on with things as they were. There was no going back.

As she felt her way towards the front door, she thought she'd step outside for a moment, see if there was anyone to chat to. She'd put up with the smell, if she could have a bit of company. Rowena often sat on her step till late at night, singing soul-songs from her homeland of Jamaica and occasionally laughing out loud in an infectious way. She always cheered Pru.

But tonight the street was silent. The rain of an hour ago

had washed the gutters free of the stench, leaving fresh air for Pru to breathe in deeply. She leaned against the wall and closed her eyes.

But the silence was broken by the sound of a car, and her heart beat faster. Abe's advances had become more frequent; he was getting impatient and more forceful. Despite everything, he had woken in her a longing for what George had given her – feelings that often visited Pru and begged for release.

She went back inside, but as she went to turn the key in the lock, her feelings burned with an intensity she couldn't deny. When she heard a knock at her door, she couldn't help herself, but let Abe in.

His large frame filled the doorway, blocking the small amount of light coming in from the street. His voice held a husky note as he enquired as to why she was in the dark. Her explanation saw him handing her some coins. 'Feed the meter and get some lights on, girl. I want to see you.'

Her body trembled as she did as Abe bid. Fear now replaced the longings she'd felt. *Don't let him try owt, please!*

Light flooded the room as the gas mantle jumped into life. Abe stood behind her. As she turned, he pulled her towards him. His need was there, pressing against her. She could hardly breathe.

'You know what I've come for. Oh, Pru . . . Pru . . .' His hand kneaded her breast. His dark eyes smouldered in his swarthy, handsome face, and his thick lips invited her.

'Abe, no. No. Don't, I – I can't.'

'There is no "can't". Not now, Pru. You know you want it. I love you, Pru. I want you. I *must* have you. I'll take care of you, Pru, I promise. There'll be no kid – I'll not make you pregnant. And there'll be no more poverty.'

'If you loved me, you would take me out of poverty without the blackmail of me having to lie with you, to pay for it. I'm not a prostitute.'

'But I can't marry you, Pru; you've said in the past that you won't convert, so that's not possible. I can't just hand out money and gifts to you – I need something in return. I have to have you, Pru. You love me, Pru, you know you do. Say it, darling; say it.'

For her sins, Pru knew she did feel a strong attraction to Abe, and submitting to him would mean the end of all she had to put up with; but it also disgusted her that she had to, and that she had once before fallen for such patter. She was better than that. Pulling away from him, the word 'No!' spat from her. 'How can I love you, when you haven't an ounce of respect for me? You want to buy me, not love me. Well, I ain't for sale!'

Abe's face changed. Pru's fear intensified. His slap sent her reeling. 'So, you want to do this the hard way, eh?'

The Abe she had suspected to exist came to the fore and showed his true colours as she stared at him, towering over her, undoing his flies. Swallowing the scream that rose to her throat, for fear of waking Freddy, Pru kicked out. Her foot caught Abe's shin. He doubled over in pain. She scrambled to her feet and ran for the door, but he was too fast for her. His large hands caught her cardigan. Her body was catapulted back into his.

A sense of hopelessness drowned her spirit, as her clothes were torn from her and she was forced towards the hearth and thrown down onto the rug. Unable to catch her breath, she felt pain searing through her, as Abe knelt across her chest and placed one knee on each arm while he undid the rest of the buttons of his flies. 'Please don't, Abe. Please.'

He hesitated. His breathless voice pleaded, 'Then do this with me willingly. Let me have you, Pru. I told you I love you. Don't make me force you.'

'No! Get out, do you hear me – get out!'

His fist landed between her breasts, taking away her breath. Already weak with hunger, she couldn't fight him off, and she felt a wetness on her thigh as he guided himself into her. Disgust made her feel sick.

Abe's thrusts were deep and violent, and his hands held her arms in a bruising grip. Droplets of his sweat fell onto her face. Sobs shook her body as repulsion overcame her, at the pleasure he was giving her. She didn't want to enjoy it. She wanted it over. *Help me, God help me.*

The words came out in a gasp as, without wanting it to, her body went into an exquisite spasm of sensations that she could not control. 'God help meeee!'

The sound triggered the end. Abe pulled from her and lay beside her, holding himself and moaning his pleasure as he reached his climax. It was a small thing to feel thankful for. At least he'd kept his promise not to give her a babby.

When it was over, he slumped down on the rug beside her. 'You enjoyed that, didn't you? Your moan told of your pleasure as you orgasmed. Ha! Well, that's the first of many that you're going to have, Pru.' He raised himself on his elbow. 'But I don't want to fight for it. Not every time. It's me right, now. You're me woman, Pru.' An ugly expression replaced the pleased-with-himself one that he'd worn, as he said this.

Pru's fear mounted once more.

'You don't know what I'm capable of, Pru. That kid of yours: you want to keep him safe, right? Well, you play ball with me, and be available when I want you, and your life will change. I'll support you both. But mess with me, and you won't have a son any more. Do you understand?'

Pru stared at him. A tear crept down her face.

'Pru, Pru, this can change your life. You be willing and loving with me, and things will get better for you. You want that, don't you? I don't want to hurt you. But I must have you when I want to. Now, tell me that we have a deal.'

Pru nodded.

Abe stood. Once dressed, he threw some coins on the table and turned as if to leave.

'I'll be back tomorrow, Pru, and we can talk then. I'll get a proper arrangement in place. You're never going hungry again, girl.'

After he'd left, Pru sat staring at the door for a few minutes, before slowly raising herself and going towards the sink. She could see that the small change on the table amounted to a couple of pounds. More than she got from the Parish Relief. As she looked at the half-crowns, shillings, sixpences and pennies, it was as if they were taunting her, telling her that she was nothing but a paid slut. That thought brought the tears once more, as she realized that her life was mapped out for her. She were nowt but Abe Manning's whore. Drying her eyes, she pulled herself up. *Well, so be it.*

After scrubbing herself in the cold water that she'd fetched from the well earlier, she dried herself rigorously, then picked up her shift and pulled it over her head, before gathering some logs from the basket and stoking the range with them. As she pulled out the damper and the fire jumped into life, she went over a few things to convince herself that she was entitled to the money, after what had happened to her. *I'm only twenty-four, and some would say as I have me life ahead of me. Well, I'm going to take charge of that life.* With

26

the defiance that entered her at this thought, she shoved the stew pot over the flames. She'd eat and go to bed. And there she would plan.

Her future was going to be different. Abe might think he had control of her, and that she would have to do his bidding, but she would see to it that he paid her well.

This brave notion didn't sit long in her. She slumped into the chair. *How did I come to this?* Her sobs were so deep that they hurt her ribs and bent her body. They lasted until exhaustion took her and she leaned back in the chair. Reaching for the towel that she'd hung to dry by the stove, she wiped her face. 'Eeh, Pru, lass, you can't change owt. Abe's stronger than you.' *And, aye, so is the pull he has on me feelings.* Another tear seeped from her sore eyes. *If this is the way of things, then I'm to make sure as I get sommat out of it. Better meself.*

It came to her then that, although she couldn't change things in the near future, she could take some steps to alter them in the long run. With the money Abe gave her, she'd pay for the education she'd always longed for, and then maybe one day she'd become a teacher. She'd helped teach a fair few in her time with learning their letters. One thing was for sure: Freddy would be cared for and would never go hungry. *I'd do owt asked of me to ensure that happened. And to keep him safe.*

27

Chapter Three

Flora jumped from the train onto the platform of Victoria Station. She'd spotted Nanny Pru through the window as they'd come into the station, then lost her again as a swirl of smoke hid her from view. She felt very grown-up, having travelled from Bexhill on her own. She'd been collected from school by Millicent's nanny, then taken to the station, where Millicent and her nanny had made sure she boarded the right train to London. The whole trip, seemingly by arrangement with Daddy – Millicent had managed everything perfectly. Mummy and Daddy would never find out that she wasn't at Millicent's house, and Millicent's nanny thought she had carried out Daddy's instructions. It had worked out just as they planned, though her tummy had been tied in knots from the moment she left the school gates. But now here she was!

She held her breath with excitement as Nanny Pru emerged from the smoke and steam, laughing and doing a little skip and jump. To Flora, Nanny Pru looked lovely in her silver-grey ankle-length frock and matching jacket. Her curly hair was topped with a darker grey felt hat with a small brim. And the dimples that Flora loved were deep crevices in Nanny Pru's pretty face.

'Eeh, me little lass, look at you – all smart in your uniform. That green suits you, but I hope as you've brought sommat a little cooler. It's a hot day, and promises to be so all week.'

It felt so good to be enclosed in her nanny's arms. No one had held her close since Nanny Pru had dropped her off at St Alfonso's Refined School for Girls in Bexhill, two years ago. Her Aunt Amelia only managed a peck on the cheek on greeting Flora, and each night at bedtime; and the one time she'd seen Mummy there had been no physical contact at all. Even Daddy didn't lift her up and hold her, as he used to, but patted her back and smiled at her.

Clinging on to Nanny Pru, Flora didn't want to let her go and couldn't help the sob that escaped her.

'Eeh, come on now, this is a happy occasion, me little lass. By, it's grand to see thee. We're going to have a good time together, you and me. I've lots lined up. But first I want you to meet someone. Let's go and get your case off the train, then I'll take you to him.'

Flora felt a little disappointment at this. She didn't want to share Nanny Pru with anyone. And as she followed Nanny into the waiting room, once her cases had been retrieved, she wondered crossly who this stranger might be. The last thing she expected was a child!

'This is Freddy. He's me son. He's sixteen months old. Freddy, this is Flora, me own little charge, and she's going to be like a big sister to you.'

Freddy looked up from his pushchair and offered Flora his wooden toy-train engine. His gurgle made her laugh. His eyes were like hers and Daddy's, very dark. His smile showed

29

two dimples, just like Nanny Pru's, and he had her curly brown hair. As she looked at him, Flora felt a deep feeling surge through her, and she knew that she loved him dearly, even though she'd only just met him. She bent down and kissed his chubby cheek. Freddy's hand came towards her and his tiny fingers caught in one of her ringlets. She giggled as Nanny Pru disentangled them.

'By, he likes you, lass. And I can tell you like him.'

'I love him, Nanny Pru. How did you get him – where did he come from . . . ? Are you married, Nanny Pru?'

Relief flooded through Flora when Nanny Pru said she wasn't married. She knew she was being selfish; sharing her with Freddy was all right, but she didn't want to share her with anyone else.

'I'll tell you all about it later. Now, let's get on our way. We've to get on the Underground to Stepney.'

On the journey, which didn't seem to take long at all, Nanny Pru made Flora feel very curious. 'I want you to be a very grown-up lass, Flora, as I have sommat to tell you about Freddy. Has your school told you owt about how babbies get here?'

Feeling a bit shy, Flora shook her head, and then remembered something that Millicent had told her. 'Millicent said it is to do with mummies and daddies. Her nanny told her a little, as she said that Millicent, who is ten already, is coming of an age. She said that they will be talking more about some things that will happen to her body. What will happen to Millicent's body, Nanny Pru?'

'We'll talk about that when we get home to mine. It's reet that Millicent's nanny is preparing her. It's a nanny's job. Does you have a new nanny when you're at home, me little love?'

'No. There's no one. Mrs Randall has a girl to help her now – she's nice, her name's Belinda, but we call her Bee. She gets my bath ready and helps me to bed. She can't read, so I read stories to her. She loves them.'

'That's kind of you, lass. And what about the boys?'

'Bee sees to their clothes, but they don't have anyone to care for all their needs. They eat with Mummy and Daddy, and they bath themselves and still have a tutor at home, though Harold is going to school next term, but not as a boarder. I wish I could be like them. I get lonely, Nanny Pru. Especially when Millicent has gone home each day.'

Nanny Pru's arm came around her, giving Flora some comfort. She snuggled into Nanny Pru's body. It wasn't as squidgy as it used to be. She could feel Nanny's ribs. She remembered Nanny Pru's love of cakes and how she'd persuade Cook to put extra cakes on the plate at teatime. Nanny once told Flora that Cook would do anything for her, as she was teaching her her letters each evening. Maybe Nanny Pru had no one to make cakes for her now.

'Nanny Pru, how is it that you can read, but Bee can't? She says she never went to school much, and not many that she knew of did.'

'I went to a day-school run by the Church. It wasn't far from where I lived. I loved school; loved chalking on me board, and forming letters. I loved books an' all. I've still got me old ones, but I've bought some new ones from the market an' all. There's a stall there that's a treasure for them as likes to read. I've a lot by Charles Dickens, and a very special book I bought for your visit, and will keep for when Freddy is older. I were lucky to get it. I asked the market trader for sommat good for a young girl, and he said as he'd

31

heard of a book only published this year. It's called *The Railway Children* and it makes you cry, and then laugh and feel good. He got a copy specially for me. I know as you'll love it.'

'Oh, I will. Do the children work on the railway?'

'Naw, but I'm not telling you owt about the story, as it will spoil it for you, so you can stop your prying, lass.'

They giggled together. Freddy began to giggle, too, and wave his wooden train in the air. 'Chuf, chuf.'

This made them giggle even more. 'Eeh, lass, I'm that happy that you've taken to me little Freddy.'

'He's mine, too.'

'He is, lass, he is. He's our little Freddy.'

Flora loved Nanny Pru's house, even though she'd been shocked by the rubbish in the street outside her door, and the smell had made her feel sick.

They were sitting in the back yard, with home-made cakes and tea. Flora felt glad that she could at least still have cakes, even though Nanny Pru didn't have any servants. The sun was hot, and the yard was trapped by the high walls. But even though the space was small, there was a row of planted pots against the back wall. Chatter in different languages could be heard, and children shouted to one another – the noise was like nothing Flora had ever experienced. A strange cooking smell floated on the breeze, which Flora wasn't sure she recognized. Nanny Pru told her it was food from far-away countries.

'Don't they eat the food that we do? What does it taste like?'

'Some of it is delicious, but some would burn your mouth out. I have a friend you will meet later. She lives across the road, and sometimes cooks me a Jamaican dish called jerk-chicken with rice, but she does make it in a special mild way for me.'

'Jerk-chicken! Does that mean that she has to shake the chicken?'

'Ha, you're full of questions – you'll tire me out. Naw, I don't know why they call it that. Reet, lass, I'll put Freddy down to have his nap, then me and you have to talk.'

Biting into the delicious fairy cake and having the cream stick to her nose resulted in Nanny Pru wiping Flora's face with her pinny, when she returned.

'Flora, lass, there's sommat as you need to knaw. But first, I want you to stop calling me "Nanny Pru". As much as it saddens me, I'm not your nanny any longer. D'yer reckon as you can call me "Aunt Pru"?'

This shocked Flora. She liked telling the other girls that she had a nanny, too, and they hung on her every word when she told them about Nanny Pru, as they all had stiff, old-fashioned nannies.

'Eeh, I knaw as that won't come easy to you, but we've to accept that we have a different relationship now. Not that we'll change with each other, but folk round here will find it strange you calling me "Nanny". Will you do that for me, eh? I've already told them as I have a niece coming to stay.'

It seemed important to Nanny Pru, so Flora agreed. 'I might slip up, but I'll try, and I can I still call you "Nanny" at school, as everyone has a nanny.'

'Aye, you can, there's no harm in that. But here I'm "Aunt Pru". Reet, start now. Ask me to pass you the sugar.'

They giggled together as, over and over again, Flora got

it wrong. But gradually, as the game progressed, it became a little more natural to call her nanny 'Aunt Pru'.

'Eeh, you've got it off pat – good, lass. Now, me next news is sommat as you have to keep a secret all your life. You must promise never to tell a soul.'

Flora couldn't speak, as this sounded very serious, so she just nodded.

'Freddy is your half-brother. Now that means that he has the same daddy as you, but not the same mummy. I'm his mummy. Your daddy gave him to me.'

This was all too much for Flora. And nothing that came after it made any sense, as she tried to work it all out. *Daddy slept with Nan . . . Aunt Pru, and put a baby in her tummy. Well, a tiny egg, and that grew into Freddy. But Aunt Pru and Daddy were very naughty to have done this, and it must never be told, or Mummy will become even more angry than she already is.* Well, that was something Flora didn't want to happen, so she agreed to keep this very strange thing a secret.

'I like that Freddy is my half-brother, it makes him special. And even if it was a naughty thing that brought him into the world, I don't think it's his fault. But maybe Mummy would be cross. She makes me think I'm bad, and I wouldn't want Freddy to feel like I do.'

'Good girl. Now, me little lass, I reckon as you've had enough revelations for one day. We'll talk another time about what happens to a girl's body to make her a woman. It's early days for you, and though I think it a nanny's job to make sure the girls in her charge know what will happen, I was a little surprised that Millicent's nanny has broached the subject already.'

'Millicent said it was because her body was changing.

34

Mine isn't, but Millicent is getting . . . well, her shape is changing and she's growing fast.'

'By, she sounds like what we call an "early developer". In which case, her nanny does reet by her, but you've no need to worry along those lines. Besides, it might be more comfortable for you if Millicent tells you about it. Now, Flora, me little love, I think you need a rest. I only have one bedroom, so you will sleep in my bed with me at night. But for now you can lie on the sofa for an hour, and then I'm taking you to the theatre.'

'Ooh, I'd love that – our school takes us to the theatre. It makes me feel as though I go out of the world and into the music. Will Freddy like it?'

'Eeh, that's a lovely thing to say about how the theatre makes you feel. And naw, my friend I told you about will look after Freddy. She'll take care of you for a couple of evenings an' all, as I've got meself a tutor and am on with bettering me education. Rowena is really nice, very funny and always singing and laughing. You'll love her. You'll meet her when we take Freddy to her later on.'

All of this sounded very exciting, but for the moment Flora had a pressing need. 'Where is your bathroom, Aunt Pru?'

'Eeh, lass, I don't have owt as posh as that. We have one lav between four houses. But you don't have to go there. I have a screen in me room with a bucket for me, and a big jerry-pot for you. I only use me bucket if I need to pee after dark, but you can use your jerry-pot any time you want to go. Come on, I'll show you.'

They passed the huge pram where Freddy slept soundly, and went through the door into the kitchen-cum-living-room. Flora had never seen a room so cosy, with its blackened, gleaming cooking range, and a deep sink with a curtain around it that matched the curtains at the window above it. To the right of this stood a dresser. Highly polished, it was hung with lovely coloured china cups, and matching plates stood on its open shelves. Each side of the fire was a comfy chair, upholstered in a patterned red fabric. The sofa was of brown leather, but had what looked like a huge curtain covering it, in the same yellow fabric as those at the windows and around the sink. A big rug lay in front of the fire, and dotted around the room were small tables, while at the back were a table and chairs. A huge vase full of summer flowers stood on the table. To Flora, this room said, 'I'm home.'

The stairs led off this room, through a door next to the table. Narrow and curved, they were soft to tread on, as each step had a pad of bright-red carpet stuck to it, with a border of highly polished wood.

The stairs led straight into the bedroom. This held a cot, a double iron bedstead, a chair and a huge dark-wood chest of drawers. In one corner of the room, next to the window, stood the screen. Behind this was the bucket and the jerry-pot that Aunt Pru had told Flora about – and a little stand containing a jug and a matching china bowl and soap dish. A towel hung on a rail that protruded from the stand. On the opposite side, a small nail had squares of newspaper stuck onto it.

'There you are, me little lass. Now, you see to yourself while I empty your case. I've cleared a drawer for your things. I see as you've clocked the newspaper; well, that's instead of toilet roll. You'll get used to it. It's a saving I make.'

It all felt strange to Flora, but she didn't want to say so.

Although she felt embarrassed with the sound of her pee hitting the bottom of the jerry-pot and wished that Aunt Pru had a bathroom, she was happy to be here and wished she'd never have to leave.

'So this is your little niece, eh? Me and you's going to get on fine, girl. My, you're pretty. Look at those lovely, big brown eyes. Them would melt anyone's heart.' Rowena's laugh filled her front room. It was a jolly warble-sound that started Flora giggling. She liked Rowena, very much.

'Oh, you have a piano! May I play it sometime while I'm here, please?'

'You play, girl? Now, ain't that something, and you not yet knee-high to a grasshopper. Come here, girl, I've gotta hug you.'

Flora didn't know what Rowena meant, but it sounded funny, and being wrapped in Rowena's huge body felt good. She smelt of the spices that permeated her home. And she and her home were a huge bundle of colour. Bright reds, oranges and greens seemed to be splashed everywhere – in the blankets thrown over the furniture, in the curtains and even in the rug, which looked like it was made of bits of cloth sewn together.

Rowena's frock wasn't like a normal frock; it was a long, deep-blue cloth with big sunflowers printed over it, which wrapped around her body from her feet to her shoulders. The same cloth swathed her head to form a huge turban. Her lovely face seemed dominated by her glistening white teeth, which more than filled her mouth.

'Do you carry things on your head, Rowena? Only we did a lesson in school about Jamaica, and all the ladies had big urns on their heads?'

'Not here I don't, girl, but back home I did as a girl, and me momma and grandmother did, too. But then me da brought me and me momma here, in a huge ship. "We're going to make our fortune in the Motherland, girl," he told me. But instead, he died of the cold, and me momma of the coughing sickness, leaving me in an orphanage.'

'That's sad, but you're all right now, aren't you?'

'Don't you be feeling sorry for big old Rowena now. I'm happy, girl. More of my folk came over and got me out of that place. I have a big family here now, and we all take care of each other. Most of them live hereabouts. We have big parties, and the menfolk all have jobs. Them's only cleaning jobs and kitchen work, but them's jobs all the same. My old man works in the kitchens of the Savoy Hotel, and he brings home a wage that would keep us for a year back home.'

Though this was said with pride, Flora couldn't help but laugh. Rowena was funny, loving and quite different from any person she'd ever met.

'Has Flora time to play me something on the piano, Pru? I'd love to hear those ivories played. My momma played, though she never read a music note in her life.'

'Oh, can I, Aunt Pru?'

'Aye, you can, me little love. We've time.'

As Flora sat and played the gentle melody of 'Greensleeves', a tune she loved – especially the line 'To cast me off discourteously', as this seemed somehow to relate to herself – there was silence, and she looked up to see both Rowena and Aunt Pru wiping tears from their eyes.

To get such a reaction filled Flora with joy, for she knew they weren't sad but were moved by her playing. At that moment she knew that music was all she ever needed, to make her feel whole. Music and the love of her Nanny Pru, because, no matter how she was to address the only woman who had ever truly loved her, she would always be 'Nanny Pru' in her heart.

Chapter Four

Determined to see Rome, on being forced to leave the Santa Maria School of Music and Art in Tuscany, Flora had booked herself onto a guided tour – a whirlwind of a few moments here and there, over a two-day trip. Today, her last, she stood gazing at the Trevi Fountain and marvelled at how quickly the years had flown by. July 1914: how did that happen? *It doesn't seem a minute since I first left home, all those years ago, to go to school in Bexley.*

The sun sparkling on the water gushing from the fountain brought Flora's attention back to its beauty, as she saw how it caused magical rainbows. Droplets danced, then reflected the colours all around her as she jostled for position with other tourists, each one eager to see their coin land in the fountain and to make their wish.

She raised her gaze to the beautiful statues, which seemed to be saying, 'We will grant your wish. Our winged horses will fly to heaven tonight and ensure that God hears you.'

Part of Flora was sad that her music studies had been cut short, and she wanted to wish it wasn't so, and that she could remain in Italy until the first day of next April, 1915

– her twenty-first birthday. But she knew that wasn't possible.

The order to leave Italy had been sudden. The college principal had burst into the concert room where the orchestra, of which she was a member, had been rehearsing, and had declared, 'You all have to leave for home. I have here a communication, dated 16th July 1914: "Due to the escalating unrest in Europe, we advise that all British citizens are to be evacuated to the United Kingdom within two weeks. The arrangements are . . ."'

Those arrangements had given Flora enough time to bring forward the plan she'd had to see Rome during the summer break, which had almost been upon them. *Not that I will see as much as I wanted to.*

Sighing, she turned round and, closing her eyes, threw her coin over her shoulder. Her wish would be what it always was, but this time she hoped it would come true: *Please let things be different for me at home. I only want to be happy and accepted by my mother.*

The tour guide broke the spell. 'Come along, everyone. We still have the Teatro Costanzi to visit, before you board your boat for home.'

Although this was going to be a highlight for her, Flora let those who were eager to please the guide file after him before she did. She wanted to watch the ripples caused by her coin and count them as they spread wider than any of the others. Did this mean her wish would come true?

Her father's last letter hadn't sounded promising:

Your mother isn't well, dearest Flora. She has asked your Aunt Amelia to take you in for a couple of years. Amelia has taken on the task of introducing you to

41

*society and we hope that you will meet a suitable
husband. I have put aside a large amount of money
for such an event, and for you to draw a generous
allowance from. I will visit you there, once you are
settled, and we will discuss my plans for your future.
    I remain your loving father.*

Loving father! Flora tossed her long, dark hair back over
her shoulder. Over the years her likeness to her mother had
become more pronounced; she had the same slight and yet
curvaceous figure, the same thick, glossy hair, and her facial
features were as clear-cut and beautiful as her mother's. She
knew, too, that her temper could flash in just the same way
her mother's did, but that she was different, in that she
didn't hold a grudge, but forgave readily. This last trait she
took from her father, but how glad she was that she hadn't
inherited his spineless attitude – always seeking forgiveness,
and wanting to keep the peace. Didn't he know that this
undermined the love he said he felt for her? She would
rather that he was still the philanderer he used to be. At least
then he wasn't a lapdog, and he stood up for her.

As for going to Aunt Amelia's home in Brighton, he
could jolly well think again! Flora had plans of her own. She
intended to go to Aunt Pru's, to live with her and Freddy.

Flora had spent a week each year with Aunt Pru. The
subterfuge of her being at Millicent's home had worked
throughout her school years, as no one took any interest in
her. Normal, loving parents would have sought more information, but no such complications ever occurred. And each
year Daddy consented without question, only occasionally
passing a remark that he hoped she'd enjoyed her visit and
had been a good girl – and that was that. After leaving

school and going to college, Flora had simply told them that she would be spending an extra week in Scotland, with like-minded students, taking part in concerts. The fund that her father had set up for her was more than enough for her needs, and for any travelling she wanted to do.

Those short stays with Aunt Pru and Freddy had been the happiest of her growing-up years, and the only time she experienced the feeling of being truly loved. Although they still lived in Stepney, they had moved to a larger house around the corner, nearer to Aunt Pru's friend, Abe. The downstairs of the house was given over to school rooms.

Flora had long since realized the extent of the relationship between Aunt Pru and Abe, even though Aunt Pru went to great lengths to hide it, when Flora visited. Freddy confirmed these suspicions on her last visit. Now fourteen and a thoughtful young man, handsome like their father, and with a love of music, like her, Freddy played the violin beautifully. She'd taken him to a concert – his first. The music had enraptured him and afterwards, whilst in a cafe drinking cocoa, he'd talked more than she'd ever known him to.

Some of what Freddy said had frightened Flora. It seemed that Abe wasn't the respectable businessman that she'd supposed, but a gangster, and wasn't always kind to Aunt Pru. 'But don't worry, Flors' – Freddy had always called her Flors – 'I keep my eye on him.'

Not wanting to disillusion him, Flora hadn't said anything, but thought what an inadequate defence he would be for Aunt Pru, if ever she needed it. She hadn't pushed for more information on what Abe did, either, but had consoled herself with the thought that Abe's funding of Pru's school for poor children in the area showed that he did have a good side.

Freddy had gone on to say, 'You know that he and Mum sleep together, don't you?'

She'd nodded and changed the subject. But now she felt glad that she knew for sure, because it was something she had to sort out with Aunt Pru. She needed Pru to know that her moving in didn't mean that Pru had to change her life, as Flora was certain had happened every time she'd visited. She knew this would be a lot for Aunt Pru to accept.

Knowing the very different circles in which Flora moved from those that she and Freddy moved in, Aunt Pru had over the years always tried to shield Flora from the way her and Freddy's life really was. But as she'd gained more understanding, Flora had realized that Aunt Pru was ashamed of how things had turned out for her. *Well, she has no need to be. She did the best she could, after the way my father treated her – making her believe she was special to him, then casting her out with a one-time payment, once Mother found out. Poor Aunt Pru should be proud of what she's achieved. Father is a beast!*

From the little she'd seen of her family over the years, Flora had been saddened by the way her father, who now owned fifteen haberdashery shops across the south of England, meant nothing in his own home. Her elder brother Harold, who still had no time for Flora and buttered up to his mother, managed three of the family shops and, Flora had noticed, was in a kind of conspiracy with her mother against her father. As for Francis, he had become weak over the years; he managed just one of the shops, and bowed down to Harold's every wish. Flora made her mind up to tackle her mother. She would try to persuade her to see the pain that she'd inflicted on her daughter, and would try to make her love her in the same way she did Harold and Francis. There would be no husband-hunting, though, as her own plans for her future didn't include marriage.

Francis wrote often. Mostly complaining letters, though his interest in foreign affairs gave her an insight as to what was going on in the world – something none of her lessons at school or college covered.

From the age of twelve, he'd written to Flora about the strategic alliances being made – Britain with France, and then later with Russia. He'd told her all he knew of the Balkan Wars as they happened. And now he feared that Britain might become involved in a war with Germany.

Re-joining the others on the tour, Flora dreaded getting back into the horse-drawn coach with them. As she was alone and the youngest, they expected her to take the most uncomfortable seat at the back of the twelve-seater carriage. The strong perfume of the women, mingled with the sweaty smell of the men, made her feel nauseous. Needing a distraction from all of this, Flora dug out of her bag Francis's latest letter, which had arrived on her final day at the Santa Maria School of Music and Art:

War is bound to happen. There is unrest in Serbia. But worse than that, the news is full of the murder of Archduke Franz Ferdinand, heir to the Austrian throne, and his wife, while on a visit to Bosnia. The Austrians believe the assassin to be a Serbian and are targeting their anger towards Serbia.

Mother has forbidden Harold and me even to talk about the possibility of war, and has told us she would die if either of us thinks of joining the forces. Well, she needn't worry on my account. I'm terrified of such a prospect!

But guess what? Do you remember that spotty girl we used to giggle at when we saw her in church – Annie, her name was. She's the daughter of one of Mother's friends. Well, she's joined the British Red Cross as a trainee. They are recruiting girls, just in case. Mother says that Annie is willing to go abroad, if needed. Can you imagine!

At this moment Flora could imagine, and she liked the idea.

Before she came to Italy to study music for a year, her continued education at St Alban's College in Edinburgh had an emphasis on music and languages, and as she'd always shone at both, it had been an easy, happy time for her. But the college had also tried to develop practical skills in their pupils. Apart from those needed to run a home, and the more genteel occupations of embroidery and painting, there had been optional courses run by the St John Ambulance Brigade. Flora had loved these lessons, and had obtained the highest level of first-aid certificate.

As a member of St John Ambulance, she now thought she could apply to them. *I, too, could train to be a nurse, and then, if the war happens, I would volunteer for oversees duty. My classical training can wait.* The more she thought about this, the more Flora warmed to the idea. After all, very few women, especially pianists, were accepted by the large orchestras, so her prospects were most likely in teaching – which didn't overly excite her, although she did relish the thought of perhaps giving some of her time to Aunt Pru's school, to bring music to the poor of the East End.

Sadness overcame her at this thought, as she pondered how few opportunities there were for women. There was nothing she would like more than to perform onstage. To have an audience hushed while she played. To hear that silence when she finished, and then the rapturous applause. She'd heard this so often at concerts, and had always wanted it to be her the audience was applauding. But then there should be more opportunities for the poor, too, and she could make a difference in that field, as her lovely Aunt Pru was doing.

The journey home took four days and, during it, Flora went over and over how she would tackle her mother. In the end she decided that direct confrontation was the only way – she would force her mother to listen to her, and to face the issues that had drawn a deep crevice between them. She so wanted them to be friends and, maybe, love would follow. How wonderful that would be.

Her mother's greeting gave her the perfect opportunity. 'Oh, you're home! Well, don't get too settled. Aunt Amelia is expecting you in a few days.'

'Mother, can I speak to you?'

'For goodness' sake, what about? I haven't much time. I have a committee meeting of the Red Cross.'

'You're part of the Red Cross? I didn't know that.'

'What did you want to speak to me about?'

This curt dismissal, cutting off any interest that she might show in her mother, always hurt. The wall between them was going to be difficult to break down, because it was a wall of hate. One put up by her mother and, seemingly, impenetrable by Flora.

'Can we go into the garden and maybe have tea served?'

'I told you, I – I have to go out.'

'Please, Mother, it's important.'

'Oh, very well.'

The warmth of the sun did nothing to thaw her mother, and her face remained stiff with anger. Flora sat down at the garden table and looked around her, hoping to gain some peace from her fraught nerves by gazing at the beautiful flowers and shrubs blooming in every corner and giving off a wonderful scent. Here, in this walled paradise, you would never know you were so near the centre of the capital city.

Grace coughed, bringing Flora's attention back to the present and reminding her that the moment was upon her. She'd planned this meeting so often that she was word-perfect. 'Mummy, I—'

'You are not a child, Flora, you should address me as "Mother" now.'

'Sorry, yes. I – I just wanted to try to clear the air between us. I wanted to say that—'

'What are you talking about: *clear the air!* We haven't fallen out. What ridiculous notion have you got into your head now?'

This wasn't going well at all. It didn't seem as if Flora's longing to have her mother as a friend would ever happen. 'Whatever I did to displease you, I want you to forgive me.'

'What nonsense is this? Has your father put you up to this?'

'No! No, I haven't spoken to Father. I'm unhappy. I want you to love me, to accept me back home. I want us to be friends.'

Rising as if her chair had burned her, Grace looked down into her daughter's face. 'You're a grown woman, and yet you still do all you can to annoy and upset me. I should

48

never have had you. You're nothing but a thorn in my side. Don't think for one moment that you will ever live under the same roof as me. I couldn't bear it.'

'Mummy!'

'"Mother!" Do you hear me? "Mother" – though I've wished a thousand times that I wasn't.' Turning and almost falling, her mother raced across the lawn.

Tears stung Flora's eyes. *Why? Why?*

Through the blur of those tears, she saw her father approaching. His walk spoke of his anger. Her mother must have gone straight to him, though Flora hadn't even known he was in the house.

'Flora, I told you in my letter that your mother wasn't well. How could you upset her, the moment you see her? I'm appalled at you. You will go to Aunt Amelia's immediately, and not spend the planned few days here.'

Flora stood. 'How nice to see you, too, Daddy.'

'Yes, well, I – I . . . it is nice to see you. But this constant jarring of your mother's nerves upsets us all, and if you cannot behave in a way that gives her some peace, then I shall have to see you when I can. That is all I can offer, Flora.'

'It isn't enough. Have you ever considered me, and my feelings, Daddy? Do you know what this rejection does to me? Do you care? You have—'

'Flora! Stop this. I have done my best, I—'

'Your best! Sending me away! Best for whom? I am your daughter, but apart from the first few years of my life, I have not spent a year in total under your roof and guidance, and I am almost twenty-one now. How is that *your best*? I have suffered because of your sin, Daddy. YOUR SIN, not mine. But you fared well, didn't you? You remained in your home,

49

while I – the innocent party – was cast out. You're pathetic, and I will never, ever forgive you.'

George slumped down on the iron garden chair so hard that it swayed and looked as though it would fall over. Instinctively Flora reached out to grab his arm. His hand caught hers. His head bent over. Huge sobs racked his body. 'I – I'm sorry. So sorry.'

Flora's heart melted. He was her father, and much in the way her mother always did, she knew she would have to forgive him. Only in Mother's case, there would always be conditions that Daddy had to adhere to. He chose those conditions over Flora's happiness. She pulled her hand away.

'You can't apologize to me, Daddy. Not until you are prepared to love and protect me.' Her own sobs joined his as she sat down. Swallowing hard, she composed herself. 'I have substituted your love with one so great you will never experience giving anything like it – or receiving it. And that is what has sustained me. You and Mother have remained a longing in my heart, but the love given to me has helped me to cope without you.'

'I – I don't understand. Your friend, Millicent, and her family?'

'No. Nanny Pru or, as I call her now, Aunt Pru.'

His face held shock.

'Yes, the woman you defiled. The woman you cast out just as readily as you did me. She has been my rock all these years, and will continue to be in the future.'

'But . . . how?'

With great satisfaction, she told him. 'You only have your lack of care for me to blame. Any normal parent wouldn't simply have accepted that I went to this stranger's house each year. They would have made enquiries, perhaps made

50

an effort to meet the family. But not you. You were just glad that I was somewhere – anywhere – that was out of sight. Well, now you know where it was . . . I – I *hate* you!'

'No! No, please try to understand . . .'

His words merged with his sobs. Whether those sobs were for himself or for his realization that he'd lost her, she couldn't tell. But at that moment, neither mattered. Rising, Flora walked away from him.

Chapter Five

'Oh, Aunt Pru, I don't believe it!'

'What is it, lass?'

Aunt Pru looked up from the papers she was studying. She was sitting at her desk in the little room to the side of the school rooms in the basement of her house, which was designated as her office. From there she only had to walk across a hall to the cloakrooms and through them to be in the classroom.

The noise coming from that direction told Flora there was a class in progress. Aunt Pru had engaged a qualified teacher, and was in the throes of trying to gain registration as a government or church school, but both criteria were high, and such recognition was proving difficult. And so she remained with the status of 'charity school' – something she hated, as she thought it somehow stigmatized those who attended and marked them as not being worthy of a place at a 'proper' school. It was a happy school nonetheless, and Pru's caring nature was a blessing for some of the little mites who attended.

Flora had settled well into living with Aunt Pru and

Freddy and loved helping out, running a music afternoon for the pupils.

'This message is from the St John Ambulance. It appears the Red Cross have been asked to send forty nurses to Belgium, because of the fighting taking place to prevent a German invasion. However, they haven't got enough fully trained personnel, and they have asked St John's to supply five of their highest-trained first-aid staff to join them. I have been specially asked to go. Even though I've been volunteering at the hospital, I never expected that I would be asked to help. It says there are five of us going to Brussels.'

'What? When?'

'Right away.'

'Eeh, lass, this stinks. You're not ready; your training was meant to last three months afore you could be accepted as a volunteer! It ain't reet. Perhaps this is sommat to do with your ma – didn't you say as how she was working on a Red Cross committee?'

'That's a possibility, but it's more likely due to the fact that I can speak French and a bit of German, as the letter says these skills will be invaluable to the rest of the group. Besides, now that I've got used to the idea, I'm excited about the prospect. And it's all to happen so quickly. I'm to report tomorrow!'

'Eeh, lass, naw. Naw, you can't go that soon. You've had no preparation.'

'I have to go, Aunt Pru. I made my mind up, before I came home from Italy, that I would do my bit.'

'But – but it's all so dangerous. I'm going to be at me wits' end while you're out there.'

'Don't be, dear Aunt Pru. I'll be safe. The Germans haven't reached Brussels and may yet be pushed back.

Besides, the Red Cross is afforded protection by all governments. We'll all be fine.'

Freddy's music interrupted them: an almost violent piece that stretched his violin strings to the limit, and pounded excitement through Flora's veins. They both listened, without realizing how close together they'd moved. Aunt Pru's hand drew Flora down, to sit in the chair next to hers. Her desk was surrounded by chairs because often the staff – cleaners, maintenance man and cook – congregated there.

The music was coming from an upstairs room, and was beautiful in its intensity. Flora had never heard it before, and guessed Freddy had written it himself. It expressed the anger that she knew his gentle nature felt at the state of the world, and his fear for her. Many times, over the last weeks, he'd begged her not to go abroad after her training. Had he heard her tell Pru that she was going tomorrow? She hoped not; she'd wanted to tell Freddy herself, and hadn't seen him when she'd come into the office.

Clutching Aunt Pru's hand, she bent close to her. 'You should send Freddy to a school of music now, Aunt Pru. He is so talented. You must protect him, and his talent. Maybe Canada? He needs to develop more refined skills. They don't have the same calibre of music schooling that there is in Europe, but he would be safe from the war, and would be learning from some professors of French origin who are renowned. I'll help to pay for it. Daddy has increased my allowance – his conscience-money, which sticks in my throat, and yet at the same time I do feel that I'm entitled to it. I haven't touched much of it and don't intend to, especially as I will be paid a sum by the Red Cross each month, which will more than cover my needs.'

'Eeh, naw, lass. You don't think it'll last long enough for them to want to take me Freddy, do you?'

Flora looked into Aunt Pru's shocked face and realized that she hadn't grasped the seriousness of what was happening.

'It's not going to be easy. You must prepare yourself, Aunt Pru. Francis, who knows a lot about current affairs, believes that, before long, many thousands of our young men will be called to arms.'

'Naw! Eeh, Flora, surely all of those soldiers will cope with it and will stop the threat to us . . . ?' Her troubled eyes stared at Flora. It was almost possible to see Pru's brain absorbing what she'd heard. 'By, Flora, what will become of us, lass?'

The music came to an end, leaving a tangible silence. Flora put her arm around Aunt Pru's shaking body. She felt sorry that she'd caused her this distress, but glad to have awoken her to the reality of what was happening.

'Think about it, Aunt Pru. Ask your solicitor to help you get Freddy to Canada. He will arrange everything. Quebec is best, as they have French traditions and their roots are in the arts and music. I would make the enquiries for you, but I have no time.'

'By, lass, you've given me sommat to think about now. I'll have a chat with Freddy. He has to have a say. But I hope that he goes. Eeh, I'd miss him. It don't seem right, asking him to move away from home, and him only fourteen. But what choice have I? It's that or risk that he has to go to war.'

This worried Flora as she knew that, despite his gentle ways, Freddy was excited by the prospect of fighting for his country when he was old enough to do so. 'No, Aunt Pru, don't leave it up to him. Make the arrangements and present him with them. Please. Make sure he goes. We must keep him safe.'

Aunt Pru's sigh told of her indecision. 'It wouldn't be reet, lass. He has a lot of your father in him, with his music and—'

'You knew about that?'

'Oh, aye, I knaws a lot about George. You knaw, he hasn't had it easy, and it ain't easy for me to talk to you about this, but . . . well, we used to meet on me day off. He'd buy me tea and we'd talk. It were a while afore owt else happened.'

Memories of the incident between her father and Aunt Pru brought a tinge of colour to Flora's cheeks. She'd always thought it had triggered her mother into turning even more against her, and had led to her being sent away to school. She didn't say anything of this, but let Aunt Pru continue.

'It might help you to knaw some of it, lass. Knawing of it helped me to forgive him some, though when I think of it all, it seems that what eventually happened was part of his plan. Making a friend and confidante of me made me feel special. I fell in love with him. Anyroad, he told me that he took after an aunt who were a renowned violinist, but she died young. Your da found a love of music, and of playing the violin, when he was at boarding school and wanted to take up a career as a musician, but his da was having none of it. He wouldn't let George practise when he was at home, because the sound broke his heart. He'd adored his sister, and George said he mourned her passing till he died.'

Flora tried to imagine life without her own music, and an empathy that she'd never felt for her father seeped into her.

'Anyroad, against his will, your da had to learn the workings of the mill that he still runs with his brother to this day.

But after his da died, he started to branch out into opening shops that the mill could supply. This led him to move to London, where he met your ma and built a separate fortune. But like I say, none of that happened until after his da died, because he never had the guts to stand up to others. He never stood up to his da, but allowed his da to crush him. And he does the same with your ma. She don't love him, but for some reason he won't stand up to her and leave. She even wanted a divorce once, but no, he couldn't face that. "Spineless" is what we call blokes like him, up north.'

'Yes, I've witnessed that. But it helps to know why he is like he is. I never knew my grandfather, but he sounds a horrid, selfish man.'

'Like Harold. I saw all of them traits in him, as a lad, and from what you've told me, they've come out more now that Harold's a man. But me point in telling you all this is that Freddy, too, could easily be forced to do sommat against his will. But I've been careful not to let that happen. I've allus given him a say in any decision that affects him. So, naw, lass. I can't make this momentous decision for him. It would be wrong. Whatever he chooses to do, I'll respect. I'll not make him spineless, like his da.'

This changed something in Flora's thinking. Her father was made the way he was by another, more dominant influence in his life, but at least he hadn't been spineless in the way he'd insisted that she was educated in a school that would feed her love of music. And she knew that arguing with Aunt Pru, on the matter of Freddy, wouldn't alter anything. But although it pained her to accept Aunt Pru's decision, she knew in her heart that it was the right thing for Freddy, although that didn't stop her laying some foundations.

Making her way up the stairs to Freddy's room, she tapped on the door. There was a hesitation before he invited her in.

'Freddy, I need to talk to you.'

'I know, Flors, I heard you tell Ma.'

This northern way of addressing his mother was the only concession Aunt Pru had made to Freddy speaking 'The King's English', as she defined the way he spoke. She'd even gone so far as to have elocution lessons for him, in the days when she taught him herself. Since then, he'd gained a scholarship to Sutton County grammar school, giving him part-sponsored education, with Aunt Pru paying a half-fee of one pound and ten shillings a term. Freddy hoped, like all the boys who attended the school, to go on to university, but Flora feared that the war might change that for this generation of young men.

'I thought you had some idea, and that is why you played that beautiful, fiery music – your way of expressing yourself, and relieving yourself of your feelings. But you mustn't fear for me, little brother. The Red Cross workers are protected. But enough of that: I want to talk to you about your future.'

By the end of their conversation Flora knew, with a heavy heart, that Freddy wouldn't be going to Canada or anywhere else . . . except, maybe, to war, if war still raged when he was old enough to join up. Her one hope was that it would all be over by then.

The excitement of the journey ahead was all Flora could think about as she boarded the Underground at Stepney to take her to Victoria Station, where she would finally meet her fellow travellers. When she arrived and stepped off the train, she stood for a moment wondering which way to go, until a voice attracted her attention.

'Hey, over here. I see you're one of us.'

The tall, pretty girl, with shining brown hair curling back off her face and hanging loose at the back, stood on the platform waving her arms at Flora.

'Hello, I'm Mags – short for Margaret – and this here is Marjella, who tells me she is known as Ella. Are you off to Belgium, like us?'

Mags oozed confidence, but Ella just gave a shy smile.

'I am. Isn't it exciting? I'm Flora.'

Mags didn't shake her outstretched hand, but took her into a big hug. 'I'm from Blackburn, and in the North we greet people properly.'

With her hat now askew, Flora turned to Ella and giggled. 'Nice to meet you both.'

Ella nodded. 'I think we will go along together well; it is nice to meet you, too.'

Flora detected an accent in the precise way that Ella spoke, but couldn't have said where she came from. Her features were precise, too, her mouth small, her nose straight and her hazel eyes didn't give anything away, although when she smiled they twinkled, and this gave the overall impression of prettiness as her face lit up. Her hair was what you might term mousy, and was fastened back into a tight bun. Both girls, like herself, wore the Red Cross armband on the sleeve of their coat.

'Come on, girls, we can get to know one another on the train; the others are in the second carriage. Apparently we are going to remain together when we arrive, so we wanted to wait here and meet you.'

'I thought there were going to be five of us volunteers, and forty or more going altogether.'

'There are, Flora, the train is full. But the other volunteers must all be assigned to a different matron and going to different places, as we were particularly introduced to this group and were told we were to keep with them.'

Flora's bones ached from the three-day journey across land and sea, but the sight of the Hotel Metropole, in the Place de Brouckère in Brussels, lifted her. She'd imagined they would go to a camp somewhere and would have to rough it, but before her was this magnificent white building.

As they entered and were booked in, her attention was caught by the beautiful stained-glass windows, through which the sun sprayed a kaleidoscope of colour. From the marble walls to the columns and pillars that lined the reception hall, this place was exquisite. Flora had never seen such luxury or thought ever to stay in such a place, although her family must have done, as Harold once let it slip, in spite, that they had an annual holiday together at such a hotel. Funny, but this thought had never hurt her, until now. Always she'd had her own secret visits with Aunt Pru, and had felt that was better than anything her brothers could have with Mother and Father. But as she stood there and imagined the four of them together, in a hotel like this, her exclusion from her family ground the pain into her heart.

The look on the faces of both Mags and Ella told her that they, too, were overcome – though Mags probably less than Flora and Ella, from what she now knew of them both. They had chatted endlessly on the journey here, until Flora felt as if she'd known Ella and Mags all her life.

Mags seemed to have everything that was needed in life,

and would one day inherit her father's fortune. She had no siblings and her father owned a cotton mill. Her jolly nature made Flora feel that, together, anything could be achieved. The way she'd talked about the workings of the mill showed her love of the world of cotton-spinning and all it entailed. Mags had been fascinated to learn that Flora's father owned a half-share in a mill in a neighbouring town to her own. 'I could run my father's business with my eyes closed,' she'd said. But there was a different side to her, too. A caring side, and this had shown in her choice of joining the volunteer aid department. 'Once I had an inkling that things weren't so good in Europe, I took myself off to join the St John Ambulance. "Mags," I said, "you might not be needed in the mill yet, but you are darned sure to be needed by the soldiers, if things are not resolved, so you had better be ready!"' She'd gone on to say, 'The St John was my best option, as they had a local branch. I've done three months with them in a hospital in Bradford, and loved it. So I may not be a qualified nurse, but I'm ready, willing and able.'

Looking over at Ella, Flora thought she still had a wary look about her. As if she had found herself where she wasn't sure she should be. Ella had told them that her nanny had brought her to England from Poland at the age of three, and had taken care of her. She had no knowledge of any family and knew only that there was a monthly allowance for her.

She had begun her training as a nurse at the age of eighteen, but after six months had been taken ill with a mystery illness that had rendered her weak and unable to function properly. Her nanny, who had become her companion, had nursed her back to health. But by that time war had been declared and so, instead of resuming her training, Ella had joined the Red Cross. She undertook further training with them and became a volunteer.

Impulsively Flora took Ella's hand. 'We're here – I can't believe it. We'll help each other through whatever we have to face. You'll see.'

Mags joined in encouraging Ella. 'We will. We'll stick together through thick and thin. Come on, let's try to bag a good room for the three of us.'

A feeling overcame Flora that she couldn't do better than have Mags and Ella by her side. The three of them had gelled well and already felt like best friends. And who better to go into the unknown with than a best friend, let alone two of them.

PART TWO
Brussels, 1914–15

~

Flora, Mags and Ella

A Terrifying Invasion

Chapter Six

Before retiring, the girls had been given their orders. Many refugees and injured soldiers had been taken to the Royal Palace, so the three of them, along with one of the trained nurses, were to be assigned positions there. Others had orders that they would be shipped to various hospitals outside Brussels. And from now on, they must wear their uniforms at all times, as much for their safety as to be ready to take up their duties whenever called to do so.

The mood had changed since yesterday – excited anticipation being replaced by efficient delegation, as news came to them that the Germans had reached the gates of Brussels.

Matron's voice boomed from the front of the assembled nurses: 'Because of this new development, there will be no need of our services at the Royal Palace. The Allied wounded there are to be evacuated. Transport has arrived to ship out those of you already assigned to other destinations, but with this turn of events, all of you have an opportunity to leave for home. If you wish to return to Britain, please file over to the left.'

Flora couldn't believe the number of girls who did so.

Mags, who stood between her and Ella, whispered, 'What's it to be, girls? I'm for staying.'

'Me, too. From what Matron has said, we're going to be needed.' Flora leaned forward and looked at Ella as she said this. Ella nodded. 'What was it you said, Mags? We go through thick and thin together? Well, that's what we'll do.'

Matron's voice brought their attention back to her. 'Right. Those remaining and designated a placement will be given a number. When we reach the station, each train that pulls in will be numbered, so make sure you get on the correct one. Those who were assigned to the palace must remain here to await further orders.'

Why hadn't new orders been decided for the three of them? A seed of fear entered Flora. This was going to be a dangerous place, if the Germans managed to invade Brussels. She'd heard talk of them not treating the Red Cross with the respect she'd been told to expect from all nations. At supper the night before, one girl had told of how her friend had been taken prisoner, along with another nurse, as soon as they had landed in Serbia. Looking at the fear on the faces of those who had elected to go home, Flora thought the story had probably contributed to them wanting to flee.

Although they had thought there were just four in their group assigned to work inside Brussels, there were seven girls left behind, once all the others had left, although she, Mags and Ella were the only volunteer staff amongst them. This seemed to set them apart from the four qualified nurses, as none of them showed any signs of wanting to be friendly.

'How about we take a walk out? See what the mood is. You speak French, Flora, you can find things out.'

'I'm game, Mags. It'll be good to see our surroundings and gauge what is truly happening.'

'Me too. I think it will be better than sitting in our room, speculating.'

With this from Ella, they linked arms and stepped outside.

The streets of Brussels were uncannily quiet. Four coaches were waiting for those assigned to be shipped out. Flora briefly wished that the three of them were part of this, but shrugged off her fear as they crossed the road and stood for a moment by the beautiful monument in the centre of the square. With its tower adorned by figures, it looked almost defiant, as if nothing could prevail against it. The sound of the water gushing from its many fountains soothed Flora's nerves.

'It was erected in 1897 to honour Jules Victor Anspach, a former Mayor of Brussels.' She translated from the plaque on the side. 'He championed the working class.'

'Good for him! I like the old fellow already.'

Flora smiled at Mags. 'Me, too. Now which way shall we go?' Looking around her, Flora loved what she saw. The square was flagged by beautiful tall buildings and many little shops and pavement cafes.

'I think we should head towards that cafe over there – it looks busy, so maybe we can find out what is happening?'

Ella's word, 'busy', didn't quite describe the one table being occupied by three women, but none of the other bars in view had any customers, so their presence made the little cafe more inviting.

Flora greeted the women as she and the others took a seat. '*Bonjour, Mesdames.*'

The women smiled a greeting. Though dressed fashionably,

and in a manner that spoke of wealth, they had what Flora would describe as a 'care-worn expression'.

On Flora asking if they had heard any news, one of the women told her that they feared the Germans would break through, and that there were rumours of many casualties lying outside the gates of Brussels. 'We are all to do as we are told and to cooperate, as Burgomaster Max has said we must. He says that we cannot fight back, as we will be in less danger if we accept the invasion and carry on as normally as the Germans allow us to.'

Although Flora agreed, she felt sad that such a fate should befall these proud women and their countrymen. But this was the least of Mags's concerns, when Flora translated the conversation to her and Ella. 'We have to go to the wounded. They need us.'

Without paying any heed to the fear that crunched her stomach muscles at this statement, Flora asked how they could accomplish this.

'Ask your ladies. Ask how we get to, and out of, the gates.'

The ladies shook their heads in unison. 'No, you must not!'

'No . . . no, it will be very bad out there. They say the fighting is intense. You will be killed!'

The third lady didn't speak, but just stared out of wide, terrified eyes.

As if to give credence to their words, a loud explosion reverberated around them, sending shockwaves through Flora. Tables were upturned. The chairs they sat on were blasted from underneath them and Flora landed on the pavement, her body bruising as she hit the ground. Shards of glass splintered all around her, as a window shattered into a thousand pieces. And then a cloud of dust enfolded her.

Flora rubbed her sore, dust-filled eyes. She could see that Ella was still standing and looking around her. Her dazed expression spoke of her shock. But where was Mags? Although she opened her mouth to call out, Flora couldn't hear whether or not she'd made a sound. Getting to her feet, she saw Mags on the floor a few feet away.

Another blast, and Flora was propelled forward. She grabbed Ella and pulled her down, to lie next to Mags.

'Always hit the ground at the sound of a blast. First rule of safety. We can do what is needed, once the threat has passed,' Mags shouted.

'I didn't have any choice, as it happened, but it's good advice, Mags.'

'Come on, there's no sight of any soldiers. I think the fighting is further away than we thought, and that was stray fire. Did any of you see what happened to the three ladies?'

This concern took away Flora's fear for herself and the others, as they all rose and looked around for the women. They found them huddled together behind a table, which they had placed in front of them as if it were a shield. Flora spoke to them and discovered that they weren't injured, just very shocked and afraid.

'Do you live far from here?'

One of them shook her head and pointed to some apartments across the street.

'We'll help you get to your homes. Don't be afraid – we don't think the Germans are near. Can you stand?'

The larger lady of the three seemed more reassured than the others. '*Oui*, we are all right. Thank you. If you could just give us a hand up.'

69

Once standing, the women were more in command of their fear. The one who'd asked for a hand now took charge.

'We will be fine. You girls get back to your hotel and safety. Thank you.'

With this, the three women, looking very vulnerable but determined, crossed the road together. It occurred to Flora as she watched them that being with friends helped. There was always the sense of wanting to protect them above yourself, and a feeling that they were there for you, watching your back. Those three women epitomized this as they clung to each other, and supported one another.

She turned to face Mags and Ella and knew that the three of them would be like that, and took comfort in the thought. 'Let's all make a run for it, eh? We'll be safe in the hotel.'

Huddled together in their bedroom, drinking the tea that Mags had ordered, they listened to the silence that had fallen. 'This can only mean one thing: someone has surrendered.'

The words had hardly left Flora's mouth when a screaming voice had them running to the window.

'What is he saying, Flors?'

For a moment, fear held Flora from answering Ella. The man's words had filled her with terror. 'He – he says . . . the Germans are coming.'

'Oh, God help us.'

'It's all right, Ella, we have international protection.'

Flora noted that even the strong and capable Mags had a tremble in her voice. The story of the Red Cross nurses in Serbia flashed before her.

As they watched, the doors and windows of every building were shuttered and barred. Shops were closed, and cafe owners hastily brought in their street furniture. Flora watched the sheets of a dropped newspaper dance – an eerie dance along the now-deserted pavement.

Then, in the distance, a sound became increasingly loud. It wasn't like anything Flora had ever heard before: the steady tramping of many feet – the Germans were truly coming! As they came into sight, Flora's heart beat with the rhythm of the marching regiments of tired-looking men, flanked by gun carriages, and mounted troops with pennons fluttering on their lances.

Though none of them spoke, the fear in the air was tangible. It was a fear that took in the whole square, as Flora imagined thousands of Belgians standing behind their shutters, watching, terrified like she was, as the enemy came upon them. As the parade came to a halt, orders were barked out. To Flora's horror, a contingency of troops came into the hotel.

An age seemed to pass, with the girls not talking, just waiting. Then the banging on their door held them suspended. Mags moved on the second loud knock and opened the door, to find the remaining four trained nurses standing there. 'We've to move in with you. The hotel has been requisitioned. It is to become the German quarters, but we have been assured, by an English-speaking officer, that we are safe from harm while we await our orders. I'm Phyllis, this is Teddy, and Jane, and Martha. As senior, I have assumed leadership. Now which one of you speaks French? We've been told that one of you does, and we've had a jolly difficult job being understood. It seems that, in their fear, none of the staff can remember how to speak the little English they have.'

'I do. I'm Flora.'

'Jolly good, Flora. I want you to go to the manager and demand that three mattresses and bedding are delivered to this room by nightfall. They will be more inclined to follow the orders of the Germans first, but be forceful: use the fact that we are internationally protected, and that any stories of our ill treatment will not do the Belgians any good, in the eyes of the Allies.'

Flora didn't want to leave the room, where she felt a small amount of protection, but she took a deep breath and marched towards the door.

'I'll come with you, Flors. Come on, we can do this.'

'Thanks, Mags.'

As they went to leave, Ella's cold hand grabbed Flora's. 'Me, too. We'll all go together.'

It felt as though a thousand eyes watched them as their tread, softened by the deep-pile carpet, took them along the sumptuous landing with its magnificent chandeliers. Soldiers stood to attention. One gave a low whistle, which set the others laughing. A hand grasped her arm. She looked up into a handsome face. In French, he asked her name. She replied in English, 'I'm Flora Roford, I'm a Red Cross Nurse and, as such, I have international protection.'

'English, eh? How many of you are there?'

'Seven. We are awaiting orders, and have been assigned one room between us.'

'Well, you had better stay in that room. Pretty girls are sought-after, no matter where they come from.'

'You insult my uniform, sir.'

He jumped back. 'Get on your way.'

A few sniggers accompanied them as they walked on.

'Well done, old thing. But why the English?'

'I didn't want him suspecting us of being anything other

than what we are. I listened carefully to that tale the other night of the captured nurse. I heard the word "spy" mentioned, so thought they might think that of me, if they knew that I spoke the native language.'

Once the girls made it back to their bedroom, they found that their beds had been stripped.

'You will take the mattresses, girls. We are senior to you.'

'Senior?' Mags sounded shocked. 'You are trained nurses, that's all. How does that make you senior to us?'

'Volunteers take second place to trained nurses. You are here to assist – it is us who have the knowledge and will guide you. That makes us senior. Now, once the mattresses and bedding arrive, you will make our beds and your own. In the meantime, we need to rearrange the room, so set to and move the beds into a row against that wall. You three will have your mattresses under the window.'

'Sorry, but no: I won't fight you over who has the beds, as it is of no consequence, but if you want them, you can move them yourselves.'

The one introduced as Teddy stepped forward. 'I agree. Look, Phyllis, we are in this together, and pulling rank is causing a rift. Once in a hospital situation, I'm sure these girls will agree that we should take the lead; but here, in a hotel bedroom besieged by German soldiers, no. We should all be equal – and friends.'

Phyllis looked nonplussed. 'Very well, I'm sorry. I was afraid and found comfort in taking charge. Of course we will muck in together. Forgive me.' A tear dropped from her eye.

Mags moved forward and took a very surprised Phyllis in her arms. 'That's all right, old thing, we all react differently in situations where we feel threatened.'

Phyllis's face was a picture and made them all laugh.

'Group hug is called for.'

'Oh, Mags, you're a card.' Flora could hardly say the words, as she found herself in a huddle of laughing girls. The tension had broken. For all she was worth, Flora felt like picking up a pillow and bashing someone with it, as often happened in the dormitory in her school days, but she resisted the temptation and joined in the banter, as each girl relaxed and they began to get to know one another.

She felt safe in the company of these girls, and a feeling of being part of something special settled in her. But what of the future? The look in the German soldier's eyes came to her as he'd called them 'pretty girls'. *Please let our orders come soon. Please don't leave us here.*

Chapter Seven

'Are you still awake, Mags?'

'I should think we all are, with this racket.'

A chorus of 'I'm awake' and 'I can't sleep' was almost drowned out by the sound of the singing Germans.

'I wish they'd shut up and go to bed. They looked exhausted when they arrived.'

'The drink has given them a new lease of life, Flors. I don't think we're going to get any—'

A scream cut off Mags. The seven of them shot up to a sitting position. The sound of a match being rasped and then light flooding the room, as candles were lit, brought some comfort, but the screaming overrode that and left Flora feeling that her blood had run cold.

Mags was the first one out of bed.

'Wait. Don't open the door. Make sure it is locked.'

'No, Phyllis, someone is being attacked – we have to go to her.'

Flora grabbed her dressing gown and was by Mags's side, unheeding of the protests from the others.

A cold draught hit them as they stepped out of the room, into a blaze of light from the chandeliers.

'Please don't, girls. You'll get hurt!'

Taking hold of one of the tall candlesticks, Flora blew out the candle and discarded it. 'I'll hit them with this if they come near to me, don't worry.'

The screaming turned to a hollow moan, giving flight to their legs, as the sound of despair put urgency into them.

Opening the door of the room from which the noise came showed a horrific sight – one of the hotel maids was being forced over the rail of the double bed. A soldier was raping her from behind.

Mags flew forward. 'Get off her, you bastard!'

His arm knocked Mags off-balance. The girl turned towards them, her face etched with pain and terror. A laugh filled the air as another soldier, naked and obviously awaiting his turn, leapt on top of Mags. Before Flora could react, her arm was clamped in an agonizing grasp.

'You will do me, pretty one.'

She looked into the lust-filled eyes of the soldier she'd spoken to earlier. 'No! No, don't touch me.'

An agonizing cry from Mags lit Flora's temper. She lifted the candlestick and brought it down on the soldier's arm. His hand loosened its grip, as he gasped with the pain of the blow, but then his stance changed and his face contorted with hate as he lashed out at her.

Landing on her back, Flora felt her breath leaving her lungs. Before she could gasp in any air, he was on top of her. 'You'll pay for that – international treaty or not. You're not in uniform now, so how am I to know who or what you are? You're a slut who came to our room to join in the fun.'

Horror seeped into Flora as she felt his hand lift her

nightdress and caress her bare thigh. She hadn't even any clothing to protect her, or to slow his advance. 'No! No! Please don't . . . don't!'

Once more Mags cried out, a sound of pain and desolation, which filled Flora with fresh anger. Lifting her legs, she kicked out. The surprise of her attack caught the soldier offguard, and he let go of her arms to defend his bare torso. Flailing with her fist, Flora felt as if a wild cat had entered her, as she saw a defeated and distressed Mags being raped unmercifully.

'Oh God. Oh, dear God, help us!'

The door behind her was flung open. '*Was ist los? Stehen um Aufmerksamkeit.*'

A disgusting group of naked, sweaty bodies stood to attention. Flora turned in horror and saw blood covering the genitals of the soldier who had hastily withdrawn from a sobbing Mags. She crawled along the floor and took Mags in her arms. There was nothing she could say.

The officer who had entered spoke to Flora's attacker. With the little German she knew, Flora understood that he'd asked who the girls were. She saw his face change to extreme anger at the reply of: '*Zwei davon sind Rote Kreuz.*' *Rote Kreuz*, she knew, meant the Red Cross.

A tirade of angry words spat from the officer. Flora held Mags's shivering body close to her. No sound came from her, but from behind, she could hear the soft whimper of the hotel maid.

Shamefaced, the officer who had attacked her, and who had spoken to them in English, translated that they were to go to their room and that nothing of this must be spoken of or reported, otherwise reprisals would be brought down on the townsfolk. 'One child will be shot, every hour of tomorrow, if this gets out.'

Flora cringed. The brutal reality of war was more horrific than she dared ever imagine. 'I will take the maid with us, and we need your assurance concerning our future safety.'

The officer looked surprised at this and sought translation. On hearing what she'd said, he nodded, but a second warning issued from him, which the soldier translated. 'In future, whilst you are in this hotel, you will not mix with the staff. You will keep yourselves out of sight as much as you can. And do not leave your room without uniform, no matter what time of the day or night. You must be recognizable to my men at all times. If you talk of this, the reprisal I spoke of will be carried out – and that goes for the maid, too. Now, leave at once and see to these two girls. Make sure they understand the consequences of anything of what occurred here being known.'

Flora nodded. Leaving a sobbing Mags to hold on to the bed, she went over to the broken maid. In French, she spoke soothing words.

'What is this? You speak French? Just who are you, girl?' A smile crossed the face of her attacker. He turned and spoke in German to his officer. Flora held her breath.

'What is your real purpose in being here, girl?'

Mustering her dignity, Flora stood to her full height. 'I'm a volunteer with the Red Cross. I've been sent here to act as an interpreter to the nurses and my fellow volunteers. We are solely here to treat the wounded of any nation who need us – yours included. Tomorrow we plan to go out of the gates, as we have heard there are wounded still out there.'

After speaking to the officer, relating what she'd said, the soldier turned back to her. 'You are to report in the morning to Herr Aldelstein, in the office that was the manager's. All of the Red Cross nurses must attend.'

Nodding her head, Flora helped the maid to her feet and supported her as they made their way towards Mags, who stood up straight and nodded at her. Flora felt the tears that had flowed during her own attack prick the back of her eyes once more, as she saw the dignity that Mags had mustered. Seeing a need in another person had helped her, and she moved forward and took the other arm of the maid. Flora managed a small smile at Mags, which she hoped conveyed her compassion.

Once outside the room, Mags seemed to collapse inwards. With the weight of the maid resting on Flora's body, she could do nothing. 'Hold it together, Mags. You can do it. Let's go to the bathroom.'

Flora took charge when they stepped inside the clinical-looking bathroom, with its black-and-white tiles and scrubbed flagstone floor, covered in a soft gold-pile matting. 'Run the bath, Mags.' And to the maid in French, 'Please don't be afraid – we will help you and take care of you. But I must ask you: did you understand what would happen, if you tell anyone about this?'

The girl shook her head. Flora related the horrific threat that the German officer had made. 'And they will do it. I have heard of them carrying out such reprisals in Serbia, so please heed what they say.'

The girl's mouth dropped open, and her eyes showed her despair.

'Try not to worry. We will have to find a way to cope, without breathing a word of what took place.'

The girl nodded, tears streamed down her bruised face

and she wiped the snot from her nose. Flora pulled her trembling body close and held her.

Mags, who had stood by as if made of stone, moved at this and silently took over, helping the girl into the bath.

'I'll fetch clean nightwear for us all, and we'll take the girl to our bedroom for the night, so that we can care for her, Mags.' Flora so wanted to hold Mags, but she had put up a wall, and Flora knew she wouldn't be able to penetrate it just yet.

'What is her name?' Mags asked, without any emotion in her voice.

'Oh, I forgot to ask. *Quel est votre nom?*'

'Aliz.'

'All will be fine, Aliz.' Flora explained to her what was happening, then left them to it. Outside in the corridor once more, she took a deep breath. A low wolf-whistle got her standing still in shock, then taking flight and running for her life to their bedroom, only to find the door locked. Banging on it as if her life depended upon it, she nearly fell over when it opened suddenly.

Frightened eyes stared at her. Ella moved forward. 'What happened? You're bruised. Oh, Flors, where's Mags? Oh, dear God!'

As seemed to happen when others showed fear, strength entered Flora now. 'I need three uniforms.' The request shocked her, but the wolf-whistle had reminded her just how vulnerable they were. 'Mags's and mine, and one other. One of your size, Ella. Hurry! Something terrible has happened.' As briefly as she could, she told the others in a low voice what had occurred, adding the threat that had been placed over them. 'Nothing must leak out about this – nothing! Promise me. Promise.'

A shocked silence followed.

'We must be brave and remain dignified, but we must obey. Don't even go to the toilet without donning your uniform, for it will protect you. We must go as one brave, united front to the office in the morning. Now promise me that you will all do as I say.'

Phyllis stepped forward. 'We will, Flora. This is devastating, but we will find a way to cope; we have to, for your sake and Mags's. Now, girls, get those uniforms. And, Flora, I left the room earlier when you were all asleep. The Germans were all in the bar drinking and singing then, so I managed to collar the manager without being seen and get him to speak English to me. He gave me all I asked for – a gas ring and a kettle, tea and milk and even sugar, as well as some mugs. So how's that for resourcefulness, eh? The kettle will be boiling on your return. Hurry along.'

In Phyllis, Flora recognized a natural-born leader, and knew her to be a brave soul who would be a massive asset to the group. An uneasy calm was settling amongst the others as they put into action Phyllis's orders. But she knew that her own language skills would mean that she must take a lead role, too. So far tonight she had proved to herself that she could, even though the horror of what had happened to her, and the others, set a shudder trembling through her.

Though she felt dirtier than she'd ever felt in her life, Flora took a moment to don her uniform before returning to the bathroom. This time the few soldiers who stood smoking at the other end of the landing turned their backs on her as she walked towards them. Amongst them was her attacker. As she neared him, he stared at her in contempt. His hand went to his crutch and he thrust his lower body forward in a gyrating movement.

Flora lifted her head and let out a laugh, something she least felt like doing. His face reddened, before showing extreme anger. Her stomach muscles clenched, but she stood up straight and walked on in a determined way. As she came up to him, the spittle gathered in her mouth. It took all her control not to spit it in his face, but she knew that would lower her to his standards and might cause his anger to tip over.

Once in the bathroom, she leaned heavily on the door. Aliz sat on the toilet seat wrapped in a huge towel. Tears poured down her face. There would be no comforting her, as there was nothing in this world that could achieve that, so Flora deliberately went into efficiency mode and instructed Aliz to put on the uniform – and the trembling girl stood and did as she was bid.

Mags sat in the steaming bath, her head resting back. Flora moved forward and stroked her wet hair off her face, guessing that she'd dunked her head in the hot water. She understood that, as she too felt she needed to cleanse the whole of herself, and not just her torso.

'Mags, the girls know. I had to tell them; we couldn't possibly hide it from them. But they also know that they mustn't breathe a word, either now or in the future, when we are assigned placements.'

Mags nodded. The despair in the gesture undid Flora and, despite having schooled herself to act in a strong manner, tears seeped from her until they were huge sobs. Mags's wet arm wrapped around her, and together they collapsed into one another and sobbed.

The hand stroking Flora's back soothed her. She lifted her head and looked into Aliz's brave smile and knew that showing your own vulnerability helped others, as it gave them the strength to cope, when they reached out to give comfort.

'We will be all right. We can forget.'

'We can, Aliz. And we will. What happened tonight, to you and Mags in particular, was a terrible thing, but we have to put it behind us and carry on. How will you keep safe, Aliz?'

'I do not have a way. And I don't see that we will have a choice, as we can't leave.'

Her situation was hopeless; Flora could see that, and didn't know how to help. 'Try to find hope, if you can. But keep safe, no matter what. The war will pass.'

'Maybe I can join the Belgian Red Cross? Maybe you could put in a word for me?'

'Have you had any nursing experience?'

'I nursed my mother until she died.'

'I'm so sorry for your loss. What about your father?'

'My father is in the French army. I fear for his safety every day.'

The pity of Aliz's life hit Flora and her heart felt heavy. 'Give it a try. You can keep this uniform – the others will understand. Go to the Red Cross tomorrow and tell them you were given this uniform by the English Red Cross nurses, to protect you from the lust of the soldiers. Tell them that you are afraid of the soldiers as you work nights at the hotel, and that you must leave your job. If you share your experience of looking after your mother, and the fact that your father is fighting for them, it might work.'

'You have helped me so much. Thank you, I will do as you say.'

'I haven't a clue what you two are talking about, but I need to get out of this water and let you have a bath, Flors.

Give me a hand, old thing.' There was a flicker of the former Mags, and Flora felt glad of it.

Once Mags was out of the water, with a towel wrapped around her, it was Flora's turn.

'I'll wash you down, Flors.'

'I can manage – you get dressed.'

'No. I need to help you.'

Flora allowed Mags to wash her down. The sensation of being cared for gave her comfort, and she thought of her dear Aunt Pru. How she would love to be by Pru's side at this moment. To feel her arms around her, and to sink into her soft, loving body and be loved.

'That's it, Mags, I'm all clean. Let's dress and get back to the other girls. There'll be hot tea waiting for us.'

But would hot tea ever soothe her again? And although she'd voiced the thought that they should try and forget all of this, she knew that she would never forget, and she knew that neither would the other two. The experience would bind them forever. She decided to give Aliz the address so that she could write to her through the Red Cross General Office, and implored her to keep in touch. War had brought them together in a vile way, but it had also cemented what she wanted to be a lifelong friendship of support and love.

Chapter Eight

A sleepless night had left Flora feeling empty. Her mind had gone over and over the events of the night before. Her heart ached for the restless Mags. Aliz had fallen into a fitful sleep, calling out and her body shaking with rebound sobs.

And now, with the early morning, Flora faced her hated attacker again. He stood next to Herr Aldelstein, behind the highly polished desk. His glare directed towards her held contempt, as he interpreted what was being said.

'Herr Aldelstein directs that you will explain your bruising as having happened during the fighting yesterday, when a stray shell hit the building across the street.'

Flora nodded and saw out of the corner of her eye that Mags – whose poor face was blighted by a swollen black eye – did, too. They both knew that the outer signs of having been hurt were nothing compared to what they were coping with emotionally, or to the pain and soreness that Mags felt, from having been violated.

This morning she'd spoken about it and had said that she was hanging on to the fact that her rapist had been interrupted, and so wouldn't have made her pregnant. She'd looked around at them all and had pleaded with them never to tell a soul. 'Not even when the war is ended. Please. I couldn't bare for anyone but us to know.'

They had made a pact. They'd sealed it by crossing their arms and all holding hands. Ella had said that she would always be there for them both, and the others had joined in saying they would, too. They'd gone into a group hug that had held love – nurtured by the situation they found themselves in – but which Flora felt would last long after they parted. The hug had included Aliz, who'd left early this morning with all their good wishes, in the hope that she would be accepted as a volunteer worker.

'You are to be put to use, while you await your orders from the British Red Cross. Herr Aldelstein has spoken to the Belgium Red Cross director, Monsieur Reynard. They are coping with the wounded from the recent engagements and need your assistance. The Royal Palace, which was being used for this purpose, has been recommissioned. There are no wounded or dead left outside the gates. The rumours about this are untrue. Monsieur Reynard will send transport for you.'

Flora was glad to get out of the office, and away from the insult in every look that the soldier gave her.

'Well, I – for one – am jolly glad to be doing something at last. But I hope our orders come through soon. Come on, girls, let's wait outside, I hate the atmosphere in here,' Teddy muttered.

Teddy had told them that her real name was Tamara Bear, but that she'd quickly been nicknamed 'Teddy' by her school friends. She seemed to Flora to be a most unlikely girl to have taken up nursing, being what you would term a horsey type. During their chats she had told of excelling in gymkhana events, and that she hoped to work with horses one day. There wasn't much that you could say was attractive about her. Her tall frame was almost manly; she had light-brown hair that she fashioned into a bun; she was short-sighted, wearing small, round glasses that she peered out of, as if they didn't really help her eyesight; and her protruding teeth did nothing to help her appearance. But for all that, Teddy came across as a good-natured soul, ready with her smile, and she was happy to go along with the crowd and do her bit.

Once outside, the sun shone down warmly on them and lifted Flora's spirits. She gazed across at the cafe where they'd sat yesterday and wondered how the women they'd met were coping. On the columns of the hotel, notices were posted that hadn't been there yesterday. One told of a curfew, another of certain buildings that were to be requisi-tioned. The Metropole was the first on the list of this notice.

Jane stood next to Teddy and was dwarfed by her. Small and quiet, she was a pretty, curly-haired girl, with freckles covering her face. She hadn't spoken much at all, but had shown concern and kindness to Mags, holding her hand and making sure she could manage her tea, when they had returned to the room the night before.

Martha's tinkling laughter could be heard as she joined Teddy and Jane. Martha was the practical sort, and got on with things without moaning about them. She had a good sense of humour and seemed to find a lighter side to everything. Blonde and good-looking rather than pretty, she was the same average height as Ella and Flora were, though inclined to a little plumpness.

Phyllis took charge again. 'Look, girls, I think we should

assert ourselves right away. We are not going to be skivvies to the Belgium lot, and neither are our volunteers. We have specific skills, and they are to use us to the best possible advantage of the patients. Flora, you will be spokesman of course, but make sure you get across that we want to work as a team and they should assign us as such.'

She had an air about her that commanded attention. Tall, like Mags, but not of Teddy's height, Phyllis was quite a striking girl, with her red hair and flashing green-brown eyes. Her features were clear-cut, and her manner was precise.

No one protested at Phyllis's air of authority. At least she wasn't being as dictatorial as she had been when they'd first met yesterday, and was showing her caring side.

Flora looked at Mags, whose pale face and pensive expression prompted her to ask, 'Are you sure you're up to going with us, Mags?'

'Yes, I'm sure. I don't feel well, but I'm not staying there on my own, Flors. Don't let them send me back.' She was broken; the spirited girl ready to take on the world had gone. Flora prayed she would come back in time.

'If it wasn't for being needed to translate, I would stay there with you. But I promise I won't let them send you back on your own. Try to buck up a little. I know it isn't easy, as I feel some of what you are going through. I was just lucky that the officer came in time to stop— Oh, Mags, I'm desperately sorry.'

A tear had seeped out of Mags's swollen eyes. Its trickle sent sorrow coursing through Flora. She hadn't known Mags long, but she had known a very different girl from the one standing beside her now. Even Mags's stance told of defeat. There was nothing Flora could say to make things right, so she tucked her arm into Mags's and huddled close to her.

A Red Cross truck pulled up and a woman alighted from the driver's seat. '*Vite, vite, Mesdames.*' A torrent of instructions followed, which Flora had a problem keeping up with. But the woman gave no leeway and hurried them on. Her glance at Flora held astonishment, as her eyes fell on her bruised cheek; but then, when she looked at Mags, her mouth dropped open. The shock registered in her voice. Flora translated: 'What is this – how did you get hurt? Are you fit to work?'

'We are, Madame.' The lie they had been told to tell, concerning the stray shell, rolled easily off Flora's tongue. To the woman's objections about them going to the hospital, Flora explained that she was needed to interpret, and then begged her to reconsider taking Mags, saying that it would be uncomfortable for Mags to be left in the hotel with the German soldiers.

The woman didn't seem to be taken in by the story. She stared at them for a long moment and then, as if making up her mind not to press them further, she nodded, before introducing herself as Madame Brecket. Then she told them that they had to prepare themselves, as there were many injured. Mostly French soldiers who, once they were well, would be sent to prison camps. 'So they are mentally and emotionally upset, too.' Looking at Mags as she spoke again, Flora translated to her that Mags would only be allowed to go with them if she agreed to work in the sluice. Madame Brecket felt that Mags's and Flora's appearance would further upset the soldiers, and so they would be required to wear a mask at all times to cover their bruising. It was as an afterthought that Madame Brecket softened and told them how sorry she was that they had come to her country to help, only to be injured.

This last comment made her human, as did her smile when she spoke. Flora could feel the tension easing amongst the others at these kind words, and an eagerness to get on with the job seized her.

The sight of the Royal Palace gave Flora a pang of homesickness, as the front of the building was so similar in appearance to Buckingham Palace, with its three sets of columns. Inside, its sumptuousness belied the purpose it was now being put to. Flora felt in awe of the gleaming gold-and-crème interior, the huge chandeliers and the polished wooden floor that shone like a mirror.

As they followed the matron they'd been assigned to, Phyllis went into her usual organizational mode. 'Look, Flora, I think we'll be best served by you not having a particular duty, but helping us all with communication. You could float and be ready to come to our aid, if needed. Ask Matron if she is in agreement with that.'

Matron agreed to Phyllis's suggestion, though Flora insisted that she first settle Mags to her tasks.

A change came over Mags once they entered the two rooms that had been adapted for their purpose. The long kitchen with a bathroom leading off it was overpoweringly hot, and full of steam. Pans boiled away on the stove, next to which stood a pile of bloodied bandages and buckets full of dirty instruments. When they walked through to the bathroom, the smell knocked them back for a moment, as bottles of urine were stacked in the bath, with bedpans of excrement piled high in a corner.

'Right, I've work to do. You can leave me now, Flors. I'll

be fine. With this lot to sort out, I'll have no time to dwell on things.'

Relief overcame Flora at this. 'You sound like your old self. But are you sure, Mags?'

'I am. There's nothing like seeing the need of others to lessen your own pain.'

A voice behind them got them turning round. 'I am here to help.'

'Aliz! Oh, Aliz, they took you on!'

'*Oui*.' Aliz held a handkerchief over her mouth against the stench.

'It takes a bit of getting used to, but that's the first rule of nursing – empty a bedpan without retching, and you know you will make it. It took me a week of doing it to cope.'

Before Aliz could answer Flora, she was swept into Mags's arms. The two girls held each other for a moment.

Flora swallowed the lump in her throat and asked, 'How did you explain the state you are in? Oh, poor Aliz, your neck is all bruised.'

'As is all of my body, and my soul. I told them that I was hurt when I fell off my bicycle, and that I no longer wanted to work at the hotel, now that the Germans were there. They understood. I told them that you English nurses had helped me, and as my clothing was ruined, you had dressed me in one of your uniforms. And that I had decided to keep it on, as it would help me to get an interview with the director. And it did! They said they had no time to train me, but that I could help with cleaning jobs and serving the meals, which is what I am used to doing. I have been given two grey dresses to wear, and Red Cross armbands. The director told me they will keep me safe. I – I think he saw through my story . . .'

'But he didn't ask you any more?'

'*Non.*'

'Well then, we have no need to worry. He must be a very wise man. The main thing is that you are all right, Aliz. Right, Mags, I have to get back. Tell me what you want Aliz to do and I'll give her instructions, before I go.'

Once more Mags showed that she was in control as she organized the sterilization of the instruments as their first job. 'We can't touch anything in the bathroom until we have done that, as we will become contaminated. Flors, can you ask for extra help for us – there's a massive task here for just the two of us.'

'I'll try, Mags, but from what I've heard, they are very short-handed.' After translating to Aliz what Mags had said, Flora left, telling them that she would be back as soon as she could.

The sights and sounds that met Flora in the makeshift ward appalled her. Men called out in agony, and it seemed to her that there was a sea of blood – beds were covered in it, as were the bandages on the men, and splashes of blood covered the walls. But there was organization, too, as nurses bustled about, cleaning up and administering to the patients.

Flora's heart went out to the broken men, and to the young nurses trying to cope with it all. Not sure what to do first, she felt inadequate, and knew at that moment that her training hadn't been sufficient. *How can I make a difference to all this?*

'Flora, over here.'

Teddy called out, and Flora ran over. Finally she was

needed, and no matter how small her contribution, it would make a difference.

'Please ask this young man to try and keep still. I am attempting to set his leg.'

How was it that these young ladies were expected to carry out such a massive task? But then, as she looked around, Flora realized there was no one else who could do so. From Matron down, the dozen or so nurses were all engaged in carrying out what would usually be done in an operating theatre: stitching wounds that gaped, digging out bullets and doing what they could for shattered limbs. In one corner a doctor sawed away at a soldier's arm, his cries of agony almost drowning the pain of the other patients.

Soothing the soldier whose leg Teddy was trying to set wasn't easy. 'Here, bite on this. Nurse Bear is strong – she can pull your leg back into place. It will hurt, but once done, it will give you a chance to walk normally again, when you have healed.'

'To *fight* again, you mean. Nurse, I need to escape or they will send us to the camps. Our lives will be a misery. Please, you must help those of us who are not so badly wounded to escape.'

Flora had been warned during her training that this would happen. They were told that they must always remain neutral. Their job was to tend the wounded, no matter what side they were on, but not to get involved or do anything other than a nurse's duties.

'I'm sorry – I can't. No doubt, when you are stronger, you will come up with a plan. But to get to that point: you have to let Nurse Bear do her job. Be brave.' She gave him a rolled-up bandage to bite on.

His hand gripped hers so tightly that the pain became

almost unbearable for her, but Flora didn't complain. Sweat dripped from Teddy as she struggled to pull the broken bones into place. Eventually she managed it, just as the soldier passed out, and as Ella called for Flora's assistance.

'You go to Ella, Flora. I can manage now. As long as he is unconscious, I can get the splint into place easily.'

Flora crossed the room and found she was needed to help a young man of similar age to herself, whose eyes held fear. '*Mon nom est Flora. Je suis Anglaise. Quel est votre nom?*'

'El – Elvan.'

Speaking in French, she told him, 'Elvan, everything is going to be all right. You're in safe hands.'

'*Non*! I – I die.'

'You speak some English?'

'A little. I am from Normandy.'

His accent was endearing. That he should try to speak her language in the last moment of his life touched her. 'We can speak French. Would you like me to contact someone for you?'

His eyes filled with tears. Speaking in his own language, his voice unsteady, he told her, 'I have my grand-mère only. Sh – she brought me up. She lives in Morlaix. Rue de Chantelle, quatorze. Her name is Louisa Garrot. Please tell her that I died a brave man. And – and that I love her.'

'Whatever it takes, I will get that message to her, Elvan.'

'*Merci*. Please . . . tell the nurse who holds my hand that she is very beautiful and has brought me comfort.'

Flora swallowed her tears.

'And – and you. You have done me a great . . . ser—'

Elvan's breath became laboured and then his eyes gently closed. Flora instinctively stroked his blond hair. His lips quivered into a small smile, giving a boyish look to his handsome face, but it quickly fell away as his last breath shuddered from his body.

Flora let go of her tears. Ella's hand came into hers, sharing her grief and shock.

No one so young should die like this, far away from home, Flora thought. But at least she had a message for his loved one. She would write to his grandmother as soon as she could. And she knew in that moment that she could make a difference.

Chapter Nine

A fortnight passed before their orders came in. They were all exhausted, but gradually the work at the palace had diminished as the soldiers were shipped out to prison camps or, in the case of the Germans, back to their homes, to re-join their regiment once they were fully recovered.

Two envelopes had been waiting for them when they returned to the hotel that evening: one was addressed to Flora, and the other to Phyllis. Opening hers, Flora told them: 'I, Mags and Ella are to go to a hospital in Charleroi, to join a British Red Cross matron and two nurses. There's no mention of you four, so I assume your orders are in your letter, Phyllis.'

'Oh, blow. I hope we are all to stay together.' Phyllis ripped open the envelope as she said this. 'Not to be. Martha, Teddy, Jane and I are to go to Marcinelle.' There was a collective muttering of regret from them all that they were to separate. It was Jane, a small girl, very shy, but with a sweet nature, who surprised them all by expressing a hope that they would meet up in the future. They all agreed, and then were further surprised when Martha, who, like Jane, hadn't expressed much of an opinion on anything up to now, suggested they all exchange addresses in any case so they would be able to make contact with each other.

Flora smiled at both Jane and Martha, and although she hadn't interacted much with them – mainly due to Phyllis being their spokesman, and Teddy's gregarious personality overshadowing them – she knew her bond with them was just as deep as it was with the more outgoing Phyllis and Teddy.

'Hold on, I'll go to the bar and see if I can get a bottle of wine. We need something to help us relax with this news, and to celebrate meeting each other.' Teddy grabbed her handbag and made for the door.

Nothing daunted Teddy, but it was Mags's reaction to Teddy's suggestion that warmed Flora's heart, as a bit of her old spark showed when she called after Teddy, 'Jolly good idea, Teddy, girl. Make it two. We're not being picked up till tomorrow at ten – we can recover by then.'

After they were all in their pyjamas, they opened the wine. As they sipped from the cups that they used for their tea, they relaxed in the convivial atmosphere.

'These bread rolls are delicious. I was starving. Flora, if you get a chance, will you thank the manager for his kindness?'

'I will, Phyllis. Now, how about a sing-song? No goodbye-night is complete without one. If I had a piano, I would play for you. I so miss my music.'

In the next hour they belted out popular numbers and giggled at silly jokes.

'Well, I don't know about you all, but I'm completely bushed.'

'Me, too, Teddy. And look at Mags – she's curled up like a baby, bless her.'

As Flora said this, Ella pulled a blanket off her own bed and covered Mags with it.

'Let us hope she has a better night, as none of us know what we have to face tomorrow, and it will be easier for her if she is rested.'

Flora agreed with Ella. 'The poor lamb has cleaned a mound of bedpans today, and she joined in the singing and enjoyed her wine, so there's every hope that she will rest well. I know I will. I can hardly keep my eyes open.'

The journey took just over an hour. Parts of it were along rough farm tracks, and caused the girls to be shaken about like rag dolls. Acrid smoke rasped the back of Flora's eyes as they finally alighted from the van.

They stood in front of the Grand Hôpital de Charleroi and looked around them. Crumpled, windowless buildings, some bleeding water as if they were tears, others belching smoke from smouldering fires, gave a picture of what had happened here as the battle to take Brussels had raged. Gunfire rumbled in the distance, putting new fear into Flora as she realized that the fighting wasn't as far away as it had been.

No sooner had they arrived than they were informed that there were no English Red Cross workers at the Grand, and were given the addresses of three more hospitals that they could try. After receiving the same reception at two more hospitals, Flora was almost ready to give up. 'I'm beat, girls, what about you? The order we received must have been out of date – our matron must have moved on.'

'We'll try the last hospital. There may be news,' Ella suggested.

They all agreed they should, and set off once more.

With her feet burning from the miles they had walked, Flora approached the last hospital on their list.

'Oh, they left here for Marcinelle a couple of days ago. It seemed their need was greater than ours, as we are getting on top of things now. The fighting has moved and we've had no new cases.'

Flora felt defeated. 'How far is Marcinelle?'

One of the nurses answered, a round-faced girl, whose smile told of her kind nature. She spoke in English, which was a relief to Flora. 'It's about eight kilometres away, but you look all in and it's getting dark. Look, I'm about to leave for home. Come with me – my mother will put you all up for the night. My name's Helga. I live in an apartment near the Sambre River, six kilometres from here. I get a lift with Monsieur Monres, who is a cleaner in the hospital and lives near me. There is plenty of room in his trap for you all.'

This kind offer almost helped to soothe Flora's feeling of utter desolation.

As the horse trundled along, the terrible aftermath of the battle was laid bare across the town. There were soulless folk with nowhere to go; others crying and trying to salvage something from their homes; and all to the background noise of shells being fired in the near distance. It made Flora think of the wounded soldiers in the Royal Palace of Brussels, who had left their mark on her.

Helga's mother made them very welcome. The apartment was on the ground floor, with a view over the river through its front window. There was one room that served as the kitchen and sitting room. Sparsely furnished, it held a scrubbed table with four chairs pushed under it, and two sofas in a beige colour. On one wall was a blackleaded stove, a sink and a dresser. A door led off the room next to the stove and this, Flora saw, when Helga's mother went into it, was a pantry, but although there wasn't much furniture, the room didn't look bare. The walls were hung with pictures and brasses, and shelving held all manner of ornaments, from a set of traditionally dressed Dutch dolls to a colourful vase.

Helga's mother was introduced as Madame Eline. She'd prepared a delicious stew, made from lamb cutlets, potatoes and vegetables. Flora felt a pang of guilt that this might have been meant to last them a few days, but she was so hungry, she ate the generous portion Madame Eline dished up to her.

Tired beyond words, they all accepted the offer of retiring after supper. The bedroom belonged to Helga and contained a huge bed that was big enough for the three of them. Helga, who had made no mention of a father, said she would sleep with her mother.

The girls lay awake for hours, chatting occasionally about what they should do, but mostly disturbed by the never-ending sounds of war.

A scream from Ella, as the house shook from a nearby shell explosion, doubled the shock Flora felt. Instinctively they huddled together, their fear tangible.

None of them spoke, as the world they used to know tumbled further into a place that held fear of their own deaths. The room lit up with a glow from houses that had taken a hit, while the space around them filled with screams of terror and despair.

Mags sat up. 'I can't stand this. Let's dress and see if we are needed.'

They all agreed, and were dressed in their uniforms in no time. Outside their room, they met Helga and her mother, who was wrapped in a shawl and was begging Helga not to go out.

In French, Helga implored her mother to try to understand. 'Look, the girls are ready, too – we may be needed. We are nurses, it is our job.'

Outside, the world had turned to a searing hell. The girls hardly knew which way to turn, but a desperate plea had them running over to a building opposite. 'Help me!'

Lit up by the fires, the night seemed as if it was day. Scrambling over rubble, they came across a woman crushed under a pile of bricks, from what Flora assumed must have been her house.

'*Mon bébé. Mon bébé.*'

Understanding this, Ella's desperate voice shouted, 'Where? Oh, Flors, ask her where her baby is.'

Helga had already done so, and Flora translated to Ella and Mags that the woman had said her child, a boy, was under the bricks. Taking charge, Helga asked the girls to do all they could to find him, while she tended to the woman.

'Flora, ask if there was anyone else in the house.'

Flora did as Ella requested and spoke directly to the woman, who was able to tell them that it was just her and her baby, as her husband was away in the army. Flora looked over at the rubble that was once the woman's house and her heart sank.

They'd been working for about ten minutes, frantically clawing at the bricks, some so hot that they burned, others

101

jagged so that they cut their hands, but nothing hindered them in their desperate bid to find the baby.

'Oh God, no!'

Flora stiffened, not wanting to ask Mags what she'd found. Turning, she saw her lift a bundle. *Please, God, don't let it be the child.*

'I've found him, poor soul.'

Clambering over the rubble, Flora and Ella got to Mags at the same time, but before they could see what Mags could, a flash from an explosion threw them all to the ground. Trembling as she spat dust from her mouth and wiped it from her eyes, Flora looked up, trying to see the others. Mags lay next to her. The bundle, now exposed, showed a dead infant, bruised and torn. A cry escaped her. Where her strength came from she didn't know, but she flailed her arms in the air, hitting out at nothing but the horror of all that was happening.

'Are you girls all right?'

Helga stood over them, her cheek bleeding. The sight of her brought Flora out of her shock, straight back into professional mode. She stood and checked the other two, who were getting to their feet, too, and found that apart from a few scrapes of their skin, they were all fine.

'How is the woman, Helga?'

Helga shook her head.

Mags still held the baby's body. She wrapped the blanket back around him. As she climbed over the rubble, they all followed her. Bending down, Mags lifted the woman's arm and placed her baby son under it.

They stood for a moment. Four nurses, who were meant to be strong, undone by the sight. An arm came round Flora and she looked up into Helga's face. Tears streamed down her cheeks. 'Did you know her, Helga?'

'Yes. She hadn't lived here long. I spoke to her for the first time this morning as I left for work. Her name was Raquel and her son was called Josen. I – I . . .'

Flora waited, as she could see that Helga was struggling with her emotions.

A group of older men came over to them. 'We have ambulances and firefighters on the way, Nurses, we'll take over here. There's a family over there who need your help.'

Somehow they got through, giving first-aid where they could and seeing patients off to hospital. Sheets were used as bandages, and various ointments and cleansing fluids, as well as painkillers, were brought out to them by the local pharmacist.

Flora wondered if she would ever feel anything ever again, other than shock, horror, fear and extreme tiredness.

The next day, as the three of them sat in the car of a friend of Helga's, having said their goodbyes to her, Flora pondered over how many young women she'd come across since leaving home. All of them were so brave in adapting to the new world they found themselves in. *Where have the lives that we planned gone? This isn't how it was meant to be.*

The car came to a halt at the request of a German soldier. The driver spoke German and took a moment to explain his business and show his papers. The soldier looked through the car window at them, then nodded. 'He says he appreciates the difficult work you are doing, far from home. He, too, is far from home and having a difficult time.'

Flora thought about the Germans she'd met at the hotel. She wound down the window and smiled at the young man.

Not much older than her, he looked uncomfortable, but then he smiled back when she used her little German to thank him: '*Vielen Dank*.'

When they finally arrived at the hospital they found the British Red Cross matron and the nurses all desperately worn out. They were told there was little equipment, and that up to fifty wounded had been brought in only that morning.

'Are there four more nurses here from England? They should have arrived yesterday?' Flora whispered to the harassed matron.

'Did you know them?' She looked up and bit hard on her lip.

Flora felt sick. 'Yes, why – what happened?'

'They were in an accident on the way. I'm very sorry, but they were all killed.'

'No . . . no . . . Oh God!'

Both Mags and Ella clung to Flora. She looked into their haggard faces and wanted to scream out the pain inside her. How was it possible? Those lovely girls. Why, why?

'Come along now, there is work to be done. I'm sorry for your loss. I didn't know them, but we badly needed them here. It is a tragedy – may their souls rest in peace. Now, I'm sorry if I sound callous, but we must focus. I need you to prepare any Germans, as they are to be evacuated. They are all in the ward across the corridor. We have been told that trucks are picking them up in about an hour. Make sure any open wounds are cleaned and dressed. Splint any obvious broken bones, and administer pain-relief to those needing it the most. There is a tray of medication over there.'

Looking at them properly for the first time, Matron

added, 'Run and change your uniforms first. I am going to assume there is a good reason for making your appearance in such a dirty condition? You can report later.' In French she shouted to an orderly, a young girl who looked no more that fifteen, 'Take these girls to the bathroom, then deliver them some uniforms from the stores, but hurry.'

Once the Germans had been shipped off, the workload eased, and Matron invited them to sit with her and, over a welcome cup of tea, tell her what had happened to them. She commended them on their foresight and bravery, before telling them to look on the German evacuation as an indication that the Allies were making headway. 'They wouldn't move the Germans out, if not. So overall the news is probably good. Now, I want you all to rest well tonight, because tomorrow I will need you to bear the brunt of the work, while I rest my nurses. I have a feeling that we, too, will be shipping out soon. As the war moves, so do we. Your first job in the morning is to heat as much water as you can. There is no running hot water here. Wash down all the mattresses that the Germans were lying on; many of the Allied soldiers are lying just on bedsprings, as there were not enough mattresses to go round and, while the Germans held the upper hand, they took precedence.'

This shocked Flora and, without asking the others, she felt that she had to speak up on their behalf. It was funny, but in the few short weeks they'd known each other, she knew they would be thinking the same as she was. 'Matron, may we do that now? I can't bear to think of those soldiers putting up with one more hour in such discomfort, let alone a whole night.'

As Matron started to protest, both Ella and Mags joined in agreement with Flora.

'Very well. And, girls, you are doing your uniforms proud. Thank you.'

The stiffness had now gone out of Matron. Her stance softened and a lovely smile lit her face, turning her from a plain care-worn woman into a lovely, approachable one.

Once they had all the soldiers settled, they made cocoa and sat together, talking about Phyllis, Teddy, Jane and Martha. It seemed they were devoid of tears and emotion, as they didn't cry, but remembered the goodbye-night and vowed they would always remember the other girls.

There were more shocks at noon the next day, as Matron announced that her prediction had come true and that she and her two nurses were to be shipped out. She wasn't sure where to, but she'd been assured it was unlikely there would be any further casualties brought to the hospital, as the fighting had moved too far away.

'I am leaving you in charge, Flora, as you speak the soldiers' language and can cope with any communications that come in, which will most likely be in French. I don't anticipate that it will be long before you are all moved on. There are plans to close our operations here, due to the lack of equipment, et cetera.'

Within an hour the nurses had left, with Matron kindly agreeing to see that the letter Flora had written to the grandmother of Elvan, the soldier whose hand she had held as he passed away, got to the Red Cross headquarters. Flora hoped that from there it would eventually reach its destination in France. This gave her closure of her time in the Royal Palace, though she knew she wouldn't ever forget

Elvan, and felt sad that he would never step on French soil again.

Turning from the open door, through which they had waved Matron and her party off, Flora sighed. 'Well, that's us carrying the cart then, girls!'

'It is, Matron Flors. Where do you want us, and what do you want us to do?'

They all burst out laughing at this. 'Ha, I've been promoted already. Nurse Mags, I want you to scrub every floor in the hospital with a nail-brush and, Nurse Ella, you are to wash the bottom of every patient!'

Their laughter rang out. Calls of 'What's so funny?' and the sound of men laughing, even though they didn't know what at, filled the two occupied wards.

'Seriously, I think I should go from bed to bed with a notebook and pen and talk to each patient. Just to make my own assessment of each one's needs. Matron indicated that it was only basic nursing care, for those left in our charge. Well, we can manage that, can't we?'

There was nothing immediate that posed more than they could manage, and Flora's confidence grew. She numbered the beds, then made a list with corresponding numbers for Ella and Mags to follow – dressings would need changing, medication would need to be given out, and general keeping clean and comfortable seemed the order of the day for most of the men.

One young man posed them more of a problem. His temperature was high, yet his body was cold.

'I'll ask the orderlies and the kitchen staff to see if there is a doctor we can call on. I'm worried about him,' Flora said.

Mags and Ella agreed. Mags, being the most experienced,

ordered that they set an orderly to douse the soldier's body in cold water, as a first-line measure.

With night orderlies in attendance, the girls sat in the kitchen, eating the delicious casserole that had been left in a pan for them.

'I don't feel a bit tired. I feel as though I'm buzzing, which is the best I've felt since we arrived in Belgium.'

'That's good to hear, Ella. I feel the same, and I'd love to stroll out and find a bar. I could just down a nice glass of wine.'

'Not sure I want to go that far, Mags.' Flora laughed. 'But, yes, I feel the same. Uplifted somehow. It was good to hear that doctor praise us, saying we had probably saved that soldier's life.'

'Yes, and good to know that there are resources out there to help us. I was relieved when the doctor decided he should be taken to a better hospital. I think it's bad form that we are left on our own.'

'We'll manage, and Matron said it wouldn't be for long. I know, how about I play that piano that stands in the hall? The soldiers will be able to hear it, if we open the doors.'

'Spiffing, as my old teacher would say. What do you think, Ella?'

Ella laughed. 'That would be wonderful. And couldn't we send the orderly for a few jugs of ale for the men?'

'Done! Come on.'

Flora was surprised when, within a few minutes of the orderly leaving the building, ten jugs of ale were delivered by the owner of the bar down the road, and by a few of his customers. 'Glad to help the men who fought so bravely, and you girls of course. We'll collect the empty jugs tomorrow.'

As Flora played tunes ranging from 'It's a long way to Tipperary' to 'Alexander's Ragtime Band', laughter, applause and even a little dancing, by the more able-bodied, turned the hospital into a place of fun.

Most of the tunes she played from memory, some she had to improvise. But however she got there, every note seared through her, bringing her joy.

Chapter Ten

Flora looked at the meagre stores left in the hospital kitchen cupboard. One bag of flour and another of dried beans – beans, which they'd eaten every day of the last week. Cook had made stews with them, bringing in an onion from her home. She had fried them, after rehydrating them, and had made a kind of pease pudding with them, but nothing really made them taste of anything other than beans . . .

Flora sighed. The order she'd put into their supplier had been refused. She was told that no bills had been paid, and the credit was already too high to continue supplying them.

Their own pay had long since ceased to arrive, and no news had filtered through either from, or about, any other Red Cross nurses in Belgium – or anywhere, for that matter – as all communication had been cut off.

They were now down to two patients, as most had been shipped to prisoner-of-war camps and some, who were not well enough to go, had gone to hospitals in Charleroi. Saying goodbye to each patient had been heart-wrenching. The remaining two were being picked up by the Germans later today, which was a relief in some ways, as the responsi-

110

bility for them would lift from her shoulders, but it also tore her apart. These two, and all the soldiers, had become their friends over the last three months.

Ella came up behind her. 'Are you Mrs Hubbard again, Flors?'

'Afraid so. Our cupboard is bare. I just don't know what to do.'

'I'll go round all the neighbours again – they helped us last week.'

'Thank you, Ella.'

Ella, always the weakest of the three girls, was stick-thin and very pale. Flora feared for her.

'Before you go, I need to speak to you and Mags. I've had bad news. You go along to Matron's Office' – they still called the office where Flora sorted out the day-to-day running of the hospital 'Matron's Office'. 'I'll go and find Mags, and we'll have a meeting about what to do next.'

'What is it, Flors?' They sat drinking the very weak tea with no milk, without complaining, chatting about this and that, until Mags brought up the subject of the bad news, with this question.

A sigh came from deep within Flora. 'I'm afraid that Hendrix has come back with a negative answer.'

Ella's head dropped. Mags just looked straight ahead. Neither girl spoke.

Hendrix was an elderly man who lived locally and had taken to coming in a few hours a day to lend them a hand. A week ago he had agreed to make the journey to Brussels to seek out the American minister, who they knew had been asked to look after British interests.

'The US Legation has said that on no account are we to go to Brussels, and that they cannot give us any money.

111

They suggest that we ask the German commandant in Charleroi to give us a pass to England, or Maastricht, via Germany.'

'They are feeding us to the wolves.'

Flora had to admit that Mags could be right. No one had bothered about them at all and, even when the communication lines were still open, very few instructions had come through, other than to complete the job in hand and await further instructions.

'I'm afraid. What about the rumours that some nurses, who were supposed to have been sent to England by the Germans, have been found in Russia?'

'That was in the beginning, Ella. There have been many talks about our standing since then, and all nations have agreed to give us immunity from capture, and freedom of movement to do our work.'

'None of that will stop the Germans; they say one thing, but do another as it suits them.'

'You're right, Ella. We need a plan, I think—'

Mags's words were cut short by a loud bang. The muscles of Flora's stomach clenched. Rising, all three went into the hall. A German officer stood there, with four soldiers flanking him. The shattered panels of the door suggested their hurried and forced entry.

With all the courage she could muster, Flora turned to Mags and Ella and told them in French to go about their duties. They had rehearsed this, after Hendrix had reported that German soldiers in the local bar had been overheard saying that the hospital was hoarding deserters. Flora had taught Mags and Ella how to answer in French, if questioned. Their intention was to pass themselves off as Belgian.

'Stay where you are!'

The officer spoke in French, but his command was unmistakable. Mags and Ella stopped in their tracks. A whimper escaped from Mags. Flora wanted to tell her that it would be all right, and to keep calm, but dared not speak to her in English. She knew the emotions that the officers' arrival would trigger in Mags, and prayed that they could keep to their plan.

The officer's next command was given in German, but once more it was easy to understand and saw Flora stepping back, as the men charged straight at her, pushing them all roughly out of the way to get into the office and begin searching the building.

'How many patients do you have here?'

This, in French again, gave Flora a little hope. So far the officer hadn't guessed that they were not what they seemed. 'Two French soldiers, who are to be shipped out today.'

'No Germans?'

'*Non.*'

'I will see for myself.'

Flora's legs felt as though they would give way, as the threat of them being arrested now seemed less likely. She was certain the soldiers would find nothing.

Following the officer, Flora watched as he checked the papers of the two soldiers, who sat in the lounge. Both still had splints on their legs, but it had been the normal practice of the Germans to ship all the soldiers out before they were fully recovered, to prevent or hamper their chances of escaping en route.

Two of the German soldiers carried out a thorough search, kicking in the doors of all the wards and breaking open cupboards that were big enough to hold a man. With the search completed, the officer stood in front of Flora and scrutinized her, without speaking. Eventually he turned on his heels, barked an order, which had his men falling in behind him, and left.

Flora couldn't believe he hadn't asked to see their papers, but then something in the way he had looked at her gave her the feeling that he had suspected they weren't all they seemed. What held him back from interrogating them, she couldn't imagine, but she was very grateful he hadn't.

Instinctively she knew they should leave, and as soon as possible. But how, and where to?

Turning, she found Mags in tears and Ella comforting her. 'Come on, girls, we need to plan our escape.' This had the effect of helping Mags, as she wiped her eyes. 'But first we need to make sure the men are all right. Pierre is terrified of what the future holds, and Jacques may need some comforting, after that experience.'

'We've a little beer left, from the last lot donated to us. I'll get them both a drink.'

'Yes, that's a good idea, Mags. Ella, do you feel up to going on your begging trip now, love? We have no food to give the men before they go – what's left of that loaf you brought back last time is black and inedible. They may not be offered anything to eat for days!'

'Yes, I won't be long. I have some houses where I know the ladies who live there will give me something, as they always do. I'll go to them first.'

Hendrix came through the door at that moment. 'Is everything all right, Mademoiselle Flora?'

'No, far from it, Hendrix. Come on through and sit down.' Once Hendrix sat down, he removed his beret, twisting and turning it in his hands. 'We need help, Monsieur Hendrix. We have to escape, and soon. I take it you saw the

Germans?' At his nod, Flora continued. 'Well, I think they suspect that we are not Belgian. They may consider taking us prisoners. We must leave the moment we have the two men fed and ready. Will you sit with them till their transport comes? And can you help us in any other way?'

'I have been preparing for this moment, Mademoiselle Flora. The rumours are getting frightening. Oh, I know that rumours are flying around everywhere – they are bound to, with no proper communication – and that some are just scaremongering, whilst others are planted by the Germans as they drink beer in our bars, so that they can keep up the level of fear that suits them, but we do have to take some seriously. I am afraid for all of you and glad that you are getting out, as it is being said that the Germans are ready to take reprisals, by shooting any nationals from enemy countries who haven't their permission to be here.'

Flora drew in a deep breath.

'What is it, Flors? You look terrified. We are safe, aren't we?' Mags asked as she walked into the office.

Flora interpreted what Hendrix had told her about them being right to move on, but didn't mention the rumours. 'He is about to tell me how he can help us, so don't worry. He has been planning this, for when we were ready.'

Keeping as calm as she could, Flora turned back to Hendrix. 'How can you help us, Hendrix?'

'There is a fund of money for helping those in need. I have asked for a sum to fund your passage, and it has been readily granted. Our townsfolk are in awe of the courage you have all shown in staying and nursing the Allied forces. Most knew you were English, but not a word has been spoken about it. Messieurs Aubert and Tompard, the owners of the coal mine, have put one of their ambulances and a driver at your disposal. He can take you to Fleurus, and from there you must go by train and tram to Liège and make your way to the market. The market women carry on a trade, taking refugees over the border into the Netherlands.'

'But what about papers?'

'One of my brother's grandchildren works as a secretary in the German headquarters, and she has managed to wangle three laissez-passer, which the Germans issue for essential travel. You are listed as sisters visiting a sick relative. But it is only valid as far as Liège, after which . . .'

'We will manage. Oh, Hendrix, I cannot thank you enough for all you have done for us. I'm overwhelmed. When should we leave?'

'You are to come to my house tonight. My wife is cooking dinner for you. Do not tell the hospital cook anything. I do not trust her. I can tell you now, but was afraid to before, that she was taking food out of here and selling it on the black market. She is disgruntled, now that there isn't any, and I know that she has petitioned the concierge of the hospital, saying that you three have overindulged the patients, and yourselves.'

'No! I – I had no idea. Oh, Hendrix. How can we be sure she won't find out?'

'We can't, but just be careful. You haven't left here for a while, so even going out will raise her suspicions. I will invite her to have a drink with me. She is partial to more than a tipple. Once we have gone, you must hurry to my house. Immediately after dinner you will leave. By the time morning comes, you will be well on your way, and Cook will receive a warning of the dire consequences of her telling anyone that you have left.'

116

Flora crossed over to Hendrix and put her arms around him. 'Thank you. Thank you so much. For everything.'

'Keep safe, and make it back home. That will be all the thanks I need.'

After he left, Ella returned with a bundle of bread and cheese. Before long, they and the soldiers were tucking into it. Flora hadn't tasted anything so delicious in a long time.

While they ate, she told Mags and Ella of the plans that Hendrix had made for them. 'We have to be strong and stick together – we can get through this. Now, let's check on our boys, they should have finished their sandwiches.'

As soon as they walked into the lounge, one of the soldiers yelled, 'Nurse, will you play again? I'd love to hear you once more, before . . .' Pierre's head dropped to his chest. Flora knew he was consumed by fear about their imminent departure to the prison camp.

Playing the piano was something she least felt like doing, but Mags and Ella goaded Flora to play. 'Let's remember this last hour together with a smile.'

'Yes, play something light-hearted, Flors.'

Sitting at the piano, she played one of her own tunes. It reminded her of her mother. She hadn't thought about her much, since leaving England. Well, soon she would be back there – with a little luck and a fair wind – but did she want to visit her home? No, she wanted so much to go to Aunt Pru, to be held by her and to see Freddy. They were her family now. As were Mags and Ella. Yes, the four of them were all the family she needed.

Chapter Eleven

The cold air managed to seep through Flora's jumper. Even the coat she had on, one of three brought to Hendrix's home by a kindly Belgian woman, didn't stop her body shivering. Part of it, she knew, was fear.

It had taken a lot of gentle persuading to get Mags to abandon her uniform, but at last she'd seen the sense of it, on the proviso that they took their Red Cross armbands with them. Not wanting these to be found by anyone interested enough to carry out a search, they'd sewn them into the hems of their skirts. From now on, the three of them were to become innocent Belgian girls.

The ambulance trundled along, shaking them as if to rattle their bones. It was twenty past midnight and, with no other vehicles on the road, Flora leaned back in relief. Some sense of being safe entered her. She squeezed both hands that were holding hers, as they all sat huddled together on the floor next to the stretcher-bed, which ran the length of one side of the ambulance. One other woman sat in the front, next to the driver. She'd been introduced as the nurse who worked in the coal mine. No other information was given to them, and they didn't ask.

'Keep down.'

Just before she bobbed down, Flora saw that they were approaching a German checkpoint. She hurriedly translated the driver's urgent instruction to Mags and Ella. Ella's head came down on her shoulder. Flora could feel her fear. Mags's grip tightened on the hand she held, as the ambulance came to a halt.

Shivering and feeling sick, Flora tried to decipher what was going on. The driver and the nurse told the guards that they were a miners' ambulance, going to pick up a patient. They were immediately asked to produce their papers.

A torch shone in through the window. Flora held her breath. Relief flooded through her as she felt the revs of the engine and the ambulance move off once more.

Dawn broke as they arrived in Fleurus. The driver gave directions to them and wished them luck.

Snowflakes danced in the gentle but icy breeze, as they made their way to the tram. They walked in silence through a broken town – eerie in the half-light of the receding moon. Jagged beams pointing to the sky, and gaping holes in the walls of houses, told the story of the fight that had taken place here; of the lives lost, and of those torn apart. Rubble littered the pavement, making their progress slow as they made their way to the tram station.

'Are you all right, Flors? You've been very quiet since we left the ambulance.'

'Not really, Ella. Sometimes I wonder if I'll ever be "all right" again. All this destruction, and you can almost smell the misery of the people – wherever they are.'

'I know. You feel as though you'd like to make everything right for them.'

'We have to make everything right for ourselves first, Ella. We've a long way to go before we get home to safety.'

In the beginning it would be Mags jollying them along, every step of the way. Now, though the strain of it weighed heavily, Flora had taken on the challenge. 'We do have a long way to go, but we'll make it. We're together, that's the main thing. Right, there's the tram station. We'll soon be in Liège.'

'What will you do when you get home, Flors?'

'Spend time with my family, and write letters to the families of Phyllis, Teddy, Jane and Martha. I still feel their loss, although I haven't spoken much about it. I hope that, even though they may have had one service for them, they will agree to me holding another one.'

'Oh, that's a lovely, if very sad and thoughtful, thing to do. Please let me know if it happens.'

'I will, Ella.'

'Me, too. I don't know about you two, but I have put it all out of my mind; it was the only way I could cope. But a service, even if it is just us three, would help to settle it all – a proper goodbye to those four brave young women.'

'You're right.'

'That's settled then.'

'But before that, I am going to contact the Red Cross and ask to be sent somewhere else, to nurse the wounded.'

Ella nodded, but Mags was shocked. 'You'd do it all again! Oh, Flors, we've done our bit. And we're not safe yet. I feel I owe the Red Cross nothing. They abandoned us.'

'Not abandoned, Mags. We were cut off. Matron couldn't have known that she wouldn't be able to contact us, once she left. Communications being cut came as a shock to us all. She did the best she could at the time; she moved on to where trained staff were needed most, and left us to nurse the last of the French soldiers. We all knew the fighting was getting further away and that no more casualties would be brought to us. I just worry where she and the others are, and if they are all right.'

'I suppose so. Anyway, I'm for leaving the service and staying at home. I've had enough.'

Flora took Mags's hand. 'You will forget, in time; at least not forget, but find it easier to live with the memory, and get back to your old self.'

'I can't ever see that happening. That soldier destroyed my soul with what he did to me.'

'You need time away from it all. I'm glad you're going home. After a while you may feel you can cope and re-join. We may even get back together again.'

'Oh, Flors, it's unbearable to be parted from you both. I've always been such an independent madam, even as a child. I have friends of course, but never have I leaned on anyone before. And it feels as though my world is ending, now we are to part.'

Flora squeezed Mags's hand tighter, unable to speak. Through the swirling snow, she spotted the lights of the tram approaching and felt glad of it. The act of boarding and getting their tickets would be a distraction from the ache in her heart. Saying goodbye would be like parting from beloved sisters.

At the first stop, German soldiers boarded the tram. Flora felt the other two move closer to her. 'Act normally.' Her urgent whisper got them moving away a little.

Her heart clanged fear around her body, as the soldiers

made their way through the passengers, checking their papers. She prayed that their passes would be accepted. She held her breath. It seemed they were in a cocoon of silence, except for the heavy tread of the soldiers' boots as they made their way down the carriage. Her silent prayers begged for help when one of the soldiers reached them. She held out her pass, hardly daring to breathe as he scrutinized it. He spoke to her in German. She replied in French, saying she didn't understand.

To her relief, he didn't speak French, so he wouldn't be able to read what the pass said. After a moment he handed it back to her, and then only glanced at Mags's and Ella's, before moving on.

Once in Liège, Flora asked a passer-by for directions to the market. She had been told to ask for Madame Velluset, and the first stall-holder they came to, a man selling pots and pans, told them to go to the fourth stall around the corner. No questions were asked of her.

Madame Velluset's wrinkled face gave nothing away, as Flora informed her they had been sent to her by Hendrix.

'Be here by three a.m. tomorrow morning. Don't be late. I have to fetch vegetables from Maastricht.'

'Thank you.'

'The Hotel Villier is along this street and to the left. They are expecting you. Go there now and stay there till morning. Here, give me three francs for these.'

Flora took the bunch of carrots and handed over the money. She knew she was paying the charge for the journey, but why the carrots? When she turned away with them, she understood the reason, as she saw a group of soldiers standing on the corner, watching them. Did they suspect the market women?

Acting as normally as her nerves would allow, she thanked Madame Velluset again and moved off. Mags and Ella followed her. 'I have our instructions. When I stop talking, giggle out loud. I want us to appear as though we haven't a care in the world.'

Both did this without questioning her. Flora pushed Mags on the shoulder in a playful gesture, as she joined in the laughter.

They made it to the hotel, where Flora felt she could finally breathe. She looked back: no one had followed them. A sigh released itself from deep within her, but the relief was only temporary. They had the worst part to come – crossing the frontier.

Their coats were no protection against the bitter wind. Flora shivered as they left the hotel the next morning. Tiredness ached through her bones, but somehow she managed to jolly the others along. An open cart stood next to the market stall, the horse waiting to start its journey, snorting its impatience. Already three others were seated in the cart. Until she boarded, Flora couldn't tell if they were men or women, but now she saw they were all female.

She greeted them in French, but they answered in English. After saying good morning, one of them whispered, 'We understand you are volunteers. I'm May Tyler, a nurse with the Red Cross. This is Jean and Betty, both nurses. We have been working in the hospital here. We just missed getting out, before all communication and travel were restricted. We've been like hermits, not daring to leave the hospital.

But we're no longer needed, and so some of the Belgium nurses arranged this escape for us.'

Flora told the nurses their story. May expressed her regret that they had been left without a helm, as she called it. They chatted on, the six of them, exchanging stories – some funny, some sad, but all just a cover for what they really wanted to talk about: the danger that lay ahead.

The cart halted, stopping their chatter. 'I can only take three through. I daren't risk any more.' The old woman's comment rendered them all silent for a moment.

Mags leaned over towards Flors. 'What is it, Flors, what did she say?'

May answered, 'Three of us have to get off and make our own way across the frontier.'

Flora could feel the tension. No one volunteered. The old woman telling them to hurry prompted Flora to say that she would walk through.

Ella and Mags immediately said they would, too.

The old woman instructed them that they should walk a little way, then cross over the field on the left and crawl under the barbed wire. The thought of this struck terror into Flora, but the thought of the others' fear gave her the strength to do it, for them. Taking hold of each of their hands, she urged Mags and Ella along, trying to keep cheerful as she chatted normally. 'I've never done anything like this before, and I thought us three had seen it all. Come on, let's go – I'm freezing.'

'Me, too, and I'm bursting for a pee. Let's make that field before I wet my knickers.'

Flora laughed at Mags; there was a glimmer of her old spirit still in her.

'I'm ready. We can do this. I feel sometimes that we can do anything as long as we stay together.'

With this willingness from Ella, too, Flora felt her own confidence boosted. She loved looking after them both, but it did become wearing sometimes. It comforted her to know they were coping.

The grass crunched under their feet as they trod the crisp frost. As soon as they were behind a hedge, they all three relieved themselves, giggling like school children.

'Come on. We're nearly there.'

Mags's voice had all the command she'd had when they first met. It was good to hear.

'Wait for me, I'm struggling with my corset.'

'You wore a corset, Ella! Ha, that's the last garment I would have put on.'

They all laughed as Ella struggled with the ties. 'Oh, blow it! If you ladies are corset-less, then so shall I be.' With this, she pulled the boned garment from around her and stuffed it in her bag.

'Throw it away, Ella. Imagine the embarrassment if we are searched!'

Instead of laughter, this brought back the fear, which hadn't been Flora's intention. The mood changed as they moved forward, keeping close together.

When they came to the barbed-wire fence, Mags said, 'Well, this is it, girls. On your bellies.'

The wire caught on Flora's coat. Untangling it gave her a deep scratch on her hand, but nothing could dampen her joy as she stood up on the other side. 'We made—'

'Halt!'

Flora froze. Her stomach turned over. Turning to her left, she looked down the barrel of a rifle held by a sentry. Her

125

body went into flight mode, but she denied it and instead whispered urgently, 'Don't run or he will shoot us.'

In French, the soldier asked for their papers. To Flora's relief, he only glanced at them and seemed happy with the German stamp, and didn't notice that the papers only allowed them to travel to Liège. 'Why are you coming this way? You must go through the checkpoint.'

Thinking quickly, Flora hoped he would believe her. 'There was a crowd – carts, bicycles and hordes of people – so we took a shortcut that we always used to take as children.'

'Well, you are out of bounds. Go back and through the correct channels.' The soldier motioned at them, sending them back through the fence.

Flora told the others what the soldier had said, then added, 'We'll have to walk as if we are going back to the road, then double-back. Once we get under the wire, we must stay down until we are sure it is clear, then run like the wind. There must be another wire fence, but I don't know how far away it is.'

'It's hopeless – we'll be shot!'

'We have to take the chance, Ella.'

'Flors is right, Ella. We can do this. Look how far we've come. It's our last hurdle, then we'll be safe.'

Flora felt she would never be safe again. Each time they approached the wire, they saw more and more sentries. 'Look, we're not far from the border now. Shall we take our chances? I have money, I'll try a bribe.'

'I don't see that we have any choice.'

'We don't, Ella. Good luck, girls.'

'That's the spirit, Mags. Now, leave the talking to me.

126

Just do as I do. But, even if challenged, don't speak. We mustn't let them know we are English.'

They stood behind a small crowd. The movement forward had come to a halt. The guard whose queue they were in was questioning a young man's papers. Flora knew this could be their chance.

'Follow me. Have your pass bent over, so that just the German stamp shows, as that is all the sentry was interested in. Look confident. Come on.'

Pushing past the crowd, she went straight up to the guard. Waving the German stamp at him, she put an aggravated tone into her voice and told him they were in a hurry. As he moved in front of them, she pressed all the money she had into his hand and smiled. He hesitated, then looked at each stamp and waved them through.

'Walk normally, girls. Keep your heads up, and look as if this is what we do every day.'

They'd barely walked a hundred yards when a sentry motioned to them that they should halt. Flora thought this was the end. She had no further tricks to pull. No money to bribe with, no papers that gave them permission to cross. Tears of defeat stung her eyes.

'Ha! I gave you a scare there. I'm Dutch, not German – just thought I would have a little fun with you.'

'Fun! You . . .' Flora couldn't continue as the tears spilled over. Her temper had released the words in English.

He replied, speaking in broken English, 'I'm sorry. Really sorry. You're English? Are you nurses?'

'Yes. And don't mind Flors – she cries for joy, more than she does in sorrow.' With this, Mags jumped forward and hugged the very surprised soldier. 'So good to see you. Are we really free?'

Recovering, the huge Dutchman hugged Mags back. 'You are. And there is an English agent in that office over there. He will help you get home to Britain from here.'

Flora's tears flowed freely once more, as she, Mags and Ella hugged one another. They'd made it!

Inside the office, a man sat bent over a desk. Flora was reminded of her brother Harold, as this man's hair was in the exact same style, his double-crown causing a few strands not to know which way to lie, so they hovered in the centre, sticking up like two spikes. The colour was the same as Harold's and her father's, too: very dark, almost black. He wore a dark suit, with a whiter-than-white shirt collar sticking out above the jacket. For some reason, Flora really wanted to see his face.

'Papers, please. Your real ones, not your fake ones.'

'We don't have any, sir, only our Red Cross armbands sewn into the hems of our skirts.'

At this he looked up. Flora jumped back a step.

For a moment he stared at her. Then he smiled. 'Don't be afraid.' This softer tone, after the commanding one he'd used, put Flora into a flutter. She couldn't take her eyes off him.

'We're volunteers.'

As Mags relayed their story, Flora took in the whole of the man: over six foot, slim, and yet with a power as if, under his clothes, he hid muscles on muscles . . . *What's the matter with me?* Making a huge effort, she pulled herself together and asked, 'W – what happens next?'

'I'm Cyrus Harpinham. I'm an officer in the British army. I'm stationed here on military business, but I am called upon to help out any British refugees who come through the frontier. I'll first need to see your armbands. What happened to your papers?'

'We had to destroy them before we left, for fear of being searched. There were rumours that threats of execution of foreign nationals were being made. Any member of an enemy country was at risk. We pretended to be Belgian.' Flora bent down and tore her armband from the hem of her skirt and handed it to him. 'Our Belgian friends helped us, or we never would have survived or got this far.'

'Very well.' His eyes bore into hers. It was strange, but somehow Flora felt that a bond joined them as they looked at one another. Her heart missed a beat. *He's beautiful . . . Oh, for goodness' sake, what am I thinking? Have I gone mad!*

As Cyrus gave them instructions on how they would get a boat to England, Flora turned from him and followed Mags and Ella outside, but he called her back. He looked again into her eyes. 'I – I hope you don't think me rude, but I'll be back in England myself in a couple of weeks. May I look you up? I – I mean, just to check you all got home safely . . . I—'

'I'd like that.' With shaking hands, she wrote her address on the pad on his desk. 'It's my aunt's address – I live with her.' He didn't remark on this, but as he reached out to slide the pad towards him, his hand brushed hers. Something in her wanted to take hold of it and never let go of it. *What is happening to me?*

Mags broke the spell. 'Flors, hurry up.'

Smiling at Cyrus, Flora went to leave. He caught hold of her arm. 'You're very beautiful.'

Her breath caught in her lungs. She wanted to tell him the same.

'I – I'm sorry. I—'

Again, that look.

'Flors, are you stopping here all day?'

Almost running out of the office, Flora wanted to hop, skip and jump. 'I've just met the man of my dreams.'

'What? Have you gone crazy, Flors? You've only just set eyes on him. He's handsome, I grant you, but you don't know him.'

'I soon will, Mags. He's coming home in two weeks and is going to visit me!'

The two girls stood staring at her.

'You really mean it, don't you, Flors?'

'I do. I really, really do.'

With that, she clasped their hands and they all twirled around, laughing and crying at the same time. Mixed emotions – relief, joy and, above all, the wonderful sense of freedom assailed them as they came into a group hug. And for Flora, there was the added feeling that her real life was soon to begin!

PART THREE
London, 1915

~

Flora and Pru

Losing and Finding Love

Chapter Twelve

Pru stood outside, waiting on her doorstep, as excitement churned her stomach. The letter had arrived a few days ago. Short and very sweet, it had just said:

Landed in England, safe and sound. Have lots to tell you. Be with you on Tuesday afternoon, as I am having to give an account of events to the Red Cross director and await orders. I have already been told that I will be given two months' leave to give me time to assess what I want to do in the future, and to give them time to evaluate all we tell them. Can't wait to see you, darling Aunt Pru.

Flora x

At last, her Flora was coming home. Oh, it had only been nine months, but she'd feared every day for her safety. She'd counted the days, the hours, and now, at last, Flora came round the corner.

'Eeh, me little lass.' Flora ran into her arms. 'By, I've missed you, and worried over you till me hair threatened to turn grey. But, lass, you look fine. I'd even go as far as to say more beautiful than you did afore you left. Oh, Flora, I'm that happy.'

'I'm so happy to be home. These tears are tears of joy. I take after you for that – you always cry when you are happy.' They both laughed as they dabbed their eyes.

'Aw, you are like me, in a lot of ways. But then I brought you up, and I'm proud of that. Now, come on in. I've a big gangly lad waiting to greet you, but he's too embarrassed to do so. You know what lads are like when they are fifteen. Not a man, but not a boy.'

'Freddy! How did you get so big and so handsome, in such a short time? I missed you so much.'

Awkward and a little red-faced, Freddy stood up. His greeting started in a high voice, but dropped to a throaty growl. Poor Freddy, his voice was breaking, his skin was spotty, his body was all gangly and as tall as a man's, making him unsure how to behave towards her.

Not giving him any choice, Flora ran to him and hugged him. 'My lovely brother, it's good to see you.'

Freddy's arms wrapped around Flora and the tension broke. 'Good to have you back, Flors. I've been worried about you. And, I know it's late, but happy birthday.'

'Ahh, thanks, little brother. I'm getting old now – twenty-one, I can't believe it. Sorry you had so much worry, but all's well now, though I had some hairy moments.'

'Ma's baked you a cake, and I got you these.'

'Daffodils! They're beautiful, and let me know that spring is truly here.' Flora once more hugged Freddy, and this time, Pru noticed, there was no hesitation on his part.

More tears pricked Pru's eyes at the sight of the love shown between the two most precious people in her life. To

134

cover up her emotions, she bustled about as she listened to Flora's tale. Most bits filled her with horror, and she felt glad that she hadn't known the extent of the danger Flora had faced. As she passed a mug of tea and a wedge of cake to Flora, Flora asked how they had all fared and whether there was news of her family.

Pru had worried about this moment. She did have news, and it wasn't good. 'Your father isn't well, Flora, lass. And it's my fault. I told Freddy about his real dad, and Freddy wanted to see him. Not to talk to him, but just to clamp eyes on him. I – I took him to your home and we waited outside for a bit. Your dad came out, and as he went to get into his car, he tripped. Without thinking, Freddy and me, we rushed forward to help him. At that moment your ma came out of the gate. She got hysterical when she saw me. And – and, well, your dad took one look at Freddy and keeled over. I – I'm sorry, lass. I – I didn't mean to be seen . . .'

'No! Oh, Aunt Pru, it isn't your fault. Oh, God, when was this?'

'A few days back. I were that worried that I got in touch with your old cook. We were allus good mates, and I knew where she lived. She told me that your dad had a heart attack and, well, it ain't good, lass. Eeh, I'm reet sorry.'

'I'll have to go right away. I'd thought I would send a message to Daddy first, get him to make arrangements.'

Pru could almost touch the pain in Flora's words. That the dear girl had to make arrangements to meet her own parents beggared belief, and broke her heart. She didn't think that, for all the face Flora put on to cover her hurt, the lass would ever come to terms with it.

'You go, love. And insist on your rights as a daughter. Don't let your ma have you turned away.'

135

'I'll be back later, Aunt Pru. And you two are not to worry. I don't hold you responsible. It was only natural that you would want to see your father, Freddy. I'm only sorry that he is like he is. He has never fully accepted his responsibilities. I have been an outcast in my own home all my life, because of Daddy's sins. But for all that, I love him very much and must go to him.'

'I understand, Flors.' Freddy had never seemed so grown-up as when he said, 'I want to go to him, too, but I can't. If he mentions me, tell him that I'm all right and don't expect anything of him. Tell him . . . well, that I love him.'

'Oh, son – I'm sorry, lad.'

'No, Ma. Don't be. I've not missed out on anything. I wouldn't have it any different. It's just that when I saw him, I felt an immediate connection to him.'

Pru helped Flora on with her coat. Her heart felt heavy. George didn't deserve any of these wonderful young 'uns, and it was his loss that he'd never known her Freddy. 'Take care, lass, and stay strong.'

Flora held her as if she would never let her go. Pru hugged Flora with all the love she felt for this girl, who had become as much her life as Freddy was. 'It'll be all right. I'm sure. Off you go. I'll get supper for about six, but I'll keep yours hot, if you're later than that. Oh, look at me. I nearly forgot. A letter came for you, lass. Here it is. Shove it in your bag – you can read it later.'

Pru didn't miss the look on Flora's face as she took the letter. She knew that blush, if she wasn't mistaken!

As she closed the door on Flora, Pru sat down and lifted her now-cold tea to her lips. 'Eeh, lad, I've brought sommat down on the pair of you. I just hope them brothers of hers treat Flora right, when she gets there.'

'I can't believe these men you told me of are my half-brothers, Ma.'

'I knaw, but you're not like them. Nothing like them. You're a good lad, and you're going to make sommat of yourself.'

Once they'd finished their tea, Pru set about getting what she would need to make a pastry crust for the meat and onions she'd cooked off on the stove.

'You've done me proud at that school you go to, Freddy. Eeh, to think the head teacher said that you're on course to get a place in university in a few years' time. By, I'm that proud of you, lad.'

'Ma, I know you have sacrificed a lot to pay for my schooling, but I told you: if the war's still on when I'm sixteen, I'll apply for training. They need all the men they can get. We're suffering heavy losses, and now the Germans are infiltrating our waters. I—'

'Stop it, lad, I can't bear it. I knaw how bad it is, but I ain't letting you go, no matter what you say. They won't take lads of fifteen and sixteen; they can't.'

'Ma. I know you're scared, but at school we had a general visit us. He told us that it may come about that they need young lads, and that we should be ready. He said that on reaching sixteen, we can apply for officer training. I want to, Ma. I want to do my bit.'

Pru felt defeated. She'd heard of young 'uns running off and lying about their age and being accepted. She'd hardly believed it, as she felt sure that checks would be made, but a lad from their own street had gone, who had only just turned sixteen. Fear had her swallowing hard. 'All right, son, we'll see. We'll not fall out about it. Let's pray that this awful war ends before you're needed.'

But deep down, she knew it wouldn't end. The talk now was of the whole world joining in, even the Americans, who had been neutral until now, but were upset and angered by the loss of one of their ships, fired on by the bloody Germans. *Why? Why?*

She didn't have long to ponder this as she began to roll out the dough she'd mixed, because the door opened and Abe walked in, cutting short her thoughts. His huge frame filled the doorway. His handsome good looks did nothing for her now. Any love she had felt for him had died within her. His bullying ways, and the control he had over her, had taken their toll.

Freddy made an excuse and left the room. He'd become embarrassed of late about her relationship with Abe, and constantly asked his mother to leave him. She knew that would make him happy. If only Freddy knew how much she longed for that to happen an' all. But Abe had made it clear what he'd do to Freddy, if she ever left him.

She knew now about his business dealings, and how he got the riches he had, although they never spoke about them. Not after she'd found out about one of his pursuits – prostituting young lasses – and had tackled him about it. That had caused her to suffer the worst beating of all the beatings she'd suffered at Abe's hands.

On the other hand, he could be gentle and kind. He was generous in his support of her school, and towards her, if she needed anything; and he cared for Freddy, and looked on them both as his family.

'What's to do with the boy? Every time I come in, he goes out! That's disrespect.'

138

'Naw, Abe. The lad's growing up. He looks on things differently to us. He loves you, I knaw that, but he's . . . well, there's things about us that he's no longer comfortable with, and he's a lot on his mind.'

Pru told him of Freddy's leaning towards the military. 'How will I bear it, Abe?'

Abe took her in his arms. Normally she'd yield to him and take comfort, even if she had no feelings for him, but her fear for her son ran too deep.

'Anything can happen. We've talked about this, Pru. Where's my spirited girl who can take on anything that comes her way, eh? You have to prepare yourself, darlin'. Even I might have to go, in the end. The news is full of how the number of volunteers is dropping. Can they wonder at it? It seems like signing your own death-warrant to me.'

'I knaw. I've read how there's talk of forcing men to go. Oh, Abe, it's all a nightmare.'

'We don't know the half of it, love. And it's bloody inconvenient. It's affecting imports now, and that has a knock-on effect on my business.'

Once more Abe held her close. She could feel his need, but she wasn't in the mood. Pulling from him, she moved away.

'What do you think you're doing? You ain't refusing me, are you?'

'It's the middle of the afternoon, Abe.'

'That's never bothered you before. Come here, I want my dues.'

'Your dues, is it? Abe, I'm not one of your prostitutes, and I'm not a never-ending supplier of your pleasure, whenever you need it! I've a lot on me plate and—'

Abe rushed at her and grabbed her arm. His grip hurt her,

his voice a threatening growl. 'Don't say things like that, ever! I don't use you. I never have. I love you. And don't you use what we have for your own gain, neither. I won't stand for it.'

Love, huh – does he even know the meaning of the word?

'A – Abe, let go, you're hurting me. I don't knaw what you mean. I – I . . . Abe!'

Her body hit the table. Resisting his strength was useless. He turned Pru and bent her over.

'Abe, naw. Don't. It's alreet. We'll go to me bed. I'm reet sorry. I didn't mean . . . Abe, naw!'

Not heeding her words, he shoved her head down, banging it on the table. Memories of him raping her in the past came to her, and she knew it gave him pleasure beyond what was normal. Her fear increased, as she thought of him tearing her as he pounded the back of her. 'Naw, naw, Abe!'

'Leave my mother alone! Get off her. You pig!'

Shock held Pru unable to move, as she felt Abe jarring from her.

'Get out of here, kid!'

'No, you get out – and don't come back. You're not welcome, and my ma isn't going to be your mistress ever again!'

Humiliated in the extreme, Pru lifted herself in time to see Abe jump towards Freddy. Her scream hurt her own ears, as she saw his fist smash into Freddy's face. Freddy's eyes rolled and his body slumped to the ground. Lifting the rolling pin, Pru brought it down on the back of Abe's head. Where she found the strength, she didn't know, but the force of the blow caused a loud cracking sound on impact.

She stood staring down at the two bodies on the floor. A

140

moaning noise, which she knew she was making but couldn't stop, filled the space around her as her mind screamed, 'Freddy, Freddy! Naw! Naw . . . !'

Chapter Thirteen

'I can't let you see your father, Flora, it will upset him too much. The stress brought on by your antics has caused this. He's been worried sick over you. Oh, it didn't help when that slut who used to be your nanny turned up here, trying to pass off her son as your father's. But you – you didn't even bother to send a letter to put his mind at rest! You're a disgrace!'

Flora cringed at Pru being called a slut, but decided to ignore it. She didn't want to deny Pru; nor did she want her mother to know the huge part that Pru had played in her life.

'Mother, that isn't how it was. I couldn't write. All communication was cut off. The Red Cross director told me that he had kept all parents informed.' She didn't say what she thought: *I doubt any letter from me would have got to Daddy anyway, as it would most probably have been intercepted by you.*

The tension in the air in Mother's sitting room eased, with the entrance of Harold. 'Ah, the Prodigal Daughter.'

'Hello, Harold. Nice to see you, too.'

'Come here.' Harold surprised Flora by crossing the

room and taking her in his arms. 'I've been worried about you. Are you all right?'

The gesture brought the tears Flora didn't want. 'I'm fine. I've had a bit of a time of it. But I'm home now.'

'Home?'

'Mother! For goodness' sake, this *is* Flora's home. What is the problem with you? Why are you so vindictive about Flora?'

Flora never thought in a million years that Harold would stand up for her. 'I'm Father's sin, that's why. Born of an apology for one of his many indiscretions, and Mother cannot forgive me for it.'

'Good God, really?'

'Stop it. Stop it! You vile girl! Oh, why did I ever have to have you?'

'Mother! No, you stop it. Stop it now. Flora is my sister – your daughter. I forbid you to treat her like this.'

'You forbid me . . . You . . . How dare you? You don't know the half of it. You think you are the heir, don't you? Well, you have a shock coming to you, as your father has a far greater sin out there that will usurp you. Then you will want me on your side, as I have always been. Then you won't forbid me to acknowledge this . . . this reminder of what he did to me – to you!'

'What are you talking about, Mother?'

Flora felt afraid to hear the answer. Something floated in her memory. A mention, when she was a child, of a son older than her brothers. *Is there another Freddy somewhere?*

'You will find out soon enough.' With this, Mother sat down and sobbed into a cushion. When she lifted her head, a tirade spewed from her, about how wronged she had been

143

by their father. How none of it was her fault, and how she suffered it all for the sake of her sons.

Harold softened. 'Mother, please. Don't upset yourself. I'm sure you're confused. Of course I am father's heir. Anyway, I don't wish to talk about it. I'll get a cup of tea brought to you. And I'm sorry, but I am going to go against your wishes and am taking Flora up to see Father. It would be cruel not to, given the possible outcome, after what has happened to him.'

Ignoring their mother's wails, Harold once more put his arm around Flora and guided her out of the room.

'Flora, we've been kept apart too long. Mother has treated you appallingly, and so has Father. Oh, I know he has kept in touch with you, but to permit what has happened to you is unbelievable. I admit I never cared much, but when I knew you were in danger, I realized how much you meant to me.'

'It wasn't your fault, Harold. Mother is Mother, and gave you a different view of everything.' Putting her arm around him, she squeezed his waist. 'I'm glad that we're friends now, though, big brother.'

Harold smiled. A crooked, funny smile – almost sinister. Flora dismissed the thought. She was being silly. Harold was being lovely to her. Why, then, did she still feel doubt about him?

'What did you make of what Mother said, old girl?'

'I – I don't know. It was all very strange. I don't think Mother is well; she's unbalanced in some way. I – I mean, she can't help the way she is.'

'No. I think that, too. She is getting stranger by the day. How is Pru? Father told me that you stay with her when you are home, and have done since you were a little girl.'

'She's wonderful.' Flora hesitated. *Should I tell him about Freddy?*

Harold's next words stopped her. 'Mother always calls her "that slut" – do you know why?'

Feeling cornered, Flora tried to pass off the remark. 'I think Mother imagines that Father took a fancy to Aunt Pru when she was my nanny.'

'Aunt?'

'Oh, it's just a polite form of address. I couldn't keep on calling her Nanny Pru. And she is like an aunt to me . . . No, more than that. She's the mother I never had. I love her very much.'

'Dear, dear, Flora, I didn't know you had stooped that low.' Before she could protest at this comment, they had reached their father's bedroom. 'Now, you are likely to be shocked, Flora. Father is very weak.'

Shocked didn't describe how she felt when she saw her father. He seemed to have shrivelled up into a little old man. 'Daddy. Oh, Daddy!'

'Flora, shush!'

'N – no, don't shush her. Flora, my darling, you're home.'

'I am, Daddy. I'm safe. Forgive me, but I couldn't contact you, as there was no means for me to do so.'

'I – I underst—' Her father's words turned into a heaving breathlessness.

'Oh, Daddy, don't try to talk. You need air. What are they doing to you, keeping you in this semi-light, with the windows all closed? It's so stuffy in here. That won't help your breathing at all!'

'Don't interfere, Flora. Mother has engaged a good, qualified nurse, which is more than you are.'

'I may not be qualified, but these last months I have done the work of a doctor, let alone a nurse. The stuffiness of this room will do Daddy no good. He needs oxygen. Open the window, Harold.'

'And what do you think you are doing? Who said you could even enter this sickroom?' A nurse bristled in from the adjoining bathroom.

'I did. I am the daughter of your patient, and I have experience of nursing. A heart-patient needs oxygen, and there is hardly any in this room. I am ordering that you keep it aired at all times. You can keep your patient warm by other means, and you can wear a coat, if necessary.'

The indignant look on the nurse's face almost got Flora giggling. But there was no further argument from the woman.

'My father isn't dead yet, and treating him as though he is can only be detrimental to him. Harold, go round to the other side of the bed and help to lift Daddy to a sitting position. Put those extra pillows behind him – that's right. There, Daddy, is that better?'

'It – it is, darling. Much better.' Flora watched her father fill his lungs with air and breathe out slowly. After a few seconds of this, some of the blueness in his face began to turn pink again.

'When is your doctor due, Daddy? What is his prognosis?'

'If you mean what is the – the outcome for me, it isn't good.'

'Daddy, just because you've had a slight heart attack – and it must have been slight, or you wouldn't be here now – it doesn't mean you are going to die.'

'Flora! How dare you give Father false hope like this? His doctor has said . . . well, he hasn't said what you are saying.

146

He thinks there is no way Father can recover. I – I'm sorry, Father.'

'Dr James is old-fashioned. His way of thinking is that a more massive heart attack will follow very quickly, but that needn't be the case. Have you even been to hospital, Daddy?'

'N – no, Mother called James in, and that was that. I've just been waiting to – to die.'

'I'll get in touch with a young physician I worked with before going to Belgium; his name's Dr Carmichael. At least let's get a second opinion.' Turning towards the astonished nurse, who stood as if turned to stone, Flora gave her an order. 'Nurse, in the meantime I want you to keep this room airy at all times. I want my father sitting up to aid his breathing, and he is to have plenty of fluids. Keep a chart, so that I can check. And check all his vital signs on a regular basis. You do have the necessary equipment, don't you?'

'I was told that it was just basic care of a dying man, Miss.'

'Well, it's not your fault. I'm sure you did your best for him, under the orders that you received, but I am changing those. I'll see to it that you have all you need. You are now looking after a patient who has every prospect of getting better, and you can help in that, with your excellent nursing skills.'

'Thank you, Miss.'

'I'll be back shortly, Daddy. Don't worry: you're going to live, so get on with planning your future, not your death.'

She was rewarded by a smile that was full of hope, and her heart went out to her beloved father.

'How dare you interfere, Flora?' The door of the bedroom was hardly closed behind them when Harold attacked her. 'Just who do you think you are – a bloody doctor, or something? You're just a bloody volunteer, and nothing more. If Dr James says that Father is dying, then he is!'

'You sound as though that is what you want to happen, Harold.'

'I – I . . . Of course I don't. But I don't want Father given false hope, either, or to prolong the agony of his dying. He was resigned, he—'

'That's just it. He had no hope and he was giving up. Well, now he does have hope. I can't say that he *will* live, but I want to give him the very best chance to. He deserves that much from us.'

'Of course, but . . . well, I don't know what to do now. I was preparing myself for taking over everything – I mean . . .'

Flora knew exactly what he meant. 'You will still have to take the reins, but if Daddy recovers, you must let him have a say; make him feel that he is needed, and that you still lean on him, even if you don't.'

The look that Harold gave her was one of a child who'd had something taken from him, and it held spite. That worried her. Her mother's words came back to her. Was it all going to be taken away from Harold anyway? She felt no surprise at the thought of another brother out there somewhere. She'd long accepted what her father was like.

'Changing the subject: where is Francis?'

'Oh, of course – you don't know.'

The whereabouts of Francis came as another shock. 'He's an officer!'

'Well, not yet. He won't pass out of Sandringham for another year. He's hoping that by then it will be all over, bar the shouting. But he thought it better to jump rather than wait to be pushed. Besides, he felt he would be safer as an officer.'

'Pushed?'

'There's talk of conscription by next year.'

Flora's mind immediately went to Freddy. But no, he would still be too young, wouldn't he? 'What about you? Will you have to go, Harold?'

'I bloody hope not! I'm thinking of relocating, to take more of a role in running the mill. It is expanding, with all the cloth needed for new uniforms and tents, et cetera. Most of those jobs are considered essential. Uncle Steven is getting on and has no heir, and the mill is expected to come to me anyway, so I'm going to try to persuade him to put me in the most-needed position on the management team, and take my chances from there. I don't agree with the bloody war, let alone want to offer my services to fight in it.'

Flora's joy at the greeting she'd had from Harold was dissolving with every minute. He hadn't changed. He was still number one, in his own eyes. He was even willing to sacrifice his father for his own aims and ambitions. Well, if she could help it, that wasn't going to happen, although she did worry that there was a possibility she was giving Daddy false hope. She didn't know how bad his heart attack had been, or how much damage it had done to her father.

'Well, I wish you luck. Now do something for me, will you? Help me to stand up to Mother, on Daddy's behalf.'

Something of the brother she'd detected when she first arrived came to the fore once more. 'Very well, old thing. If it will please you, but I'm not saying that I agree with you.'

He was complex, this brother of hers. The age difference between them had not mattered too much when they were younger, but she detected that, despite Harold's indifference to her then, he had loved her, and still loved her now. But mostly, she suspected, it would be on his terms. For some reason it seemed to suit him for the moment to be seen to defy their mother; for what reason, though, she couldn't imagine.

'Flora, I might need your help, too. Let's go into the morning room before we approach Mother, so that I can explain.'

'I need to get in touch with Dr Carmichael first. It is imperative that we act quickly.'

'Well, send one of the maids with a message. We can tell Mother we have done as we saw fit, and then she can't object.'

'One of the maids – how many do we have now?'

'Oh, I don't know. Never seems enough for Mother. There's one called Susan. She has her wits about her, I'll send for her.'

Harold seemed very familiar with the girl, to call her by her first name, or even to know what her name was!

With the message on its way, Flora asked Harold to tell her how she could help.

'I'm worried about what Mother knows. She has said that Father had an affair with Pru. Do you know anything about that?'

'I'd rather not say, Harold. It isn't for me to tell you.'

'That means it is true. And has Pru got a child that could be Father's?'

'Harold, this conversation isn't one you should be having with me. I can't tell you anything. Anyway, how will it help you to know?'

'I need to know what competition I have. Am I the eldest

or not? You heard what Mother said: that someone could usurp me. That sounds as though Father has an older son.'

Flora couldn't answer this. Harold's words resonated with what she'd heard as a child and what their mother had said today, but it might just be Mother rambling on. 'I don't know any more than you do. Anyway, if it's true, there's nothing you can do about it.'

'Oh yes, there is. If he exists, then I can find out if Father has recognized him as his son. I can make Father word his will in such a way that I still inherit.'

This all sounded so cold and selfish to Flora, and yet she understood. 'I'm sorry, Harold. If you are asking me to ask Father, then I can't. I just can't.'

'No, but you could ask Pru.'

'I know that Pru doesn't know. I remember . . . Look, I'm sorry, I lied about not knowing that Daddy and Pru had an affair.' She told him of the night their father had visited Pru, and how what their mother had said about Daddy's mistress had hurt Pru. 'She thought she was the first one – the only one – and she believed that Daddy loved her; Pru was devastated just to be one of a number. So, no, I'm sure she doesn't know anything about this child that Mother talks of.'

'I must find out. I must!'

'Then you must ask Mother or Father. It is your only way. But given Father's health, I would ask Mother. Tell her why you need to know – I think that will do the trick. Though I think she seems ready to tell you anyway.'

'If she isn't now, she will be by the time I'm finished.'

There it was again: that sinister side to this brother of hers. Flora shuddered. Something told her to be careful in her dealings with Harold. This made her feel sad, because

151

not an hour ago she'd been full of joy at having rediscovered him.

By the time Flora left her parents' home, her hope for her father was soaring. Dr Carmichael had attended him immediately, explaining that he was just going off-duty when the message arrived. 'I remembered you, Flora, and had heard tales of you being out of contact behind enemy lines. I came as much out of relief for you as anything. So don't let anyone read anything else into my haste. It doesn't mean that I think your father is dying.'

She'd been flattered, but she hadn't responded to the look Kenneth Carmichael had given her, although she had hung on his every word as he'd related Father's statistics to her and had given his prognosis that a good recovery was, in his opinion, very possible. 'His heartbeat is steady, and his pulse is strong, which doesn't indicate that anything sinister is going on. I would say the kind of attack he had was brought on by shock. Now, that's not to be taken lightly, and he will need nursing back to health, and medication.'

In no time, Father had engaged Kenneth to see him back to good health, and Flora felt she could relax. She had warned the doctor that he would come up against objections from her mother and her eldest brother, but Kenneth had shown that he was up to coping with them – by handling Harold firmly, and by putting Mother in the picture; he also pre-empted Mother by saying how pleased she must feel, to know that her beloved husband was going to be all right.

On the train back to Pru's, Flora remembered the letter she had received. How could she have forgotten it? On taking it out of her bag and tearing it open, its contents got her heart soaring. Cyrus was coming to visit her:

I have two weeks' leave, Flora. And I want to spend most of that with you. I know you will think me forward, but I can't help myself. I have thought of nothing other than meeting you again and getting to know you. Well, to be honest, I've thought of nothing but you, since you came into my office.

Flora held the letter to her heart. Cyrus was coming next week!

Chapter Fourteen

To Pru, space wasn't nothingness, for in the nothingness there was something – patterns. They formed as she stared, unblinking, at the figures lying on the floor.

She sensed, rather than saw, the movement of one of them and prayed it was Freddy. Stealing herself to focus, she felt relief flood through her as she saw that it was.

'Ma? Ma?'

'I'm here, son. You're all reet, lad. Get yourself up. Hold on to the chair. I – I can't help you, I'm too shaky.'

As Freddy rose, she saw him hesitate. His eyes fixed on the bulk that was Abe. 'Is – is he dead, Ma? What happened?'

She told him what she'd done.

'Oh, Ma . . . Ma.'

She knew Freddy must feel groggy, because he swayed, but she didn't move to steady him. She couldn't. She had to stay sitting or she would collapse. 'Don't worry, lad, we'll sort it.' *Sort it! How am I ever to do that?* 'Have a check, will you? See if he's breathing.'

The silence that followed held all her future years. Would there be any? Or would she hang for Abe's murder?

'No, I can't feel him breathing. He – he . . . Oh, Ma, he's dead!'

'He tried to rape me, then he hit you, Freddy. It was self-defence. I – I didn't mean to kill him, only stop him. Go for the doctor; go on, take five shillings out of me purse and tell the doctor he has to come at once.'

Before Pru registered anything further, she was being questioned by a doubting policeman. She couldn't stop her tears. She cried for Freddy, and for Abe, and she cried for herself. The policeman took no notice. He'd been summoned by the doctor to attend a suspicious death, and now he thought he knew it all, without listening to her.

'Look, Missus. You need to tell me the truth. Everyone knows that you were Abe's woman, and now you're trying to say he raped you? That's like saying a husband rapes his wife. It don't sound right.'

'He hit my son. My son tried to stop him—'

'Your son said he saw you bent over the table, and that he asked Abe to stop. Any son would say that, if they saw their mother in such a position.'

'Aye, and any mother would protect their son – and that's all I did. I hit Abe to stop him attacking my son.'

'But your son can't remember you hitting Abe, so he must have been unconscious, which would mean the threat to him had passed, and yet you still hit Abe with an instrument that was likely to kill him. That is cold-blooded murder. I'm arresting you, Prudence Hatton, for the murder of Abe Manning . . .'

Flora's jubilation had her skipping along the road. She couldn't wait to tell Aunt Pru about Cyrus, but as she rounded the corner she was surprised to see Pru's house in darkness. Coming up to the door, she saw a note pinned to it. Under the light of the street lamp, she read: *I'm at Aunt Rowena's, Freddy.*

A frown creased Flora's brow. Why should Freddy be with Rowena? Had Pru been called away or something? Unable to think of a reason, but knowing that something was wrong, she ran around the corner to Aunt Pru's old street and banged on Rowena's door.

The news that met her saw Flora standing rigid with shock. 'No! No, how . . . ? I mean . . . Oh, dear God!'

A sniffle gave her the realization that Freddy was near. Rowena called out to him, 'Come through, me darlin', come and see Flora.'

The door to the kitchen opened slowly. Freddy sidled through, looking afraid. His red face and swollen eyes spoke of his anguish. His bruised chin and cut lip shocked Flora.

'Freddy, it's all right. I'm here for you. We – we can sort this all out.'

'How? Oh, Flors, how?'

She couldn't have said how it happened, but Freddy was in her arms. Stroking his hair, she tried to soothe the sobs that racked his body. 'We'll find a way, I promise you, my darling brother, we will. I'll find a good lawyer, and I'll get Daddy to pay. I'll make him – even if we have to blackmail him with exposure as your father.'

'No, I can't do that, Flors. He's ill and, well, I—'

'Not even for your mother? We can, and we will, Freddy. Listen to me. Aunt Pru needs all the help I can give her. It all looks bad for her, but we know she would never have done this if . . . well, if she wasn't forced to.'

'You think it's my fault, and it is. I shouldn't have inter-fered.'

'I would think less of you if you hadn't, and I'd have come home to find that Aunt Pru had been hurt by Abe and you had done nothing to help her.'

'I – I liked Abe, Flors. He was all right most of the time. He was good to us, though I think he has hurt Ma before; she had bruises sometimes, but this time I – I think it was me that made him angry. You see, once I realized what was going on, I lost my respect for him and couldn't bear to be in the same room. I – I shouldn't have treated him like that. It led to this, I'm sure of it. I heard him shout about me being disrespectful. I should have—'

'Stop it, Freddy. This isn't your fault. Everything you are saying is quite natural. I felt the same, when I realized. I lost respect for them both at times, but I was away most of the time at school and I coped with it. Then I began to under-stand more, as I got older. You shouldn't expect anything of yourself, other than to have been repulsed by how Abe used your mother. Because he did.'

It came to Flora then how damaging Freddy's view of everything was, for Aunt Pru's case. He must have said things without realizing how harmful they would be.

'Freddy, I will get that lawyer, I promise. Now, listen to me. Until you have spoken to him, you are not to speak to anyone – not even a policeman, if he asks you questions. You need help to sort out your thoughts. Abe's actions were never kind. He did what he did so that he could have what he wanted from your ma. There's proof of that in how he didn't marry her, and give Pru her rightful status. Aunt Pru was vulnerable when Abe took advantage of her; she was poor, very poor. She couldn't even feed you. Abe knew that

157

and used it. Don't like him. Don't ever like anything about his memory. Try to think of everything from your mother's point of view, and then you will be instrumental in helping her prove her innocence.'

'Oh, Flors, I've already said things.'

'They can be unsaid. You were in shock. We'll save Aunt Pru.' As she said this, Flora wasn't sure it was the truth. The hopelessness of how everything sounded, when Rowena had told her what had happened, struck her once more and her own tears spilled over.

As sobs racked her body, Freddy implored her, 'Don't cry, Flors. I promise I will do all you told me to. You've helped me. And whatever it takes, we will save Ma. We will.' And Flora was reminded of what had often happened behind enemy lines: that showing weakness helped those weaker than you to become strong.

'I'm thinking, girl, that the pair of you could use a drop of me rum. Home-made it might be, but it finds the cold places that need tickling, and I think you both have those at this moment.'

'Oh, Rowena! Maybe you're right. I've had a funny "return-home" day. I've felt despair and happiness, and complete devastation, all in the space of a few hours.'

Taking the small glass, and not objecting to Freddy taking the one that was offered to him, Flora drank the treacly liquid in one gulp. Her own coughing and spluttering on doing so were nothing compared to Freddy's, as he copied her in downing his drink in the same way. And this, despite everything, got them all laughing. It gave Flora the hope that Freddy did have the strength to get through this. She wondered how she would fare, but then she had the prospect of Cyrus coming to see her, and that would help her.

Pru woke from a fitful sleep. The stale air of the cell clawed at her, but now there was something different about it – alcohol? The cold steel of the handcuffs that bound her sent a chill through her body. *God help me. God help me!*

But no answer came to her prayer. The dank walls of the dark prison cell only echoed her despair.

The sound of drunken breathing came to her. Peering through the half-light, she saw a woman lying on the bench opposite. Her snorts told that she was asleep, but the moment Pru moved and the chain around her ankles clanged, the woman sat bolt upright. 'What's your game?'

'Nowt, I haven't got a game – I'm just getting meself comfortable.'

''Ere, I knows you. You're Abe Manning's woman, ain't yer?'

'I'm Pru Hatton, as runs a school for the poor kids.'

'I knows that, but I also knows yer sleep with Abe Manning. Everyone knows it. What're yer doing in here then?'

Pru didn't answer. Inside she screamed against the way she was perceived, and against the vile things that had happened, and asked God: *How could this day, which had started so wonderful with the return of Flora, end so horrifically?* And then she begged of Him once more: *Help me, help me . . .*

'Cat got yer tongue, then? Here, are yer crying? That's not going to 'elp yer. Not in 'ere, it ain't. Yer've to be strong, or the bastards 'ave the upper-hand.'

Pru knew the woman: a bag lady, who lived from one

drink to the next, often stealing from the local shops, but for all that, not a bad sort. 'I've done sommat terrible, Ivy, lass. I've killed Abe.'

'What? Killed 'im? Good riddance. It were 'im as put me out of me 'ouse. I were only a few weeks behind on me rent. But if what you say is right, you're in for it, girl. And to my mind, you shouldn't be admitting it. In 'ere, you have to be crafty. Never admit anything. Now, tell me: how did this all come about?'

Somehow it was a relief to Pru to unburden herself.

'That ain't murder; it's self-defence, and defence of your young son – and under provocation, too. I know these things. I've bedded in these cells with the best of them, thieves, murderers and prostitutes, and I've learned a thing or two. Now, have you told the bobbies that you did it?'

'Naw, I haven't said much at all. I've said I had to save me lad, that's all, but they weren't for believing me.'

'That don't matter. They have to have proof. You need someone to sort them bobbies out for you. You need a good lawyer, girl. But they cost money.'

A small grain of hope took root inside Pru. She had some money. It wasn't much, but maybe she could borrow some more to put towards it. Her thoughts turned to Flora. Now that Abe was gone, the lass was the only person Pru knew who had money. Flora had an allowance that she hardly touched. And if she could, Flora would help her, Pru knew that. She had to – there was no one else she could turn to. *Oh, aye, I've plenty as would stand by me and speak for me, I knaws that, but none of them could do owt to help me predicament.* But then would speaking up for her even help? Didn't it all look bad for her? Even Ivy identified her as the woman who slept with Abe Manning.

How would that sound, in a court of law? *It's hopeless, hopeless . . . I'll hang! Oh God, no! . . . Help me – please don't let me hang!*

Chapter Fifteen

'I'm glad you came, Flora, Father's been asking for you.'

'How is he?'

Harold looked less than pleased as he told her that Father was making remarkable progress.

'Is Mother in?'

'She is, but you know how it is with her. She must have seen you coming up the path, and screamed out that she doesn't want to see you. Sorry, old thing.'

'If you are sorry, Harold, why have you got that smirk on your face?'

'Don't take it out on me. I'm not Father's horrible reminder . . .'

Hitting out at him, Flora had to laugh.

'I'd like to see Father alone – do you mind, Harold?'

'Why? You're not going to upset him, are you?'

Flora didn't answer this, but skipped up the stairs and left Harold. When she looked back, he had an annoyed look on his face. For a moment she thought he would follow her, as his hand stretched out for the stair rail, but he dropped it by his side again and turned away.

Flora's heart pounded. Taking a deep breath, she knocked on the door. *I have to do this, for Aunt Pru's sake.*

The night before had been agony. Not allowed back into Aunt Pru's house, she and Freddy had spent the night at Rowena's. For all that had happened, it turned out to be a jolly evening, helped by another tot of rum each. But through it all, her soul had ached with worry for Pru.

First thing this morning she'd asked the family solicitor to recommend someone who dealt with criminal law. She'd lied and said that she wanted help for a nursing friend. It had worked, and Graham Taylor, of Taylor, Taylor & Brompkins, Solicitors, had recommended one Henry Chamberlain, whom he called an eminent lawyer with a high success rate in wrongly-accused cases.

It turned out that Henry Chamberlain's office was in the same building as Graham Taylor's. Flora had found Henry easy to talk to, and very interested in Pru's case. Hope had filled her, until he'd told her how much he charged. 'My fee is inclusive – it doesn't fluctuate with how difficult the case proves to be. It also includes the fee of a private detective, if I need to engage one, as seems likely in this case.' For all that, one hundred pounds was a fortune and was more than she could afford on her own.

'Flora, I'm so happy to see you. Look at what you have done for me!'

Her father sat in a chair by the window; his skin had a normal tone, but bluish veins stood out here and there on his face, giving her a tinge of fear, though his eyes shone as he spoke. 'I feel as fit as a fiddle – and that after just one day on the medication, and with the new nursing regime. Thank you, darling girl. Now come and sit down. I need to ask you something, before you tell me all about your adventures.'

What he asked surprised Flora, and yet paved the way for what she had to say. 'The boy that Prudence had with her: is he mine?'

'Oh, Daddy, he is, and I—'

'What does Prudence want of me? I cannot recognize him publicly, or privately, as my son – that would kill your mother.'

On hearing him say this, Flora finally realized that her father was heartless. She'd always tried to keep faith that somehow she was mistaken about his character, and had tried to forgive him, whilst blaming her mother for everything. But now she knew. Feeling no pity for him, she told him what had happened to Pru. 'I therefore need you to make out a cheque for me for one thousand pounds, so that I can see to paying for everything Aunt Pru needs, and for bail, if it is set, besides engaging a very good lawyer for her.'

'But – but . . . Oh my God! Will it get out who the boy is? It – it mustn't . . . A murderess! I can't be associated with her, and neither can you. I forbid it, Flora!'

'Then it *will* all come out. How you took one of your servants and then banished her, when you were found out by your wife. And how you left her to fend for herself and tend to her young son – *your son*! Even . . . Daddy! Oh, Daddy—'

Her father had slumped forward. Acting quickly, Flora opened the collar of his nightshirt and began to massage his heart, as she had seen being done in the hospital in Belgium.

Within minutes he sat up. 'I'm all right. It wasn't an attack – I had no pain. I just collapsed with the shock of what you said. Flora, you are my daughter, how could you threaten me with all of this?'

Flora hung her head.

'Tell me, you didn't mean it.'

'I did mean it, Father. Aunt Pru and Freddy mean more to me than you do, because you killed my love for you a long time ago. Oh, it came back to me when I saw you in need, but the way you have just behaved . . . well, I don't think I can ever love you again.'

He was silent for a long time. Flora remained standing by his side. Her stance was resolute; she had to win this battle, she had to.

'Very well, I will have the money transferred to your account. But it may take a few days. I will have to send for my bank manager. I cannot let Harold get involved in this. I have an account that no one knows of; it is not linked to my business, and is used to make private payments that I don't want anyone to know anything about. But I am disappointed in you, Flora. That you should put these people before me – that hurts.'

'They are not "these people". Aunt Pru is the mother I never had, and Freddy is my half-brother – your son.'

'Oh, for goodness' sake, don't be so melodramatic! The boy is nothing to me, and Prudence is even less. She knew what she was doing. She had visions of getting above her station. Her actions since prove that. You say that she slept with this man that she killed, for money? Well then, doesn't that tell you something?'

There could be no argument with this. And to Flora's chagrin, she knew that the way her father put it was exactly how Pru's life would be perceived – a son born out of wedlock, and a kept woman who eventually killed her 'innocent' lover. *Oh, Aunt Pru, how can I save you?*

Looking down on her father, she wanted to say that it was

all his doing. But she could see that he was shaking in every limb. 'Father, let me help you to bed.'

'Don't touch me. Leave! Leave my house now, and never come back! You have chosen a whore and a bastard boy over your father, who has loved and cared for you. I no longer have a daughter. This payment, to which I will add a further sum, will be your last from me. I will cancel your allowance.'

Pain zinged through Flora's heart. But she stood tall. She didn't care about the money, but to lose whatever threads she had of her father, and of her home, broke her heart.

'Daddy! No! Don't do this. I – I . . . you're all I have. I will be an orphan.'

'Of your own doing. You are heartless. Yesterday I was dying, but that doesn't matter to you, does it? Oh no, only that precious whore matters to you. All your life you have caused your mother heartache, and now me, when I am at my most vulnerable. Get out of my sight!'

The door opened. 'What is happening? What have you done, you wicked, evil girl?'

'Mother, I—'

'Flora! What the blazes! Mother, send for the doctor – Father doesn't look at all well.'

'Just get her out of this house, Harold. She is never to step foot in here again.'

'Father!'

Harold's reaction would have been comical, if it wasn't for the tragedy of Flora's situation, as his head bobbed on his neck and he looked from one person to the other, completely dumfounded. 'Flora, why?'

'I can't explain, Harold. I have given Father a shock, but I didn't expect this. Oh, Harold.'

'I'm appalled, Father. Appalled at Flora's treatment.

Come on, old thing.' Flora was grateful to take Harold's arm. An ally that she least expected, but a welcome one. 'I'll get my driver to take you back to Pru's, old thing. But look, give me the address, so I can contact you.'

Flora hesitated, but then decided against doing so. 'Here, this is my Red Cross address – they accept post for us all.' She handed Harold a card with the address written on it. 'Let me know how Daddy is, won't you?' She turned and opened the door, as Harold came to the doorstep with her. 'And, Harold, I had to do what I did to Daddy, for Aunt Pru's sake. You will read about it in the paper. I can't tell you any more, but keep in touch and give this address to Francis.'

'But, Flora, what is it all about? Tell me. Don't let me get another shock, on having to read about it.'

Briefly she told him what had happened to Pru. 'I needed to get her a lawyer, Harold, she's innocent.'

'And you took the risk of harming Father, for that slut? How low have you stooped, Flora? "Aunt Pru" . . . ? For God's sake, she was your nanny, a lowlife; and she's gone further into the gutter, by the sound of it. I forbid you to get involved. And I will forbid Father to help her out financially, as I guess that's what you wanted from him.'

'You can't forbid me anything, Harold.'

'Then I will have to take the same stance as Mother and Father. Here, keep your poxy address – it is nothing to me. I can't think why I wanted to get on better terms with you. All it has done is show me who you really are. Goodbye, Flora.'

The door slammed shut.

Flora stood there, looking towards the gate. Behind her the closed door signalled the end of any life with her family

– no matter how tenuous that thread had been, it cut a deep hurt into her. And in front of her, the only family life she'd gleaned any happiness from had now been fragmented. Inwardly, she folded, unsure what to do. But then a picture of Freddy came to her. Freddy needed her. She would have the money now to pay for help for Pru's defence, and to set up home for her and Freddy, because neither of them could go back to their old home. They wouldn't be able to bear it, after what had happened there. No, she'd see to it that it was closed down, once the police let her in; and she would begin to make a new life for Freddy. How long that would be for, she didn't know. And there were so many other considerations, too. The Red Cross, for one. And Cyrus.

Yes, she'd only met him the once, and for a few minutes at that, but he was a consideration in whatever happened from now on. Tomorrow he would be here. Tomorrow she would have to face him, with all that was going on in her life. More than likely he would turn away and leave her. No man wanted the troubles that she had, put onto his shoulders.

As she closed the gate, a tear plopped onto her cheek. Looking up, she saw her father's bedroom curtain move. He was watching her, she was sure of that. Watching his only daughter walk out of his life. Well, it was his sins weighing her down as she went.

Something in her wanted to scream at him, but instead she lifted her shoulders and put her head back. She would go forward without them all. She would seek her own happiness. Would that be with Cyrus? *Oh, I hope so. For it doesn't matter that we only met the once. I know our lives are entwined more deeply than they could be if we'd known each other a lifetime. Because, with one look, Cyrus has embedded himself in my heart.*

As this thought died, Flora knew that any future happiness would be less than perfect, if she didn't manage to get Aunt Pru off all the charges. That would be her aim. That and taking care of her lovely half-brother, Freddy.

Chapter Sixteen

Pru stood in the dock the next day. She looked over to the public gallery and saw Flora and Freddy. Freddy waved. He had a look of hope on his face. *Eeh, lad, what have I brought you to?*

But she wasn't without hope herself. The lawyer who'd been to see her that morning had brought her a change of clothes, and had insisted that she be allowed to wash. When she was ready, he'd talked her through what was happening today. He'd managed to pull in some favours and had got a quick bail hearing for her.

She'd told him all that had happened and how she came to be in Abe's clutches, and even who Freddy's father was. He'd listened without comment, scribbling notes on a pad. Then he'd said that she was not to worry, he would sort everything for her. *That is sommat to hope on, ain't it?*

'All stand.'

Pru found herself compelled to look towards the bench. An old man walked in, bedecked in robes and a raggedy-looking wig.

What followed was a lot of talking, some whispering and

what seemed like an argument between her lawyer and the judge, but most of it went over Pru's head, as she found herself cocooned in another world from the proceedings. In this world she was enslaved to Abe. And she had flashes of Flora's and Freddy's father jumping in and out of her head, his mouth open in a laugh, his eyes like a mad man's. Abe appeared as if he was the Devil, taunting Pru and telling her that she would hang for doing him in. Her body shuddered and she opened her mouth to scream, but a muffled sound came out, which was lost to her as she fell into a blackness that held no fear for her.

'Pru . . . Aunt Pru.'

'Ma, Ma, you're free!'

The words came to her as if from a long distance away and spoken through a tunnel. Echoing. Bouncing off the pain in her head.

'Aunt Pru, wake up. We love you. Aunt Pru!'

Opening her eyes, it seemed that she was in a world of white. 'You're in hospital, Aunt Pru. Don't be afraid. We're here. Me and Freddy. You're all right. You have a fever. But it's good news. You don't have to go back to the cells. You can come back to Rowena's with us, once you're well, and until I can find us a new home. Oh, I've so much to tell you, Aunt Pru.'

'A new home, lass?'

'Yes. Just for now. You don't want to go back to your house – not yet.'

No, she didn't; not yet, not ever. But what would become of her school and the kids? She was so close to it becoming a recognized school. Pru's head hurt again. 'Eeh, me lad, and me Flora, I have to sleep.'

'I'll stay with you, Ma, you rest. I'll be here when you wake. Only Flora has to go. She's meeting her young man.'

'Freddy! I told you, I barely know him. He – he's just a friend.'

Pru couldn't understand any of this, nor why they both seemed so unconcerned and cheerful. But something of what they'd said swam around in her tired brain. *I'm free. Eeh, thank God. But for how long? Dear God, for how long?*

As Flora walked towards Aunt Pru's home, the nerves that she hadn't had time to feel clenched at her insides now. She wished she could have contacted Cyrus and asked him to meet her elsewhere, but there hadn't been time. He'd said he would be at the address she had given him between four and five o'clock.

As she approached the house, a figure moved out of the shadows. 'Flora?'

For a moment she couldn't answer. Then her voice came out, all squeaky, making her feel silly. 'Yes, it's me.'

'Thank God. I thought you'd had me on a wild goose chase. I didn't expect you to live in a house like this, and when I found it all closed up, I – I, well, I . . .'

She was close to Cyrus now, swimming once more in his deep, dark eyes. The reflection of the lamplight made them even more beautiful than she had remembered. She swallowed hard. 'Well, I do live here. *Did.* Look, I can't ask you in. I . . . There is such a lot to tell you. So much has happened. I don't think you will want to know me, once you hear it all.'

'That won't happen.' His low voice caused a reaction in her as if he'd taken a feather and run it along her spine.

'Cyrus, can we go somewhere we can talk? I don't know

172

anywhere. I've been away from here for most of my life, and only stopped here with my Aunt Pru on odd weeks.'

'Flora, you look troubled. When you say that a lot has happened, you don't mean good things, I take it. Are you grieving? Have you lost loved ones? I – I don't want to intrude. I . . . well, I just knew I had to see you again. Does that sound cheeky?'

'No, it doesn't. And no, I'm not grieving the death of a loved one through the war or anything, but I am sad and worried, and my life has taken a turn I never expected it to. It is a lot to unburden onto you, but I – I feel . . . I feel you are a friend, even though we only met the once.' To her horror, the last word came out on a sob, and tears stung her eyes.

'Flora, what is it? Look, come on. I have a cab waiting. I hoped you would let me take you to dinner.'

'I'd love that.' Secretly she felt glad that she had dressed for such an event. Rowena had been allowed into Aunt Pru's house to fetch clothes for them all. And Flora had been able to plan her outfit with care. She'd chosen her dark-blue coat, for warmth, and because it covered the outfit that wouldn't have been appropriate for where she'd been today. But once it was discarded, she hoped Cyrus liked the ankle-length slim-fitting skirt with a matching jacket, which buttoned up to a pretty neckline and was in two layers: one that came to her hip with a slight flare, and a short, bolero-type top layer. The fabric was wool, but very finely woven, in a thin blue-and-white stripe.

His eyes told her he approved, once they reached the hotel where Cyrus was staying for his two-week leave and he removed her coat.

As they entered the dining room she felt warmth seep into

her for the first time today. It had taken a while to get to the City of Westminster. The streets were crowded with carriages and buses, filling the air with dust. The smell of horse dung had been overpowering. And she'd felt sorry for the poor animals pulling all the vehicles, as they were steered this way and that way by angry, shouting coachmen, trying to avoid collisions.

The shops were a distraction, especially Harrods. It was lit up and glowed like gold in the dark. Flora had never shopped there, but she loved to see the hustle and bustle of those who did as they thronged its doors.

The Brompton Coach House and Inn offered a welcome respite from the busy London streets. 'I stay here if my mother is away,' Cyrus told Flora. 'She often visits her sister in Switzerland. My aunt has a lung condition, so she lives there for the quality of the thin air.' He pulled out a chair for her at an elegantly laid table in the corner of the room. 'Elegant' was a word she'd also use to describe the hotel.

'What a nice place – I like it.'

'That's a good start then. Have you looked up at the ceilings? I find them fascinating and see something different in them every time.'

Flora looked upwards. Her eyes feasted on a collage of scenes from Roman times, depicted in the busy wallpaper that covered the ceiling. Carved cornices formed a border, making it appear as if a large framed picture hung above them. 'Very interesting, and not what I expected, given the rest of the room. Though the columns in each corner really set it off.'

A waiter hovered around them. 'Shall I order for you? I know what's really good.'

Flora nodded her assent. She didn't feel that she could

have done so herself, judging by the huge menu cards and how she was feeling.

A confusion of emotions was attacking her. Was it just yesterday that her family finally got rid of her? And just hours since her darling Aunt Pru had collapsed under the strain of what was happening to her? *And yet I feel the warmth of deep happiness drifting me along, as if I was made to be by Cyrus's side.* Had she only known him for an hour? It couldn't be possible; she knew nothing about him, and yet she knew everything . . .

'We're having lamb chops. Ha, I know – such a huge menu, and I choose something we could have every day, but these chops are different. They trim them from the bone and they are cooked in the most delicious sauce. The meat melts in your mouth.'

'Mmm, I'm convinced. Thank you.'

Cyrus laughed. His face lit up. Picking up the glass that the waiter had filled with a crisp white wine, he raised it to her. 'Here's to us.'

It seemed such a natural thing to reciprocate with 'Us'.

His eyes held hers as they sipped. The churned emotions inside her settled into one – one that gave her a deep love for this man. After a moment she broke the spell. 'I think getting to know one another might be a good idea.'

'Me, too. I want to know everything about you. Especially as I'm going to make you my wife.'

Flora's heart pounded happiness through her body as she asked, 'Can it really happen like this? Is it possible that one look can seal a lifetime?'

'I think so. No, I know so, as the moment I looked into your eyes, Flora, I knew.'

'So did I.'

Cyrus's hand reached out to her and took hers. The touch tingled through Flora. Nothing in her objected to, or questioned, the way she felt. And that feeling seized her whole being as he lifted her hand to his lips. His eyes were telling her of his love for her.

Smiling, she gently took her hand away. And, trying to lighten the moment, she said, 'I'll start by interrogating you.' His laughter shivered through her as, taking a deep breath, she asked, 'So, you stay here when your mother isn't at home, but where is home?'

'In Bexleyheath.'

From that beginning, Flora was astounded by the coincidences to her life that followed, as she discovered that Cyrus had been to the same school as her brothers and – this almost seemed a coincidence too far – had studied and loved music, only he played the violin, not the piano. 'My mother couldn't afford to send me to the school, or for extra music tuition, but my grandfather – my father's father – left a sum for my schooling and a monthly allowance for me. She told me that his one stipulation was that I was encouraged to learn and to love music. You see, my father was killed in the Boer War when I was five, and his father died within a year. I have a picture of them together with my gran, who died before both of them. I'll show it to you one day. I would have loved to have known both of them, but will forever be grateful to my grandfather for taking care of me. My mother, though a handsome woman, never married again, but she manages well. She was left a legacy from her own parents. So, you see, I am not much of a catch financially. Though I do hope to take up a career in banking once the war is over – if I don't get taken on by a well-paying orchestra.'

'Is someone trying to catch you, then?'

They giggled. 'Just letting my future wife know where she will stand. Unless, of course, she brings riches with her.'

It was as if the proposal was accepted and acceptable; she hadn't questioned it, and didn't want to – her only need was to confirm it. 'I'm afraid I don't, so we will just have to manage as best we can.'

Cyrus reached for her hand again, and for the first time showed his own surprise at how quickly everything was happening to them. 'So you feel the same way? Really? Truly? You would marry me, after not knowing me for a day yet?'

'I would. I know you are the one for me, Cyrus. I know very little about you, and yet I feel I have known you forever. It is as if you are the other half of me.'

His smile melted her. She wished so much they weren't in a public place and that she could go into his arms and have him kiss her lips.

The waiter brought them back to reality, as he began to prepare the table.

'Oh, I forgot to say. Besides the lamb, we are having a warming broth to start with. It's made with beetroot and beef; it is delicious, but not filling.'

'Thank you. It sounds lovely.'

'So, Flora. What about you? I know something troubles you. Time to unburden yourself, if you think you know me well enough now.'

'My story is difficult to understand. I can only tell you it exactly as it is. I hope it doesn't put you off. I'm the daughter of a very wealthy man and a well-bred mother, and have two brothers who went to the same school as you. But I am an outcast, and I live with my half-brother and his mother, who is the most wonderful woman in the world, but at this moment stands accused of murder.'

Cyrus's expression went from astonishment to bewilderment. She knew what she'd said was an extreme test for him, as it probably shattered the illusion he had of her being a girl of gentle birth, loved and cosseted, who had enough guts to go to war, but remained feminine and protected from the real world.

She waited for him to say something. Her heart clenched in a vice of uncertainty as to whether the happiness that had flooded it would seep away into a swamp of dissolution.

'My God! Poor darling, that sounds horrific.'

The endearment helped. As did his tone of deep concern. 'It is. But my aunt's plight is the worst part of it all. Aunt Pru isn't my real aunt.' She explained their relationship. 'It is a long story, but best told from the beginning. Are you ready to hear it? It isn't easy telling, and it won't be easy for you to feel the same about me, once you have heard it all.'

'Nothing could make me feel differently about you, Flora. You have hit me like a bolt of lightning. You are me, and whatever you come wrapped up in, I will accept.'

They were eating their third course, of 'berried pears' – a lovely dish of poached pears topped with fresh berry compote – by the time Flora had finished telling her story and answering his questions. Throughout, Cyrus had shown his hurt at what she had been through, and now he reached for her hand. With the comfort it gave, she opened her heart to him. 'I once visited the Trevi Fountain, Cyrus. It was at the end of my time studying music in Italy, and I wished to be loved and said that I was only seeking happiness. In you, I think I have found both. I know I still have to deal with Aunt Pru's and my half-brother's situation, but I feel strong enough now to do that. And as far as my family is concerned,

I have given up seeking their love. And you have filled any remaining void inside me.'

'My darling.'

The words sealed his loyalty to her and made them as one, as once more Cyrus kissed her hand. 'So that is us, knowing the ins and outs of each other's life, and now there is "us", going forward from here. And we will make that future around music and the theatre. Do you like the theatre?'

'Oh, I do. I love it. And Freddy, the half-brother I mentioned, does too. He plays the violin, like you, and we both love to compose music. I write pieces for the stage, too – musicals. No one has ever seen them, but when I can, I play the music from them and dream of the production.'

'I do that, too! Darling, we were meant for each other, and I can't wait to meet Freddy. We will keep our shared dream alive, and one day we will work towards it happening. But in the meantime, I have my posting orders. I'm to be second-in-command of our army in Artois, northern France. We are pushing the Germans back, but have suffered heavy losses.'

'Oh no, I can't bear it. I've only just found you.' Neither of them had said the words, but they came to her now. 'I love you, Cyrus. I can't be without you.'

'I feel the same, darling. I love you. I can't understand it, or put any sense to it at all, but I love you so deeply it hurts. Will you marry me before I go? I only have ten days left of my leave. Please say you will marry me, Flora, my love.'

'I will. I will, Cyrus. But when . . . where, and how?'

'A lot of my fellow men have obtained special licences to marry. They only take forty-eight hours to arrange. We can do it on our own, or ask your aunt and half-brother. Do you

179

know, I feel as though I know Freddy. I think I'll ask him to be my best man, as all my friends are serving abroad.'

'Oh, he'd love that. And Aunt Pru can be my maid-of-honour. It will give her something to look forward to. And they can both be our witnesses.'

'From what I've heard, your Aunt Pru needs some good news, but will she be well enough, as I'm planning on applying first thing in the morning for the licence? If all goes well, we can be married in two days' time! Ha. I can't believe it, and yet I *can* believe it, as it is so right that we seal our love in this way, as quickly as it came to us.'

Happiness flooded not just Flora's heart, but her whole body, and with it came a trickle of excited anticipation. What would it be like to lie with Cyrus, to feel his arms around her, his hands touching her body, and to have him make her completely his? As if guessing her thoughts, his hand tightened on hers. 'I think I will ask for the bill. I need to hold you, and I can't do that here.'

Outside the cold air bit Flora's cheeks, but couldn't make a mark on her warm, glowing body. Gently pulling her into the shadows of the building, Cyrus took her in his arms. Had she ever thought herself at home anywhere in this world? Well, she knew now that she was mistaken, because here, close to Cyrus's body, was her true home. She clung to him, and thrilled when his hand lifted her head and his breath touched her cheeks, like a light, warm breeze. As his lips touched hers, it was as if she was given life for the first time ever. And yet she couldn't say that she was complete, as there was more that she needed from him. Her body cried out for him.

His whisper told her he felt the same. 'Only two nights to wait, my darling.'

It seemed like a lifetime. 'I wish it was now.'

He held her tightly, his groan telling her that he was fighting against making it so. But she didn't want him to fight it. She wanted him to go against what she knew was his honourable nature, and take her to his room and make love to her.

Cyrus resisted. Taking control, he stepped back from her. 'I'll call a cab to take you home, darling. We must wait. We would regret it forever if we didn't. Can I call for you tomorrow?'

'We'll meet somewhere – it will be easier. In the afternoon, as I have to look for a place to rent tomorrow. I have to get Freddy settled somewhere, and bring Aunt Pru back to it.'

'Oh, yes, I forgot. You never said that Aunt Pru was in agreement with that – are you sure she wants to move?'

'Yes, I'm sure. Initially we may have to go to a hotel. Rowena, who I told you about, is going to Pru's house again, to pack up all our personal things. And then I'll engage a removal firm to do the rest.'

'Why not this hotel? That would be so convenient for our plans, too. We could arrange our wedding breakfast here. Then, my darling, you can move into my room on our wedding night.' His arms enclosed her once more, and the flame that had become a burning ember relit inside her.

'Yes.' The word came out as a hoarse whisper, and could have meant so many things. She wanted to say yes to all that his body demanded of her.

'Oh, Flora, you must go. You must. I'll book you all in here from tomorrow.'

'Thank you, darling. I'll bring them along tomorrow afternoon. By then you should have our licence. Oh, Cyrus, I can't believe all this is happening, but I know it is right that it should.'

He pecked her on the nose. 'That's my goodnight kiss. I dare not give you another proper one.' He laughed as he pulled her out of the shadows and hailed a cab. 'See you tomorrow, darling.'

What had been difficult to believe while she had been with Cyrus now became impossible, as the horse gave a snort and the cab moved away. The rush of traffic had slowed, and the streets had quietened of people, giving Flora a more relaxing ride home. During it she said over and over to herself: *How can this be? What! No. Me – a married woman in two days* . . . A giggle escaped her and she pulled her coat around her, as if to hug herself, as excitement zinged through her. Not one jot of doubt entered her, only the realization that the happiness she'd sought was about to be hers.

But then a group of soldiers came into view, heading for the station, and the thought of Cyrus going off to war hit Flora, and her heart seemed to deflate. How was she to bear it? Only one idea occurred, and that was to return to nursing. Only it must be here in London, as she needed to be able to care for Freddy and Pru. *Dear Aunt Pru, what will the outcome be for you?*

As her mind turned to the awful recent happenings, she wasn't without hope. Henry Chamberlain had told them that he was going to work on bringing the charge down from murder to one of manslaughter, but then he hoped to go further and plead self-defence. 'But,' he'd warned, 'the circumstances of the relationship between Abe Manning and your aunt will be a hindrance to whatever case I bring, as she will already be perceived as a sinner by the righteous lot that sit in judgement and usually make up a jury.' He'd shaken his head and said that although he would do his best, Pru was to prepare herself for a prison term.

The thought of that marred Flora's happiness, as it was a bitter pill, and one that was so undeserved.

Chapter Seventeen

The two days passed much quicker than Flora thought they would. Having so much to do helped. Her one fear – that she might have to ask the consent of her father – hadn't materialized. Having turned twenty-one years of age, she was able to give her own consent to the marriage. She had never made a decision so easily and so readily, and this surprised her. She'd never had a boyfriend to compare the feelings that she had for Cyrus. She just knew he was the right one for her. She knew that her life would be empty without him in it. She knew she was in love.

Rowena had come into her own, on hearing the news. Rummaging through her stack of materials, she had made a gown so beautiful that tears had run down Flora's cheeks at the sight of it. Its simplicity gave it its beauty, with an Empire line, and the dress flowing to her ankles in the palest pink silk.

Flora already had a perfect, sheer silver-grey over-jacket from another outfit that lifted the gown from simple and elegant to a thing of beauty. Rowena made it even more so, by adorning it with tiny pink flowers that she'd made from the same silk as the gown. The frock had tiny straps over the shoulders, but the jacket had three-quarter sleeves, with layers of frills at the cuffs. The effect was stunning and was enhanced when Aunt Pru, now feeling much better, had dressed Flora's long hair in a swooped-back style that hung in a bunch of ringlets falling from her crown to her neck.

'Sommat blue and sommat borrowed is the order, lass. Wear these pearls. I bought them out of me first wage. They were on a market stall, and I knew they were good 'uns, but the market trader hadn't seen their value; she had a second-hand stall and sold everything for a penny. Me best buy ever!'

'Oh, Aunt Pru, they were! They're beautiful.'

'I had to clean them up. They looked as if a coal miner had worn them on his shift, but one rub of me finger, as they lay there amongst the rubbish she had, and I knew. Someone had thrown the baby out with the bath water – as we up north say about such a find.'

Flora laughed. It was good to see Aunt Pru looking relaxed and happy. 'I'll take great care of them.'

'Eeh, lass, I canna get over it. My Flora – a bride. I'll say one thing. No grass nor weeds grow under your feet, lass. But I don't blame you. If I'd seen Cyrus first, I'd have grabbed him.'

'Oh, Aunt Pru!'

Their laughter died down as Pru's tears overflowed.

'It'll be all right – we'll get through. I'll always be here for you and Freddy, Aunt Pru. Always. And you can be nanny and grandmother to our children. We'll be a happy family. We will.'

Rowena finished fussing over the gown and stood up. 'My, ain't you the pretty one, Flora, girl?'

'That's down to you, dear Rowena, and Aunt Pru – thank you. You've worked so hard for me.'

'Been a pleasure. Now you all have a lovely day, and don't forget old Rowena; come and visit often – me door's always open.'

'But you're staying, aren't you?'

'No, thank you kindly, but I'm not comfortable in a place like this. Them's all right with me while they think I'm a serving woman, but they won't accept me as a guest.'

Flora was shocked at this. 'Whatever do you mean?'

'I'm black. It's as simple as that. As long as I don't over-step the mark in this country, then them's happy, but if I step over the line drawn, them's not happy. And I don't want that on your wedding day, darling girl.'

'But . . .'

'Leave it, Flora, lass. We can't change things. We would only make Rowena unhappy by insisting.'

Aunt Pru's reaction shocked Flora, but deep down she knew that Pru would never say such a thing if she could help it.

Holding Rowena as if she would never let her go, Flora wallowed in her big arms and the soft hug of her body, fighting the tears. 'I love you, Rowena. You are one of the nicest people I know.'

'I know that, honey – well, the bit about you loving me. And I love you. Now, have a happy day. I'll see you at the church, but that's as far as I can go. You'll be telling me all about it when I see you. Well, not *all* . . .' Rowena's happy laughter followed her from the room.

'I'm sorry, lass, I wanted so much to stand by you and insist, but I know there is a strong possibility that the management would refuse to serve Rowena, and I didn't want that embarrassment for her – or for you. Now, put it out of your mind. Rowena has long since accepted her lot, so you can an' all.'

Although Flora was blissfully happy throughout the proceedings at the church – a cold, huge but beautiful place that seemed to swallow up the four of them – and at the wedding breakfast around the same table that she and Cyrus had first eaten at together, the incident stayed with her. It was one she couldn't understand, and she would do all she could to change it. But what that could be, she didn't yet know. There was a war raging, and people were more concerned with that than with social justice. But maybe after the war . . . Maybe then she could try to right the injustice of the way in which black people were treated.

'Well, Flora, I must say, you look stunning. A prettier bride I couldn't wish for. I only wish my mother was here to see you. I've written to her and hope she understands. I told her that once the war is over, we will have a proper affair, so that she can invite all her friends to it and introduce you to the rest of our family.'

'That would be lovely, and thank you for the compliment, darling.'

'Shall we raise our glasses? To my new family, and to us – and to absent friends.'

Flora giggled, and happiness glowed from her as they clinked their glasses.

Aunt Pru spoke next. 'And me and Freddy raise our glasses to you both, and welcome you, Cyrus. By, lad, you're a lovely addition to our lot.'

They all laughed.

'I don't even know what your mother looks like, Cyrus.

Are you sure she won't be cross, and blame me for us marrying so quickly?'

'No, Mother's a bit of a bohemian; anything is acceptable. I have a picture of her.'

Dressed in a flowing, many-layered frock, Olivia – as Cyrus told them his mother was called – looked like someone Flora would like very much. Her pose was impish, and her face held a cheeky smile that spoke of someone who loved a lot of what life had to offer.

Olivia looked so much younger than Flora's own mother, whose beauty had faded under the pinched-up sourness that had taken root in her. Cyrus's mother was graceful, like a ballet dancer. Any fear of meeting her, or of how she would accept what had happened, left Flora as she gazed at her new mother-in-law.

'I'll send her some photos of today. I know she will love you, darling. All of you.'

For a moment Flora thought of all that was going on and wondered if Olivia would be accepting of her son's involvement with her and Aunt Pru. But the feel of Cyrus's hand taking hold of hers, and of him leaning close to her, stopped these thoughts. 'Won't be long now, darling.' These words, whispered into her neck, sent a shiver of anticipation and a little fear through her. But no, she was being silly. Not knowing what to do didn't mean it would go wrong. Cyrus would guide her, and she was sure it would all come naturally, as she wanted nothing more than to give herself fully to him.

'Well, it's time me and Freddy got on our way. Eeh, I'm that excited, going to the theatre. That were thoughtful of you, Cyrus, getting them tickets. It would have been a let-down to us, after such an exciting day, to have nothing to follow it.'

'I've asked for the cab to pick you up at five-thirty, so enjoy it, both of you.'

'And wrap up warm – it's freezing out there.'

Aunt Pru's smile made Flora blush. It came with a knowing nod. She smiled back, and then found herself in Aunt Pru's arms. 'Me little lass. I'm that happy for you.'

As Aunt Pru released her, Flora could see that her emotions were about to spill over, but Freddy stepped in. 'Come on, Ma. I can't wait to get to the Palace; we don't want to be late.' With this, there was a quick peck from Freddy, which she turned into a hug, much to his extreme embarrassment, and they were gone.

'Just us two now, darling. They'll have a wonderful time – don't worry about them. I thought it might have given us all an awkward moment if I didn't arrange something specific for them.'

'It was a genius idea, Cyrus. As you say, it would have been uncomfortable, with them just having a bedroom to go to, and none of us knowing how to bring the proceedings to an end. Now they are excited to have a second event to look forward to, and we have each other.'

'We do, Mrs Harpinham.' With this, Cyrus stood and, taking Flora's hand, helped her to rise. It gave her a moment when the enormity of what she had done hit her.

Mags and Ella came to her mind, and she wondered what they would think when they received the letters she'd sent to them: *You know that man we met on the frontier? Well, I'm marrying him tomorrow!* A giggle bubbled up in her as she imagined their faces; they'd be so shocked, and would have a thousand questions for her.

'Something amusing you, darling?'

'Just my thoughts about the reaction of Mags and Ella – the two other nurses with me at the frontier – when they hear about us.'

'We've that to face with everyone; some will say we are mad, and I think we are a little, and others will tut and wait for us to fail, which we won't. But who cares? Fate brought us together, at a moment that left us no time to do things the conventional way, courting for a couple of years. So, here we are.'

These words sent a tremble through her. *No time! Please let there be years and years ahead of us.*

'Hey, no glum faces today. I only meant that we are destined to be apart for a time and that we—'

'Shush! I don't want to think of that now. We have eight days before you have to report, so let's enjoy every minute and not talk about the war.'

Without another word, Cyrus guided her through the dining room. Once they were outside his bedroom door and he'd opened it, he bent and lifted her into the air. The shyness that had overcome her vanished with the gesture, as they both burst out laughing. 'It's traditional for a man to carry his bride over the threshold.'

'I know, but through a narrow hotel-room door?' She scrunched herself up in his arms so that they could get through. Once they were, Cyrus didn't put her down until they reached the bed. Here, he lowered her gently onto the softest bed she'd ever lain on.

'Champagne?'

He had thought of everything. A table under the window held two glasses, one on each side of a beautiful arrangement of flowers, and on a stand next to the table stood an ice-bucket holding a bottle of champagne.

The popping of the cork made them giggle once more. But as Cyrus brought the full glasses over to the bed and they linked arms to sip, they became quiet, each looking into the other's eyes. 'To our future – a long and happy one.'

As she sipped, these words of Cyrus's sent a feeling through Flora that turned her heart as heavy as lead, and with it came a premonition that something was going to go wrong. Shaking the feeling from her, she smiled as Cyrus took her glass and lifted her to stand in front of him.

His kiss was gentle at first, but deepened to a passionate one, giving himself to her with every touch of his lips. Moving from her mouth, he kissed her eyes, her nose, her cheeks, her hair, then back to her lips, exploring her mouth with his tongue, sending thrills through her that had her wanting to beg him to take her.

He gently slid each garment from her body, until she stood naked before him. Nothing of the shyness she thought she would feel visited her. Instead, every part of her felt alive and full of love and need.

Helping him undress was as natural as if she had been doing it all her life.

Looking at him, she found him beautiful. Never before had she thought this of a man's body as she'd bathed men on their sickbeds, and it had never occurred to her that she ever would, but her Cyrus was beautiful. His skin wasn't a stark white, as she'd found with many men who never exposed themselves to the sun, but a lovely tanned colour. He had just a small tuft of hair between his contoured chest, and his stomach was flat. As her eyes took in his desire of her, her own need increased to the point where she cried out as he held her and lowered them both to the bed. There Cyrus took in every part of her, with his eyes, his lips and his hands. 'Oh, my darling. You're beautiful. I love you.'

With these words, he lifted himself onto her.

The moment was here, and Flora was ready.

The entering of her wasn't without pain. Cyrus helped this with his gentleness, and his words of love. But the pain didn't last, and soon she took Cyrus fully into her and felt a joy sweep over her. And now she wanted to give to him. Holding him close, she moved with him, increasing her own feelings of deep pleasure, which grew into an urgency she couldn't deny. When the urgency reached its peak, she heard herself holler Cyrus's name over and over, as her very soul fragmented, then came together to make her complete.

Feeling his lips kiss her face, and his tongue lick her neck and breasts, she relaxed. This she knew instinctively was a time he needed – an abandonment to his own pleasure, his own fulfilment. When it came, he called her name in a moan that spoke of his soul releasing itself to her.

They clung together afterwards. Their sweat mingled, their bodies trembled. Life had just begun for them both.

Was it too exquisite to last? This thought trembled through Flora as she held her Cyrus. *Don't let it be . . . Please God, keep my Cyrus safe.*

Chapter Eighteen

'Hello, you.'

Flora felt a peck on her nose and opened her eyes. She came out of her dreamy state and looked up into Cyrus's face.

'I've been watching you. You have a funny little breathing pattern as you sleep. Two gentle breaths and then a snort.'

'I don't, do I?'

'Yes, it goes like this: brrr…brrr!'

Laughing, she put her hands on his chest and pushed him. Sitting up, she was about to protest when she saw his expression. 'You're teasing me!'

He laughed out loud, before taking her in his arms. 'I have a surprise for you. We're going to Brighton for three days.'

'Oh? But—'

'No objections. Pru knows all about it and has packed a case for you. She checked with that lawyer fellow, and nothing will happen for at least three weeks regarding her court case. *And* she has an agent looking out for a property for you all, as Pru has put hers up for sale. There! Everything is sorted out, darling. Except, I need to make love to you again, before the breakfast that I ordered arrives.'

When she could, Flora asked how Cyrus had managed to pull off such a secret, and why keep it till this morning?

'While you were being dressed yesterday, I popped out to the Cook's travel shop and they arranged it all. Then I got hold of Pru, by sending Freddy for her.'

'Oh, I remember; he popped his head round and said that he couldn't fix his cravat and would she help him?'

'That's right – Freddy was in on it. They left the table earlier than they needed to, to get to the theatre, and that is when Pru packed your case. And, with my spare key, she popped it in here, under the bed. Take a look.'

When Flora leaned over the side to look, Cyrus snuggled up to her once more. 'I'm so happy, darling. I don't have words to express how much.'

Leaning back into his body, Flora felt another premonition. She trembled.

'What is it, darling? Don't be afraid for me. I'll be fine. I promise to take care at all times; it will take more than the Kaiser to harm me!'

'I don't know why I keep feeling this dread, but I suppose it's natural. Let's do as we said, and put the war and all it entails behind us and enjoy the three days you have planned. Thank you, thank you so much.'

As the train pulled out of the station, leaving Pru and Freddy waving them off, a tear came to Flora's eye. Pru looked so vulnerable, so afraid and yet courageous, as she stood tall, waving as if her life depended on it.

'Don't worry, darling, everything will be fine, I'm sure. When I spoke to Pru, she told me how Abe had bullied her for years, and how she had others who could testify to that. And Freddy is strong; he will be a good witness for her, too.'

'But Henry Chamberlain said that she still may have to go to jail for a short term, and how will she face that?'

'She will. She will have a future to come out to. She'll have you at home with her, and Freddy, and she's talked of starting a new school. She's making plans, and that's good. In the meantime, the selling of her home and finding a new one will take up her time. It's a new beginning for her.'

'I wish that she could meet someone who would love her, like you love me. She's been used by men all her life.'

'Yes, that would be wonderful. I haven't known Pru long, but she means a lot to me.'

'You have a habit of falling for women very quickly, Mr Harpinham – it has to stop.'

The joke lightened the moment, as they made their way along the corridor of the train, searching for a carriage.

'This one's empty. And the train doesn't stop, so we will have it all to ourselves.'

As she watched Cyrus lift their cases onto the rack above the seats, she marvelled at how, with everything they did, it seemed as though they'd done it together for a lifetime; as if something they couldn't see had always joined them together.

Their time in Brighton had been magical. The sun had shone for them and, yes, the rain had rained on them, but nothing had marred their joy of each other. Whether splashing in the puddles, or walking along the stony beach, all that had mattered was the complete love they had for one another.

But now it was over, and Flora was standing on another platform, this time waving Cyrus off. If it was possible, he looked even more beautiful in his uniform.

Flora had dressed in the same outfit she'd worn on their first date, minus the coat, as this late April day was a warm, sunny one.

They'd promised that they wouldn't cry, but would hold each other and smile, so that the last picture they had of each other, till they met again, was a happy one. Keeping that promise wasn't possible for either of them. Their tears mingled as they kissed.

'Goodbye, my love, stay safe. Please stay safe.'

'I will, my darling.'

Their hands held as the train pulled slowly away, and until Flora was almost running alongside it, and then she was alone – lost and alone.

Pru stood on the doorstep of the hotel. She'd seen Freddy go happily off to school this morning, his first morning back after all that had happened, and had paced the floor of her bedroom, hoping that he and Flora would be all right. Now she was waiting for Flora's return.

The sadness she felt was for her lovely Flora and Cyrus. Theirs was a love story of fairy tales, and now they had been forced apart. Flora would need her. However, it wasn't Flora she saw coming towards her, but Henry Chamberlain. Her sorrow turned to fear.

'Good afternoon, Pru. There's no need to look so scared. I have news that I think will help your case.'

They'd just sat down in a small room off the main bar, called 'the snug', when the hotel manager showed Flora in, and promised that they wouldn't be disturbed. Flora's flushed face told of her tears. Pru's heart went out to her. She stood up and took Flora's shivering body in her arms, holding her close.

A cough from Henry Chamberlain brought them out of the hug. Both women dried their eyes. 'Commiserations, Flora. Pru told me where you've been and why. I have a son fighting in France. We have to be strong for them.'

Flora nodded. Pru knew she was having difficulty in speaking. Guiding her to a chair, she told Flora that there was good news. 'Let's hope it's so good that it cheers us both up, eh, lass?'

'Right, I'll get on with it. I've had a man digging into the ins and outs of Manning's businesses, and what he's come up with will make your hair curl. Abe Manning crossed a lot of people – two murders have even been laid at his door. These people feel that you have avenged them, and they are willing to testify. We have a woman who was beaten near to death because she refused to prostitute herself when she couldn't pay her rent.'

Pru's head drooped. Shame washed over her. She hadn't refused, when Abe offered her a way out of her poverty. She'd given in and taken the easy life. Flora took her hand. Henry Chamberlain seemed not to notice anything amiss and carried on.

'We have a man who will say that he saw Manning brutally murder a young girl, when she had nothing to give him after two weeks on the streets. She'd spent the money on drink. He made an example of her. But everyone kept quiet, afraid of what might happen to them.'

A tear ran down Pru's cheek as memories of her own beatings came back to her.

'And a neighbour who will testify to hearing you scream-ing on occasions, and Abe shouting vile, abusive language at you.'

Pru looked up. She'd never really admitted to herself the

extent of Abe's abuse. She'd brushed it off as her own fault. Before she could say anything, Henry Chamberlain further shocked her. 'And, best of all, we have Abe's sister, Rifka, and his brother, Eilam. They will testify to how he has abused Rifka for years. Eilam knew and had witnessed it, but lived in fear of his brother.'

'Naw! Naw!'

Flora's grip on Pru tightened, but Pru didn't speak. But then what could she say? Lass hadn't thought ever to be involved in such degradation. Not like Freddy, poor lad. *But now I've pulled Flora down to my level, and I never meant to – I didn't.*

'You should be happy, Pru. All this is going to help your case tremendously. It makes what you say happened into a truth. It backs you up, until there can be no other verdict but self-defence. You're going to go free, Pru. Do you understand?'

The word 'free' lifted her, as she knew it did Flora. Without knowing how it happened, they were both standing and holding each other, and then doing a little jig. 'Oh, Aunt Pru, I'm so happy. But, Henry, why does she even have to face a court case? Surely the case can be dropped, if the prosecution sees all this new evidence?'

'It's not that simple. A man has died, and they have to be seen to look at all the facts and hear all the evidence. Don't forget: the prosecution will have some evidence of their own to bring. It's called justice, and it's the right of every man – even vile creatures like Abe Manning. The hearing will bring closure to the matter, bring it out in the open and in a proper manner. A jury will decide after hearing all the evidence, after which the case can truly be closed and a certified reason for death issued. In this case, I am sure it will be

"Died at the hand of a victim of his violence, whilst that victim was trying to defend herself".'

Everything he said was music to Pru's ears. She wanted to sing out in her happiness. She only wished that her joy wasn't marred by the sadness in Flora.

Three weeks later they walked out of the court arm-in-arm: Flora, Pru and Freddy. They walked in the direction of Blackfriars station on Queen Victoria Street. They were going home.

Flora had thrown herself into finding the right place, and had found an empty house in Brixton. The area was a little posh and pricey for them, but this three-bedroomed house with its own bathroom had been standing empty for a while. The money that her father had put in the bank for Flora helped to speed things along, and although there was a lot that needed doing, they had moved Pru's furniture into the house. Pru was to pay Flora half of the money back when she sold her place, but this house was to be hers: her name on the deeds, as Flora argued that her father owed Pru that money.

'I have enough money for myself, after Henry's fees are paid. You know that he halved them, don't you, Aunt Pru?' Flora said. 'And besides that, Father had put a lot more into the account than I asked him for.' On saying this, she had persuaded Pru to go ahead. The house was all they needed.

It had surprised Flora to find that, besides her father's money and the back-pay she received from the Red Cross, she'd been given notification of a weekly allowance from Cyrus's pay; that, as well as having secured a paying job in the military wards of Moorfields Hospital, through the Red

Cross, meant that Flora would soon build up her funds, to enable her to look for a home for her and Cyrus.

Keeping busy had helped her to cope. As had her first days on the ward, as she was called on to assist in all manner of caring for the badly damaged soldiers. Some were affected by the gas that Germany had used – a horrific tactic that hadn't lasted long as a weapon for enemy use in warfare, as the wind had changed and more of the Germans' own soldiers had been injured than had the Allies'.

But one of the best happenings of late was the happiness that she saw in Freddy, which she knew today's news would compound. For Freddy, everything in his world had come good. His ma was no longer in the clutches of the vile Abe. He had moved from an area where he was often bullied for being different, and was engrossed in his military training at school – something that gave Pru and Flora worries.

'Let's treat ourselves to a bun and a nice hot cup of tea on the way home, Pru. We deserve it.'

They'd walked along Pocock Street on leaving the Crown Court, and had turned towards the station. 'Eeh, let's get the train afore we stop. I want to be as far away from this place as I can get, lass.'

Back in Brixton, they went into the first cafe they came to, with the apt name of the Corner Cafe. The bell that rang as they opened the door had a homely sound. The tables covered in green gingham added to this, as did the fire roaring up the chimney.

They sat eating their iced buns and licking sticky fingers, until the door opened again, sending a cold draught around Flora's legs and making her look up.

'Harold!'

'Flora . . . I – I. How are you? And Pru. You're not in prison, then?'

Pru reddened.

'No, she's not. I suppose you have read about it in the papers? Well, you will read tomorrow that she was found innocent of all charges, and the verdict was "self-defence under extreme provocation".'

'Oh, I'm glad. Well done, Pru. And this is?'

'Me son, Freddy.'

'Ha, he looks like our father, Flora.'

Flora could have hit Harold. But Freddy surprised her with his answer, 'That's because I am his son. And I'm your half-brother. How do you do?'

Harold's mouth opened and closed again. He didn't take Freddy's outstretched hand, but looked at Flora, his face telling of his outrage, his teeth gritted together as he snarled at her: 'And so, this is what you wouldn't admit to? Though I had guessed. Do our parents know?'

'Father knows, but Mother doesn't.'

'Is this the news you upset him with? Sometimes, Flora, I think Mother is right about you. You're nothing but trouble.'

'She ain't reet. Flora has never done owt to your ma; your father did it all, and Flora suffered for it. I were just a young lass and in awe of him – he were me master. He took advantage of that, and left your ma in their bed and came to me. He made me feel as if I were special and had a future with him. I were daft to give in to him, but I weren't the only one. Your ma screamed at him that he had broken her heart by producing a son with his mistress afore she had you.'

Harold's expression had changed. His anger shook his body. Pru had just confirmed his worst fear. Flora saw the

201

control he had to use as he tried not to show how Pru's words had affected him. He turned to Pru. 'Do – do you know who the woman was, and where her son is?'

'Naw, that's all I knaw. Except that your dad pacified your ma and made her think it would never happen again.' Pru went on to explain how Flora became hated by her mother. And although she and Harold had talked about it previously, it all sounded more convincing coming from Pru. She'd tried to make Harold understand, but it seemed he'd since chosen to believe their mother's version of her character.

'Sit down, Harold. I'll order another cup of tea.'

He did as Flora bade him, his face ashen. 'What do you know of this other son, Pru? Where is he, and did my father recognize him as his son?'

'I knaw nowt, lad, I told you. I were kicked out. Oh, your da gave me a pay-off and I managed to get meself a place, but I were pregnant and had no prospects. I weren't thrown quite into the gutter, but near to it.' As if aware of Freddy for the first time since she'd spoken up, Aunt Pru added, 'But I had one thing more precious than money, and that were me Freddy.'

Harold looked uncomfortable. He didn't look in Freddy's direction, but kept his head down. Flora expected him at least to apologize for their father, or express his own sorrow about what happened, but Harold's self-centred core came to the fore. 'How does one go about finding someone? I must find out more about this supposed older brother. I *must* know if Father recognized him, Flora – it's vital.'

'Vital to what? Whether you inherit or not; or to make him your brother, as you appear not to want to do with Freddy?'

'Oh, for God's sake, why should I? If Father hasn't done

202

so, then there is no need for me to. But if Father has recognized this other son, then my life as I expect it to turn out will change, and that's not fair.'

What Harold perceived as fair was a lot different from what Flora did. She looked at Freddy and smiled at him. 'You're better off without people like this half-brother of yours in your life, believe me. He only wants to know if you are of any use to him, or might be a threat to him. I know – I have experienced Harold's way of loving.'

'Flora!'

'It's true, Harold. You gave me your love, and took it from me, within two days. Anyway, what brings you to these parts? I'm curious.' The words had hardly left her lips when the doorbell rang again and in walked Susan. 'Oh, like Father, like son?'

'Shut up! It's nothing to do with you.'

Susan stood in the doorway. Flora could see the shock on her face and wanted so much to go to her and to beg her not to trust Harold, but Harold was up and making his way towards her. He took Susan's arm roughly and hurried her out of the cafe.

'History has a way of repeating itself. I take it, by the way she were dressed, and by Harold's reaction, that the girl is one of your ma's maids?'

'Yes. Not sure what she is doing around here, though, but Harold's up to no good, and that worries me.'

'It might just be that this is far enough away from home. But didn't you mention that your da had opened a shop in this area?'

'There was talk of it, but I don't really know where all the shops are. I just overheard Father and Harold talking about business once. You know, they never discussed anything in front of me, and yet I am surely entitled to know.'

'I don't think you are, lass. It's a man's world, and the female members of the family have no rights.'

'Do I have any rights, Ma?'

'Not unless your father recognizes you as his son. And I'm sorry, lad, but that ain't going to happen.'

'It doesn't matter. I have something of my father – I have his love of music, like Flora has. I heard today that I passed my grade-three music and violinist exam.'

'Eeh, Freddy.'

'Oh, Freddy, that's wonderful. You know, Cyrus plays too and is very accomplished. One day, you, me and Cyrus will form a trio and make wonderful music together. Cyrus writes music and lyrics, too, just like us, so we'll put on a concert of our own music.'

'Oh, Flors, as me ma would say, that'd be grand.'

They all laughed. Harold and his exploits and self-centred ways now forgotten, they regained their previous joy, and Flora was glad of it. Nothing could lift her heartache, but like millions of others, she had to get on with life as best she could, she knew that.

Looking for a home for her and Cyrus would help. She'd save every penny of his money towards it, so that he felt as if he had bought it; and she'd have it ready for his return. *Please God let him return.*

'Now, lass, no sad faces. Not today. Head held high with courage, and let's take the next step of our lives, eh?'

'Yes, we've a lot to look forward to, and to celebrate.'

'Aye, we have our worries an' all, but life's like that.'

As they walked along arm-in-arm, Flora realized that Aunt Pru must be worried. She had no means of earning an income now and, with the fees for Freddy's schooling to find, she had a tough time in front of her. 'Have you any plans, Aunt Pru?'

'I haven't given much thought to it all, I daren't, I was never really sure as I'd come out of that court a free woman. But I have to plan now. Somehow I have to make a lot of money. Freddy's schooling is important.'

'Ma, I only have another term left. I can leave now and get a job. One more term's not going to make that much difference.'

'It will, Freddy. You won't complete your exams, and you have to go on with your schooling after that, to get to university.'

'Ma, that's an impossible dream now. Where would we get the money?'

'I could ask our father.'

'No! I want nothing from him, Flors – nothing. You getting what you have for Ma is enough. I want to forget that he and the rest of them exist. I have you, and that's enough. And, Ma, I want to go to fight. I have to. You have to come to terms with that.'

The 'no-sadness-today' pact they'd made was broken. Sadness hung over them like a cloud as they reached the door of their home. For Freddy to join up was unthinkable, and yet the latest news was that the war would rage on for years, and they all knew it was inevitable that he would go.

Chapter Nineteen

A week had passed since Christmas. With each day Flora's heart had sunk further, as the promise in the last letter she received from Cyrus hadn't materialized. Now, the birth of their child was on her, and agonizing pains wracked her body.

'Flora, lass, one more try, come on, you can do it. That's reet, lass, push, Flora, push.'

A scream came from deep within Flora as the pain gripped her. Sweat ran off her face, her teeth clenched and her neck strained. *Oh God, let it be over soon, I can't bear any more.*

With this thought dying in her, her next was a curse as she felt as though she would split in two, but then a cry filled the room and her heart swelled.

Our baby. Oh, Cyrus, if only you were here . . .

'Let it all out, me lass. You've sommat to cry over, but sommat to rejoice over an' all. There, you have a lovely little lass. She's reet bonny. Eeh, you're a clever lass.'

Flora looked down into the blood-covered face and felt a love fill her that warmed her whole body. 'Oh, she's beautiful. Beautiful!'

'She will be, when I've cleaned her up and put her in her layette that I've all ready for her. Oooh, come here, me bonny wee one. I'm your Aunty Pru, and I love the bones of you.'

'You're not just her aunt – you're her namesake, as she is to be called Prudence Alice, only we will use her second name, to avoid confusion. Alice is after Aliz, a girl I met in Belgium who I want to remember.'

'Aw, that's lovely. Reet, me little Alice, a bath for you and a nice cuppa for your ma. Then I'll clean you up, lass. Eeh, I'm going to have me hands full, with the pair of you.'

Flora smiled, a weak, tired smile. Her body reacted to the hours of labour and trembled with exhaustion. She lay back. An awareness of what she held in her hand came to her and she opened it, gasping in horror as she saw how she'd crumpled Cyrus's photo. He'd sent it to her a few weeks back, in a letter that was full of hope:

We had a great victory today, darling. We secured a ridge that is a strategic advantage. Not only that, but defeating the Germans meant so much to the men. Though, sadly, our casualties are still high and we are not getting the replacements we need.

This means that those still fighting are very tired. Maybe now, with this victory, we can rest for a few days. There's always a lull when a battle is won, while our enemy regroups and we begin to see their next move.

I'm enclosing a photo taken when a fellow officer and I snatched a few hours and went into Artois; we had a good time, and got a little drunk. A French lady took the picture, and in no time returned to the bar with it developed. She studied photography and tries to earn a

*living taking shots of the war and of soldiers, and
selling them to newspapers. How resilient people are.*

I made sure I bought this one for you.

*Your last letter took me to heaven with your
wonderful news. A baby – we made a baby: how
amazing is that? Oh, my darling, I wish you didn't
have to cope alone and I could fuss over you, and do all
the things a normal expectant father would do. But these
are not normal times, and won't be for a long time.*

*Though I do have some news that cheers me, and I
hope gives you something to look forward to. I may be
home for Christmas! To our home, our very own. Clever
girl, you, finding a home and sorting everything out.
I cannot wait.*

*You say you are due early January? Just maybe, our
little one will be born while I am there! Wouldn't that
be wonderful? I cannot wait to meet him, or her. I have
no preference, by the way. I just want you and our baby
to be well.*

*I love you beyond loving, my darling. You are never
far away, because you are me.*

Your loving and devoted, Cyrus x

Every word was etched on Flora's heart, increasing her
pain as Cyrus hadn't made it home, and she didn't know
why. The photo, which showed Cyrus's wonderful eyes glit-
tering a little too much with the effect of the alcohol, had
made her smile, remembering the night they reached Brighton
and had drunk too much champagne and Cyrus was all silly
and giggly. Oh, how her heart longed for him. And now she'd
crumpled the bottom half of his photo.

A wail came from her, shocking her and bringing Aunt

Pru running up the stairs. After she placed the baby in the cot at the foot of the bed, the mattress sank as she plonked herself next to Flora. 'What's to do, lass? Eeh, me little love.'

Flora could only show her the photo.

'Well, you've made a mess of that, but it's a nice mess. Cyrus's lovely face is still intact, but it's as if he has been holding your hand throughout all the pain and helping you through it. I could iron it, to make it a bit better, but I'd treasure it as it is, lass. Show him that he was with you when he most needed to be.'

This calmed Flora. Aunt Pru was right. Holding the photo had helped, and the damage to it would be a reminder of that – and something to show Cyrus. He would love that.

'That's reet; smiles are better than tears, and better for the little one, too. A happy mam makes for a happy babby.'

Sitting up a few hours later, with Alice feeding from her breast for the second time, Flora was overcome with a sense of complete fulfilment. Her hand stroked the soft down of her baby's brown hair. How complete her life would be if Cyrus were here. With her and his daughter, in their own home.

Home . . . how thrilled he'd sounded that they had their own home. She hoped his expectations weren't too high, because with finding herself pregnant and having to give up work, she hadn't been able to save Cyrus's money, but found she'd had to live on it. That had meant she had had to greatly lower her budget to buy this house.

A one-up, one-down in a much less desirable part of Brixton than Aunt Pru lived in was all Flora could afford, though she had managed to get permission to build a bathroom on the back of the house, which led off from the kitchen. This was essential to her, as the thought of a shared lav at the bottom of the garden filled her with disgust. She'd had a high fence erected to hide the lav, and had the now-enclosed yard paved. Pot plants broke its starkness and gave them a haven all their own, although, with a layer of snow covering it at the moment, it wasn't a place to linger.

At least with only two rooms – a kitchen-cum-living-room and a bedroom – she hadn't needed a lot of furniture and, scouring the second-hand shops, she had managed to find some elegant pieces that gave the house a richness and made her feel it was her home.

'Can I come up, love?'

The voice made her jump. *I'll never get used to how the women around here just walk into each other's homes.* She called out to Mrs Larch that, yes, she could, and then found the woman in the doorway at the top of the stairs before she even had the last word out!

'I heard. A little girl then? Congratulations, love. I brought you a casserole. I stuck it in the oven before I called out. It'll be ready for your supper, and will give you the goodness you need back in your body. Now let me look, then I'll make you a nice Rosy Lee.'

Flora smiled. Mrs Larch was the kind of woman you would describe as the salt of the earth. 'Thank you, that's very kind of you. I'd love a cup of tea.' Not really the truth, as Aunt Pru had served her a total of four cups, before leaving to make sure Freddy was home from school – 'restless Freddy', she called him, and she lived in fear of him having joined up and announcing that he'd done so, leaving Aunt Pru with nothing she could do about it.

'You're welcome, love. Now, let me look. Ooh, she's a bundle of joy at a time like this. Poor Mrs Randall at the top of the street had one of them brown envelopes. Her Tommy copped it. Poor woman. She's demented with grief. To lose a lad, just eighteen years old. I could kill that Kaiser bloke. They should let him loose in our street, then he'd know it.'

This news devastated Flora. The tears that had found a permanent home between her throat and eyes, causing her to swallow hard to keep them from flowing, now won the battle once more and streamed down her face.

'There, there, you let your heart rule – it does no harm. We've all cried for the lad. But the whole street's rejoicing that a baby has been brought to us. That northern woman told us. We were all having a natter and comforting each other, when she came out and, with a little skip and jump, told us you'd delivered. We told her that we'd all watch out for you, when she couldn't be here. I've made enough of me casserole for her and her lad, as she said she'd be back with him later.'

Through her sobs, Flora thanked Mrs Larch. The kindness of the woman, and the way she and all her neighbours had accepted her into their fold, had been something she couldn't comprehend and yet welcomed.

With Alice taken from her and settled back in her cot, Flora sipped the hot tea, knowing she'd be glad when Mrs Larch left, so that she could use the pot behind the screen. Going downstairs was not allowed, on the strict instructions of Aunt Pru, but oh dear, all the tea had made her nearly fill the pot!

'Please give my condolences to Mrs Randall. Tell her she's welcome to come and see little Alice any time.'

'She's in no fit state, love, but I know she'll be comforted by you having said it. You're different to us – you talk posh, and you, and your inside lav, is something we were all shocked at having amongst us, love. But for all that, we're your neighbours, and neighbours should stick together and look out for one another. That's our way.'

'I'm glad of it. I know I seem different, but my Aunt Pru brought me up in a neighbourhood like this one. So I'm not so different in my outlook, and I want to be a part of the community.'

'Your Aunt Pru told us all about you. She likes a natter, that one. Though she talks funny, she's a good girl.'

Flora knew from experience that you had to be in your fifties, or thereabouts, for these cockney women to call you a woman. Pru, at just thirty-seven, was still classed as a girl.

'She told us all what happened to her, as well. Poor girl. We all reckon as she could do with finding a good man to take care of her. Now, I'm off. Mrs Harper will pop in, in an hour, if we don't see your Aunt Pru is back by then.'

This was something Flora had to get used to. She hoped that Cyrus would, too. For although she'd said that she was used to the ways of streets like this, she wasn't really. The times she had been with Aunt Pru, the neighbours had mainly been from foreign lands and didn't have this London way of going on – except for Rowena, of course.

When the next visit happened, it was Mrs Larch again, only this time her voice had a different note. 'I'm coming up, love.'

Flora couldn't say why, but the tone this was said in sent a chill through her and told her there was much to fear, as Mrs Larch appeared in the doorway.

'Oh, love, it's come. The one we all dread. I took it off the delivery boy and brought it to you meself.'

'No. No! Oh God, nooo!'

A big, fleshy arm gathered her into a huge, soft bosom.

A hand stroked her hair. 'Read it first, love; it may not be all bad. Some are just missing or injured. It may not be what you think.'

Flora tore open the brown envelope. Her life had come to a halt, and all sound, all movement and all feeling were locked in her world of pain and silenced:

It is with regret that we inform you that your husband, Second Officer Cyrus Harpinham, has been taken prisoner . . .

Though it was not what she wanted to read, Flora breathed once more, releasing the relief that she felt at the news not signalling the complete end of her world. She read on:

We have information that he is to be taken to Beeskow, near Berlin – a prison camp for officers. We believe he will be reasonably treated, in accordance with international agreements.

Flora's heart dropped. Those words gave her little comfort.

'There, he'll be all right, love. Think of it as him being safe. Especially with him being an officer. That Mrs Harper, she can read, you know, and she has a paper delivered. We all go for a cuppa Rosy Lee in the afternoon and listen as she reads snippets out to us. There was an article on prisoners-of-war. It said officers had beds, and the lower ranks to take care of them. That they were fed well, and the conditions were good. There was reports that their only suffering was boredom, and that they played sport to help them with that.'

'Really? Oh, I hope so, Mrs Larch. I didn't know, as I have avoided reading too much about the war. I've tried not to think of it.'

'Well, you know first-hand. We all know how you went out as a Red Cross nurse to Belgium, and we all think you're a brave girl. You're going to need to be, for your baby, love. We'll all be 'ere for you, but in the end you've to call on the strength that took you to 'elp the Allies that were wounded. We're all proud to have you amongst us.'

Aunt Pru has been gossiping – is there anything about me that my neighbours don't know? But them knowing about her, and how different she was from them, and yet still accepting her, brought Flora comfort. And the strength Mrs Larch spoke of did enter her, and made her determined to get through this, as Cyrus had to. And at that moment an idea occurred to her of how she could fill some of her spare time and give something back to her community.

'When I've recovered from the birth and this shock, I'd like to help you to learn to read, if you would like that?'

To Flora's surprise, tears sparkled in Mrs Larch's eyes. 'Oh, love, I would. Mrs Harper 'as never offered. We all think she likes the status it gives her – her being the only one who can read. But to be able to lose meself in one of them *People's Friend* magazines, which she reads us a serial from, would be lovely. I could curl up on me own sofa whenever I 'ad a mo, instead of waiting for her to have the time to read the lovely stories to us. She considers the news is much more beneficial to us. Well, I'd like to consider what *I* want to enjoy, and it ain't always what is sad about the world. Ooh, love, I'll tell the others, and you'll have a class of us to deal with in no time. Perhaps we could use the church hall, eh?'

Taken aback by Mrs Larch's enthusiasm, Flora laughed, despite the ache in her heart. 'Yes, we can arrange that, and Aunt Pru is a teacher, so she will help.'

Poor Aunt Pru; she'd found it impossible to get a position teaching in a school, and had taken three jobs to help her cope. Mornings were given over to two cleaning jobs, and her afternoons to working in the tearoom at the corner of Flora's street. Though whether she'd still have that, after taking this afternoon off, Flora didn't know. But she'd been glad that Aunt Pru had taken to calling in to see her every day before going to the cafe, especially today.

Left alone once more, Flora was assailed by mixed emotions. Yes, it might be years before she saw Cyrus again, but if what Mrs Larch said was true, he would be safe. The constant worry of wondering if he was dead or alive would leave her. And that would be a blessing. But a huge part of her wished there had never been a war, and for her Cyrus to have never left her side. *Oh, Cyrus, my love, my love . . .*

PART FOUR
The Somme, 1916

~

Flora and Freddy

Hearts and Lives Torn Apart

Chapter Twenty

'He's gone – oh, Flora, he's gone.' Aunt Pru's scream as she came through the door of Flora's home got her staring in shock.

It took a moment for her to reply. 'When, how? Oh, Freddy, no. No.'

'I came home to find this. It were propped up by me milk bottle, and there was a bunch of flowers next to it. I were that angry, I threw the flowers into the grate. Eeh, Flora, what am I to do, lass?'

Flora didn't know what to say. The appeals for young men to join up had moved to an almost brainwashing pitch, with posters everywhere pointing an accusing finger, and recruitment officers visiting factories, upper schools and universities. She and Aunt Pru should have known that Freddy wouldn't resist and should have been more vigilant with him.

'How can they take them so young – Freddy's only sixteen! I thought the conscription of married men had made the difference they needed. Oh, Aunt Pru! We will have to contact the powers that be and tell them his real age.'

They were in each other's arms, clinging on to their love

219

to help them, but it didn't, not really; nothing could ease the desolation they felt.

Aunt Pru pulled away and shook her head. 'Naw. I must let him take this step. I've allus said as he's to make his own decisions. All we can do is pray he will change his mind once he gets in the thick of it – a lad who used to be at my school did. He told the truth of his age and they sent him home. But oh, Flora, what if he doesn't? I can't bear it, I can't.'

'You will find a way, Aunt Pru – we women have to.'

'Eeh, hark at me, and you haven't heard nowt in these last six months about your Cyrus, poor lad. I'm sorry, lass. Like you say, we're to get on with it.'

'I wish I could hear. I have sent parcels to the Red Cross for him, but haven't heard from them as to whether they were able to get them through. Anyway, we have a more pressing need, in what Freddy has done. We need to contact him and . . . well, Aunt Pru, you may not like what I'm going to say, but we need to offer him our support. He will need it.'

'Aye. I'll go and put his flowers into a vase. Will you come for your tea? It's nice enough to sit out. A lovely June day, and here we are in the doldrums.'

'That will be nice. I'll see you later.' The hug Aunt Pru gave her held tension. For all her brave words, it was going to take a lot for them to come to terms with Freddy going and, she knew, a lot of agonizing in the future after he was posted.

As they sat in the garden, Flora broached the subject that had been on her mind for a while. 'Aunt Pru, I would like to go back to work. I was wondering, now that Alice is weaned from my breast, if you would become her nanny? It would be full-time. And you would have to take over the reading lessons in the church hall, but Alice is used to going to those and loves all the attention she gets.'

'Oh, Flora, that would be my salvation, lass. Aye, I would, but can you afford to pay me? You knaw as I would do it for nowt, but I'd have to give me jobs up. Eeh, I'd love to do the class an' all. I've envied you doing that, while I were at the cafe working.'

'Yes, I can manage to pay you. I'll match what you get now and a bit over, and the women are getting on so well, especially Mrs Larch, so I would hate for the classes to have to stop. They pay ten pennies a month – well, those who can afford it. They buy their own pencils and notebooks, though some make the best out of anything they can get their hands on: the backs of letters, and sheets ripped out of their grocery order books. One came in stinking of fish one day. She'd only cut up the wrapping off the fish she'd brought from the fishmonger – there was a ruckus about that, I can tell you!'

They both laughed. For Flora, her laugh held relief, for she had longed to get back to work. She'd gone into the hospital and had played the piano once a week for the injured – those nearly blind and the poor souls who were fully blind, who had found solace in her music, and they all loved to hold Alice. But that had only served to show Flora just how short-staffed they were at the hospital, and had set up a need in her to get back to doing more for the war effort.

Flora found that she was readily taken on at Moorfields Hospital, and her step was light as she approached it a week later. But her heart lifted with joy when she entered the ward. 'Ella! Oh, Ella, what are you doing here?'

'Flors! Flors – oh, it's good to see you. I was going to try to look you up, but I've had no time.'

The tut-tut of the sister in charge had them moving out of their hug and standing to attention.

'I gather you two know each other?'

'Yes, Sister, sorry, Sister – we were in Belgium together.'

'Well, I have to say: well done for that. We all heard about the plight of the Red Cross nurses caught out there.' She looked at the watch pinned to her frock. 'I expect you need to catch up. Pop along to the canteen, but don't take long. Bedpan duty will be in ten minutes and I want you both attending to it.'

They almost tripped over each other as they rushed out of the door into the corridor. 'Ella, I can't believe it. Where have you been? Did you get my letters?'

'Only just, and I was going to contact you. I've been working in a field hospital in France. I have been sent back here to learn how to look after those with eye injuries. I will be going back in about six weeks, but I am a bit frustrated, as Sister uses me more as a ward orderly rather than letting me near any treatment. I have contacted the Red Cross General Office about it. But what about you? Married – and to that bloke we met at the frontier! You dark horse – are you happy?'

As they sipped the strong, stewed tea, Flora told her own and Cyrus's story. Ella was so sorry to hear of Cyrus's plight, but was thrilled to learn of Alice and asked question after question.

'Hey, I feel as though I'm being interrogated here.'

'Sorry, just one more. Have you heard from Mags, Flora?'

'Not much. It saddens me, but she doesn't seem to want to know. All I can glean is that she is helping her father. She hasn't met anyone, and doesn't intend to. I wish I could help her.'

'I will write, too, while I am here. Maybe on one of our weekends off we could travel up to the North to see her?'

'That would be lovely. I have a brother who goes up regularly to the family-owned mill. He's thinking of living up there. I see him occasionally – well, you know how my family situation was, and it has worsened since, but for some reason my oldest brother seems to want to keep in contact. I sometimes wonder if he is my father's spy, keeping an eye on what I am up to. Anyway, I could ask him to take us.'

'Oh, let's. That would be wonderful. I'll write to Mags later today and put the feelers out. In the meantime, you can seek out your brother and see if he will help us.'

'I will. Oh, Ella, it's good to see you. You seem to have grown – not in height, but in confidence, and it's good to see.'

'I could do with a few inches, but no, I'm stuck as I am.' They giggled at this. 'Joking apart, I have seen some terrible things, Flors. Far worse than we ever experienced. I have had to toughen up and stand on my own two feet. You're often called upon to make life-and-death decisions, and can't always defer them to others. You should come out, Flors: we need you.'

This last sentence settled in Flora, and she pondered it for most of the day. Could she? *It would be a wrench leaving Alice, but she would be fine with Aunt Pru. I so need a huge distraction from the heartache that is my constant companion.* But then hadn't she read that the Red Cross wouldn't take married women?

Harold flirted with Ella on the journey up north, hardly taking any notice of Flora. He knew of Mags's family and

223

their mill, and when Flora had asked him for a lift, he'd told her, 'I heard that Witherbrook had a daughter who thinks she could run his mill. Ha, women today think they can do anything. Give me a feminine woman, who just wants to run my home and sit and sew, or something.'

'And who lets you have your mistresses.'

He'd become angry at this retort from Flora. 'That's another part of a man's life that a woman is advised not to interfere with. Mother has made that mistake.'

She'd been surprised that he hadn't mentioned the mysterious older brother again, but was glad when he had agreed to take her and Ella to see Mags. And even more pleased to hear that Mags wanted to see them.

Harold's attention towards Ella had worried her, as she knew Harold would eat the Ellas of this world for breakfast; but his reaction when he met Mags was as if someone had hit him with a sledgehammer. Even more disconcerting, Mags had the same reaction to him.

They stared at each other, and hardly took any notice of her introductions. Before Ella and Flora could say hello to Mags, Harold had invited them all out to dinner with him that evening. She and Ella exchanged glances. Ella's held amusement, but to Flora it seemed like a clash of giant personalities that would end in hurt for Mags, and she intended to disillusion both girls about her brother.

Once he'd left to go and see to the business he had at the mill, the three of them hugged, shed tears and chatted, all at the same time.

To Flora, it was like coming home for a second time; home to her sisters, as she'd never stopped thinking about them in that way. It felt so good to be with them again.

Mags took them into her beautiful home, surrounded by

magnificent scenery of rugged, mountainous hills and green fields. The house was more a mansion, and yet had a homely feel, smelling of polish and fresh flowers, with bright colours giving it a light, airy look. The furnishings were modern, ornate and grand, with high-backed chairs with thick gold velvet cushions in an elaborately carved wooden frame giving a touch of elegance.

Mags's mother was welcoming and an older version of Mags herself – tall and self-assured, giving the impression that she was in charge of any situation. She greeted them as Mags had done when she first met them, with a big hug, before showing them into the garden.

Once they were seated under a sunshade, Flora looked at Mags and thought how different she looked in her summer attire. Her dress was of cream cotton, with a pattern of tiny rosebuds in pinks and yellows. It was cut to fit the bodice, with long sleeves and a feminine neckline that showed a tiny glimpse of her cleavage; the skirt flared out and flowed to the floor. 'You're looking so well, Mags. With so little news of you, I've been frightened as to your true welfare.'

'I'm all right, Flors. Sorry, but I found it difficult to write. My pen wanted to go on its own and pour out things that I didn't want to revisit, so I avoided picking it up and instead threw myself into my work. Sometimes I had the feeling that I wanted to forget it all, and that meant both of you, too. But that passed and I've loved hearing all your news, and am so happy that you asked to come up and see me.'

'We wouldn't have given up on you – we understood.'

'I know. And as for your letter about your marriage, well! Though none of it surprised me really. You are impetuous

225

and you fell in love at first sight. We knew that, didn't we, Ella?'

Ella nodded and smiled.

'Well, I'm jolly glad it has worked out for you . . . I – I mean . . .'

'No, don't worry, Mags. I don't want you to feel awkward at talking about Cyrus. I *want* to talk about him. I long for the day he will come home. I just wish I knew how he was being treated.'

'I've read that officers are treated with respect, Flors, so try to hang on to that. And what about you, Ella, going back into the field? I couldn't do that. I so admire you.'

The chat went on for a while, mostly about their exploits in Belgium, which now seemed to have been an adventure, instead of the terror-filled hours they really had been.

It was Mags who changed the subject. 'Tell me about your brother, Flors. I was surprised when you wrote that he was bringing you, as I thought, when you said you were now fully estranged from your family, that you meant all of them. I'm glad you didn't. I think Harold a handsome man, and it's interesting to me how much involvement he has in the mill industry. Is that why he hasn't gone to war – essential work, and all that?'

Although Flora wouldn't want Mags to fall for Harold, she was glad to hear her taking an interest in any man. She'd had the impression that, since her terrible experience, Mags had avoided any romantic entanglement. 'Oh, he's all right. I wouldn't say he's avoided the war – well, maybe. But although he's handsome, I'd advise any girl to give him a wide berth; he's not great husband material.'

'Hmm, maybe he can be brought into line.'

They all laughed at this.

'Anyway, I bet it would be fun trying. Have you told him anything about what happened – you know . . .'

'No, Mags. We made a pact, and I've kept it. Not even family, we said.'

'Oh, I was just making sure. I shouldn't have mentioned it. Anyway, your turn, Ella, tell us what it's like in France. I mean, what it's really like: is it hell?'

Listening to Ella, the urge that had seized Flora before revisited her. *Would it be possible for me to go? Could I be parted from Alice for that long?* But then she decided that, as nurses were needed so badly, she had a duty to try, and made her mind up that she would make enquiries. This was compounded in her mind when Ella said, 'I'm not supposed to say anything, but you know that the Red Cross is fore-warned of where they are most likely to be needed next? Well, there is a new field hospital being constructed in Dieppe, in Normandy. I suppose, from that, we can deduce that a new offensive is being planned, as that is usually the case when we are on the move. I have been told that, after the training I am undertaking at Moorfields, I am to be posted there.'

'They must be expecting a lot of casualties to have a hos-pital constructed. What is it like working in tents?' As she asked this, Flora thought of Freddy and her arms pebbled with goosebumps. What if he was sent there? It was then that she made her mind up. If he was, then she would go, too.

'It's muddy most of the time. France is having a wet summer. And chaotic, as it's difficult to bring any proper order to things, because new casualties are arriving all the time. You just get everyone settled and some sort of routine in place, when you hear the guns start in the distance and,

227

before long, convoys of ambulances arrive, or a hospital train. But they mostly come in during the night. And it isn't just the living wounded that they bring; there are those that didn't make it, who need cleaning up and identifying, by tagging them. I dread that duty. All those young lives. And those whose bodies are brought to us are considered lucky, I know; a lot are just left where they fell, and have to be hastily buried during a sort of truce that takes place for that purpose. And that's because there are so many wounded to transport that the dead have to be left behind. At least the dead that are brought in have a decent burial in a marked grave, and their families know where they are and receive any belongings they had on them.'

They were all silent after listening to this. Flora sipped her tea, not touching the chocolate biscuit that had been served with it. She hadn't the stomach for it, as once more the reality of war had touched her, with the vivid descriptions Ella had given. How could she not offer her services now? She would feel as if somehow she had betrayed Cyrus, if she didn't go to the help of the men he'd been forced to leave behind. Yes, she would miss Alice – it would feel as if only half of her was going; but when Alice grew up and was told why her mother had gone, she would understand. And she couldn't be left in more loving care than with Aunt Pru, who adored her.

At dinner, the worry Flora felt about the attraction that Mags and Harold had shown for each other grew. They looked as if they had known each other all their lives. Having so much common ground, with the daily life of running a mill to discuss, made their conversation flow, and even she had to admit they made a handsome pair, and that each seemed to bring the other alive in a way she'd never seen before.

Their engrossment in each other gave Flora time to talk to Ella about her plans. Ella was more than a little surprised.

'Really? You mean you would seriously try to get to work in France?'

'If they will have me, yes. I have a lot to offer, but I have heard they don't take married women.'

'In theory, no. But in practice they can't turn them down, as they need all the hands they can get. If you're serious about this, Flors, then apply.'

'I am serious, Ella. It will help me, as well as me helping others. I need to be stretched to my limit, to get through the years ahead of me. I thought going out to work would do it, but it isn't enough. It isn't. I have to seek out something that will take me so far out of my humdrum routine, and will drain me, so that I cannot think, let alone feel.'

'Oh, Flors, does it hurt that much?'

'It does. It hurts so much that only inflicting more hurt on myself can possibly get me to the other side of the pain. Tearing myself away from Alice, and coping with what you have described, will do that. Does that make sense?'

Flora didn't think it did make sense to Ella, even though she nodded her head. But it did to her, and that's what mattered. On her return to London she would put the wheels in motion and do all she could to make going to work in France a reality.

Chapter Twenty-One

It had taken a lot of interviews, and standing her ground, for Flora to get accepted. As part of her application she'd had to sit an exam.

She'd had to write a brief history of a case of enteric fever during the third week, giving a temperature chart; and tell how to prepare a linseed-meal poultice, an ice poultice and a mustard poultice, and indicate their use. Another part of the exam had asked about 'crisis and lysis' and in what illnesses respectively they occurred. And she'd even had to describe how to make a peptonized beef-tea.

After passing this exam with a 100 per cent score, Flora had finally been accepted. And now she had the letter in her hand that she knew contained her orders.

Sitting down at the table that still held her breakfast dishes and the remains of the porridge that Alice had refused to eat, Flora listened to her child gurgling away as she sat, propped by cushions, in her high chair, happily banging her spoon on the tray.

Tears stung Flora's eyes, as what she'd planned was now becoming a reality. What had made her think that she could walk away from Alice and do this? But doing so would help her get through the pain that was her constant companion.

A further incentive to carry it all through had been Freddy arriving home last night. To her, he had grown in stature and become a man. But her fear for him had deepened as they had gathered at Aunt Pru's, and Freddy told them that after a three-week leave he was being deployed to Picardy. For she knew a battle was raging there, and that it was the bloodiest and hardest-fought to date. The newspapers were full every day of the thousands of deaths and wounded. Poor Pru had almost fainted at the news of Freddy going there, but had found enough courage to regain the strength she needed. 'Eeh, me lass, I've prayed as they wouldn't accept you,' she told Flora, 'but now a part of me is glad, as to knaw as you're there will ease me mind some, as you can watch out for me lad.'

Freddy had put them both right. 'I'll be watching over myself, and over my fellow soldiers, as much as I can. Flors cannot come onto the battlefield with me, and cannot be responsible for anything that might happen to me, when I am engaged in fighting the enemy. But that said, Flors, it'll be good to know that, when I can get away, I can come and see you, so I'll be hoping you are sent somewhere near to me – though I wish with all my heart that you hadn't embarked on this madcap idea in the first place.'

She understood that, and questioned her own sanity and the impulse that she'd allowed to drive her, but here she was, holding the letter that would tell her one way or the other. Tearing it open, she read:

231

Dear Volunteer Flora Harpinham,

Please arrange to meet Matron Hugby at Victoria Station at eleven a.m. on Monday 31st July 1916. Matron will be just inside the station, and in uniform.

From there you will catch a train to Newhaven and, after an overnight stay, will join a ship taking you to France. Your final destination will be hospital no. 16 at Le Tréport, near Dieppe.

Your rank will be Assistant Nurse, as you have proved your capability in the excellent service you gave in Brussels and in the results you obtained in sitting the exam. You will find a blue stripe with the uniform and equipment that will be issued to you once you arrive.

To distinguish your rank, you are to wear this on your right sleeve below the shoulder at all times while in uniform. This is in addition to the war-service stripes, worn on the left sleeve on indoor and outdoor uniform. You will also be issued a gilding-metal badge of the letter A, and this you will wear on the bib of your apron, a quarter of an inch above the Red Cross in the centre.

I take this opportunity of thanking you for offering your services and of wishing you well.

The letter was signed on behalf of the Director of the Red Cross.

For a moment, Flora held the letter to her breast. Her hands felt the rapid beat of her heart. Her throat tightened. It was really going to happen! *And I shall be with Ella.*

Reaching for the map of France, which she had pored over time after time, looking for the places reported in the newspapers, she located Dieppe. Her heart sank as she realized it was about sixty miles from the nearest battles that were now being fought. A long way for the wounded to travel, but disappointingly, too, a long way from where Freddy was likely to be. But he would have leave-days; she'd read that the soldiers were rested often and a rotation system was used, so that they weren't charging into battle every day, but did different duties in the trenches some days, and were free to do as they pleased on others. She'd try to arrange for the ambulance drivers to take notes to him; she'd sort it out with him before she left.

Finding herself on a station platform once more, and facing worse than she had when heading to Belgium, Flora stood quietly behind the matron as more and more girls joined her. The chatter was of excited anticipation. Flora wanted to bring them all down to earth and tell them what it would be really like, but she didn't; she kept quiet. Her emotions were in a turmoil, making it difficult for her to join in and begin to make friends.

When she arrived at the hospital, Ella greeted her as if she hadn't seen her for a lifetime. Coming out of the huge hug, Flora began to feel the knot that had tied her stomach loosen.

'Well, here we go again, Flors. I can't tell you how good it feels to have you by my side. All the girls here are good sorts; the atmosphere is one of a lovely community and the order of the day is to stay cheerful, no matter what, so that the lads feel there is hope.'

As Ella showed her around, Flora detected more a feeling of despair than of hope, from both the staff and the wounded. The noise was the familiar one of men calling out in pain seeking attention, though some, too weak to do that, moaned in a low, agonized sound that cut into Flora's heart. Doctors called out for a nurse, and nurses called out to volunteers. The smell was a mixture of carbolic and chlorine, which didn't quite cover the stench of rotting flesh.

Ella sighed and shrugged her shoulders, as if apologizing for her fib. 'We're just so understaffed. But we do try.'

'I'll let you get back to work, Ella. I wish I could help you, but the sister said that, apart from familiarizing ourselves with the place, we weren't to do anything until we had been properly briefed and received our kit, and shown where we are to bunk. I'd better get out of your way and go along to the rallying point now.'

It seemed that the first month passed without Flora having engaged in it, and yet she'd worked harder than she'd ever worked in her life. Her weight had dropped by almost a stone, her body ached constantly, and she felt she was constantly swimming against the tide.

Looking into the eyes of the man whose hand she held, she read his despair. Both of his legs had been amputated, and he had frequent screaming nightmares. 'Joseph, do you think you can go back to sleep now?'

He shook his head, and his eyes stared out at her. Sweat beaded his forehead.

'It's all right. Don't be afraid. I'll stay a little while longer. Try to close your eyes.'

'T – tell me about home.'

'You'll make it back – you will.'

His head shook.

'You're a cockney, aren't you, Joseph? Well, I've spent a lot of my life in Stepney and now live in Brixton. It's just as you left it: noisy, busy and full of small communities pulling together even more than they did before the war. Big Ben still deafens us on the hour, and ships come in up the Thames. Smoke hangs heavy in the air, bringing down terrible smog, and some streets stink of the old cesspits that are still in use. Ragged-arsed kids play hoop-and-stick and pester you for a penny, and barrow boys tout their wares through the streets. At night, the lamplighter goes along lighting the way, and the evening news is shouted from every corner. Is that how you remember it . . . Joseph?'

His eyes didn't blink.

Oh no. Oh God, no. Standing up, Flora felt her body shake. She should be used to losing a soldier by now, but she wasn't. Running along to the night sister to report Joseph's passing, she found herself crying and unable to say the words. She could only point.

'Oh, my dear. It was Joseph Carter you were specializing, wasn't it? I gather he has left us? Leave it to me. Go along to the canteen and take half an hour – it's quiet at the moment.'

'Thank you, Sister. I – I'm sorry.'

'Don't be. A nurse who has no feeling is no good to me, or to the men. Off you go.'

Flora didn't make it to the canteen, but stood behind the tent designated for that purpose and tried to compose herself. The opposite happened. More tears flowed and her body weakened with the weight of her longing for Cyrus and Alice, and the pity of all the suffering and loss around her.

An arm came round her. 'Hey, what's all this, you'll make yourself ill.'

No words would come to answer him, and she didn't resist when the man who had spoken to her pulled her into

235

his arms. 'I'm one of the ambulance drivers, and it strikes me you're in need of some comfort.' His lips brushed her neck. For a moment she imagined it was Cyrus and a calm came over her. Then she lifted her head. The touch of his lips on hers startled her. A sob made him release her.

'No. Get off me! Don't touch me.'

'You seemed willing a minute ago. You want to watch how you tease men – some won't take no for an answer.'

'I'm sorry, you caught me at a bad moment. I'm not . . I don't . . . You see, I'm married, and my husband is a prisoner-of-war. I – I left my child to come here; and my patient died a few moments ago . . . I—'

'Well, I'm sorry if I was mistaken. I only tried to offer comfort, and then you seemed as if you wanted more. God knows, any man in camp would give it to a willing woman. You won't report me, will you?'

His obvious distress saw her reassuring him. He wasn't to blame. 'No. I understand how you mistook my actions. My name's Flora, what's yours?'

'Jim – Jim Skelby. I just brought a couple of wounded in. They're in the clearing tent now, and I have to get back. I reckon there will be a few casualties tomorrow, as there's another push planned.'

'Can you do something for me, Jim? I need to get a message to one of the soldiers, my half-brother.'

'You do know there's a thousand or so of them out there, don't you?'

'Yes. Is there no way of locating one of them?'

'I suppose I could try. What's his name and what regiment does he belong to?'

'Freddy Hatton, of the Essex Regiment, Second Battalion.

236

Please try. I need to know that he is safe, and then arrange to meet him when he has his leave-day.'

'Leave it with me. I'm attached to that regiment. If I don't see you on my return, I'll leave a message. Look, I'm sorry about just now. You caught me at a weak moment. I'd never behave like that normally.'

'Please forget it – I have done. I wasn't willing, you apologized and that's good enough for me.'

'Look, love, I don't know if it will help or not, but like you, I'm missing folk back home. My mother and my brothers, and especially my young sisters, but I turn that around to help me get through. I imagine it is them needing help, and relying on a stranger to give it to them. That makes me be strong, and I treat every young lad like I'd want my lot to be treated, if they were in the same situation. It makes me so engrossed in my job that I don't dwell on it too much. Try it.'

'Thanks, Jim, I will. I'd better go, I'll see you another time.'

As he walked away, Flora felt that she'd made a friend. Yes, he would have taken advantage of her, if she'd have carried on showing the willingness that she had at first, but she couldn't blame him for that. *Whatever possessed me?*

Whatever it was, Flora shook it from her and, feeling stronger, walked determinedly back to the ward tent.

Chapter Twenty-Two

It rarely occurred, but Flora and Ella were off-duty on the same day. Too tired to do anything other than walk along the clifftop, they had braved the spitting rain and the unseasonal cool, late-September wind that held the threat of a heavier downpour, and walked arm-in-arm towards Dieppe.

'I have news of Freddy, at last. He will be on leave for two days next week, and I've cleared it with Sister that I can have that time off, too. Jim has sorted everything. I'm catching the train to Albert, and Freddy can get a lift to there. He's just outside Thiepval.'

'Oh, how lovely – give him my love. I sometimes think I'm lucky, knowing of no family; even though it tears me apart at times, I have no one to worry over. After this is all over, I'm going to try to find out where my allowance comes from, and if the trust is part of a will or from someone who is alive.'

'Sometimes, being women, we are treated as if we have no rights. If you were a man, you would have access to so much more information. The bank wouldn't be able to tell you to go away when you made enquiries.'

'Maybe I should marry, and make my husband my attorney.'

'Oh, anyone in mind? I see you getting on well with Jim, and he always seeks you out.'

'Mmm, we'll see. I'm afraid of attachments made under the pressure we find ourselves in. It's so easy to mistake comfort for love.'

Flora felt herself blush, as memories of her first meeting with Jim prickled her. She'd long since admitted to herself that, for a fleeting moment, she had been ready to seek the comfort of Jim's arms. But she'd had no such thoughts since; the moment had been one of her lowest. And Jim had become a good friend, often bringing them things from town, as his work sent him to many places as he transported the wounded. But she suspected his feelings were more than those of comfort, where Ella was concerned.

'You're quiet.'

Flora pulled her cardigan round her. 'Oh, just thinking. I agree with you: a few of the girls have boyfriends amongst the walking wounded, and you wonder where it can lead.'

'Oh, and doctor–nurse relationships are a great source of gossip, too.'

'Ha! Keeps us all going.'

'Let's go to the docks, there's always something to watch there, and that little bar serves some delicious seafood.'

The docks of Dieppe were the highlight of a free day. There – apart from when the hospital ship was in, and the sight of patients being taken aboard meant they still had their work in view – the nurses could watch fishing boats going out and other boats offloading their catch, or see the women mending the nets.

Today, the grey sky gave the tall buildings an eerie look,

and Flora shivered. Life here carried on, despite what was happening a few miles away, and the horror of the field hospital.

'You're not yourself today. What is it, Flors?'

'I – I . . . well, I just keep thinking that days off for the soldiers follow the days when they've been over the top. How often we hear them say, "And it was my day off tomorrow."'

'Are you worried that Freddy will be in the thick of it before you see him?'

'Yes. A week is a long time, and during it he has so much to face. I just can't shift this feeling that I have.'

'It's natural. Take deep breaths of this lovely fresh air. It helps to clear your mind. Remember, we only see the casualties of the war. And they are only a fraction of the men fighting, so Freddy could just as easily be one of those who survive unscathed.'

'Yes, knowing him, though—'

'Right, stop now. You'll convince me soon, and I plan to marry him.'

'What!' Flora burst out laughing. 'Oh, Ella, he did have a crush on you the moment he met you.'

'He did. He was waiting for me outside the hospital once, and we walked together. Freddy's lovely, and will get through this and meet someone perfect for him, and live happily ever after.'

'I think he wants to go into politics. At least that was his latest idea. But of course he always comes back to his plans for a musical career. I think he was swayed this time by an urge to put the world right. I sometimes think he believes he can achieve that single-handed. Boys are funny, when they reach that stage of not quite being a man. I remember

Francis . . . Oh, well, that was another lifetime. No more reminiscing. I'm starving.'

Ella's hand squeezed Flora's arm. 'Let's hope that the catch this morning was a good one and that Monsieur Douple has managed to buy the best of it. I can smell Madame Douple's bread already.'

Relaxed and ignoring the niggling voice inside her, Flora drifted off to sleep that night; the fresh air and the walk had tired her in a different way from the exhausting shifts. Her dreams were of Freddy playing with Alice.

Coming out of a deep sleep, she tried to manage what was happening in her dream, as now Freddy was waving and Alice was crying; she didn't want that, but everything floated away from her and she couldn't bring it all back to the way she wanted it. She couldn't make her world well again, not even in her dreams.

A bell tolled, clanging fear into her that shot her up to a sitting position. 'Come on, everyone, all hands are needed on deck. There's a large intake, and more expected.'

Responding immediately to this shout from one of the nurses, who'd popped her head into the dormitory tent and left, Flora donned her uniform, splashed her face in the cold water she'd left in a bowl by her bed and rushed to the main station, where she knew orders would be given out.

'Assistant Nurse Harpinham, take charge of minors; you go with her, Grendan.'

Putting a volunteer in charge of any department meant that this was a really big affair, and all the qualified nurses would be needed for the more serious cases.

Brenda Grendan was a good and capable volunteer, and Flora knew she would fare well with her by her side. 'Brenda, when we get to the tent, I'll assess, while you make sure there are trays ready. I can apply stitches where needed, so make some trays up for that purpose, too.'

The talk amongst her patients was of tanks being used for the first time, and how the German barbed-wire defences had been smashed. And although in pain, the soldiers were jubilant about this new feature of the war. It was as if hope had entered where there had been none. But to Flora, their tales gave a reason for the high numbers of wounded, as it seemed that, buoyed by this extra support, many had taken risks they normally wouldn't have.

A man calling her name got Flora straightening from where she'd been bent over a young soldier, who to her seemed no more than a boy, removing a piece of shrapnel that had only just pierced his leg, and cleaning and dressing the wound and stitching the gaping tear. 'There you go. Take a crutch from the corner there and report to tent nine. You'll be kept there for a couple of weeks, to make sure there is no infection. You've been lucky.' *Lucky? Is he really? In two weeks he'll be back on the front line.*

Wiping her brow and going outside the tent, Flora saw Jim making his way along the tents, calling her name.

'Here, Jim. I'm here.'

'I've bad news. I've brought your brother in. He's in a bad way. He's in—'

'Oh no . . . No! Oh, Jim.'

'Follow me. Hurry!'

'I can't leave my post. Oh, Jim. I – I have to find the sister in charge.'

'It's bad, Flora, I'm sorry. Get to him as quick as you can. Ella's with him. I told her who he was, but she said she knew and sent me for you.'

'What's going on, Nurse Harpinham, why have you left your post? Those boys I left you in charge of may only have minors, but they are frightened and traumatized. I trusted you to take care of them, and I find—'

'Oh, Sister . . . My – my brother . . .'

'Oh, dear girl.'

Jim told the sister what had happened.

'Run along, Nurse Harpinham. Go. We'll manage here.'

Jim ran ahead. Flora couldn't register whether she was running or walking, for her soul was already with Freddy.

At the tent entrance, Jim took her hand. 'I have to go, but remember, I'm here for you.'

'Thank you, Jim.'

Entering the tent seemed like walking into hell. Blood ran along the floor, screams mingled with sobs, and cries of 'Help me' tugged at her heart.

Flora sought desperately which way to go, and then caught sight of Ella as she stood up from bending over a patient. 'Ella!'

'Flora, this way. Oh, Flors, I – I'm sorry.'

'Is – is he . . . ?'

'He's alive, but, Flors, he – well, he hasn't got long.'

'No, no, no . . . No! Ella, oh God. Ella, no!'

'Be brave for him, Flors. Freddy needs you. We told him you were coming. He's afraid, and he needs your strength.'

The words filtered into her. The worst kind of bravery was needed of her now, but she would find it in herself, for her darling Freddy.

'Freddy, I'm here, my darling brother, I'm here.'

His lovely face was untouched by his injury, but ashen. His dark eyes stared out of deeply sunk sockets. His voice was just a whisper. 'Flors . . . I don't want to die, Flors.'

243

'You won't, my darling. You're badly injured and have a long road ahead of you, but you won't die. Your ma will see to that, once they ship you home.'

His body relaxed. What was left of it, that was, as Flora could see that he was just a torso, no legs. A trickle of blood seeped out of the corner of his mouth as she watched him. As she went to wipe it away, he coughed and a torrent of his blood splashed her face. Taking Freddy in her arms, she lifted him. 'Someone, come quickly!'

Ella was by her side. 'Hold him in that position, I'll get the doctor.'

'Flors . . . Flors, I – I love you, Sis.'

'And I love you, with all my heart, Freddy. Now don't try to talk.'

'Tell . . . Ma . . . Fl—'

'Freddy, no. Oh, Freddy . . . Freddy!'

His head had flopped onto her arm. His face slackened, and she knew that he had gone.

Resting him back on the bed, she lay down beside him. Her heart screamed her pain, but she kept quiet; the last thing the staff and the poor dying boys around her needed was for her to give way to the agony that encased her.

Ella came back and stood next to her, stroking her hair. Tears streamed down her face. But responding to a call, she left without speaking, pulling the curtain around the bed as she did so.

Flora smoothed Freddy's hair. 'My darling brother. My lovely boy . . .'

Getting off the bed when the doctor appeared a few minutes later, she waited until he had carried out his tests. No hope entered her that he would find any sign of life. Looking up at her, he shook his head. 'I'm sorry. But try to take comfort from the fact that he had you with him. We have lost ten so far, and most of them died alone, without even a nurse with them.'

There was a little comfort in that for Flora, but also a deep sadness for those other boys. 'I'll take my brother to the morgue and take care of him, Doctor.'

'No. You are needed by the living. The orderlies will do that. You must carry on with your work. Besides, it will take away his dignity in death, to have his sister wash him. We will call you once he is ready.'

Breathing in deeply, Flora kissed Freddy's still cheek and somehow found the strength to walk away.

Hours later, she and Ella went together to visit Freddy. Until then, Flora had kept herself together, but when she saw his body, with his possessions folded neatly on top of it, she turned and ran.

Holding her skirt, she ran and ran and didn't stop until she reached the cliff edge, where she fell onto the cold, damp grass and beat it with her fists. Her tears mingled with her snot, her throat rasped out terrible screams as she denied God, and the Devil, and all mankind.

When she fell quiet, Ella's voice came to her. 'Flors, my poor Flors.'

'Oh, Ella, Ella. How am I going to let Aunt Pru hear this, without me being there? I want to tell her myself. I want to take Freddy back with me.'

'That's won't be possible, Flors. He will be buried here, with his fellow soldiers. We will give him a good send-off, eh? For your Aunt Pru's sake.'

'But I don't want her to get that awful telegram. I don't . . .'

'I know, but it will be out of your hands. It is the official way, and that's how it will be done. Write at once to her, Flors, so that your letter gets to her soon after.'

'I want to go back. Oh, Ella, I want to go back.' Her sobs brought the words out, but Flora knew they were not just because of her sorrow. She couldn't stay here – she had to be with her Alice and her Aunt Pru.

'I don't think anyone would stop you, Flors, and I think it is the right thing for you to do. Your emotions are worn ragged, with all you have on your plate. We can't always help ourselves by helping others, and you will be needed at home. Let me help you up.'

The last post sounded all around Flora, but didn't touch the thick wall she'd put up around herself to shield her from what was happening. A row of coffins sat in a long grave. Freddy's was the fourth one along. In his hand he held a locket, with a picture of his ma in it, and laid on his chest was a wreath of wild flowers that she and Ella had made.

Moving forward at the bidding of the chaplain, Flora picked up a handful of earth. The noise it made as it hit Freddy's coffin shuddered through her. But she turned and walked with dignity to stand by Ella's and Jim's side. They manoeuvred her between them and both put their arms around her, but neither spoke.

Her bags were packed, and tomorrow she would board the ship for home.

She'd done all she could for the war effort; now it was time to be with her family.

Chapter Twenty-Three

It seemed to Flora that her Aunt Pru had shrunk. Her body was bent over, and her stature was that of a woman in her sixties rather than one approaching her forties. Never an overweight person, Pru had little fat that she could afford to lose, but the pain of her loss had ravished her body and left her almost skeletal.

They clung together on the station. Flora had been surprised to see Pru there, waiting to meet her.

'I couldn't go another minute, Flora, without seeing you. Rowena is watching Alice. By, she's grown, and she's crawling everywhere and into everything.'

'I shouldn't have left – I know that now. I could only see my own pain and wanted to rid myself of it, but I haven't. I've added to it.'

'I'm glad you went. My Freddy didn't die alone, like them other poor lads you told me of. That gave me a lot of comfort to know that he was in your arms, lass.'

'Dear Aunt Pru, I'm so sorry. So very sorry.'

'Aye. Well, don't start me blubbing here, lass. Let's get home. Little Alice needs us, and we need her. She's kept me going, I can tell you. Without her to care for, I'd have gone mad.'

They linked arms and walked through the usual crowd of young soldiers and older ones, and wives kissing them goodbye. Flora couldn't think about what they all had to face. She just wanted to get home.

When they reached Rowena's house, Flora's heart was in her mouth. 'Do you think Alice will know me? Will she want to come home with me?'

'Aye, she'll know you. I sewed that photo of you onto the tummy of her favourite teddy, and she is always kissing you and saying, "Mama".'

The tears threatened, but Flora swallowed them down. When the door opened, Rowena stood there, with Alice in her arms. 'Well, you're home, love, and welcome – so welcome. We've missed you. Look, Alice: Mama.'

Alice held her head down shyly. Her eyes looked up into Flora's face. Flora wanted to grab her and hold her to her, but she waited. Alice looked from her teddy to Flora and then whispered, 'Mama?'

'Yes, darling. Mama's back.'

Alice put her arms out and stretched towards her. Dropping her bag, Flora took hold of her. 'I'm sorry, my darling, so sorry I left you. Forgive me.' As she spoke, she kissed Alice's face and neck and cuddled her to her. There was no resistance from her daughter. 'Oh, Alice, I'm home . . . I'm home.'

Two more pairs of arms came around her, and at that moment she felt so loved. What did it matter that her parents had rejected her – what did any of it matter? She had a family; she had the best family she could possibly have.

* * *

'I'm staying at yours, Flora.' They were in a cab on the way to Flora's home. 'I've looked after it all for you, and I took me bedding over these last three weeks, to get Alice used to being in her own home again. But I can't go back to my own place, not yet. I want to stay with you.'

'I wouldn't have it any other way, Aunt Pru. We need each other.'

'I'll want to hear all about how me Freddy went, but not yet. I'll tell you when I'm ready.'

Flora didn't answer; she only hoped that when Pru was ready, she would be, too.

'There's a surprise for you on the table, when you get in.'

'Oh, Aunt Pru, have you been baking?'

'Naw. I've not done owt like that since I heard. Though I've fed Alice of course, and taken care of all her needs.'

'You have to eat, dear Aunt Pru, you have to build your strength up.'

'I can't. Me lovely Freddy can't, so I can't.'

A tear fell silently down Aunt Pru's face. All Flora could do was to squeeze her hand, as the sleeping Alice held her arms captive.

The surprise on the table made Flora squeal with joy, like she thought she would never squeal again. There was a pile of letters, tied with a red ribbon.

'Shush, now, you'll wake Alice from her nap, and she can be a grumpy thing if she doesn't have her sleep.'

Flora's breath caught in her lungs. 'Tell me that they are what I think they are, Aunt Pru!'

'Aye. They are. They all came together, about five days ago. They were tied with string, but I found that bit of ribbon. Give Alice to me, and you take the letters to your room. I'll put her in her cot and make us a pot of tea.'

Sitting on her bed, Flora kissed the bundle before untying it. She checked the postage, but there were no clues as to which one to read first, so she opened them all and spread them out. The first had been written just after Cyrus's capture and told of his anguish, not for himself, but for her. He said the camp was not fully built and they were to work on building it, but he welcomed that, as he wanted to be busy.

Later letters showed how he was counting the months to the birth of their child, and then that he knew the birth had taken place and longed for news.

The next one told her that he'd received her parcel, and how his heart had swelled to know that he was the father of a baby girl.

None of them told her much about his life, except for the boredom that he suffered, and the agony of not being with her. But they all spoke of his love. And so beautifully expressed that she could almost hear his voice.

'Oh, Cyrus. My Cyrus.' With the letters held to her breast, she could feel him in the room with her. Though she wanted to curl up in a ball and cry and cry, she gained strength from them. She had a job to do. She had to help Aunt Pru, and she had to be a mother to Alice – a proper mother, nothing like her own mother – and never going away and leaving her again. A tinge of shame coloured her cheeks. How had she made such a decision, and what would Cyrus think of her?

She'd make it up to Alice, and to Aunt Pru. And she would beg Cyrus to forgive her for abandoning their child.

In the days that followed, getting to know her little girl gave Flora the lift she needed, but her worry for her Aunt Pru increased. More than once she'd heard her vomiting and had rushed to her side.

'You have to go to the doctor, Aunt Pru, I'm worried out of my mind about you.'

'It's me grief, lass. From the moment that envelope came, I've felt ill. Before that, I was fine and nothing ailed me.'

'It could be the shock and, like you say, your grief. I have a sick feeling inside me, and have had since it all happened, but for you it is much worse. And you're not eating, love. You're not getting any sustenance. You need to have a check-up. Between us, we can afford to have the doctor call on you.'

They hadn't discussed money since she'd returned, but there was a worry niggling away at Flora. On her visit to the bank, she had found that her funds were very much depleted. She'd arranged for Aunt Pru to collect a weekly sum to keep her and Alice while she was away, and knew that she had to keep taking care of Aunt Pru for a while, as she couldn't possibly work to take care of herself.

At least the Red Cross owed her a few months' salary. And she had her allowance from Cyrus's army pay to collect, so maybe things wouldn't be too bad, but she would have to consider getting a job. That couldn't be nursing. She knew she could never do that again. But if not that, then what else was there for her? Her music maybe? There must be a way to earn a shilling or two playing the piano.

She was jolted out of these thoughts by Aunt Pru's sobs. 'Oh, my dear, let me help you.'

With Aunt Pru leaning heavily on her, they made it to the sofa. Alice looked up from where she was playing on the rug in front of the fire and her bottom lip shook, before she let out a wail, then crawled over and tugged at Flora's skirt.

251

Lifting her onto her knee while keeping Aunt Pru supported wasn't easy.

'Aunt Pru is not feeling well, darling, Mummy needs to help her.'

Alice offered her teddy to Aunt Pru, who took it and held it close to her breast, rocking backwards and forwards.

'Talk to me, dear Aunt Pru. Would you like to hear how Freddy died? Would that help you?'

'Yes, tell me what happened, lass.'

Missing out the part that haunted her – Freddy saying he didn't want to die – Flora told of how he was in her arms, and how he said that he loved her. And she added to what she knew he would have said, if he'd had time. 'His last words were "Tell Ma I love her."'

'Oh, my Freddy, my Freddy . . .'

Flora held Aunt Pru with her one free arm.

'What made me lad die? I – I mean, what was the cause – how was he hurt?'

This Flora had dreaded. But she knew that *she* would want to know, as knowing as she did gave her peace, thinking that she wouldn't have wanted Freddy to live, just to suffer all his life. Once more she left out what she thought would be too much for Aunt Pru, and told her how Freddy had died of a massive haemorrhage that had covered her with his blood.

'H – his legs . . . Oh, Aunt Pru, I'm sorry, but they did all they could. Ella was his nurse, you remember her? My friend, who I met in Belgium and again at Moorfields? She loved Freddy, and Freddy loved her, but she couldn't save him.'

'Eeh, Flora, the letter said that he was one of the bravest young men his officer had ever known, and a very nice, willing and pleasant young man. He said me Freddy would be getting a posthumous medal for gallantry, as he took actions that saved his friends, but he didn't say what, he just said, "Above and beyond the call of duty." That makes me proud.'

'I didn't know that. That's our Freddy, eh? Always thinking of others. We're going to miss him.'

'I'd give owt to hear him play his violin once more. And the music he composed.'

'Would you like me to play some of it on the piano for you, one day? If you dig it all out, I will try to learn it, though composition for a violin is different from a piano.'

'That would be grand, lass. And I'd like a service for him – a memorial – to help me, as I wasn't able to be there for his burial.'

'Yes, that would be a good idea. We'll set about arranging it. Now, will you let me call out the doctor to examine you, Aunt Pru?'

'Naw. I think I'll be reet now, lass. I feel me grief and allus will, but I feel that a peace has settled in me, now that I knaw how Freddy died. You see, I can thank God for taking him, as I wouldn't want him to suffer for years and years in pain, and not being able to walk; and worrying about him not having someone of his own, as not many lasses would take on a man so badly injured. And to knaw that he were calm and accepting, and able to tell you that he loved us. And to think that you were with him – being me, so to speak – and that the nurse who tended to him loved him an' all. Aye, it's all given me a peace, as I were in turmoil, with me imagination showing me horror.'

'It's like his doctor said to me: we're to think of him as lucky that he didn't die alone. Around us at the time were a dozen or so bodies of young men, and most had died without anyone at their side; and those who did have someone, it was a nurse or a doctor, who they'd never met before.'

'Aw, their poor mams – what a thought. What a terrible thought. Aye, I'm to think on that, and give thanks. Now, d'yer knaw sommat, lass. I'm hungry. I could eat a scabby cat, I'm that starving.'

Flora laughed. Alice copied her and laughed and clapped her hands.

'Eeh, me wee one, there's not a lot to applaud, but there's sommat, and it's enough to help me go forward. Shall we have some fish and chips for supper, eh? Our Freddy loved fish and chips for his supper.'

'Mmm, yes, please. What do you say, Alice?'

'Mmmm,' Alice gurgled, and her mimicking of Flora whilst nodding her head had them both laughing.

The queue at Ma Tatley's house for her fish and chips stretched around the corner of her street, when Flora joined it. Ma Tatley cooked the delicious meal in her front room. She had two huge cast-iron pots full of lard bubbling away, and a bowl of batter on her table. Next to the bowl was a pile of flour, for coating the fish, before she dropped it into the batter and then the hot fat. Her childlike son, Billy, sat next to the table, peeling dozens and dozens of potatoes and cutting them into chips. Sometimes, if there was a child in the queue, he would carve the potato into a face and do a puppet show, mimicking different voices and making everyone laugh.

The air had a nip in it, reminding Flora that winter would soon be upon them. For some unknown reason, she thought of her parents and her brothers. Would they ever know the pleasure of eating fish and chips out of a newspaper wrapping?

254

Would they ever enjoy the delicious smell, or feel the vinegar catch their throat, or chase it down their chin? She doubted it, and she knew in that moment just how much she too would have missed it, if she had been loved by them. Life would have passed her by, too – real life, that is. And she felt glad. Glad to be part of this gossiping queue, and to be accepted by them. Everywhere she went she was welcomed back, and commiserated with; told how much pride they had in her and, yes, asked if she would start up the classes again, as Pru had left them off when the news had come through.

Mrs Larch came towards her. ''Ello, love. 'Ow's Pru?'

'She's doing all right, thanks, Mrs Larch. Well, better than all right – she's hungry, which she hasn't been for weeks. That's why I'm here.'

''Ere, you lot, let Flora come to the front. Pru's feeling hungry, and for the first time since . . . well, you all know what 'appened. Shift yourselves.'

'Oh no, it's all right, no . . .'

Calls came of 'Come along, love' and 'You're welcome, you're our hero', whilst people moved out of her way and, with their hands on her back, propelled Flora forward.

'You needn't, no, really.' But they were having none of it. Behind her a voice started singing, 'For she's a jolly good fellow, for she's . . .'

Flora blushed, but had a feeling as she smiled at them that all she'd done and all she'd been through had just been made worthwhile.

It was lovely and warm in Ma Tatley's front room and brightly lit. The woman who had just been served turned. 'Flora, it's good to see you.'

'Hello, Mrs Clark.'

Jostling the bundle of fish and chips in her arms and putting

255

them back on the table, Mrs Clark picked up one of the pieces of newspaper that were ready for wrapping. 'Look, hold on a minute. I've been practising. "The use of tanks at—"'

'Stop!'

'Oh, I'm sorry, I'm sure.'

'No. No, I didn't mean . . . I – I'm very pleased with your progress – you have done me and Pru proud. Well done. It's just, well, I can't hear about it, as it brings it back . . . I—'

'Oh, I'm sorry. That was thoughtless of me. Forgive me.'

Impulsively Flora took the woman in her arms. 'Don't worry. I'll heal.' Mrs Clark was bright red when Flora let her go. Flora was reminded of how she had felt when she'd first met Mags. She laughed. 'Sorry, we're not used to showing our affection for each other, are we? We should all move up to the North, they all hug up there.'

A voice said, 'They 'ave to, they're all bloody freezing.'

'Well, I'm freezing now. Give us a hug, Mazie.'

'Gerroff, Bert Smith, what's your game?'

Everyone burst into laughter at this. Flora joined in with them and, as she did so, she knew she was one of them, and wanted to be. Forget her posh schooling and having been looked after by maids – that was a cold place to be. Here amongst the cockneys she was loved and welcomed and, yes, needed.

'I haven't got all day, yer know. What's you wanting, Flora?'

'Two fish and chips, please. Thank you.'

'And they're on the house, love. A gift from me. But will you do sommat in return for me?'

'I will, Mrs Tatley, anything.'

'Will you teach me son how to play the piano? He loves his grandma's piano that stands in me back room, and makes a nice sound when he sits at it, but I think he could learn proper notes, and I 'eard as you play.'

'I would love that.'

'I'll pay. I don't expect you to give your time for nothing.'

Knowing the proud cockney way, and sure that Mrs Tatley could afford it, Flora accepted. 'We'll discuss terms when I visit. I'll pop round tomorrow, when you're not busy cooking.'

'Ta, love. And I'll add all the fish and chips you and Pru want, into the bargain.'

As Flora left, more than one person caught her arm and asked her if she would teach their child, too. Most said they couldn't afford much, but had a piano in their front room and wanted to hear it played. Flora suspected that the pianos would all need tuning, but she could deal with that later, so she nodded her head and began to feel that maybe she was being taken in the direction that was meant for her – to share her music knowledge with others.

Before she left them, her future seemed set, because other people had asked her to start up the reading lessons again, and many more than had previously attended were saying they too wanted to learn. As she said goodbye, she told them that she would be in touch soon and would put a notice on the church-hall door, as to when lessons would be.

Walking home, holding the warm fish and chips close to her body, Flora felt a little more secure about the future, and her mind returned to her family and the privileges they had. And she knew that she would never want to go back. But she would ask Aunt Pru to find out from Cook how they all were. A part of her needed to know that.

* * *

257

It was a few weeks before she found out. Preparations were well under way for Christmas when Cook paid them a visit. It was good to see her, to find that she'd often thought of Flora and to hear her say, 'All the staff that knew you are always asking me to get news from Pru about you. It hurt us a lot, how you were treated.'

Flora listened with shock to find out that, only two weeks ago, Harold had been conscripted.

'But you know him, he got out of it. None of us know how or why.'

This was typical of Harold. 'And Francis, is he abroad?'

'Yes, he's been in France for some time. Your mother has took to her bed and refuses to get up. Your father is weak in his body now, as well as in his mind . . . Oh, I beg your pardon, Miss. I—'

'No, it's all right. Don't worry. My father is a weak man, but tell me more about his health: how does he manage?'

'He has a man to look after him. Mr Symans. He lost three of his fingers in the Boer War, and since then has been working as a manservant in various houses. He tells us that he was always ridiculed for his affliction, so he looked for a position in a smaller household. He quietly lords it over us all. But he's not a bad man, and he thinks a lot of your father. He takes him for walks in a bath chair, and goes with him two days a week when your father insists on going into the office.'

All of this made Flora feel sad. She wished she could help her father with his businesses and be of some comfort to her mother, but she wouldn't dwell on it. She had made up her mind where she belonged and, unless they asked for her help, she would never go back.

Not having heard from Mags for a long time, she asked, 'Has Harold or Francis taken up with a young lady?'

'Not that I know of. Mr Harold spends most of his time up in the North, so he may have a girlfriend there, but I don't know.'

This concerned Flora, because although she knew Harold made frequent visits up north, he hadn't ever spent most of his time there. He was bound to have been in contact with Mags, as they had got on so well. Flora wondered if she would rue the day that she had introduced them.

As Cook left, she promised to come again. 'And I'll tell them all back there how well you are, and how lovely little Alice is. And, Prudence, I know they will all be sorry to hear your sad news.'

'Aye, well, tell them all thanks, and give them me regards.'

As she closed the door on Cook, Flora turned to Aunt Pru. 'Ha, we have a spy in the camp. Though it seems a bit underhand, but you know, Pru, something in me still wants to know how they all are.'

'Blood's thicker than water, lass. It's only natural. What ain't natural is how they don't seem to want to bother about you. That breaks me heart. But then they don't knaw what they're missing. Come here and give me a hug.'

In Aunt Pru's arms Flora found the comfort she had always found, and a soothing of the pain caused by being rejected by her family. A hurt that she tried to deny, but knew was always there.

With Aunt Pru, and with her little Alice, she was almost complete. *If only the war would end and my Cyrus would come home.*

PART FIVE
London, 1918–19

~

Flora and Cyrus

Let No Man Put Asunder

Chapter Twenty-Four

'Pass those cakes along, Flora. Do you want them all to yourself?'

Flora laughed as she passed the plate of iced fancies along to Mrs Larch. The sound of the children chattering away as they sat on the long benches, at the equally long table in the church hall, was deafening. Aunt Pru came towards her with a huge pot of tea in her hands. 'This is for the grown-ups. Come on, lass, I've all the cups laid out on that table at the back.'

'Oh, Aunt Pru, give me that before you drop it. You couldn't have put the table further from the kitchen, could you?'

Aunt Pru let out a howl of laughter, her too-thin body shaking with the force of it. 'You know me. Allus working backwards.'

As she followed her, Flora let her worry over Aunt Pru drift from her as she took in the bunting hanging from the ceiling, and the balloons floating around, as the children hit them from one to the other. All around her was a sea of joy.

Flora thought she would always remember this day,

Wednesday, 13th November 1918, the first day they could all gather to have a tea party to celebrate the end of the war, with the signing of the Armistice two days ago. Her own joy gripped her stomach. Surely her Cyrus would be home soon?

But home to what?

How things had changed in the last couple of years. After her allowance from Cyrus's pay had stopped about a year ago, with no reason given – other than that there was an error in the authorization, so payment was suspended until such time as this could be sorted out – she and Aunt Pru had eked out a living from what they could earn teaching, which was little more than a couple of pounds a month. Aunt Pru could only manage one lesson a week: a one-to-one with the shopkeeper's son, who, though he went to school, struggled with learning to read. She was doing an amazing job with him and was finding a way to unlock his understanding. As for herself, there was the class in this hall, which was thriving; and her music lessons, which had recently brought in more money, as she was teaching the children of a wealthy family, who could afford to pay the proper going rate. It had been one of her neighbours who had got her the job. She cleaned for the family and had told her employer about Flora. Her hope now was that this kind of work would grow, as word about her spread amongst the better-off.

Getting a job wasn't easy. Aunt Pru's health had never recovered; if anything, it had deteriorated, and she wasn't strong enough to look after Alice full-time. And so the work that Flora did get had to be somewhere she could take Alice with her or, as with her pub job, work at night when Alice was asleep.

One of the measures taken, to help her cope, was to sell her house and live in Aunt Pru's, which was bigger. That had been a wrench for them both. Aunt Pru had never wanted to return there, and Flora had so wanted to have a home for Cyrus to come back to.

The price she got for her house was far below the market value, and she'd only been able to put a small amount in the bank, after paying the debts she owed. But that had dwindled weekly and was nowhere near enough to set up home again in the near future.

'Eeh, lass, that were a big sigh. I thought we said we'd forget our troubles for the day. You can't change owt by worrying, lass. Perk up and enjoy yourself.'

As she smiled at Aunt Pru, a voice called over to her, ''Ere, Flora, 'ow about we clear the tables and you play us a tune. Let's have a good old London sing-song, eh?'

'Yes, that's a good idea, Mrs Harper.'

Flora's playing of singalong songs at the local pub had been another source of income for her, over the last few months. She'd mastered such songs as 'My Old Dutch', 'Down at the Old Bull and Bush' and 'On Mother Kelly's Doorstep', as well as many more, and always enjoyed her weekly stint. It had become a good source of income, if unpredictable. Not being a drinker as such, she refused the offer of drinks from the locals, but had put a saucer on top of the piano. The odd farthings they dropped in for her made a difference to what she earned. The landlord gave her an amount according to his takings; if they were good, then she would receive three shillings, but if bad, then she had been paid as little as one shilling.

By the time the party came to an end, all the adults, apart from Aunt Pru, Mrs Larch and Flora, were rolling drunk.

'Eeh, look at the mess. We'll be here till dawn, but it was worth it. What a night!' Aunt Pru looked exhausted as she sat looking around the hall.

Mrs Larch nodded, her hands on her hips and giving her big smile. 'And to think, our boys will be com— Oh, I'm sorry, Prudence. It's that drop of beer I had, making me tongue loose before I think what I'm saying.'

'Naw, don't be sorry – we should rejoice about those returning. Me lad gave his life and it cut me in two, but these lads who are coming home have done just as much. We're to take care of them when they get back. It'll take a long time for them to get reet, after this lot.'

'Look, I don't know about you two, but I'm tired to my bones. Let's lock up and come back in the morning. We can get more willing hands then, when they've all slept off the drink.'

'You're reet, Flora, I don't reckon as I can lift a finger to owt. I just need me bed. Give me your arm, lass.'

Though there was nothing of Aunt Pru, the weight she put on Flora's arm as she tried to help her up deepened Flora's worry about her health. The strength seemed to be ebbing from Aunt Pru as the days went by. There had never been anything specific that Flora could put her finger on, to say what was wrong with Aunt Pru's health. She ate regularly, though little; she no longer vomited, as she had when she first began to fail, but she was weak, lacked energy and tired easily. But as Flora looked into her Aunt Pru's face now, fear gripped her. Aunt Pru's lips had turned blue. Her heart! *Oh no, I should have realized. The symptoms were staring me in the face!*

If only they could have afforded a doctor's visit. But in reality there wasn't too much that could be done for a weak heart, other than the care she already gave Aunt Pru. But now that Flora was sure she knew what was happening, she would take even greater care of her. And, in the hope that something could be done, when her darling Cyrus returned and was able to claim his back-pay, she would ask to use some of it to get Aunt Pru seen by Kenneth Carmichael, the physician who had attended her father.

As the weeks went by, very little news filtered through about the prisoners-of-war. Trainloads of soldiers, both able-bodied and wounded, arrived every day, and families were reunited. Always there seemed to be a party going on somewhere, as people felt the need to celebrate every homecoming. For Flora, this brought in extra money, as she was engaged almost every night to play the piano. Every part of her ached from the long hours, but the ache in her heart was the hardest to bear.

She longed to hear that Cyrus was on his way home, though the latest that she had read yesterday had given her hope. It appeared that the regiments of British soldiers who had got to Germany were beginning to reach the prisoner-of-war camps and organize medical care and the return home of the prisoners. But it warned that this would take some time, as the processing of prisoners wasn't an easy task. *At last! And whatever else, at least now I know that Cyrus is truly being cared for and treated well.*

But there was another worry that seemed to outweigh all the joy of the war ending, and was posing a greater threat to life than the war itself had done: the spread of flu. The papers had been full of its devastating effect across the globe, and now London was in its grip, with the pandemic escalated by the returning soldiers probably carrying the virus home with them. Already hundreds had died, the hospitals were full and there was a backlog of bodies in the morgues, as the funeral directors couldn't cope.

And now the flu was in their street! A young boy, who lived only doors away, had been taken ill. Terrified for Alice and Aunt Pru, Flora decided that playing at the pub and for parties had to stop. There was too much of a risk, amongst the crowds of people. If she could, she would lock her door and keep it locked, but as always the spirit of everyone was to keep going, no matter what.

As if her thought had been heard, a loud banging on her door made Flora jump. The door handle turned and Mrs Larch walked in. 'It's me 'usband, can you come and 'elp him, Flora. 'E can't breathe.'

Flora stood still, unable to react.

'You're a nurse, you must be able to 'elp, love. Please, I'm at me wits' end!'

Looking from Alice to Pru, Flora's heart told her not to do this, but she couldn't refuse, even though she knew there was little she could do. 'I'll get my coat and be along in a moment – you get back to him. Aunt Pru, don't touch the door knob, and keep Alice away from where Mrs Larch stood, as she may be carrying the virus. If you feel strong enough, get a bowl of hot water and disinfectant and wash the door knob and the door. I'll be back soon, but neither of you are to come near to me until I have bathed and put my clothes in the boiler.'

'Eeh, lass.'

'I know, but try not to worry. As long as we take precautions, we should be all right. I'm taking this tea towel with me, to use as a mask. I'll be back soon.'

The sound coming from Mrs Larch's living room was

pitiful. The heat in the room was stifling, as a fire blazed up the chimney. Mr Larch lay on the sofa, his body covered by a blanket. His hoarse gasps as he struggled for breath echoed around the room.

'I'm going to tie this tea towel around my mouth, Mrs Larch. Now don't worry, it is normal nursing procedure to wear a mask, and you should do the same. But, first, open all the windows and doors.'

'But he's cold.'

'That's the fever. I think he has pneumonia.'

'Oh, God love us, no . . . No!'

'Do as I say. And then help me to strip him. We have to bathe him in cold water to bring his temperature down. Have you any aspirin? They say it is helping with the symptoms if a patient takes a higher dose than normal, every four hours.'

As Mrs Larch went round opening windows, Flora stripped the blanket from Mr Larch and began taking off his soaked pyjamas.

'I have aspirin. I never thought to give it to 'im. I take it for me 'eadaches.'

'Right, we'll deal with his temperature first. Bring me a bowl of cold water, then get as many pots of water boiling on the stove as you can. Once we have cooled him down a little, we need to close the windows and then fill the room with steam, for his breathing. But at the same time keep dousing him in cold water, to cool him.'

'Will 'e live?'

The question, asked of her many times in the past, was one she couldn't answer. 'Let's do all we can to give him a chance. Do as I say – and hurry.'

Her tone was one of command and Mrs Larch responded.

An hour later, with her body soaked in sweat, Flora thought she heard a change in Mr Larch's breathing, but not for the better. Now it was even more laboured, and when he exhaled, a distinct rattle could be heard. *Oh God, help him.* But in her heart she knew there was no help to be had, as this was what they termed the death-rattle. Within minutes it ceased, and a silence filled the room.

'I'm so sorry, I—'

Exhaustion, and grief for Mrs Larch, caused Flora's tears to tumble and, as she thought of Freddy, the pain in her heart increased and racked her body with sobs. Mrs Larch's arm came round her. 'You did all you could.' After a moment, as the shock of what had happened ground into her, Mrs Larch began to sob. 'Bert . . . Bert.'

Flora pulled herself together. 'I'll make you a cup of tea, and then go for the doctor. They are duty bound to come to certify a death, even if we can't pay.'

'Ta, love, and ta for all you did, for my Bert.'

'Cover him with the sheet, and then, when I come back, we need to scrub the room from top to bottom, and you need to bathe, and boil your clothes and all the bedding. It may be wise to burn Bert's pyjamas. I – I know all of that is the last thing you want to do, but we must. The virus spreads like wildfire, and we have to take every precaution we can.'

Mrs Larch nodded. 'I'll make a start now. Forget that tea, love, you go and fetch the doctor.'

As Flora left the house, despair entered her. *Why, why? Haven't we all been through enough? Didn't enough people die in the war?*

Mr Larch had worked hard throughout the war years. His job on the railway was considered an essential one, but one

270

he had to do with very few other workers, as the younger ones had volunteered to go to war.

He and Mrs Larch had no children, and now she was going to be truly alone. Except that maybe, as she was the heart of the community, looking out for others and like a surrogate mother to all the kids, they would rally round her and make sure she was all right. Yes, Flora knew that would happen, and the thought comforted her.

But how many of them would this flu epidemic slaughter before it was finished? *Please God, keep us all safe, especially Aunt Pru and my little Alice.*

Chapter Twenty-Five

Weary beyond endurance, once she was home, Flora forced herself to bath and to boil her clothes and the towel she'd used. She even scrubbed her shoes, praying as she did so that she hadn't brought the virus to her home.

Aunt Pru was asleep in the chair next to the dying fire, and Alice was curled up on the sofa.

'Aunt Pru, I'm home.'

With a snort and a little jump, Pru opened her eyes. After a moment they held a question.

'No, I didn't save him – he died two hours ago.'

'Oh, lass, does it never end? Let me get you a cup of cocoa, I'm rested now. I managed to clean everything down. You put little one to bed.'

Flora didn't protest. Sometimes she had to let Pru do as she wanted to, and she knew that what made her happiest was taking care of her and Alice.

The clock struck midnight as they drank the hot, steaming cocoa. Too tired to talk much, they sat in silence for a while. Flora thought over the night's happenings and how, when the doctor arrived, he had assured Mrs Larch that what had been done was the correct procedure. This had pleased Flora, as there was always a danger that Mrs Larch, who had objected to everything at first, could have begun to think that, instead of helping, Flora had made things worse.

Aunt Pru brought her out of her thoughts. 'Thou knaws, lass, I often think as I've dragged you down. You should be living in a nice house, looked after by servants and the like.'

'What brought that on? Never think like that, Aunt Pru. I chose to live with you. I chose the love you gave me over all the comforts my Aunt Amelia could have given me. They would have been cold comforts anyway, as she never made me welcome. I was a ticket for her to get money out of my father. I hated every minute there.'

Flora leaned forward and took Aunt Pru's cold hand in her own. 'You were the saving of me, and I love you, Aunt Pru. More than I can tell you. None of the struggle we have is your fault. You're not well, you can't help that.'

'What do you think is wrong with me?'

She'd dreaded this question. 'I think it may be your heart, my dear. I think what you have been through has taken its toll on you. Though that alone wouldn't necessarily cause heart disease.'

'I had rheumatic fever as a child.'

'Oh, that's probably the cause – if I'm right, and we don't know that I am. And, you know, patients with damaged hearts can live on for years. It's just a matter of taking care, not over-exerting yourself. I shouldn't have asked you to clean down tonight. I was just so afraid of the flu virus getting into our house.'

'Well, I don't do much, as you won't let me, lass, so I

doubt it hurt me, though I took a long time to do it. I just have no energy, and me breathing's troubling me of late.'

This set up a further worry in Flora, but she had no time to ponder it, as the second knock of the night sounded on the door. This one was followed by an impatient rattling of the door knocker.

'Oh, for goodness' sake, who's this now? I hope it's not anyone else in distress. I'm exhausted.'

Flora went to the door as she spoke. Opening it left her speechless for a moment and then squealing out, 'Cyrus! Oh, Cyrus.'

She didn't register how thin he was or his gaunt face, but flung herself at him, laughing and crying tears of joy, all at the same time. To be in his arms took away all the hurt and pain, and rolled the years back. His voice came to her over and over, 'Flora. Flora, my Flora.'

'Eeh, lass, bring the poor man in out of the cold and get the door shut.'

Flora laughed. The way Aunt Pru had said this, you'd think Cyrus had only been to the shop and back, instead of being away for almost four years. Taking his hand, she pulled him inside, her gaze never leaving his beloved face.

It was as the light fell on him that the pain of all he'd been through registered with her. 'Oh, my darling, you're home now. We'll soon have you well. Let me take your coat.'

'I'm fine, my darling. Everything in my world came right the moment you opened the door.'

'Come away and sit down, lad. You can have my chair, as I'm off to bed. But, by, it's good to see you.'

'And you, Aunt Pru. Let me help you – you look worn out, what have you been up to?'

'Lass'll tell you everything, lad. And ta. I could do with a help up.'

Flora saw the look of concern pass over Cyrus's face, but her own concern was for him. His cheeks had sunk in, his eyes had the stare of someone very weak and his clothes hung on his body.

'I'll help Aunt Pru. You sit down and get warm, my love. I'll not be a mo.'

With Aunt Pru tucked up, Flora bent to kiss her head.

'By, lass, you've to tread carefully. He's damaged in his body, but he could be so in his mind, too. Take things steady, and don't force him to tell you owt as he don't want to. Just love him tonight. That's all he needs.'

'I will, Aunt Pru, don't you worry. I'll smother him in love. Now you get off to sleep.'

Downstairs, she found that Cyrus had rested his head back and had his eyes closed. As quietly as she could, she moved the kettle over the hob and set about making another cup of cocoa. She hoped he liked it.

This thought told her how little she knew of him. They'd had so few days together, and had spent most of them making love.

A tingle went through her, because thinking this awakened feelings she'd long since suppressed. Cyrus opened his eyes. His look was full of love. His hand came out to her and he pulled her down onto his knee. She could feel his thigh bones digging into her, but any worry she might have had about how emaciated he was disappeared, as their lips met. With that touch, her world came right again.

She didn't want ever to pull away from him, but she could feel how uncomfortable he was, so she took her lips from his and rose. 'We have our life in front of us, darling. Let's get you stronger first.'

His smile was apologetic.

'Darling, nothing is expected of you. To have you back with me is all I asked for. Everything else can happen when it does. Don't feel that you have to do anything other than be here. And we have such a lot to talk about and to catch up on.'

'Yes, I need to talk. Some of my fellow prisoners never wanted to, and even on the way home they said they would never speak of what happened to us, but I want to. I want to write it all down and cleanse myself of it.'

'It was that bad, darling?'

'It was. But I'm home now. And I'm determined not to let the experience colour the rest of my life, as I fear many will. I'm going to deal with it, then put it behind me.'

'That's what I try to do. But you already know most of what happened to me. I could write it in my letters, but I knew there was more than you could write.'

'They censored our mail. They wanted to create a propaganda message that it was better to surrender and become prisoners-of-war than be killed fighting for what they termed a lost cause.'

'Yes, we were aware of that message, but none of us believed that conditions were good for you.'

Cyrus took the cocoa and sipped it. 'When I've had this, can I peep at our little girl? I've dreamed of the moment I set eyes on her. And I have dreamed of making more babies with you, my darling. So, when I'm stronger, you had better watch out.'

They both laughed. Flora sank onto the mat in front of Cyrus, and he stroked her hair with his free hand.

'I was so sorry to hear about Freddy, darling. A lovely young man – taken. What a waste of life. So many . . . So many.'

She didn't want to cry, as she'd done so much of that, and this homecoming wasn't going to be spoilt by tears of sadness. 'I know. It's going to take a lot of getting over, and we have another threat, with the flu pandemic reaching us, but we are to stay strong.'

'What about your Aunt Pru? She's not well, is she? What do the doctors say?'

'We haven't been able to afford one. But even if we did, I don't believe there's anything that can be done.'

'Not afford one? Why not?'

'I don't want to tire you with details, darling, not tonight, but things have been very difficult, moneywise, for a long time now.'

'But you never said in your letters.'

'How could I? You had enough on your plate. I tried just to tell you the good things, except when I had to tell you about Freddy, of course. But the main reason was Aunt Pru not being strong enough to care for Alice while I went out to work, so I had to get whatever work I could that allowed me to take her with me. Most of it was very low-paid. And the second reason, which may turn out to be a blessing for us, is that your pay was stopped.' She went on to explain, hating talking about such things when he'd only just arrived home, but knowing she couldn't avoid doing so, as he wasn't going to let it stay in the air until the morning.

'My God! What authorization did they need? I gave them all they asked for.'

'Don't worry about it now. Like Aunt Pru says, no use worrying at a time when you can do nothing about it.

Anyway, think, my darling. You have been without pay for almost three years. All of that is owed to you – less what they did pay me. That simply means that even more is owed to you, so we will be all right, now that you are home.'

'I have other money, too, darling. I told you about my grandfather's legacy, didn't I? Well, when we docked, we stayed in barracks for two nights. I had no way of contacting you to let you know that I was home safely, but I needed various things and was taken to the bank. I found that my allowance had built up to a tidy sum. We can open our own home up again, and get medical help for Pru and—'

'I had to sell our home. I lied in my letter, when I said I'd closed it and moved in with Aunt Pru. I'm sorry.'

'Don't ever say sorry for whatever decisions you had to take, darling. It doesn't matter. I'm home now, and I have more than enough to set us up again. Now, no more talking. I'd say that our future looks bright. Let's go to bed. I want to hold you, and to feel your body next to mine. I – I don't know if I can—'

'Shush, darling. We've already visited that. Nothing is expected of you. I just want to lie with you, too. My only stipulation is that you have no clothes on!'

'You hussy.'

Once more they laughed as they linked hands and went up the stairs.

'This is Alice's room. Tread quietly now, don't wake her.'

They crept into the tiny room, lit by the moon shining through the window. Its light fell across Alice's bed, showing her screwed up into a ball, with no covers on; her thumb was stuck in her mouth, with a picture of Cyrus on her pillow.

His gasp told of his love. His arm pulled Flora to him.

Had she thought her world had been made right, on seeing him? Now she knew it was truly complete, as the circle of her family came together.

Cyrus didn't want to leave the room, but she gently persuaded him to. 'Alice will be frightened if she wakes. We'll make a game in the morning for her. I'll get up and chat to her about you, as we always do, and then I'll build up to her knowing that you are here. You don't look too different from your photo, which she has with her at all times.'

'It looks a bit crumpled, she must hold it a lot.'

'That happened when I was giving birth to her. I held it and didn't realize that I was squeezing it. I imagined that it was your hand.'

'It was, darling. Whenever you've needed me, I've only been a thought away. As you have to me.'

Taking his hand, she led him to her bedroom. Aunt Pru had insisted that she have the double room. She was so glad of that now.

They curled up together, their bodies touching in all the places they could touch. And then what Cyrus had feared wouldn't happen, did happen. His need of her gave Flora joy beyond anything she had imagined, as they rekindled the feelings they had experienced in those first days of meeting.

When Cyrus entered her, it was as if no time had passed since he'd been coupled with her before. She clung to him, manoeuvring him onto his back, so that she could give of herself to him. Nothing stopped the love flowing from one to the other. No barriers existed. The sensations that racked her body seized her whole being and fractured her into a thousand pieces, before bringing her back as a whole person, the person she was meant to be. Loved deeply by this man. No time apart had erased or even splintered any part of that.

Chapter Twenty-Six

Waking next to Cyrus brought heaven to Flora's heart. She watched him as he breathed, enjoyed the beauty of his face. A beauty not marred by the small changes that being underweight had wrought in him. She wondered what he'd been through, and was glad he'd made up his mind to cleanse himself of it and to look forward, without letting the past drag him down.

Creeping out of bed, she looked in on Alice. She lay looking angelic, on her back with her arms up, as if surrendering. Her right hand touched Cyrus's photo. Flora wanted to lift her up and twirl her round in the air, such was her joy.

But instead she crept along to Aunt Pru's room. It was eight o'clock, and Aunt Pru liked to get up at this time. Sometimes she needed help. But often, after a cup of tea in bed, she felt she could manage. On those days Flora filled a bowl of water for her and put it on a stand next to her bed, before placing to hand everything she would need.

Unusually, the room was still in darkness. 'Are you awake, Aunt Pru?'

The silence pebbled Flora's arms with goosebumps. Fear

trickled through her. Switching on the light made that fear a truth. 'No . . . no!' Reaching the bedside without knowing she'd moved, Flora lifted Aunt Pru's cold hand and looked into the waxen face. A face as beautiful in death as it had been when she was a young woman. With all pain gone, there was a peace in her expression that told of her passing away in her sleep.

'Oh, Aunt Pru . . .' Flora was on her knees, her head resting on Aunt Pru's still chest. 'I hope you are with Freddy. I hope that he came to fetch you, and that your passing was something you welcomed. Did you wait, my darling, for me to be happy?'

Somehow, as she said these words, she knew that was what had happened. Her dear Aunt Pru had hung on and on, not wanting to leave until Cyrus was safely home to take care of her.

'Oh, my dear, dear mother, I will miss you so much.'

Calling Aunt Pru her mother came naturally to her, as that is what she had been. A tiny regret entered her, that she hadn't done so when Aunt Pru could hear her, and hadn't given her the status of grandmother to Alice. *But in death there is always a regret for those left living, and that is such a tiny regret for me to live with.*

Flora stood up and went back to her bedroom, as the deep pain cut into her.

Cyrus was awake and smiling. 'Good morning, darling, I'm being good and staying put, like you told me to. Is Alice awake – does she know about me being here? I can't . . . Darling, what's the matter? You're crying!'

Running to him, Flora flung herself onto the bed and lay across his chest.

His arm held her. 'Aunt Pru?'

'Y – yes, sh – she's gone. Oh, Cyrus. Why, just when everything was going to come right for us?'

'Maybe that is why. She felt that she could let go. She was very ill, my darling, I could see that the moment I looked at her. I'll get up and go for the doctor. Is it far from here?'

'No. But I can get Billy to go. He'll be standing by his gate as he does every morning. He's the son of Mrs Tatley, who runs a fish-and-chip business from her front room. They only live on the next street, where our house stood. Billy . . . well, he has a simple way of looking at life, and he loves to run errands for everyone when he's not helping his mother. I'll write a note and give it to him. He's very reliable and knows where to go. I won't be two minutes. Alice is still asleep.'

'Let me do it. What if Alice wakes and you're not here, and neither is her Aunt Pru? Oh, my darling, you're shaking.'

'It was such a shock. I can't think straight.'

'Look, what about the neighbour: will she take a note to this Billy?'

'Yes.'

'Well then, I'll see to that. I'm home now, darling, you have no need to shoulder the burden of everything. I'm here for you.'

These words soothed some of the pain that racked her heart. For a moment Flora clung on to Cyrus and didn't want to let go of him, but he helped her come to a place where she could cope, by gently talking her through the practicalities of what she had to do.

'Aunt Pru has been everything to you, my darling. Now you must do all you can to help her on her last journey. She is with Freddy, I'm sure. But she'll want to look her best for him, so pick out a nice outfit for her and prepare to wash her and get her ready. We will give her a good send-off.'

Cyrus's words held wisdom. Yes, she needed to do all of that for her beloved Aunt Pru. 'I'll get Alice up and, while we wait for the doctor, she can start to get used to you, then you can take her to Rowena. Poor Rowena, she's going to be devastated. Everyone is – Aunt Pru was so loved.'

'And what better legacy for her to leave behind? I know I wasn't in her company for long, but I loved her, too. She had that effect on people. If she liked you, she took you to her heart.'

'You're so right. Now, are you sure you feel up to all of this?'

'Very sure. It is what I have dreamed of for almost four years, though I wouldn't have wished for the sadness that's befallen us. I want to slip into the role of husband and father, and take care of you both, darling. So, no trying to mollycoddle me.'

Flora smiled through her tears. 'I'll go and get Alice up.'

Alice was full of questions while Flora dressed her. 'How did Daddy get out of the picture to be here?'

'He didn't, darling. He came on a ship. Remember, Mummy told you that he couldn't come before, because he had to stay in another country until they let him come to us?'

'Yes, and he loves us, doesn't he, Mummy?'

'He does, darling. And now he can give you that cuddle I told you he was saving for you.'

'Aunt Pru loves him, like we do, doesn't she? Will she have a cuddle?'

'She had one last night, when you were asleep, darling.

Then she said, "I'm going to Freddy, now that you have your daddy to look after you."'

'But Freddy's in heaven, and Aunt Pru is sad when she looks at his photo.'

'Yes, darling, she was sad because she wanted to be with him, but she couldn't leave us because we needed her. But in the night, the angels came and took her to Freddy.'

'But I didn't say goodbye. I don't want her to go. I want Aunt Pru to stay. Did Daddy want her to go, now he has come home?'

'No, darling, he was planning to get a special doctor to Aunt Pru to try and make her well again. But, darling, that couldn't have happened. Aunt Pru's heart was very poorly and she would have suffered such a lot.'

'I don't want Aunt Pru to be in pain any more. If the doctor can't make her better, can Freddy?'

'Yes, he can. And he has. Last night Aunt Pru had the worst pain she had ever had, and Freddy had no choice. He thought about leaving her till morning so that she could say goodbye, but he couldn't bear for her to suffer and knew that you would understand, and would have all the memories of her that she gave you. And so he asked the angels to fetch her to him.'

'I'm glad he did, Mummy, but I have a sadness inside my chest, and I want to cry.'

A noise on the stairs told her that Cyrus was back. 'Well, I have someone who will take that sadness away, just as Freddy knew he would. Freddy knew you would let him have his mummy with him, because now you can have your daddy with you. What do you think of that?'

'Will my daddy like me? He's only ever seen me from his photo. What if I'm naughty? Will he think I'm a horrid girl?'

'No, I won't, my darling little girl. I will love you, no matter what you do. But I will hope that you will try to be good for me and Mummy.'

A shyness came over Alice, as she looked from the photo to Cyrus. Flora held her breath.

Cyrus opened his arms. 'I brought a cuddle for you.'

Alice smiled. 'You came out of your photo.'

'I did. Come to me, my darling. You and I have to get to know each other.'

As Alice went to him, her voice was shy. 'But I do know you. Mummy told me everything about you. I know that I love you, Daddy.'

A tear ran down Cyrus's face as he held Alice to him. She clung to him, then put her head back and looked at him. 'Your nose is bigger than on the photo.'

They all laughed, and it felt right to do so. Aunt Pru would have loved this moment, and maybe she was sharing it with them.

'Don't worry, it will shrink again, now that I am home with you and Mummy. Where I have been, there wasn't much food, and I have lost a lot of fat that plumped out my cheeks and hid my big nose. But you and Mummy are going to feed me up, and make me handsome again.'

'We don't have a lot of food, Daddy, but you can have mine.'

Cyrus's face fell at this. His eyes found Flora's. His frown told of his deep hurt.

'It doesn't matter now, darling,' she said to him. 'You could have done nothing about it. We had enough. Alice has been fed well; she is just repeating snippets she's heard Aunt Pru and I talk about.'

He stepped forward and held her with his free arm. As he

did so, Alice leaned towards her and held her around her neck with one arm, while still holding Cyrus with the other. To Flora, this was a moment she'd longed for: the three of them in a cuddle. It lifted her and made her smile.

Aunt Pru would have loved to have seen it too. But it wasn't to be. It was enough that she knew it would happen. That she felt able to go. Because Flora could now admit that Aunt Pru couldn't have gone on a moment longer. Getting her to bed last night had shown that. *Dear Aunt Pru. Rest your weary head. Say hello to Freddy for me. Tell him how much I miss him.*

'Don't cry, Mummy. You said we would all be happy when Daddy came home. I'm happy.'

'And I am too, my darling. These are tears of joy.'

In a way, it wasn't a lie. For part of her was joyful that Aunt Pru was at peace, but oh, she was going to miss her. She was going to miss her so much.

As they had stood next to the open grave, Flora had looked around her. So many fresh mounds of earth reminded her of the toll the flu epidemic had taken.

With the numbers so high, they'd had to wait three weeks for today's burial of Aunt Pru's body in its final resting place. During that time three elderly residents had died in the street from the flu. But since the last one passed, two weeks ago, there had been no fresh cases. Everyone hoped it would not return.

As she'd looked at the sea of faces, swimming in the well of tears in her eyes, Flora had felt a comfort that so many had loved Aunt Pru, and had turned out, despite the warning of not gathering in numbers, to say their goodbyes and pay their respects.

And now here she was playing the songs they all loved to sing. How, she didn't know, but Aunt Pru deserved a good send-off, and she would have loved the knees-up that her wake had turned into. Belting out 'Mother Kelly's Doorstep', Flora had to smile as she saw Cyrus dancing with Mrs Larch.

A voice came into her head. *'Eeh, lass, it's a good do, ain't it? You've done me proud.'* Flora's smile widened. *We have, lovely Aunt Pru. I hope you and Freddy are dancing. Goodnight, my beautiful ma, goodnight. Sleep tight.*

A further smile played around her lips.

Yes, if I had given Aunt Pru her proper place as my mother, I would have called her 'Ma', as Freddy had done. How I wish that I had.

Chapter Twenty-Seven

Flora and Cyrus held Alice's hands as she skipped along between them. Flora couldn't believe they were taking her to her first day at school.

They'd found a day-school for infants in what was termed the 'Posh End' of Brixton. The fees were just affordable to them, as Aunt Pru had left her house to Flora, which meant they hadn't had to use any of their funds to house themselves. But if Cyrus didn't get a position soon, then they might have to rethink, and educate Alice themselves for a time.

'Our little girl is growing up, aren't you, darling, and is soon to have a baby brother or sister.'

'I want a sister, really, but I don't mind a brother, Daddy.'

'Well, we don't have much choice in the matter, so whatever it is, we'll all love and welcome him or her, won't we?'

'Yes, Daddy. When will you fetch the new baby?'

Flora bent her body so that she could whisper to Alice. 'Any day now. Might even be here when you get home from school.'

'What! Are you all right, Flora? Has something happened?' The panic in Cyrus's voice made her giggle.

'I'm fine, but yes, I am having niggles. Little pains in my back.'

'But my mother doesn't arrive for three days!'

'Well then, you'll have to take care of us, darling.'

'Of course I will, but it will be nice for you to have another woman with you. I'm dying for you to meet Mother. I just know you will both get on so well. You both have the same independent spirit. Mother won't interfere, or anything like that; she's not one for bothering how others run their lives, but she will be happy to help, if you need it. She can't wait to meet you and Alice.'

'And I'm looking forward to meeting her and getting to know her.'

They fell silent then, as they reached the gates of the school. And as she had done every day, Flora thought about Aunt Pru and how proud she would have been to see Alice take this next step in her life.

Smiling heavenwards, as Alice was taken by the hand and led into school by a young teacher, Flora remembered Aunt Pru's own little school and how she'd helped so many children in Stepney, and then adults in Brixton. And how she'd brought Alice into the world, but wouldn't be here to bring in her second child. *Oh, Aunt Pru, I miss you. I miss you so much. Has it only been ten months since you left me?*

'You're quiet, darling. Don't worry, Alice will be fine.'

'I know. I worry, though, that she might just get settled and make new friends and we have to take her out of school.'

'I'm hoping that I hear from Willingborough Bank soon. My interview with them went well. The manager served in the same regiment as me, though he joined a year later, so

I didn't know him, but he's keen to help a fellow officer, and my qualifications stood the test for the position of accounts clerk. And then I can study and take further exams, in the hope of rising to bank manager myself.'

'But you are a violinist, not an accountant! It's so sad that you can't find a position with an orchestra.'

'There is a possibility; a friend I studied with is thinking of forming his own orchestra and he mentioned you; he knows you are a pianist. It would just be part-time for a while – well, mainly rehearsing of course – but he has a backer, so there would be a small payment for each musician. He plans to stage concerts, so there's a chance we could gain popularity. I'm very excited about it, but I wasn't going to say anything until after the baby is born, as you have enough to think about.'

'Oh, that would be wonderful . . . Ooh!'

'What is it, darling? Flora! Oh dear, what shall I do?'

As Flora clung to the railings of a house, pain clutched her like a vice, but she couldn't help but smile as the usually calm Cyrus began to flap and panic.

'I'll run for a cab . . . but, no . . . I – I can't leave you. Oh, Flora, why did you even think of coming out of the house?'

'Free spirit, darling. No new baby was going to keep me from seeing my first child take the next step of her life. There, the pain has subsided and we're nearly home. As soon as we get there, run for Rowena – she's standing by, ready to help.'

'Not the doctor?'

'No, you goose, he'll charge the earth and make a huge fuss. We women can sort this out. Don't worry, darling.'

* * *

A week later, with their son sleeping peacefully in his cot, having arrived in the world, kicking and screaming, just an hour after they had reached home, Cyrus's mother arrived.

Just a short time in her company explained to Flora how it was that Cyrus was so beautiful to look at, as well as being a beautiful person, because his mother was both of those things. Tall and slender, she was the picture of elegance, from her dark hair with hints of silver strands running through it, which she wore rolled back from her face with a centre parting, to her dainty feet, encased in slipper-type shoes that matched whatever she wore. On this September afternoon a pink frock fitted her shapely figure, and a flowing chiffon over-dress floated around her, giving the impression of a butterfly.

As they sat in the garden together, Flora felt dowdy in comparison, as her tummy hadn't reduced much with the birth, and she'd had to wear one of the shifts that Rowena had made for her to wear during her confinement.

But then, better that than her nightdress, as should have been the case, because she really should be in bed, according to convention. New mothers were meant to stay bedridden for at least ten days. But thank goodness Olivia – as her mother-in-law had asked Flora to call her – did not stand on convention. She'd swept into Flora's bedroom an hour ago with a bowl of hot water. 'Up you get. Fresh air will do you more good than a stuffy bed, my dear. Wash yourself and dress, and I'll get tea ready. We'll be really naughty and sit in the garden.'

Flora ventured downstairs shortly afterwards.

'That's better. I haven't seen you dressed before, and you look lovely, my dear. And don't worry. I'll keep popping in to take a peek at Frederick. Lovely name. Cyrus told me you called the baby after your brother, and that he will be known as Freddy. Poor Freddy: was he your only brother, dear? Are your parents still alive?'

'Oh, Cyrus hasn't told you?'

'I asked him about you and your family, but mysteriously he said that I must ask you?'

'Well, my story is a little strange, and he probably thought I should tell you what I want you to know. But I don't mind you knowing. I think it best not to have any secrets. Freddy was my half-brother, born of an affair my father had . . .'

Olivia didn't interrupt or react in any way; it was as if the way Flora's father carried on was normal behaviour to her.

'Anyway, it appears that my nanny wasn't the only one my father was unfaithful with. He had an affair and another son, whom I've never met. When my mother found out, which must have been when that son was a few years old, as he is apparently older than my eldest brother, my father tried to make up to Mother, and I was the result . . .'

By the time Flora had finished her story, tears were running down her face. She hadn't realized she still cared so much.

'I'm sorry. But, well, I – I need to know something. You say that your brother runs a mill in the North and is afraid of losing it. This may seem a strange question, but are the shops your father runs haberdashery shops?'

'Yes, do you know him?'

Olivia had turned deathly white and her hand shook as she put her cup down, almost missing the saucer, causing the high-pitched sound of china against china.

'Are you all right, Olivia? Are you not feeling well?'

'I – I . . . Oh dear, I think I've had too much sun.' Taking a lace hanky from her sleeve, she dabbed at her eyes.

She's crying! Olivia's crying, but why? For some reason, Flora felt fear clench her. 'Shall we go inside? It's cooler in the front room, as it doesn't get the sun.'

When Olivia stood, it was as if she had shrunk and aged. She had the look of someone who'd suffered a shock.

'Let me help you, Olivia, hold on to my arm.'

Before Flora could take the outstretched arm, Olivia bent forward and was sick. 'Oh dear. Oh, I'm sorry. How disgusting of me.'

'No, you're not well. You couldn't help it. And nothing like that embarrasses me. I was nursing for a couple of years, remember? Now, hold my arm and let's get inside, where it is cooler.'

The fear wouldn't leave Flora as she settled Olivia in an easy chair and went to fetch a glass of water for her. Olivia's symptoms were those of someone who had been exposed to too much sun, but that wasn't the case. It wasn't that hot today, and they'd only been outside for a short time. It seemed to be something that had been said that had upset her, but what? Did Olivia know the woman with whom Father had a child? How amazing that would be, as it could lead to her meeting her second half-brother. Maybe even becoming close to him, as she had done Freddy. But dared she ask Olivia? *No, I must wait for her to volunteer the information, as I might upset her further.*

'Is that better? Maybe you could put something cooler on, once your legs feel steadier, or perhaps you would like to lie down?'

'N – no, thank you, my dear. I'll be all right in a moment.' Olivia put her head back. More tears seeped out of her closed eyes.

'Can you tell me what is upsetting you, Olivia? Sometimes it helps to unburden yourself, and I'm a good listener.'

'Thank you, b – but no, I c – can't tell you. I'll be all right. May I have some time alone, my dear?'

'Of course. Just call up to me if you need me. I feel more tired than I thought I would, so I'll slip back into bed. I'll take Freddy with me, so there's no need to worry. Take all the time you need.'

Once in bed, Flora lay back on her pillow and went over the possibilities of why her story had upset Olivia, because she was sure it was what she'd said. Olivia had become very agitated after she had told her what Father did. It was as if it triggered knowledge in her – something she knew, but didn't want to. Surely it must be that she knows who Father's mistress is? *But how do I ask her, without appearing very rude and intrusive?*

There wasn't a chance to talk the incident over with Cyrus until they were in bed. It was he who brought up the subject of his mother not looking well.

'I think telling her about my family upset her.' Flora related what had happened.

'But why? Why should Mother be upset? I mean, any kind and caring person, as she is, would feel compassion for you, but to the extent of crying and actually being sick! I'll have to talk to her about it. There must be something in what you said that worried her.'

'It happened when she asked a little more about Father, and what his work was.'

'This just isn't like her. What on earth can be troubling her?'

'Whatever it is, we need to give her time. We want to help her, but clearly we can't yet. I'm sure she will come to us when she can. Let's not worry her any further, but carry on as if nothing has happened, until she feels she can talk to us.'

'You're right, darling. Yes, we'll arrange a nice evening for her tomorrow tonight. We'll have a good dinner, and then you and I can play for her. I want to practise something with you that I have written for the piano and violin. I have to go for a second interview at the bank tomorrow, which sounds hopeful, and thought you might find time to read the score and maybe have a little practice of it?'

'Oh, the one I have heard you tinkering with? It sounded lovely. I will, I'll spend some time on it. Clever you. I wish I could write for the violin. I have so many pieces for the piano.'

'We'll take a look at them one day, darling, and see if I can adapt them. Now, no more talk, I need to snuggle up to you. If I'm going to present my best tomorrow, then I have to get to sleep. And you, darling, are still in recovery, after giving me my wonderful son. And it will soon be his night-feed time, at this rate.'

His kiss awoke in her feelings she didn't think she would feel this soon after giving birth, but she suppressed them. She could hear in Cyrus's voice how tired he was.

Sleep didn't come to Flora for a long time, as her mind went over possibilities. It even occurred to her that Olivia might be one of her father's conquests; but no, if that was so, then Cyrus would have thought of the possibility. In any case, Olivia didn't seem like the kind of woman who would have affairs. Why should she? She had been widowed for many years and could have remarried, but hadn't done. It was all a mystery, but the most likely answer was that

Olivia knew Father's mistress. What an exciting prospect that was!

Although Cyrus tried to get Olivia to tell him what was troubling her, she wouldn't. She only said that she needed to go away for a couple of days to sort out something very personal to her, which for the moment she couldn't talk about.

This upset Cyrus, and for some reason further unnerved Flora, but they both knew they had to give Olivia the time she needed. So there was nothing they could do; they could only hope that Olivia felt better once she returned.

Chapter Twenty-Eight

'Flora, I have a letter from our bank. I'm to go in to speak with the manager.'

Flora looked up from sorting the dirty linen. She'd filled the copper in the corner of the kitchen, set up the mangle and grated the soap in readiness, though she hadn't relished the task, as she was feeling tired before she'd even begun. Wiping her brow with her arm, she looked up at Cyrus. 'Oh, what can that be about? We've not spent money we don't have, have we?'

'I don't know. We shouldn't have, but the letter does say, "to discuss your current financial position". Which sounds ominous.'

'Oh dear, and we have Christmas upon us and I have put in a large order at the grocer's, as your mother's coming.' Worry flared up in Flora. Yes, money was tight because, apart from the little they both earned teaching music and doing the odd concert with the new orchestra they had helped to form, the only other money coming in was Cyrus's allowance. But with no rent to pay, they scraped by, especially as Olivia had taken over the payment of Alice's school fees.

Thinking of Olivia, it still niggled at Flora that they'd never got to the bottom of why she had been so upset that day. She'd insisted that she'd had too much sun, or eaten something that hadn't agreed with her, and they'd had to leave it at that. But the more Flora pondered over it, the more she was sure that there had been more to it.

Cyrus moved closer to her and put his arm around her. Feeling him close comforted her. She gazed up at him. He looked so much better now, as he'd filled out to his normal weight and was in a good place mentally. His nightmares had lessened, too. But now he had worry lines around his eyes as he frowned. 'You look peaky, darling, you're not overdoing it, are you? I'll always leave what I'm doing to help you.'

'I know, but I can manage. It's just . . . well, it's early days, but I think I may be pregnant again.'

'So soon? Oh, darling, that's good news, but do you mind? I mean, Freddy is barely three months old.'

'No, I'm thrilled. All the children we are blessed with will be welcomed by me, and I know by you, too. I was made to mother your offspring, darling.'

'Oh, Flora, my darling. I do love you so much. And now I want to show you how much.'

The usual sensations flared up and filled her with his love, as he gently took her breast in his hand. His lips brushed her neck, and she was lost. Taking her hand, he led her to their bedroom. There, they made love in a way that told of their abandonment of everything, no matter that it was morning, and the washing was waiting to be done. No matter that they had worries about money. For this moment in time, there were just the two of them, taking each other to exquisite heights in an outpouring of their love for one another.

As they lay quietly, both exhausted, their hands entwined, Cyrus looked over at Flora. 'I'm so sorry that I haven't been able to get employment yet. I really thought I would have got that job I applied for at the bank. It shocked me when they told me that I hadn't been successful. I'll make a renewed effort, and work in one of the factories, if need be.'

'No, my love. I'd never have you doing that. Everything will be all right, I'm sure of it.'

'I'm not so sure. This notice from the bank reads more like a demand for my presence. I feel something has gone wrong. I'll pop in there this afternoon and make an appointment. I can only think that it has to do with my allowance, and that maybe the money from the will has run out. I've never given much thought to how long it would last; and lately, when I have, I didn't want to trouble my mother about it. She seems to have enough on her plate. Anyway, if that is so, well, it will force my hand. I will have to find some work.'

'But your writing is important. And your teaching and composing. As well as the work you do in preparing the concerts – all of that is important to who you are.'

'I know, but none of it is more important than you and our children.'

Flora had dropped off to sleep in the chair when Cyrus came back from the bank the next afternoon – the first appointment he could get.

The morning had been a busy one for her, and Freddy had been fractious. But her worry wasn't for him, as it was just a teething problem ailing Freddy, and she'd managed to soothe him and get him to sleep. It was Alice who was worrying her.

Alice had started a cough just over a week ago, and it was getting worse. There had been no soothing her, but eventually she'd dropped off, snuggled under a blanket on the sofa.

Flora had sat down for a few moments, intending to reread the letter she'd had from Mags. It had been addressed to her old address, and the new owners had dropped it off for her.

She'd felt a pang of guilt at not keeping in touch with Mags, but life had taken over. She'd never heard from Ella, but often thought of them both. Reading Mags's letter had upset her a little, as she was going to marry Harold. Mags and Harold! Somehow Flora couldn't be happy about it, especially as the letter said that Mags was sorry she couldn't ask her to the wedding, but hoped they could continue to be friends and write occasionally to each other. It felt as though Mags had crossed over to the other side, though part of what she wrote denied this:

I'm always thinking of you, Flors. And it is jolly beastly the way your family treat you, but no matter how much I badger Harold, he just won't agree to making things up with you. He says that everything is best left as it is. That you have made a life for yourself, and that's that. He tells me you have two children now . . .

Just before she'd dropped off, Flora had thought that Cook was a double agent, and then she had smiled. None of it mattered to her now. She had all she needed in life.

'Oh, did I wake you, darling? Sorry. Are you feeling all right? Is Alice all right?'

'Yes, I'm fine. And Alice is asleep. Though I'm hoping for good news from you, darling, as I think Alice needs to see a doctor. How did it go?'

In her heart, she knew. She could see by Cyrus's face that he was even more worried than he had been before he'd left for the bank.

'Not well. It was as I thought. The allowance stopped in September, and no one thought to let me know. Several of my cheques have been sent back. One to the grocer, I'm sorry to say. Last month's account hasn't been paid. And one to the coal merchant.'

'Oh no. I've orders with them both. What are we going to do?'

Cyrus hung his head. 'I don't know. I just don't know.'

Standing up, Flora went to him. His arms opened and enclosed her, and she could feel his despair.

'We'll think of something. There's things we can sell, and there is the Christmas concert in the church hall – the tickets for that are going really well. And I can go to the pub and ask if I can play there again. I used to go down really well.'

'If only they liked violin music, I would be there like a shot. But couldn't you teach me those London songs on the piano? I hate to think of you going out at night.'

'I don't see why not, as they are all simple chords. And we'll come up with more ways of making money, I'm sure. We just need to sort out something for the immediate future, so we can pay the grocer and the coal merchant and receive my orders for Christmas.'

'I can pawn my watch, and my second violin.'

'And I have that bracelet you bought me in Brighton.'

'Oh, Flora, I love you. I'll make a renewed effort, once Christmas is over, to get employment. Something must

301

come up. I wish now that I hadn't taken my discharge and had stayed as an officer.'

'No, I couldn't have been apart from you any longer. I'm sure something will happen; we'll get through this together. We can always sell the house and live in rented accommodation.'

'That's a last resort. I'll go to the pawn shop today. We need to pay the grocer and coal merchant as soon as possible. We have to eat and be warm over Christmas.'

A heavy feeling settled in Flora. How had it come to this? Her mind went to her parents, and how they and her brothers would have everything they needed over Christmas, while their daughter and grandchildren had practically nothing. But then she and Cyrus and their children had everything, as they had love. With this thought, she cheered up and helped Cyrus dig out what they owned that the pawn shop would be interested in.

When Olivia arrived, it was with more bags than Flora expected her to have. She looked a lot thinner than she had on her visit in September, and her face had a pensive expression.

'Mother, dear, are you unwell? Why didn't you let us know? You could have come sooner.'

'No. I – I have to talk to you, Cyrus. How I am going to say what I have to say, I do not know. You will hate me, and yet what I did, I couldn't help. And now I have been abandoned.'

Flora sensed that whatever it was that troubled Olivia was going to have a devastating effect on her and Cyrus, but while she didn't want to hear what Olivia had to say, she felt compelled to facilitate her saying it. 'I'll take the children upstairs for a while, and you can talk to Cyrus, Olivia.'

'Oh, just let me hug them first. Oh? Is Alice not well? What is it, darling? Tell Grandmother.' Alice had stirred and smiled a weak smile at Olivia as she lifted the child. 'There, there, have you a cold, my darling?'

Flora's trepidation at what her mother-in-law had to say to Cyrus left her, as her attention was taken by Alice. Coming out of a hug with her grandmother, the child began another fit of coughing.

'Dear, dear, Alice, my poor darling. How long has she had that cough? It sounds like the croup! Has she seen a doctor?'

'No, Mother, but she does need to. Flora has tried everything, but Alice's cough refuses to respond to all the usual treatments: inhaling friar's balsam, beef teas, and hot-water pans applied to her chest. We had planned a talk to you, too. My allowance has run out, and we were hoping you can help us out a little, just to get a doctor for Alice.'

'Oh, my darling son, I can't.' Tears filled Olivia's eyes. 'I – I need to sit down, I have to tell you . . . I—'

Helping Olivia to a chair, Cyrus asked Flora not to leave the room. 'I think we should both hear what Mother has to say, darling.'

Flora couldn't speak. She could sense Cyrus's fear and it compounded her own. 'Alice, darling, Mummy and Daddy need to talk to Grandmother in the front room. Do you think you can snuggle on the sofa in here for a short while?' The coughing bout had passed, but as Flora looked at the too-pale face of her daughter, her heart felt torn with anguish. 'I can't leave her, Cyrus. Whatever you have to say, Olivia, will have to wait. I need to be with Alice.'

Olivia nodded. A silence fell. It was fraught with tension. Cyrus sat next to his mother, holding her hand for a moment, but as soon as Olivia calmed, he came to lean over

Alice and stroked her hair. 'She's very hot, Flora darling. I'm worried for her.'

'I know. Will you get me a bowl of cold water and a flannel, so that I can sponge her? That might bring her temperature down.'

As Cyrus went through to the kitchen, Olivia stood up. 'I'll keep an eye on Freddy, maybe take him for a walk, if that's all right.'

'Yes, if you're feeling better, of course it will be a help.'

'He's beautiful. Is he always asleep?' There was a lighter tone to Olivia's voice, which gave Flora a little hope. *Maybe it's something and nothing that's troubling her.*

'He is a sleepyhead, which is just as well, as I'm constantly tired. Oh, and I have some news for you.' Flora smiled, though she least felt like it, but her news was happy news. 'You may hear me vomiting in the mornings.'

'What! No! So soon? It can't be – it mustn't be!'

'Mother!' Cyrus had come back into the room just as Olivia said this. 'That isn't the sort of reaction we expected from you. Flora and I are very happy that another child is on the way. What is the matter with you?'

Instinctively Flora picked up the blanket that had been wrapped around Alice and enclosed her child in it once more. Holding Alice close to her, she kept part of the blanket over the child's ears.

Olivia pulled a chair from under the table and sat down heavily on it. She leaned her arm on the table. 'I have terrible news for you.'

Flora tightened her grip on Alice. There was no resistance from the child. She seemed weaker than ever, and not interested in anything going on in the room.

Cyrus came and sat next to Flora, his arm around her.

304

'I – I'm sorry. So sorry; please don't hate me. I love you both and need you.'

'Mother, please!'

'I have no easy way to tell you. You share the same father. You are half-brother and sister.'

Flora felt a scream rising within her as her world crashed around her, but all that came from her was a hoarse whisper . . . 'No. no. Please God, no!'

Beside her, she felt Cyrus's body tremble. 'Oh God, no! Mother, what are you saying?'

'I had an affair with George Roford. I was never married. I have been in love with George – and he with me – for thirty-five years. The picture I gave you of your father, Cyrus, was a cousin of mine, and he did die in the Boer War, and it was his parents in the picture with him. I only had my sister left in the world, and she agreed to keep to my story. Our parents had been only children and they died when we were in our twenties; they didn't leave us a penny, only debts. My affair came to an end when your father was taken ill, Flora. It broke my heart. It was like a bereavement. But, poor darling, his health meant that he could no longer get away from home to spend time with me.

'He loves your mother, Flora, and always has. He is a man capable of loving two women. When you told me about your Aunt Pru and Freddy, it devastated me. But then I worked out that his affair with Pru happened during the time George and I were estranged. Your mother had found out about me. Her own sons were five and three at the time, and George broke off our relationship. I didn't see him for years, but he continued to take care of us, paying an allowance into a bank account that I set up for you, Cyrus; and for me too, into my own account.

'I contacted George through his solicitor when I realized who you were, Flora. All I got back was a letter saying that George was disgusted with me, for not telling you who your father was, Cyrus. He said that if I had done, this incestuous marriage couldn't have taken place. He said that he was going to cut all ties with me, and stop both allowances. I – I have nothing. No income, and I will soon have no home, as I am unable to keep up with the rent payments on my apartment. I have been given two months to pay up or leave. I – I need help, and you are all I have to turn to, and yet how can you ever forgive me?'

Flora felt as if she would faint. She couldn't breathe, such was her shock. She stared at Olivia, and then at her beloved Cyrus. *This can't be happening. It can't . . . Oh God! Oh God, help me!* Her body filled with silent screams that she dared not give vent to, for fear of frightening Alice and waking Freddy. Cyrus's arm tightened around her, the trembling of his body now a violent shaking. Olivia had her head on her arm, leaning over the table. Sobs racked her, as if she were a rag doll being shaken by an invisible hand.

A spasm of coughing from Alice broke the terrible spell that had held them all.

Looking down at her, Flora saw a trickle of blood run down her chin. 'Cyrus, oh, Cyrus, help me. We have to get Alice to hospital.'

'What?' Cyrus was in the grip of shock concerning what he'd heard. He looked at Flora as if she'd gone mad.

'Darling, our daughter needs us.'

Alice coughed again. Blood sprayed from her. Cyrus jumped up and helped Flora to rise. Not knowing how she stood on legs that trembled beneath her, Flora made herself walk towards the door. 'Olivia, you have to look after

Freddy. Alice is desperately ill. We have to take her to the hospital. We'll deal with everything else later.' Flora didn't want there to be a later. For now, her worry for her daughter consumed her. She could think of nothing else. 'Run to the end of the street, Cyrus, and get a cab. Go, darling. I know you're in shock, but we have to save Alice.'

Chapter Twenty-Nine

When the cab came, Flora implored the driver, 'Get us to Lambeth Road Infirmary, as quick as you can.'

In her haste she hadn't covered the blood, which was now staining Alice's blanket. 'What's wrong with the child, Missus? I don't want to catch anything.'

'Please, please don't refuse us – my child's life is at stake.'

'Well, all right, but I'll 'ave to keep the windows of the cab open.'

In the few minutes it took to get to the hospital, Flora was frozen to the bone, but she took no heed of this and jumped from the cab, leaving Cyrus to pay the driver. When Cyrus caught up with her, she was at the reception desk, imploring the nurse on duty to get a doctor for Alice.

'There isn't a doctor here, love. This is a hospital run by the board of the Poor Law. A doctor only visits once a week. We have an isolation ward free; your daughter will be admitted there, and we will take care of her as best we can, but we're short-staffed and have very little equipment or medication. Your best bet is to take her to the London General, which used to be St Gabriel's College, on Cormont Road.

It's a military hospital, but they have a sanatorium. They'll charge you, unless you're military, sir?'

'No. I was, but I was discharged.'

'Well then, try the Royal London on Whitechapel Road. They make a charge, but not as much, and they have everything your daughter will need. Can you afford to pay?'

'We'll get the money. Thank you.'

Outside there were a number of cabs. 'I don't know if I have enough money to pay for a journey of five miles or so, Flora. Oh God, what are we to do?'

'We'll take the cab to my parents' house first. I'll beg my father for some money to pay the driver, and for the hospital. Surely he won't refuse, for his only granddaughter?'

Saying this brought back to Flora the devastating news that Olivia had given them, but she didn't devote her attention, or any of her emotions, to this. She had to block it all out. Alice's life was at stake.

With a dread that caused her heart to ache, she admitted to herself that Alice most likely had tuberculosis of the lung. A fatal illness, if not treated properly, but even then, her chances of survival would be slim. No matter what it took, she had to try to give her daughter that slim chance.

As her family home came into view, Flora began to pray for courage. Alice stirred in her arms and coughed. This was enough to drive Flora forward. Shouting at the driver to wait for them, she dashed out of the car to the front door and rang the bell.

To her surprise, Francis opened the door. He jumped back, embarrassment seeming to leave him unsure what to do. 'Flora! Why have you come? It isn't a good idea. I – I think, well, Father isn't well . . .'

'Oh, so you remember my name, eh? Having a good life,

are you, Francis? Forgot you had a sister? Most convenient. I need to speak to Father, and I'm not leaving until I do. It's a matter of great urgency!'

'If it is about your incestuous marriage, dear sister, we all know and are disgusted with you, even if we did think it a surprising act of revenge. You seem capable of doing anything to disrupt this family.'

Harold came towards the door and pushed Francis out of the way, as he said this.

Flora looked up at him. 'Our child is very sick and we need some money for her treatment. That, and that only, is the reason I have lowered myself to step over this doorstep. Now I haven't much time, please let me speak to Father.'

'No. I absolutely forbid it!'

Before Flora could speak, Cyrus gently pushed her out of the way. 'Well, I – as the eldest son – overrule you. Get out of my way. I want to see my father.'

The enormity of Cyrus's words hit Flora hard. *Oh God, I can't bear it! I didn't want it to be the truth.*

'So your slut of a mother informed us . . . Hey, let me go!'

Cyrus held Harold by the collar and pushed him against the wall. 'Do you know what the worst thing is, about what I discovered only tonight? That you are my brother – you disgusting excuse for a man. Now, get out of our way.'

'Don't let them in, Harold . . . Francis . . . Stop them!'

'Mother, please, our child is dying. Please help me.'

'What is happening?'

'Go back into the withdrawing room, Mags; please, darling. And you, Mother, I don't want you involved in this.'

'But, Harold . . . Flors! Oh, Flors, are you all right?'

'Help me, Mags, please, please help me. My little Alice

'. . . she's dying. I – I haven't any money for her treatment. I came to ask my father, but they won't let me in.'

'My God! Harold? Why not?'

'It is none of your business, Mags, please leave this to us.'

'My business or not, I'm not standing by and letting a child die! Nor am I going to refuse to help my dearest friend. Flors, I'll come with you. I have some money, and I can arrange as much finance as you need.' Mags turned to the maid, who stood, white-faced, looking on. 'Please bring my coat.'

As the bodies in the doorway parted, Flora saw who the maid was, and for a fleeting moment felt triumph over Harold as she said, 'Oh, I see you still have Susan in tow?' But she felt immediate remorse as Mags looked from the cringing maid to Harold, and a shadow of doubt and hurt crossed her face.

'You vixen! And you wonder why none of us wants you near to us. Get out! Get out, do you hear me? You have broken the law, dear sister, and I am going to inform the police that you are cohabiting with your half-brother! You're disgusting!'

'No, Cyrus!'

Cyrus had raised his fist, but stopped at this shout from Flora.

'Leave him, I shouldn't have said what I did. All of this is wasting so much time, and Alice has so little. Will you help us, Mags? I don't know what else to do.'

'Yes, I will, dear Flors.' Mags turned and took her coat and purse from a mortified Susan.

'I forbid you to, Mags. As your fiancé, I forbid you to go with these . . . these . . .'

'Your sister, Harold?'

'She has never been like a sister to me.' He turned and took their now-sobbing mother in his arms. 'Nor a daughter to our mother. She has always caused pain and trouble.'

'I – I haven't. I haven't, I was never allowed to be your sister . . . I—'

'Oh, don't come up with that trash; you were destructive and had to be sent away, or our mother would have become even more fragile than she already is.'

'Harold, I think we have a lot to talk about, but in the meantime I am not turning my back on Flors, or her husband and child. If that goes against your wishes, then I am sorry, and you will have to do as you see fit. Come on, Flors. Let's get Alice to the hospital.'

Alice was taken from them when they arrived. The sister in charge told them they must wait while an assessment of Alice was made. It might be that they would have to call in a specialist, but whatever their decision, they would inform the family as soon as they could.

With Alice taken from her, Flora collapsed inwardly and gave vent to all the pent-up feelings that had strangled her heart.

'Oh, Flors, what a mess. How did it all come to this? Though the way Harold acted was driven by how his mother shaped him. Well, shaped both her sons. She is manipulative in the extreme. If she doesn't get what she wants, she feigns illness.'

'I know, but I thought Harold had her under his control.'

'He does, but what has gone on down the years has made Harold what he is. He bats for the side that he thinks most beneficial to him. I believe, when he was all right towards you, that he saw you as a weapon he could use against his father, to get what he desired – to be put in charge of the mill, and so be in an essential job that didn't require him to go to war. But he's made some bad decisions, and he is failing. That is where I come in. I have what he wants – a successful mill that will prop up his mill. Or at least my father does and, as his son-in-law, Harold will get what he needs to boost his business.'

'And, knowing all of this, you still love him, Mags?'

'Love is something we cannot help. I would have thought you would understand that, Flors.'

'Oh, I do. And I know that it can surmount everything, but . . .' She reached out and took Cyrus's hand. 'How we will surmount the bombshell that has landed in our laps today, I just don't know. I haven't been able to give my mind to it at all. I'm so very worried about our little Alice.'

'You mean you truly didn't know until today? Nothing that either of you said to the other even gave you a clue?'

'No, why should it?' Cyrus replied. 'We met out of the blue, and in a foreign country. We had an immediate and very strong attraction to each other, which hit us both hard. Yes, it was love, but not brother–sister love. Oh, there were a few coincidences in what we learned about each other later on: my music, and how Flora's father was gifted at playing on the violin, as I myself am. Me having been to the same school as those I now know are my half-brothers. But I completely believed that my father had been killed in the Boer War and that my allowance came from my late grandfather's will, which is what my mother told me and my aunt confirmed. As did the picture they gave me, of my supposed father and grandparents. I didn't have an inkling that I wasn't who I was told I was. It is devastating news.'

'I believe you, and I am so sorry. But Harold is afraid, and is acting irrationally because of his fear. He has convinced himself, and the rest of the family, that Flora set out to find you and married you incestuously, to spite them all. They found out, because your father had a relapse just after he'd asked for a letter to be sent to his solicitor. Harold read the letter that your father was answering. It was from his solicitor telling him what your mother had found out. Harold verbally abused your father, saying that his so-called daughter had had the last laugh, by marrying his bastard son. Your father admitted that he had been paying an allowance to his son and his mistress, whom he still loved and would have gone to for good, but for his illness.

'This set your mother off, Flora. She was hysterical and a doctor had to be called. Your father had a relapse, and Harold forced him to sign a letter to the bank to stop the payments to you, Cyrus, and to your mother. And then ripped up the letter your father was going to send, and wrote one himself to his father's solicitor, and made his father sign that, too. He is now consulting solicitors as to the impossibility, and the illegality, of you being recognized as the heir to your father, Cyrus.'

Bitterness entered Flora. 'Did none of them think that if they had not rejected me, this wouldn't have happened? That, in the normal run of things, I would have brought Cyrus to our home to meet my family; and that Father, on hearing all about Cyrus, would have realized the truth and the marriage would not have gone ahead? They are to blame. They forgot they had a daughter and a sister, and left me floundering on my own. But none of this matters at the moment. Only that you believe us, Mags, when we say that we are innocent of what Harold accuses us of. And, even more than that, we love each other so very much, and at this moment are facing the awful prospect of losing our daughter, and each other.'

'Oh, my darling Flora, don't think of either of those things happening. We will find a way. We have to,' Cyrus urged her. 'I can't bear to be apart from you, and can never be a brother to you. You are my wife, my everything.'

'Flors, I'm so sorry. Try to hold on to the fact that Alice is in the best hands possible. As for yourselves, there will be a way, as Cyrus says. You will have to be very careful not to be seen to be carrying on as husband and wife, now that you know what your true relationship is. Then, as soon as you can, you must go away somewhere, where Harold cannot do you any harm. He is very bitter at the moment, and could take action that could see you both going to prison and your children taken from you. I have been very worried for you since news of this broke. I didn't know what to believe, or what to do. I should have warned you and kept faith in our friendship, Flors, but Harold is powerful, when he sets his mind to something.'

'Please don't worry. None of this is your fault, Mags. But, you know, although I don't like to admit it, I am like Harold in some ways, because I would ask you – even though it is a terrible betrayal of our friendship – to use the power you have over Harold to help us.'

'How can I do that? And what power?'

'By threatening to leave him, if he carries out his threat of going to the police. You say he needs to marry you? Well, that gives you power over him to help us – please, Mags. And, if you can, please forgive me for asking this of you, but I cannot bear to see Cyrus go to prison, and the threat of that hangs over me, too. And to lose our children . . . Oh God. What have we done to deserve all that?'

'I will help you. I will, Flors, but I will make conditions. These are to secure my future happiness with Harold. I won't blackmail him, but I will help you financially, and make sure that he does, too, to get away – somewhere abroad, where the law of England cannot touch you, and no one there will know your status, thereby enabling you to continue to live as man and wife. But you must do something for me. You, Cyrus, must renounce all claim to your father's fortune.'

This shocked Flora, but as it was a way out for them, she was willing to agree. However, she had no time to, because the door to the waiting room opened. 'Mr and Mrs Harpinham, the doctor would like to talk to you.'

'Sister, is our daughter all right?'

'I'm sorry, Mr Harpinham, but I cannot speak to you about your daughter's condition. You need to ask the doctor. Please come this way.'

'M – Mags, come with us, we may need you.'

'Who is this lady? Is she a relative?'

'Soon to be my sister-in-law, and aunty to Alice. We would like her with us.'

'Very well, come this way, please.'

Flora held on to Cyrus's hand as if her life depended on it. She had nothing else but his love. Her mind cast aside for the moment the thought that they could be forced apart, as they were still together and facing something much bigger than any of their other problems.

'I'm sorry, Mr Harpinham, but your daughter is dying. How long has she had a cough? Did you not seek to have her medically checked out? There might have been a chance.'

Cyrus folded. This gave Flora strength. 'She had a childhood cough. I have been a nurse, and I thought it was croup. I – I did what was necessary . . . I—'

'Oh, where did you train? Why did you think that being a nurse gave you enough skill to diagnose your child and treat her?'

Flora wanted to say that she loved her child, that she didn't want Alice to die, that she would give her own life for her, but all of this sounded hollow in the face of the neglect that the accusing voice seemed to level at her. Her head bent over in defeat.

Mags spoke up. 'You are talking to someone who single-handedly ran a hospital in Belgium, after the Germans invaded, with only two other volunteer nurses and a few staff to help. In that situation she often had to be the doctor, and did a sterling job of saving many lives. Not only that, but when she got out, she then went to the Somme and gave of her all there. She is a devoted mother, who has fallen on hard times. If you doctors gave of your services to those less fortunate, as my friend has done, this situation wouldn't have arisen!'

The doctor was taken aback for a moment. 'I apologize. I see a lot of cases of neglect. I misjudged the situation.'

'Neglect or an inability to change things, Doctor?'

'Madam, I am not on trial here. I want to help these parents and their child. There are charitable organizations . . .'

'Please, it doesn't matter. I accept your apology. Please, Doctor, tell me and my wife what, if anything, can be done for our child.'

Flora was relieved at this intervention by Cyrus, but felt a little pride at how Mags had reacted. This was the old Mags, the spirited Mags. She would always do the right thing as she saw it, and would fiercely defend those she loved. Flora just wished she didn't number Harold amongst them.

'I have to say there is very little that can be done. Living

317

in a country where the air is full of oxygen, such as Switzerland, is one treatment, but I'm afraid this would only delay the inevitable. I regret to say that tender care is all that can be offered. We have an isolation ward where this can take place.'

'I want her home. I want to nurse her myself.'

'That is very noble, and I am sure that you are highly capable, but, my dear, you have to consider how TB spreads. You have to think of yourself, your husband and any other family you may have.'

'I am, and I will. I will isolate one of our rooms at home. I will take every precaution that the nurses here will take, when entering and leaving that room. I must take care of my own child. I have done so for so many other mothers, and I need to do this for my own child.'

'Very well, I will discharge Alice to you. And, because of what your friend has said, I will visit and prescribe medication at no cost to you. You, young lady, have awoken my conscience and that isn't a good place for me to visit.'

The doctor and Mags smiled at each other, but Flora couldn't smile. Her world had collapsed.

Chapter Thirty

By the time they reached home, Alice's breathing was labouring so badly that Flora's fears for her increased. Mags had insisted on coming home with them to help them set up the isolation room for Alice.

They found Olivia asleep in the chair by a dying fire. On waking her, Cyrus sat with her and told her what had happened.

As Flora and Mags worked to turn the front room into a sanatorium, they could hear Olivia's cries of despair. Flora blocked out the sound as much as she could, as she directed and helped Mags and Cyrus to fill buckets of hot water and scrub the room clean. Between them, they moved furniture, taking one of the sofas into the living-room-cum-kitchen, leaving one for Flora to sleep on, and bringing a bed downstairs for Alice.

The carpet was rolled up and the wooden floor scrubbed, and all the lace curtains were taken down from the windows of the house, then made into a tent for the bed by nailing them to the ceiling. 'This will enable me to keep her out of a draught and yet have the windows open, so that she has a constant supply of fresh air.'

Through all of this, Alice slept on the sofa, helped by the drugs given to her at the hospital.

When everything was ready, and they had all scrubbed their hands clean, Flora hugged Mags goodbye and waved her off as she got into the cab, which she'd paid to wait for her.

On closing the door, Flora clung to Cyrus, telling him as they came out of the hug how much she loved him. 'This must be our last physical contact for a while, for fear of spreading the infection. I will bath and prepare myself, then you must bath. All our clothes will have to be boiled, and we must constantly wash our hands. I will make more masks out of the edges of lace curtains that are more closely woven, and which I cut off for that purpose. I will leave these on a chair outside the room.'

Speaking to both Cyrus and the now-calm Olivia, Flora told them that they must always wash their hands and don a mask before entering the room, and wash their hands on leaving, then boil the mask they had used.

'I can help make the masks, Flora.'

'Thank you, Olivia.'

'F – Flora, I—'

'Don't say anything. We none of us blame you. It was a million-to-one chance that Cyrus and I should meet as we did. Especially as you had moved away from London. I do have a lot of questions, after what Mags has told me happened once you contacted my father. And I wish you had spoken to us before you did that. But I have to give all my attention now to looking after Alice. We will talk at a later time. For now, I want you to stay. We both need you, as will our little Freddy.'

Olivia nodded in a way that showed her relief.

After her bath, Flora donned the nurse's frock and one of the many aprons lent to her by the sister at the hospital, as being so much easier to keep her from spreading infection. Next, she put on one of the masks; these, along with other items given to her that she might need – a bowl for sterilizing, a bedpan, a pack of disposable paper gloves and a feeding cup – showed that Mags had worked a miracle with her outburst, and that not only the doctor's conscience had been pricked.

With Alice still asleep and now tucked up in bed, Flora looked down at her and allowed despair to creep into her heart. *How am I going to bear losing you, my darling? How, how?*

The door opened. Cyrus stood there in his pyjamas, wearing a mask. 'I haven't got a uniform, but I thought, as these are boilable, I could come in wearing them and take my turn, or sit together with you. Please don't shut me out, Flora, my darling. I can't live through all of this without you by my side and being unable to hold you.'

'Oh, Cyrus, I don't know what to do. We have to face it that, whatever we decide to do, we cannot save our darling child. But I want to protect Freddy, and you and Olivia. I have been reckless bringing Alice home. I thought only of my own pain, and of hers, if she should wake and neither of us was there.'

'I understand. But I also know that we need each other at this time.'

'We do. Oh, we do, darling. But we must take every care that we can.'

'We will. Please agree, darling.'

She was in his arms, a place she didn't think she would be for a long time, if ever again. 'I do, I know that I cannot get through this without you.'

Coming out of the hug, Cyrus looked down at her. 'Let's sit a moment.' He guided her to the sofa. 'I'm sorry, I know it doesn't seem like the right time, but there is an urgency in our situation, and we must talk. I think that both your own and Mags's solutions were good. I can never miss something that I didn't have, so I don't mind renouncing my entitlement to any inheritance that might have come my way. I know that your father – our father – has treated you badly, but until he was forced not to, he continued to take care of me.'

'That hurts me, as he cut me off so easily. But then he still loved your mother, so maybe he wanted to please her.'

'Yes, that would be the reason. And was probably why I was sent off to school, so that I wouldn't be in the way of any visits he made. Was he away from home a lot?'

'I think so. I have so few memories of my time at home, and none of them happy.'

'Life has been so unfair to you, my darling.'

'It has to all those of us in our age range. But don't forget that I had dear Aunt Pru and Freddy, and they filled my life with love and caring. I miss them both so much.'

Cyrus held her close once more. 'How are we to bear everything on our shoulders, darling? Our little Alice . . .'

There was a sob in his voice, which caused her own tears to spill over. They clung together, trying to give and receive comfort and strength from one another.

A loud knocking on the front door shot them apart. 'Police! Open up!'

'Oh, my God! Harold has done it. He's informed on us. Oh, Cyrus. Go – go out of the window. You can get away down the alley. I'll tell them that we split up the moment we heard. Go to Rowena, she will help you. I'll contact her when I can.'

'But I'm not dressed!'

'Never mind that, go!'

The knocking persisted. Grabbing a pair of paper gloves, Flora ran from the room, putting them on as she went. Olivia came down the stairs leading to the kitchen just as Flora got there.

'I'll see to it. Cyrus has gone. We are to say that after we came back from the hospital, he left to try to find alternative accommodation.'

When Flora opened the door, the policeman standing there, with an oil lamp in his hand, jumped back. 'Sorry, Nurse, I wanted to talk to Cyrus and Flora Harpinham.'

'Come in, Officer. I am Flora. I am nursing my dying child. I am dressed like this to prevent the spread of the TB that she has. Cyrus does not live here, from today. I think you may have come here regarding the unfortunate position that Cyrus and I found ourselves in. Sit down, and I will explain everything.'

'I have a warrant to arrest you.'

'Please don't, my child's life depends on me.'

'Well, in the circumstances I'll hear you out, and take the information back to my sergeant. We have a report that you are living with your brother in an incestuous relationship, and that you married, knowing that you were kin. Is this true?'

'Not wholly, no.' Flora told him the truth of how they had only found out about their relationship today, and how their daughter had been taken ill; and then added the lie that Cyrus had left as soon as he could, after their return from the hospital. She told of their shock and that they knew they could never live together again. 'You have to believe me. We didn't know. We met . . .'

At the end of her story, during which the officer took several notes, he said he would have to search the house to make sure Cyrus wasn't there. 'Do you have anyone who can verify your story, Miss?'

'I can, Officer, and so can Flora's father,' Olivia said. 'I informed Flora's father – my . . . lover – when I realized the awful truth. I didn't know how to tell Flora and Cyrus. I did wrong. I should have told them the moment I knew.'

She went on to explain how the war had separated her and her son, and how she had spent most of it in Switzerland with her sister, while he was in a prisoner-of-war camp. 'I only knew that he had married a girl called Flora. I didn't know her surname, or that George – her father – had a daughter. He only ever told me of the birth of his sons. He . . . well, he said he had broken off intimate relationships with his wife, and I believed him. It was a shock to hear that he had a further child with his wife, and one with another mistress.' Olivia continued telling the whole story, leaving nothing out.

'Your story has the ring of truth to me, and gives a reason why Harold Roford would be so vindictive as to tell us a different story. He obviously wants his older half-brother discredited. I have written down what you have said, albeit in a brief way. I need you both to sign your statements. I will do my search of the house, then report back to my sergeant.'

'Thank you, but I must insist that you protect yourself

from infection by putting a mask on when you go into the front room, which is now a sanitized room for my daughter.'

'I'll just pop my head around the door. I'm very sorry for your plight, Miss, and hope that you and your . . . well, Mr Harpinham, are not prosecuted, but that's not down to me. I would speak to a solicitor as soon as you can, if I were you.'

After he'd gone, Flora leaned on the door. Her legs felt as though they would give way and her heart held an avalanche of tears – tears that she could not give way to. 'Thank you, Olivia, it must have been very difficult for you to admit to everything, knowing that it may become public, if all of this goes to court.'

'Do you think it will?'

'Yes, I think it has to, if only to put an order on Cyrus and me that forbids us to live together as man and wife.'

'I'm so sorry. I have never seen my son happier than he is with you. The love you share is unique and has never shown any cracks; you were made for each other.'

'We'll find a way. We have to. We cannot live without each other. And as you know, I am with child again.'

'Oh, my dear, how can you bear it all?'

'I haven't been given a choice. Now, I must get back to little Alice. Try to get some rest. Cyrus is with Rowena; he may come back later, so don't be frightened if you hear a noise.'

During the few times that the policeman had agreed to her going to check on Alice, Flora had been encouraged to see her child sleeping peacefully and her breathing less laboured, but as she entered the room now, she found Alice agitated and plucking at the sheet that covered her.

'What is it, darling? Mummy is here.'

Alice smiled. The smile turned to a cough. Blood splattered the white sheet. Flora gasped as she saw Alice's eyes roll back into her head as she went to breathe in. But the air didn't fill her body.

Flora grabbed her and held her daughter to her. 'Alice, breathe. Breathe . . . Oh, Alice, no . . . Noooo . . .'

Collapsing into the chair beside the bed, Flora rocked backwards and forwards, holding her child's body close. All of who she was drained from her. Nothing mattered any more. Nothing would ever matter again. In that moment she was filled with hate: hate for her brother, and hate for her mother and father; and yes, hate for God, whom she'd begged things of so many times in her life, and who had left her alone and abandoned. For in His act of taking her child, He had cut her loose, and that filled Flora with dark despair.

PART SIX

London, 1920

~

Cyrus, Flora and Harold

Jealousy Knows No Bounds

Chapter Thirty-One

Flora stood in the Salvation Army church hall. The delicious smell of stew cooking in the large pans mingled with that of unwashed bodies and clothes, as the poor and misplaced persons lined up to be fed. Some, she knew, had been put out of their homes for non-payment of rent, due to their man not coming home from war, and the slowness of the powers-that-be in sorting out widows' pensions. Others were ex-soldiers who were no longer able to work. Their bodies or minds, and sometimes both, were broken. It was all a pitiful sight.

Her own plight was such that she had been forced here, seeking food for herself and Freddy. But she had ended up becoming a volunteer when she realized that, as bad as her own situation was, there were others much worse off.

In doing so, she had found solace for her heartache, a way of coping with all she had on her plate. But then her heart was so fractured that she'd found her pain too deep to visit and had kept it locked within her.

As she filled bowl after bowl with the stew, the folk holding them out to her merged into a mass of human need that seemed insurmountable. And yet the room wasn't a cheerless place, but held laughter and kindness, and a sense that she'd always found in the East End: that we are all in this together.

Here, the worries about her bills, and the loneliness that engulfed her at home, faded and became almost insignificant.

'When's the baby due then?'

The woman in front of her, whose hair was matted to her head, and whose teeth showed decay, smiled out from a weather-beaten face as she asked this.

'Oh, not for months yet. I am just about five months pregnant.'

'And you have the lad there, too. Not much between them, is there?'

Flora blushed at this.

'Sorry, Miss. I didn't mean anything. Just passing the time of the day.'

'No. It's all right. I – I, well, I am coping with a lot at the moment.'

'You are? Well, you should try walking in my shoes.'

Flora could only give a weak smile. To this woman, in her ragged, unwashed state, without a bed to call her own, she knew she must appear to be one of the privileged. Without warning, her smile turned to tears.

'Oh, I – I didn't mean . . . Are you all right, Miss?'

Flora shook her head. 'I don't think I will ever be all right again, but I'm trying to cope, like the rest of you. I *am* walking in your shoes, more than you will ever know.'

'Carry on, Gladys, get some bread from the basket and go and sit and eat your dinner.' Emma, one of the soldiers – as members of the Salvation Army were called – took Flora's arm. 'And you sit down and have your meal, too, Flora. Have you eaten since you last came here two days ago?'

Swallowing hard, Flora shook her head. 'Freddy has, though. I am taking care of him.'

'We know you are. Don't look so scared. We all admire what you are doing, and how you are coping. You have been through a lot. You know, we would feed you without you having to work for it.'

'I know. But I feel better for helping those worse off than me.'

'Take your bowl of stew into the kitchen. Then, if you feel strong enough after, you can help with the washing up. Like I say, you needn't do anything, but I can see that wouldn't sit right with you.'

Freddy didn't stir as Flora ate her stew. The incident had rocked her and touched her vulnerable side, leaving her exposed to her emotions and bringing her troubles into focus.

For three months she had coped by suppressing her feelings, existing solely for Freddy and trying to keep her head above water. Her neighbours had been wonderful, and many mornings she had woken to find a box of coal or a sack of potatoes on her doorstep, besides the odd loaf of bread, freshly baked and wrapped in greaseproof paper. Mags had helped, too. She had given Flora regular sums of money, but didn't know the extent of the debt that Flora was in. And a little money had come in from Cyrus, who had found some music-teaching work.

She had vowed that she would pay Mags back every penny, and somehow she had persuaded those she owed money to – the coal merchant, the grocer, the bank and others – to accept promissory notes until her house sold.

But now everything was coming to a head. Later today she would see Cyrus, her beloved. Would that be a help, or a rubbing of salt into her wounds, as their meeting would be brief, and then he would have to return to his mother's? *Oh, how I wish the courts would decide, one way or another, what is going to happen.*

However, this paled against what she had to do when she left here – visit her darling Alice's resting place.

When she left home later, leaving Freddy in the care of Rowena, who had been more than happy to help her out, Flora didn't relish either of the ordeals facing her. One was upon her now, as she stood in the churchyard, gazing down at the mound of earth that covered her child.

The wind howling through the trees that shielded the graveyard from the road sounded like the wail of the hundreds of mothers whose children lay in this earth. As it whipped around her, the wind mocked her, lifting her skirt, and trying to remove her hat from her head. But Flora paid no heed to its antics, for her inner self was detached from her body and lay in the little box, with her Alice.

When she fell to her knees, the rugged ground snagged her stockings, but she didn't care. Today she was here to tell Alice that the grandfather she had never met had died three days ago. 'Today is his funeral, and I have been told to stay away until everyone has gone. And then your daddy and I have to be at the reading of the will, by order of his solicitor. Most likely that is to hear that we are cut out of it. But, Alice, I can't feel an ounce of sorrow. Even remembering my father before Aunt Pru took me off to stay away from home and live at school – the only time that I felt loved by him – doesn't give me any sadness at his passing, only a bitterness that consumes me, and has done since you left me, my darling.'

Not one of her family had sent their condolences to Flora, or had attended the funeral of her child. But for dear Mags, Alice would have had a pauper's funeral.

'I'm selling our home, Alice. I have to. Now that you no longer skip from room to room with your joyous cries of happiness, the place is dead to me, too. I don't know what I am to do. Nor what will become of little Freddy and your new brother or sister, who is now moving in little flutters, to remind me that he or she is going to arrive in a few months. I don't want to leave you here, but tomorrow I will hear the judgement of the court and may have to run away, once I have the money from my house sale. You see, Alice, my darling child, I cannot live without your daddy. I can't . . . I can't. These last weeks without him have been hell.'

'Flora!'

Turning, she saw Cyrus standing on the path. He walked towards her. 'I knew that I would find you here, darling. Let me help you up, you look like a lost soul.'

Cyrus looked more beautiful than ever, with the rays of the sun lighting up his body. For a moment Flora thought he was a mirage, but then the touch of his hand on hers trembled through her. 'Oh, Cyrus. Cyrus.'

They clung together. 'I've missed you so much, my darling. How cruel that we had to part, when we most needed each other. Mother has had almost to lock me in, to keep me in her apartment with her. But we jeopardized so much if we didn't make our parting seem absolute.'

'I know. Your letters arriving every day helped me. I was glad to hear that you have managed to earn a little, to keep you and your mother going, but you shouldn't have sent any to me. I've been all right.'

'Oh, my darling, I had to. You and Freddy are my world. And . . . our darling little Alice. Oh, Flora, it is so painful.'

She wiped his tears.

When he was calmer, Cyrus lifted his head. 'There is some good news, darling. It is earlier than we thought, but after it was accepted that we had told the truth and the decision was made not to prosecute us, the solicitor that Mags engaged moved everything along, using our grief as leverage to get our case heard more quickly than would normally have happened. It has been judged that we should live apart, and that the children should stay with you, but can make visits to me and my mother each month.'

'Oh, Cyrus. Cyrus. I – I can't do that, I need you by my side.'

'I know. I need you, too. We have no other options open to us but to run away. Once the house is sold, we will go to France. No one can touch us there. And with us both speaking the language, and having the colouring of the French, we can merge into that country without being too noticeable.'

'Yes, yes, let's do that, but we must tell no one. Not even your mother or Mags – no one.'

'We can't do that to my mother. She will know, and will visit us from time to time, but she is being forced to give up her apartment and is going to live with her sister permanently, so she will be safe from letting anything slip.'

'And, thinking about it, I can trust Mags. I overreacted. I know she would never tell Harold. And we may need a contact here. I will also confide in Rowena. I want her to visit Alice for us, and keep her grave tidy.'

'Yes, darling, it is difficult to cut ourselves off from everyone who loves us. I know it hurts that you have never heard from Ella. Maybe, one of these days, you will. Now, are you ready, darling? We have to go to the dreaded wolves.' Bending down, Cyrus kissed his hand and touched the earth covering Alice. 'You are always with me, my darling child. I carry you in my heart, and will take you wherever I go.'

This brought comfort to Flora, and she did the same, for Alice *was* always with them; they weren't leaving her behind. And, with this thought, Flora felt stronger.

'"This is the Last Will and Testament of the deceased, George Howard Roford, and witnessed by me, his solicitor, John Henry Wright. This Will supersedes all others written before 11th November 1918 . . ."'

A collective gasp from Flora's mother, Harold and Francis interrupted the proceedings for a moment. Mother stood up. 'What date did you say?'

John Henry Wright repeated the first two lines of the Will that he held.

'But that isn't my husband's Will. I have a copy of his Will dated June 1902; he changed it to cut out F— I mean, that was the last time he updated his Will, to my knowledge.'

Pain zinged through Flora. Her mother had been about to say that her father had cut her out of the Will while she was still a child. *What kind of man was he, to burden me with his sins?* She looked over towards Cyrus, who was seated with Olivia on the opposite side of the room. They were all in her father's study: Cyrus, his mother, Harold, Francis and herself and Mother. Mother had, until this moment, behaved with dignity. The kind of dignity that said she knew something with which she would triumph over them all.

Flora suspected this was the only reason Mother had agreed to sit in the same room as Father's mistress and her son, or even have them in her home. There could have been nothing else that would have persuaded her to do so, other than that she must have thought she could finally banish them – and her daughter – from her life, and do so in a grand manner, by sending them packing from her own doorstep. Now she looked crumpled, and older than her years. Her eyes held fear and her body trembled. For the first time ever, Flora felt a small amount of pity for her mother, as she suspected there were shocks ahead for all of them in the revised Will.

'I can assure you, Mrs Roford, that while I extend my sympathy to you for your loss and for what you are about to hear, this is the only, and, valid Will of your late husband. I drew it up personally, to his instructions, and witnessed both the validity of it and the fact that he was sound in mind and body at the time.'

The room fell silent.

With the rest of the formalities read out and out of the way, John Henry Wright cleared his throat.

'"To my wife, Grace Mary Roford, I leave the house and all contents therein, plus a yearly income of one thousand pounds, which shall be paid from a trust fund set up for this purpose. On her death, this trust fund shall be closed and all assets remaining shall form part of her estate."'

There was no protest from her mother following this. Flora could see her, and could almost feel the tension emanating from her pensive body.

'"To my son, Harold Michael Roford, I leave my share of the Roford mill and all assets and shares in that business that are held in my name at the time of my death. And the sum of five thousand pounds . . ."'

The pause held a horror-filled gasp and an uttered 'What! God, what was Father thinking? Mother, that cannot be right!'

Flora feared for her mother, who had gone deathly pale.

'Please allow me to continue, Harold. "To my son, Francis, I leave the sum of three thousand pounds."'

'Well, that sums up what he thought of me, the pig-headed sod!'

'Can I please get through this without any further interruptions? Thank you. "To Olivia Harpinham"' – another, more painful gasp from Mother – '"I leave the apartment in which she resides, all contents therein, and one thousand pounds annual income, from a trust set up for this purpose."'

Flora was shocked. So her father had been Olivia's landlord, and yet had made her pay rent and would have forced her to move out. Did he intend to change his Will again, but was not given the chance to do so? Or did he decide to leave it as it was and punish Olivia in life, but make up for it in his death? She sighed. *I will never know.*

John Henry Wright carried on, despite the noise Harold was making as he tried to comfort Mother, and despite Mother's agonized wails. '"After a number of small legacies left to staff, all of which total one thousand pounds and are named in a separate list: to my son and heir, Cyrus Peter Harpinham, I leave the entire residue of my estate, with the proviso that he takes care of my beloved daughter, Flora Mary Roford, for the rest of her life."'

The room fell silent. All Flora could think of was that her father had called her his 'beloved daughter', and had left her welfare up to Cyrus. *He couldn't possibly have known back then, could he?*

'I will contest it! This is preposterous! That man is a bastard son. I am the legal heir. My father couldn't have been sound in his mind even to have considered wording his Will the way it is worded. It is cruel. Cruel, beyond words, to my mother!'

'I'm afraid there is nothing to contest, Harold. I'm very sorry. I did try to talk your father out of this, and advised him to set up a lifelong trust fund for his illegitimate son, and for his daughter, but he would have none of it. I have carried this burden for a long time, and many a time hoped that he would outlive you, Grace. I am so very sorry that you should have had to sit through that.'

Cyrus stood up. 'I'm sorry, too. I agree that it was very cruel and humiliating, to both your mother and mine, Harold. I didn't know our father, but I'm glad of that. I would very much like to meet you all, once I know the extent of my inheritance, as I would like to make things right.'

'You – you bastard, born of a whore – can never make things right!'

This, from Francis, shocked Flora. She would have expected it from Harold.

'I'm glad that my father is dead! I hate him more in death than I did when he was alive. I'm ashamed to be his son.' Francis ran from the room. Flora wanted to go after him, but stayed still.

'Get out! Get out all of you!' Mother's words turned into hysterical screams. Spittle sprayed from her mouth. Her eyes stared out, giving her the appearance of a wild animal.

Flora's nursing instincts came to the fore. She jumped up and slapped her mother.

'You vile creature! How dare you hit my mother.'

'I – I only wanted to stop her hysterics, Harold. I didn't hit her for any reason other than a medical one. Mother, are you all right? This has all been a terrible shock.'

'Just go. All of you. Just go!'

Cyrus hurried his mother out of the room. Flora ran after them. As she came up to them, she heard Cyrus say, 'That was dreadful. Mother, how could you have liked such a man, let alone loved him?'

Looking pale and shocked, Olivia clung to Cyrus, then turned and hooked her arm through Flora's, too. Flora looked over towards Cyrus. 'Cyrus, don't. We know ourselves how love can make you accept any situation.'

'We do, but to actually plan that humiliation. Not that he could have known that his wife would outlive him, but his sons were most likely to, and were always going to hear that he didn't think enough of them to leave them equal shares in his estate. I'm astounded by it all, and by my legacy, and cannot take it all in.'

Flora had often thought she had traits of her father and brother in her, and at this moment she knew so, because although she did feel sorry for them, she wanted to shout for joy, because at last her father had recognized her, and had made up for all he'd not given her in the past. And a small part of her felt that her mother and brothers had got what was coming to them.

Cyrus broke into these thoughts, his kindness putting her to shame. 'Let's get away from here and let them come to terms with everything. I'll contact John Wright tomorrow and make an appointment to discuss all the implications, and exactly what I have been left. I want to make it right for all of them, to the best of my ability.'

Without telling him her real feelings, Flora agreed. 'Yes. They don't deserve you to, but I would expect nothing less of you, darling.'

As they made their way to the waiting cab, Olivia spoke for the first time. 'You are right, Cyrus. How could I have loved such a cruel man? To insist that we were all together like that, and to have treated his family so unjustly. I wouldn't have cared, if he had left me nothing but happy memories. Now they are all tainted, and have been for a while, since I learned of Pru and Freddy. I need to be as far away from all of this as I can.'

'I'll put you on a train to Bexleyheath tomorrow, Mother, and will contact you as soon as I know what is happening. I need to sort everything out, before I leave here. Flora, darling. We can't be seen together, after I drop you off at your home. It's going to be so difficult. But as soon as I can, I will get some money to you. How have you really fared? You never said in your letters, and I've been worried sick.'

'I know; and I know you asked me, but my answer would have worried you even more than not knowing.' She told him how difficult it had all been.

'Oh, my poor darling. But all of this will come to an end. Once everything is sorted, I will look for a place for us in France, as we spoke about earlier. No one will keep us apart.' He pulled her to him. His mother averted her eyes and stared out of the window. 'Always remember that I love you. I will see you tomorrow, as we now have a legitimate reason to meet up, as I am officially your guardian.'

Flora managed a small smile. But as the cab took them away from her, and she stood outside the home she'd once loved – the home that had resounded with laughter, and yes, worrying times too, but mixed with family love – a feeling of foreboding shivered through her. It didn't last long, as a deep loneliness shrouded her.

She ran up the path and opened the door. Rowena stood there with her arms open. Going into the huge cuddle, Flora let her body empty of the tears that she'd locked deep inside her.

Chapter Thirty-Two

Flora waited outside her home. When the cab appeared, her heart beat faster. As soon as it came to a standstill, she jumped in and fell into Cyrus's arms, relishing his kisses on her face and finally on her lips.

'Oh, darling. I – I've been so lonely.'

'Me too, darling. I hope you don't mind coming with me, but I want them all to see that you are in agreement with me.'

Two days had passed since the Will-reading. Cyrus now knew the extent of his legacy. He was the owner of twenty-five thriving haberdashery shops, plus investment portfolios and properties, and cash in saving accounts worth a total of one hundred and fifty thousand pounds. There were also keys to some safe-deposit boxes, the contents of which were unknown.

'What I propose to do is to sell the shops and divide the money up between the four of us and your mother. I have been told that the total value of each shop is around four thousand pounds, including stock, all fixtures and fittings and the buildings, which are owned outright. And of course the goodwill should add a little more value. However, the amount may vary and could be considerably less, depending on whether they are bought as an entire business or individually, as all prices are negotiable. That will give each of us, approximately, twenty thousand pounds, on top of what we have already been left. And, darling, despite the annulment of our marriage, to me you are still my wife and everything that I have is half-yours. I somehow think our father must have found out about our situation, and kept quiet and made arrangements accordingly.'

'Yes, I think that, too. It is too much of a coincidence that he put me in your care, as a stipulation of his Will. But how? And why did he keep quiet about it?'

'We will never know. Maybe he had you watched over, but if so, I think it could have been that he hoped my mother would never find out, as she didn't know you existed. But if that is the case, it was very naive of him. Did he think you would never meet and talk? I think it will all have to remain the mystery it is. Anyway, darling, are you in agreement?'

'Yes, I am. I think it is very generous of you. And it will mean that Mother's, Harold's and Francis's fortunes will be greatly changed. And we can go off to France and forget about them, as that is all I want to do.'

'I am surprised that they agreed to meet us, and at their home, too. I wanted the meeting to be in the solicitor's office, but they were adamant that it should take place at your mother's house.'

'I find that not only strange, but a little frightening.'

'Me, too, but John Wright couldn't change their mind. I wanted him to come along, but he said he couldn't. He said he'd received a message to say that Mags will be there and will act as mediator.'

'Oh? Well, that makes me feel a little better. Though now that Harold is coming into some money, I wonder if he will bow down to her wishes much. We need to be very careful, Cyrus. I don't trust any of them.'

'Maybe we should call it off? Tell them that the meeting is to take place only on our terms.'

'No. I just want it over with. Neither Mother nor Harold is noted for giving in. Let's take a deep breath and get it over with.'

They were asked to attend the drawing room, a room that Flora loved as a child. It was always light and bright and, being across the hall from her father's office, it had French doors that led into the garden. The garden was lovely to look at, with tall pine trees edging the bottom of the long lawn, and the garden dotted with flowerbeds, borders and rockeries. All year round something flowered, giving colour.

Flora felt a moment of nostalgia as she remembered playing with Francis on the lawn. Always it was 'Cowboys and Indians', and he was always the victor of the wars that broke out. At least she had that one good memory.

Mother stood near the fireplace. Harold sat on a high-backed chair, and Francis seemed almost huddled on the sofa, his whole persona giving off the sense that he was in a very cross mood.

Mags greeted Flora with a hug and a kiss on the cheek. Her hands enclosed Flora's and she gave her a look of encouragement.

After she had greeted Cyrus in the same way, she set proceedings off by saying. 'Obviously tensions are high amongst you, but I think we should all be adult about this and approach it in a businesslike manner. We understand, Cyrus, that you wish to discuss with your brothers and Grace a plan that you have to even everything up a little, and to make fair the very unfair and unjust terms of your father's Will.'

To Flora, it felt as if she and Cyrus were on trial, but she understood Mags's approach and welcomed it.

'Yes, I have a proposal to put to you all. Well, it is more than a proposal, as it isn't up for discussion: you either accept it or do not. I will put all the shops up for sale . . .'

No one spoke as Cyrus outlined his plan. Flora was almost lulled into the feeling that all was going to go smoothly, when suddenly her mother lunged at her. 'This is all your doing, you nasty, vile person!'

Stepping back, Flora almost lost her balance. Her mother clawed at her. She saw Cyrus move, but before he could get to her, Mags leapt forward and pushed Flora's mother off her. What Mags said as she did so mystified Flora: 'I know your plan. Well, it isn't going to work.' From where Flora lay on the floor, she saw Harold go towards Cyrus, but his progress was stopped by Mags. 'No! I know the plan, and I won't let it happen.'

'You're as bad as them!' Flora was astonished at this comment from her mother, and hurt for Mags, as Mother continued, 'I don't like you – and never have. My son is only marrying you to get what you have.'

Flora tried to rise from the floor as her mother attacked Mags. But then she watched in horror as her mother teetered backwards, losing her balance.

'Harold, grab Mother . . .'

Harold stood as if made of stone. Flora saw Mags step

345

forward, making an effort to catch Mother, but it was too late. A sickening thud brought a stillness to the room.

Flora stared at her mother's motionless body.

'It – it was an accident. I didn't mean to . . . I – I only tried to push her off me. Oh, God, please don't say that she's— Flora, she attacked me . . .' Mags stuttered.

Flora didn't know how she got to her feet, for it wasn't a conscious act, but she rushed to her mother and, although she felt for a pulse, she knew she wouldn't find one.

A moan came from Francis that Flora likened to a cat that had been trod on. He rose, and his eyes stared from one to the other. 'You're all evil. Evil!'

'Francis . . .'

'Leave him; he's been fit for nothing but the loony bin since he came back from the war. Is Mother. . . ?'

'Mother has gone, Harold. Why? Why did this happen, I – I mean . . . Oh God!'

Harold shot a look at Mags, who was in complete shock. Flora wanted to ask her what plan had been hatched, but none of it mattered now.

Harold took charge. 'We have to deal with this. I'll send someone for the doctor and the police, but we must all stick together and defend Mags. We all saw that it was an accident.'

Flora looked at Mags and was reminded of the time of her friend's rape. Like then, the strong woman that Mags was had gone, and the vulnerable, frightened and shocked woman was back. 'Harold's right – it was an accident, Mags. Don't be afraid; we all saw what happened.'

Although Harold had seemed to be in charge in the immediate aftermath of the accident, when he came back into the room it was as if he was a child again. He went over to their mother's body and sank onto his knees. His sobs were pitiful.

Mags still didn't move. Flora went to her. 'Come on, Mags.'

Cyrus took her other arm. But his concern was for Flora. 'Are you all right, darling. I was so shocked, I couldn't move. The baby . . . ?'

'I'm fine. A bit bruised, but nothing else. Don't worry, darling.'

'What a terrible thing to happen. I feel responsible. I only wanted to put everything right.'

'I know, but—'

'*You* are responsible, you bastard! Bastard by birth and bastard by nature. Coming here, lording it over us all, with handouts of what should rightfully have been ours anyway. And now my mother is dead. It's all your fault – you and that rotten sister of mine are to blame for everything!'

Harold's outburst showed Flora the reality of what had happened. Something in her wanted to find a way of making everything right. She walked towards her brother. 'Let me help you, Harold.'

'The only way you can help me is by staying out of my life.'

'Oh, Harold, how twisted your mind is. You see me as the enemy, but I'm not. I never was. I didn't want to be out-cast—'

'Don't come that story again. I've heard it that many times from you. You gave Mother nothing but pain.'

'You will never see the truth, will you?'

One of the maids entered and showed in the doctor, with a policeman following shortly afterwards, stopping all con-versation. After the doctor had declared Mother dead, the policeman asked what had happened.

Cyrus spoke. 'It was all a terrible accident, but a long story. You see . . .'

When he had finished telling it all, the policeman asked the doctor if the death was consistent with the story told. 'Yes, everything would suggest that she was pushed backwards.'

'And will you examine the woman who is meant to have done this?'

Mags looked up. 'I am the one. I am so sorry. I didn't mean this to happen.'

'Let's begin with your name.'

'Mags . . . Margaret Witherbrook. I – I was trying to defend myself. They—'

'We all saw it. We wouldn't defend her if she had done it on purpose – that is our mother lying there, for God's sake.'

As he ranted, Harold rushed over and sat on the arm of the sofa next to Mags and put his arm around her. Flora saw, from her position next to Mags, that Harold had taken hold of the back of Mags's neck. Not in a way that made her protest, but to Flora it looked as though he was trying to convey something to Mags. A feeling seized her that Harold was trying to control Mags, no doubt stopping her from revealing the plan she had spoken of.

'I am sure, sir, but I have to present all the evidence. Please allow the doctor to examine Miss Witherbrook. I am sure it won't take long. Nothing here looks as though anything different from what you have all said has occurred, but I need to present the coroner with the facts, backed by concrete evidence.'

The doctor declared that the scratches on Mags's face were consistent with her being attacked in the manner described.

'And now you, Miss . . .'

'Harp— I mean, Roford. Miss Flora Roford. I am the daughter of . . . That's my mother!'

'She attacked you first, I understand?'

'Yes.'

The doctor looked closely at Flora's face. He shook his head. 'I've always pitied your situation, Flora. Oh yes, I knew all about it, before what you have all told me today. Your mother was mentally unstable, and was not responsible for all of her actions. I think it might help you to remember that. It's shocking, what has gone on here; and to learn that what your mother always ranted about, concerning your father, was the truth. If I had believed her, I might have treated her differently.'

Flora nodded. His sympathy for her had almost undone her, as she too felt the pity of her mother's life.

'Right, I have all I need. Your mother's body will be taken to the police-station morgue in Chapel End Street, where another doctor will examine it. If everything is as you have told me, then what I have gathered today, and his report, will go to the coroner, who will issue a death certificate. After that, you can make arrangements to have the body collected. I'm very sorry for your loss.' On saying this, the policeman bowed and left.

'I'll just clean your wounds, ladies, then I will go,' the doctor said. 'The hearse shouldn't be long in coming to collect your mother. I'm very sorry for all you have been through. This is a bad blow, coming so soon after you lost your father. I hope you can all sort out everything that you were speaking of.'

This last he directed towards Cyrus, who, since giving all

349

the facts, had sat down on the opposite sofa from where Flora sat, and kept his gaze to the floor.

When the doctor left, Harold stood up. 'Shall we go into another room? My father's office?'

On this, he took hold of Mags's hand and, to Flora, looked as if he almost forced her forward. The feeling Flora had had earlier niggled at her again.

When they reached the office, Harold spoke gently to Mags. 'Sit down, darling. You heard what the doctor said – Mother was unhinged. Please don't think twice about what she said. It isn't the truth; if it was, now that I have the money coming to me to rescue the mill of which I am a full partner, then I would bring our relationship to an end. I can't do that, because I love you.'

Mags sat down and looked up into Harold's face. Her look was one of complete trust. Flora shuddered.

'Now, Cyrus. Can we continue? I know it may sound callous, but I also know that you want an end to this, as I do. I – I'm sorry for my outburst. I was deeply shocked, and have been since I found out about your existence. I hope you understand.' He wiped his face with a large white hand-kerchief.

'Yes, if Flora and Mags are all right with that. But I think Francis should be found and taken care of and, if he is up to it, should be involved in whatever we agree.'

'Of course. I expect he has gone to his room. He isn't well, but he won't accept it, so that makes it difficult for us to get help for him. He has nightmares and behaves in strange ways. M – Mother, was at her wits' end with him.' Harold pulled the bell-cord. 'I'll send a maid after him, as I don't want to leave Mags.'

Mags lowered her head.

350

'Can I get you anything, Mags? Do you want to get some fresh air with me while the men discuss everything? I have already agreed everything that Cyrus plans to do,' Flora said.

'No! I – I mean, it is too cold,' Harold insisted. 'After a shock like you have both had, it won't do you any good to catch a chill. Besides, darling, I don't want to be without you by my side. I need you with me.'

Mags looked lost. But she agreed with Harold.

'I'll pour us all a drink.' As Flora crossed the room to the drinks tray, a maid knocked and entered. Harold instructed her to seek out Mr Francis and ask him to come and join them as soon as he could.

When Francis came in, he reminded Flora of how he was as a boy. Petulant is how she would describe him, but her heart went out to him. Harold, having avoided fighting in the war, had no concept of what war was like. She and Cyrus understood. 'Francis, come and sit down, and try to understand that Cyrus is only trying to help you both,' she urged him.

'Yes, that is all I want to do. I don't want to lord it over you, but I am in the position I am through no fault of my own. I didn't like what happened, regarding the Will, and I would like a chance to try to balance everything a little more fairly. I have already outlined how. I want your agreement to it, and then I will instruct the solicitor who is the executor of the Will to carry out the sale.'

'I can't say that I am in agreement,' Harold said. 'My father, Francis and I built up the business to what it is. We have put in a lot of hard work, and we stood for a lot from our father. Then you come along and take the lot away from us. I think the only fair way is for you to sign the shops over to Francis and me, to do with them as we will.'

In a shaky voice, Francis agreed with this. 'That's how it should have been. What have you ever put into those shops? Nothing! You didn't know they existed, until you and she—'

'That's enough. I won't stand for any of you attacking Flora. You know the truth of what happened. Now, I will only agree to signing the shops over to the three of you: Flora; you, Harold; and you, Francis. And I will appoint an accountant to oversee Flora's interest in the business. And that is my final offer.'

After a moment Harold snapped. 'Then, I for one, will take your first offer. I don't want to be in a partnership with someone who contributes nothing and yet takes a one-third share. Sell the bloody lot and have done with it!'

'Francis?'

'I agree. Flora won't do anything to help run the shops, so why should she have anything of them? She shouldn't even be getting a share of the sale!'

'Flora is owed a lot more than you will ever be. You have been taken care of and given a home. That should have been done for Flora; it was her right, too.'

'I can see that she has fed you a load of lies. She hasn't told you how she haunted our mother's every waking hour, has she?'

'Yes, but she didn't commit the sin that hurt your mother – your father did. Anyway, I don't see the point in discussing this further. I'm disgusted that you, as her brothers, never offered her any protection, or stood up to your parents on her behalf. I want this finished with, and then I want you out of my life. I will never call you my brothers. I am too ashamed to.'

Francis jumped up, but Harold caught hold of him. 'Leave it. We know the truth. Mother always told us, didn't she? We'll have the last laugh. Mother's Will leaves every-thing to us. She showed it to me. So, that means we have the house, as well as what Father left us, and our share of the sale of the shops, so I think we have done very well in the end.'

'Harold, you can't hurt me,' Flora insisted. 'I bear a deep hurt that nothing you can do will ever surpass. I want nothing of Mother's. I'm proud of Cyrus, but I can never be proud of either of you. Cyrus, shall we leave?'

'Yes, I will get everything drawn up as soon as I can. You will be hearing from John Wright in due course.'

As they turned to leave, Mags called out Flora's name. Flora turned to see Harold pulling her roughly back into her chair. She went over to Mags and knelt beside her. 'Mags, don't go through with this, please don't.'

'I – I need to tell you—'

'Mags, for Christ's sake!'

Despite this from Harold, Mags continued, 'I need to tell you, Flora, not to lose touch. You have my address.'

Flora somehow knew that wasn't what Mags had intended to say. She was sure now that a plan had been hatched to bring about something bad to Cyrus, but that Mags had intervened and it had all gone horribly wrong. She decided that, whatever it was, it was best left now. She patted Mags's hand. 'I'll write. Don't worry about it all – I understand. Take care.'

As they left, Flora had the feeling that she might never see Mags again. What had happened today had placed Mags firmly in Harold's clutches. But she decided that she would let Mags know where she was in France, and that she would always be there for her.

This thought brought Ella into her mind. She had been

negligent, where Ella was concerned. The moment they were settled in France, she'd write to the address she had for Ella, so that she knew where to contact Flora, if she wanted to. She hoped Ella did, for although time had changed her, she still thought of Ella and Mags as her sisters.

Chapter Thirty-Three

Flora felt no grief for the passing of her parents. She had grieved for them a long time ago. But agony encased her days and nights for the loss of her little Alice, and this was compounded by separation from her beloved Cyrus, when she needed him more than she had ever done.

They dared not meet often and, when they did, it was usually in the company of the solicitor. They feared the harm that Harold might do to them. He knew that they were seeing each other, as they had to, to sort through the legal tangles of the Will; but they both longed for some private time together.

Three weeks had passed since the day her mother had died. There were to be no further investigations. From the medical reports and the statements given by them all, the coroner had concluded that Grace's death had been accidental, during a family argument, and had been contributed to by the deceased's own actions. Flora hadn't been invited to the funeral, and only knew it had taken place through a notification in the paper.

And now as she stood in her kitchen – the place of so

much love, happiness and, yes, deeply ingrained hurt – she stared at the box on the table in front of her. It had been found inside one of the many safe-deposit boxes left by her father. Most had contained either cash, which he hadn't declared in his tax returns, or share certificates in various names, and the address of the broker who would access these and sell them for Cyrus. One box had been for her, and another for Olivia.

The letter inside the box lay on top of a bundle of notes that amounted to one thousand pounds, and a beautiful diamond necklace, earrings and bracelet set.

Reading the letter reduced her to tears. Not of sadness, but of anger and frustration with a man who had cast her out for the sake of his own peace. A peace he sought through revenge on his deathbed:

My dearest Flora,

By now you will have had the day that I planned for you – the reading of my Will. I will rest in peace, knowing that your mother will hear the truth of my feelings and see that I hadn't forgotten you. It will hurt her even more that I linked you with my eldest son. I need to hurt her. She has inflicted so much pain on me.

I know that my son's existence will have come as a surprise to you, but he was born of my great love for his mother, Olivia, whom you will also meet.

Flora sighed. *Oh, the webs we weave. How shocked you must have been, Father, to hear that Cyrus and I knew each other more than you could ever dream we would. A shock that finally killed you.*

I could not go so far as to leave you something in my Will, not publicly, as I didn't want to inflict more pain on you, because you would have suffered at the hands of your brothers and your mother, as a way of getting back at me.

And so I chose a channel for my love for you, through the son who doesn't know me, or you or your brothers, but most importantly hasn't been influenced against you by the wickedness of your mother.

I haven't been able to prepare you or him, or his mother, as I could not admit your existence to my beloved Olivia. She has always believed that I was living in name only within my marriage, as divorce wasn't possible for me. But the truth is that I did love your mother, but she eroded that love over the years. All this is her fault. If she had been a loving wife, I would not have strayed.

Flora lifted her eyes heavenwards. *In that lay the basis of your weak personality: that you blame everyone for your own failings. Your words show that you didn't grasp how much you would hurt Olivia – and did hurt her – when she found out about me. The hurt at that time was doubled, as she also found out about my dear nanny, Aunt Pru, and how badly you served her.* The letter went on in the same vein:

But let me address my treatment of you, as you are now hearing the truth about your mother. She black-mailed me into treating you the way I did. She would have ruined me, and inflicted hurt on my beloved Olivia. My final casting you out was your own fault, as you well know.

357

A tear plopped onto Flora's cheek. *So, your own pride and survival meant more to you than me? As did saving Olivia pain?* 'I WAS JUST A CHILD . . . A CHILD. AND YOU WERE MY FATHER! YOU SACRIFICED ME!' The words screamed from her. Her hand shook the letter in the air. All the pain that her father had made her suffer came from her, as she wailed and ranted at him, screaming the words she would have liked to have said to him in life.

Calming herself, Flora thought that she could almost hear Aunt Pru: *Don't worry about what you can't change, lass.* And she knew that none of what was upsetting her could ever be changed. Taking a deep breath, she read the final paragraphs:

> *But I forgave you, as my actions now have shown. The necklace set I bought on your twenty-fifth birthday. As I could not give it to you, I placed it in this box for you to receive after my death, when you will know the extent of my love for you, which I hope you now realize, from the actions I have taken.*
>
> *The money is in the hope that you meet someone to love, and is to fund your wedding day, as it is a father's duty to pay for such an occasion. If you are already married by the time you get this, then have a second honeymoon on me.*

Reading the last lines of the letter, Flora felt strangely released from a burden she'd carried all her life – the burden of her father's sin.

> *And so, my darling daughter, with all the hurt laid to rest, I hope that you have a happy life, safe in the*

knowledge that I loved you very much and was always
very proud of how you rose to the challenge of the war.
    Your loving father x

The kind of love George Roford gave wasn't the kind of love that she, or anyone, needed. Flora knew that now. It was manipulative and self-centred. He and Mother had deserved each other.

Closing the box, she decided that she would never wear the necklace set. Now that she was secure in her finances, she would give it to the Salvation Army to auction, to raise funds for them. There was still so much of the aftermath of war to address: homeless people, invalided men who couldn't work, and families with no man to care for them. Flora had always wanted to help them in some way, but had ended up needing the same help they did. And, before she left for France, she would give the thousand pounds to the Red Cross. *That is my goodbye to you, George Roford, because even in your final act of making sure I was taken care of, you haven't redeemed yourself.*

Going to the sink that stood under the window, Flora scooped some water from the bucket standing on the draining board, which she had collected rainwater in, and swilled her face with it. As she dried herself, the door next to the kitchen sink opened.

'Can I come in, Flora, love? I've brought half of the pie I baked. I thought that you and Freddy would enjoy it. I can't stop making enough food for two.'

Flora smiled. She knew this was an excuse. Mrs Larch, like the rest of her neighbours, liked to make sure she ate. They didn't know that her circumstances had changed. She must think of a way that she could thank them, before she left.

'How are you, love? I can see your pain. Only none of us have liked to bother you too much.'

'You've all been wonderful. I'm all right. Getting through each hour as best I can. As you know, it's the only way.'

'It is, but you've 'ad more on your plate than most. I – I, well, I've brought the *Evening News* in with me. There's a lot of people shocked by the latest 'appening. We can't believe it, of you and Cyrus, so I've been asked to . . . Look, we don't want to 'urt you, love. We know as there's a mistake 'appened somewhere along the line, but . . .'

Flora's heart missed a beat. 'What is it, Mrs Larch? Have you read something in the paper?'

'I 'ave. And but for you and Pru, I wouldn't 'ave been able to, a few months ago. Though I dare say as Mrs Harper would 'ave brought it to our attention. Anyway, there's an article as says that you and Cyrus—'

'We didn't know. Please believe me. We weren't charged, because the police knew our story to be true. We only found out on the day that Alice died. Our marriage has been annulled.'

'Oh, poor love. I thought it would be something like that, only the paper indicates as you knew and still went ahead.'

Flora took the paper and scanned the short piece about herself and Cyrus: 'Couple Found Out in Incestuous Marriage . . .' The wording was very clever, in that it indicated that their sources had informed them that the couple lied their way out of being prosecuted and jailed; and yet there was nothing in the article that they could be sued over:

Court records show that the marriage has been annulled and that the couple are not ever to live together again.

360

*However, our source tells us that they are still close –
closer than a brother and sister would normally be
expected to be.*

Harold! His jealousy of Cyrus knew no bounds. *So, dear
brother, you choose revenge. Well, two can play that game!*

'By the looks of your face, love, I reckon as the so-called
"source" had better watch out.'

Flora smiled at this. 'The important thing is that you, and
everyone, believe me. Sit down, Mrs Larch, I'll make a cup
of tea and then tell you how it all happened.'

'It's none of mine or anyone else's business, love. I just
wanted to 'ear from you that it weren't true.'

'I know. But I want you to hear, as further things have
happened that will take me away from you, and I haven't
thanked you or any of the others for the help given to me
over the terrible time of Alice's passing, and . . . well, the
food and coal and everything. I am so grateful. I – I have
been through so much that I have just been accepting, and
not letting you all know how grateful I am. You have all kept
me and Freddy fed and warm. I love you all.'

'And we love you. All of us. It broke our hearts to see all
that landed on your doorstep. You've done so much for us
all. We're proud to 'ave you as one of us.'

'Thank you. That means a lot to me. Tell me how you've
been, while I make the tea, and then I want to tell you my
story.'

By the time she had finished, Mrs Larch was in tears. ''Ow
can your family treat you in that way? They ain't fit to have
kids. If only . . . Well, "if onlys" don't 'elp, but I would 'ave
loved a daughter like you. I reckon as Pru were the lucky
one.'

'No, I was lucky to have Aunt Pru. She was a wonderful nanny and took care of me all of my life, until she died.'

'I reckon as she's still there for you, me darling. Come 'ere, let me give you a cuddle.'

Flora hadn't expected this, but welcomed it. It felt good to be held by someone who loved her.

'You won't forget us, will you, love?'

'No. I will never forget you.' She hadn't told Mrs Larch that Cyrus was going to France with her, only that she needed a new beginning for herself and Freddy and her unborn child, and that, as she spoke French, she wanted to go back there, where no one who wished her harm could reach her. It felt bad not to tell the truth, but Mrs Larch and all of her neighbours were what she termed 'straight as dye' and wouldn't be able to forgive such a sin. She couldn't bear for them to think badly of her.

'It must be a wrench, leaving Alice's resting place, though you'll take Alice with you, as those we have lost live inside us each time we think of them. I talk to my Bert all the time. Look, I'll tell you what I'll do. I'll organize a team of us that will keep the little one's resting place tidy for you. 'Ow's that, eh?'

Flora went back into Mrs Larch's arms and held her close. Her emotions were so wrecked that she found she was dried of tears, but her heart bled just the same. 'Thank you. Thank you so much.'

Something that had occurred to her in the last few days now came to her mind. Knowing that, in this area, they were averse to immigrants moving in, Flora thought she would broach the subject. Coming out of Mrs Larch's embrace, she looked her in the face, wanting to read her reaction. 'There is something I wanted to tell you. It is an idea I have had, to thank someone who has been a dear friend to me since I was a child. I know you have all seen her coming and going, but how would you feel if she and her family lived in this house?'

'You're talking about that Jamaican woman, aren't you? Rowena?'

So far, no disdain. 'Yes. She lives in a squalor not of her own making. She is a good housewife, but her house is damp, and some of her neighbours are not fussy about what they throw in the streets. There is no proper sanitation in her area, and I fear for her health. And so I would dearly love to give her this house, but I don't want her – or any of you – to be unhappy.' Flora held her breath. This had been the most difficult conversation, as it felt as though she was classing her dear Rowena as a second-class citizen, who needed permission to live freely where she wanted to. But it wasn't like that; she just wanted everything to be all right for Rowena, if she went ahead with her plans. There was so much prejudice in certain areas of London.

'Well, I can speak for myself, and I would love to 'ave her 'ere. Me and her 'ave chatted on many an occasion, and I find her a lovely, jolly person. I'll see to it that she's treated right.'

'Oh, thank you. Thank you so much. And something else: Rowena can play a wonderful honky-tonk piano.'

'That settles it then. We've missed our singalongs.' Flora found herself hugged again. 'We're all going to miss you, love.'

With this, Mrs Larch went out of the door. Flora stood still for a moment. Her heart was heavy. She would miss Mrs Larch and all of her neighbours. How she wished she could stay amongst them. But the pull to be with her Cyrus was too strong, even though it might mean eternal damnation for them both. In life, they had to be together and live as husband and wife.

Chapter Thirty-Four

Cyrus had bought a car. A lovely deep-maroon Wolseley. He'd picked Flora up from where she'd waited, three miles from her home, in a little cafe they both knew. They hadn't driven long, before Flora mentioned the article and what was on her mind.

'Cyrus, I don't want Harold to have a share of the sale. I am sure it is he who has sold our story to the newspapers. Last night I had mud thrown at my window. Mrs Larch heard the noise and chased the boys off, but it was very frightening. I am convinced it was Harold who informed the paper.'

'Darling, you are speaking out of temper and are not being rational. If we cut Harold out, it will make him want to seek revenge even more. It is a bitter pill, but we have to swallow it. I really want you to think about the consequences for us. We are powerless – we intend to break the law of the land, and of God. If Harold ever found out, he would crucify us with that knowledge.'

'I know you are right, my darling, but I am angry and do want to punish him.'

'Isn't that what has been wrong in your family for so long? This need to punish?'

Flora was mortified at this comment. She stared at Cyrus. 'How dare you! I – I cannot forgive you comparing me to them.'

'Oh, Flora, you look even more beautiful when you are angry. I should make you so more often.'

'It isn't a joke, Cyrus. That hurt me.'

'I know, and it was meant to. Well, not hurt you, but wake you up to the fact that you are behaving exactly as they do: wanting revenge, wanting to punish. I don't like it, and I don't want you even to think like that.'

Flora felt her cheeks colour with shame. 'I'm sorry. You're right. But you're one of us, don't you ever feel those traits in you?'

'Now you have hurt *me*. Flora, do you look at me and see a brother?'

'No! No, I see the man I love – the man I want to spend the rest of my life with. My husband. Oh, why are we bickering? We never used to talk like this to each other. I love you beyond all things, Cyrus. I miss you so much. I miss lying with you, being held by you, kissed and—'

'My darling. We are under a lot of pressure. We shouldn't take it out on each other. If only I could hold you . . . Come on, darling, let's go inside. The sooner we have everything to do with your father's Will sorted out, the better everything will be for us.'

They had reached the office of John Henry Wright, Solicitors. They walked up the steps to the entrance without speaking or allowing their bodies to touch. And yet Flora wanted so much to take Cyrus in her arms. To run with him to a place of safety and have him take and give of himself to her. Sighing, she followed him inside.

'Good morning, both. Well, today is a good day, as I believe everything is ready to be finalized. A buyer has been found for the shops! He has offered a little below the market value, and has graded the shops according to where they are situated and the takings of each one. He has come up with an average figure of three thousand pounds per shop. What do you think?'

'No, we won't take that.'

'But, Cyrus, it will mean . . . I mean, I think it is a fair offer for someone to make who is proposing to take all of the shops off our – your – hands.'

'It is a first offer. A tentative one. Please go back to the prospective buyer and ask for three and a half thousand, on average. Which means he is getting the shops for five hundred pounds each below the true value, and that is to include all stock. I don't want to be bothered with inventories, and it comes with the stipulation that the deal is sealed within a week.'

'A very good move, if I may say so. I can send a runner now to my agent, as the buyer is waiting with him. I think you will get what you have asked for because, like you, I think the first offer was given in a lot of hope, but not much faith.'

After the runner had been instructed, Cyrus asked, 'How quickly can my part of the deal be concluded? I need to complete all of the business to do with the Will as soon as possible.'

'My agent has a contract already drafted. If the offer is accepted, the figure will be added to it, along with wording that will state that the price includes everything. Once you sign that, I can do the rest. Your brothers have given me their bank-account details for their shares, which you so generously are gifting to them. I, of course, have your details, Cyrus. But what about your share, Miss Roford?'

Flora wanted to say that it could go into Cyrus's account, but knew that she couldn't. She gave the name of her bank and the details.

'Very well, today should conclude our business. It has been a pleasure working with you, Cyrus, and I hope that you will engage my services in the future, maybe under better circumstances.'

'I most certainly will, for you have made a difficult job easy. Now that you have Miss Roford's details, will you please arrange for an allowance to be paid to her? I will put the money that her father stipulated, in his further instructions to me, into a trust fund, and as you are administering the other trust funds that he set up, I would like you to handle that one, too. Also, I would like you to send all communications to me to this address. It is a friend of mine, and I am willing to sign anything that you need, in order to authorize my dealings with you to go through him. Always mark them "Private and confidential", as I don't want him to read anything, but I am going to be travelling and he will know where my next port of call is, to enable me to receive post. I have instructed my bank, and any other party who may wish to contact me, that they are to do so through you. I know that I can rely on your strict confidence. And an annual billing arrangement for your services would suit me, if it does you?'

'I will be honoured to act for you. And the annual payment is in order, too. Thank you. While we wait, I will get my clerk to draft that into a contract between us. My fee is thirty-five pounds a year, plus any postage costs or out-of-pocket expenses incurred. I will bill you each year, as the fee for my services so far will be payable once you sign the contract that we are expecting today.'

By the time they left the solicitor's office, Flora was full of admiration for her Cyrus. He'd thought of everything, and now it was all completed. Happiness settled in her. Soon they would be together again.

'Cyrus, how do I put my house in Rowena's name?'

'I don't think you should, darling. I think you should draw up a contract between you both, which will be just as legally binding as using a solicitor, but more confidential. It should give her and her husband permission to live in your house for life, rent-free, but on the death of them both – or at such time as they don't need it – it reverts to you. It will be an insurance policy for our future, if our new venture should fail.'

'Venture? I thought we would have enough money just to live out there in France.'

'We do, but what kind of legacy is that for our children? We need to build them a new future in France, and one that will sustain them after we have gone. We need to show them that life is about working for what they need. We have tried our best in that field, but now we have a chance to do more.'

'What have you in mind?'

'A vineyard. I have been reading about growing grapes for wine and the regions that are best for this, and how the wine is made.'

'It sounds very difficult, but exciting. But what about our music?'

'We will find a way of incorporating that into our lives.

Once we make friends, we can hold concerts. But if we devote our lives to music, it may put us in the public eye, and we don't want that. Sadly, the dream we share of owning our own theatre and writing musical plays, and putting them into production, is one dream we have to forgo, for the sake of never being discovered.'

'Yes, I can see that. Well, we can entertain each other with our music, and we will make wine-making our new dream. Oh, Cyrus, I can't wait; when can we go?'

'I have to go first, to find us somewhere to live and—'

'No! I'm not going to be separated from you again, please, Cyrus. Besides, my pregnancy is progressing and there may come a time when I can't travel, and then the baby is too young and . . . No, please. I can't go through all of that alone. I have no one but Rowena and my neighbours now. I need to be with you.'

'Oh, my darling, I hadn't thought of that.'

They sat in a tea shop, drinking tea, and had ordered a cake each. Under the table she felt Cyrus touch her leg with his. His mouth moved and silently spoke the words, 'I love you.'

Aloud he said, 'What you have said changes everything. I will go into Thomas Cook and ask them to book our whole journey from here to the south-west of France, including hotels to stay in on the way. We will drive over in my new car.' His eyebrows went up and his lips curled in an impish smile.

'Ha, you sound like a little boy with a new toy.'

'That's what it feels like to me. I could pinch myself. I know I have dealt with everything in a businesslike manner, and as if doing so was an everyday thing to me, but inside I do feel like a child at Christmas-time, eager to open the next present. I've always wanted a Wolseley car, and to think that I now have one is unbelievable.'

Under the table she sought his hand and held it tightly, never wanting to let it go ever again.

'Darling, couldn't we go sooner than all that will take? Couldn't we get a train to Dover and stay in a hotel together there, where no one knows us, and arrange everything through Thomas Cook down there? I'm sure they will have a branch there. Please agree, Cyrus, I am desperate to be with you. The nights are long on my own, and my grief eats into me.'

'Oh, my darling Flora. I have been so busy that I haven't had time to think about . . . No, that isn't true. I haven't let myself think about our loss. Or how you are coping. I'm so sorry. I couldn't face the pain.'

'It's all right, I understand. I have tried to block it all out, too. But I can't do it. It crowds me during my long hours alone.'

'Then it must come to an end. We will do as you say. I cannot see anything that could stop us. Mother has left for her sister's; her finances were sorted out very quickly, as they were nothing to do with the main body of the estate, but were set up separately. She is keeping her apartment, even though it hurts her to think how callous the man she loved was, in letting her think the apartment he'd found for her and me was rented from an agency. And she will visit us when we are settled. So that just leaves your house. How soon can you sort Rowena out and be ready?'

'Rowena is at my house now, taking care of Freddy. I can write out the contract for her, and she will help me pack my clothes.' She told him how the neighbours were going to look after Alice's grave. 'And they will tidy Pru's grave, too.

371

I couldn't refuse the neighbours. Rowena wanted to do it, but she understands and she will be part of the group undertaking the work.'

'It will be a wrench leaving our little Alice.' Cyrus's eyes suddenly filled with tears.

Flora told him what Mrs Larch had said. 'Wherever we are, Alice will be with us in our hearts, and I'll pack her knitted doll that she loved, to take with us.'

'I can't bear it, Flora . . .' His tears flowed freely.

When they walked outside, the wind whipped around them. Cyrus put his arm round Flora and pulled her to him. 'Cyrus, no – not in public.'

'I don't care; if we are seen, I am merely protecting you from the wind, as would be natural. Look, there's a flower stall: shall we buy some flowers and take them to Alice and Pru? It might be the last time we can do so for a long time.'

They stood by Alice's grave. Neither spoke. Cyrus's tears flowed freely once more, but Flora was empty of tears, though full to the brim with pain. She wanted to scream the feeling out of her and pound the earth with her fist, begging it to give her daughter back to her. Her arms ached to cuddle her darling Alice.

Cyrus pulled her into his body once more. He shook with sobs. Together they laid the flowers on the diminishing mound of earth. 'What will we do about marking the grave, darling? Look over there: there is a little boy's grave with an angel statue on it. I'd like something like that for Alice.'

'I would, too, Cyrus; and one of those oval-shaped stones for Pru. And something else I would like to do: I'd like to detour to Dieppe and visit Freddy's grave, and see the area, now that there is peace there. I think that will rest my mind of all the horrible images that haunt me.'

'Yes, we can do that. Let's get you home, darling. I've seen a stonemason's shop nearby, so I'll go in and arrange the headstones. What would you like inscribed on Pru's?'

'After her name and details, which I will write down for you, I would like: "A woman who cared". That's all, as it sums up Aunt Pru. For Alice: "A child loved dearly, now with Jesus and safe from pain".' Saying the words gave Flora some comfort.

'That's lovely. I would add: "A child loved dearly by her mummy and daddy and brother Freddy, and missed every day".'

Flora thought this nice, but far too long; but, as her daddy, Cyrus had a right to have what he wanted, too. And it was all so true. Alice was missed so very much.

Chapter Thirty-Five

'You sure are full of surprises, Missy! My, you mean it? Me and my old man can move into this lovely house and stay forever?'

'I mean it, Rowena. I'm going away. I can't tell you where, because I don't know yet, but it is going to be in France. I just haven't settled on where in France. No one must know. Not a soul. I am only telling my closest friends, of which you are one. I will miss you, Rowena.'

'I'm going to be missing you, too. But I hope as you're taking the lovely Cyrus with you. You two are made to be together.'

Thankfully, before she could answer, a knock on the front door interrupted them. 'I'll get it, honey, you have work to do. It'll probably be someone trying to sell something.'

'Thank you, Rowena. I'll pop upstairs and make a start. Is Freddy asleep?'

'He is – he's been one little monkey today.'

Reaching the landing, Flora stopped in her progress towards her bedroom, as a familiar voice came to her.

'What are you doing in my sister's house, black woman?'

Harold?

'And who are you to ask me that? And, for your information, I know I'm black – you don't need to tell me that I am, Mister.'

'Step aside, you filthy negress.'

'I'm as clean as the day I was born, Mister. And I ain't stepping aside until I knows who you are and what your business is here.'

'It's all right, Rowena, it's my brother. Let him in.'

'Oh, one of them as cast you out? Well, that ain't nothing to be proud of, and none of us black folk would do such a thing.'

'Rowena, Freddy is crying – please go to him, love. I'll take my brother through to the kitchen.'

'The kitchen! Hasn't this awful place got a withdrawing room?'

'I have a front room, but I wouldn't allow you to step inside it, Harold, as it is where my daughter died, and you would taint her memory with your presence.'

'Charming! I see your pregnancy is showing. Good God, Flora, you should be ashamed of yourself. With your own brother! Disgusting.'

'You have done all you can to me on that score, Harold, so there is nothing more you can hurt me with. I know you gave the story to the paper, thinking that I would be hounded out. Well, it didn't happen. My neighbours are good people, and they believed me when I told them the truth of Cyrus and me not knowing. And the masses didn't take up the story, so it didn't go further than London. A failed operation, I would say.'

'Worth a try. I would do anything to bring you and that so-called "brother" of ours to your knees.'

'We know that.'

'I know you are still seeing him.'

'I have to. He is my guardian, so to speak, as Father made him so.'

'You know what I mean.'

'You are mistaken, and if that is all you have come for, I think you should leave.'

'It isn't. We are selling the parents' house. And there is the question of Francis. His mental state is worsening and, as his sister, you should take responsibility for him. I want to bring him and his things here – you must have room.'

'That's not possible, Harold. Did Mother leave a Will?'

'I told you that she did, and there was nothing for you; you aren't even mentioned.'

'I didn't expect to be. Is Francis joint beneficiary?'

'Of course, why?'

'And has he agreed to the sale, knowing that he will be homeless? Won't he have enough to buy himself a place, or enough to rent somewhere?'

'He is too ill for that. And I have power of attorney over him, so I can sell the house without his say-so. You don't know what he has been like, since he came home from war. He has shaking and screaming fits. He runs around naked in the garden. He digs trenches; he wakes the household at night with his nightmares. The staff have coped admirably with it all. But, after the sale, I am going north to live, and then Mags and I will be married. I can't take Francis with me. You have to have him.'

Flora was shocked to hear just how bad Francis's condition was, as she hadn't considered it. But she couldn't take care of him. She couldn't give up her plans for him. None

376

of them could ask that of her. 'I refuse. You will have to find a home for him.'

'You callous bitch! This is your brother you are talking about.'

'Neither of you has been a brother to me for a long time, and I owe you nothing. Nothing! Do you hear me? I don't care if I never see either of you again.'

To her surprise, Harold slumped into the chair next to the fire. 'How did it come to this, Flora? How did we let our parents divide us in this way?'

'Because you wanted it all. You are like Father, and you sacrificed our relationship to make up to Mother and Father. But it didn't happen the way you planned it, and now you are jealous of me, and of Cyrus; and you are plotting all the time to wreak revenge on us. It has all gone sour for you. If I had my way, I wouldn't give you what Cyrus is planning to.'

'And you are all Mother said you were. I offer you an olive branch, and you shove it right back in my face. Mags is going to be very upset. She hoped we could be friends, but she just doesn't know you.'

The realization came to Flora that, from the moment Harold had sat down, he'd decided on different tactics. He'd tried the 'I'm really a loving brother' act before and hadn't meant it, and it wasn't going to work this time.

'I doubt that's true. Mags knows me far better than you do. Anyway, what about Francis – will you put him in a home? There are some good private ones for officers who are impaired, physically or mentally, due to their war service. He can afford to pay for himself, and he will be much better cared for by professionals than by me, here.'

'I've tried that, but he refuses. Would you at least come and talk to him? He may listen to you.'

Flora was afraid to do this. Afraid that she would weaken, if faced with Francis's plight. Going to France was the only hope she and Cyrus had. She had to resist this emotional blackmail. But her heart ruled her head and, reluctantly, she arranged for Rowena to stay a little longer, and donned her coat and went with Harold.

'Is Mags still at the house?'

'No, she has gone home. She is very upset and fragile over what happened, and I am anxious to get to her.'

'Poor Mags; in some ways she is very strong, but in others she can become almost childlike.'

'Has this happened before? You seem to know a lot about how she is feeling.'

'We went through a lot together, that's all; there were some very bad situations, and we all had breakdowns at times.'

Flora stared out of the window of the car, willing herself to be strong. She had to resist, no matter how much Francis needed her. He had to be persuaded to go into a home, if he was as ill as Harold described; it was the only way.

Flames lit the night as if it were day, as they turned into the street where the house stood. 'Harold, that's our house. Oh God, it's on fire!'

'That bloody idiot! Christ, I didn't believe he'd do it.'

'What do you mean – Francis? Did he threaten to do this?'

'Yes, the stupid bugger. Francis said that rather than sell the only home he had, he would burn it to the ground.'

'You pig, Harold! You forced him. He was of sound

enough mind to refuse to sell. How could you? No wonder his condition has worsened. Well, Francis has had the last laugh.'

'Only if he isn't in the house. If he is, then I will laugh all the way to the bank, with Mother's trust fund and the insurance money – and no more mad Francis to bother me.'

'You're vile. Vile! I'm ashamed to be related to you.'

Harold laughed as he pulled up outside the house. 'Lovely blaze – well done, Francis. Good job.'

As they got out of the car Flora screamed at him, 'For God's sake, we have to check if Francis is safe, and get someone to go for the firefighters. And what if the staff are trapped? This isn't about you and your gains. People could die! Francis could—'

'Oh God, no . . . I hadn't thought. Susan! No, not my darling Susan!'

Flora felt as if she would collapse. History was repeating itself. The saying 'like father, like son' was coming true. She'd been sure Susan and Harold were continuing their relationship, and now she knew they were. And his mistress meant more to him than the safety of his own brother. A sick feeling took hold of her. She wanted to claw at Harold, to make him realize the path he was taking and how much pain it would cause, but she had no time to deal with that now.

'Get back into your car and go for the firefighters, Harold. Quickly!'

A distant clanging of bells stopped him. 'Sounds like someone already did that. I'll go round the back to see if anyone got out.'

Flora followed him, the heat from the burning inferno scorching her face.

'Oh, Master Harold and Miss Flora. Oh, thank God!'

'Cook, is there anyone in the house?'

'M – Master Francis, he – he . . . Oh God, he smashed things, then he set fire to the furniture, and it all went up so quickly. I – I tried to stop him, but it was no use. I screamed to everyone to get out, but no one has come out this way, and I couldn't get back in. I sent the gardener's boy running for the firefighters.'

Flora took hold of Cook and held her shaking body to her. She couldn't speak to try and comfort her, as her own fear was strangling her.

But Harold's reaction was what she would expect. 'Never mind all of that: where is Susan?'

'I – I don't know.'

Anger gave Flora her strength back. 'There's more than just Susan to worry about, Harold. Cook, how many staff were there in—'

Screams of 'Help me. Help, I'm up here!' stopped Flora from saying any more. Susan appeared at an upstairs window. 'Help me, Harold. Help me!'

Her desperate plea spurred Flora into action. 'Get the ladder from the garage, Harold – hurry.'

'What? No . . . no, wait, the bells are louder now; the firefighters will be here any moment. Leave it to them.'

'That may be too late. Look at the flames around Susan. Please, Harold, I'm not asking you to go up to her. I'll do that – just fetch the ladder!'

To Flora's despair, her cowardly brother stared back at her, and she realized that his fear had frozen him and she'd have to take charge. 'Cook, come with me. Come on! We can carry the ladder between us.'

Thankfully, Harold had left the garage door open. And as it was a separate building from the house, it wasn't in danger of catching fire. The inside of the garage was lit by the flames, helping them to locate the ladder quickly.

'You grab that end, Cook, and I'll get the other.'

When they reached the house, Susan could no longer be seen.

'Oh no. Help us, Harold, help us.' Still Harold didn't move. 'We'll have to do it ourselves, Cook. Put the ladder on the ground, then we'll get hold of the middle section and lift it into place. That's it; now, hold it steady while I go up.'

'No. Please don't, Miss Flora. Harold should do it. You may harm yourself, or your baby.'

Flora didn't have time to try to persuade Harold, but lifted her skirt, thanking God for the new fashion of shorter clothes, and headed up the ladder. The heat was unbearable. Smoke stung her eyes and made her cough, but she wouldn't give up. 'Susan? Susan, can you hear me? I have a ladder. Come on, Susan – please make a last effort. Please.'

Susan's head appeared, her coughs pitiful to hear.

'Climb out. I'll steady your footing, then I'll stay behind you to guide you down. You can do it, Susan. You can!' Susan sat on the ledge and swung one foot out. 'Turn around, as you have to come down backwards – that's right, good girl.'

Praying that Cook could hold the ladder steady, Flora guided Susan's foot down to a rung.

'That's it, Susan. Now the other one; you can put your weight on this foot, as you're on a rung of the ladder.' Susan managed to get her other leg out. 'Now, I'll lift your foot and put it on the next rung. This foot that I am tapping now.'

Three rungs had been negotiated when the ladder slipped. Flora screamed out, 'Ha . . . rold, help us!' The ladder slipped again. Susan screamed. 'Hold on, Susan, but keep still.' The clanging of bells now drowned Flora's words. 'Oh, thank God!'

The ladder slipped again, this time more than it had done previously. Instinctively, Flora put her hand out and grabbed at the ivy clinging to the wall. It came with her, but then stopped. She clung on, praying to the God she had long thought had forsaken her.

'Grab the ivy, Susan. It needs the strength of us both to hold the ladder still.'

'I can't. I can't take my hands off or I'll fall.'

Below them, Flora could see firefighters running towards the ladder. But too late, for the weight of Susan was too much for her to stop the slide. Flora's grip on the ivy loosened and the ground came hurtling towards her. Her scream merged with the blackness that seized her.

Chapter Thirty-Six

From a distance a voice called, 'Open your eyes, Miss. You're all right. We caught you. You fainted. We've got the young woman you were helping. She's badly burned, but hopefully she'll make it. Well done, you're a very brave young woman.'

'M – my baby.'

'Is your baby inside the 'ouse, darlin'?' This was another voice. Flora patted her stomach.

'Oh dear, she's in the family way. Let's get her to the ambulance. Don't you worry, I'm sure everything will be all right.'

The other man spoke then. 'In my book, though you were foolish to put yourself and your baby in jeopardy, you're a 'ero, Miss. A true 'ero.'

'Sh – she saved lives in the war, Officer. She's one of the bravest women on earth.'

Dear Cook.

'Is she going to be all right?'

'She is, love; now move yourself. Let's get her into the ambulance.'

Showing no concern for her, Harold shouted, 'Officer, there are others in the house, and one of them is my brother.'

'I'm sorry, sir, there's nothing that can be done for anyone in there. My officers will concentrate on bringing the fire under control.'

Harold's protest was meant to show concern, but to Flora it was sickening, as she knew how hollow his pleas were.

Poor Francis. Harold knew you had threatened this action, and probably took himself out of the way to give you a chance to do it. Using me as an excuse for why he was out.

Harold came into Flora's view. 'Officer, the girl who's burned – can I go with her to the hospital? She needs me.'

In that instant Flora felt rage enter her. A noise came from her, rasping her sore throat and giving her the taste of the smoke she'd inhaled. 'I HATE YOU!'

Harold's face registered his shock. *Is he so self-centred that he can't see what he does to others?*

'Now then, don't go upsetting yourself. I don't know what has 'appened between you and this gentleman, but, darlin', you have to think of your unborn child. He's had a jolt and must be scared stiff. He don't want his mother giving in and sending bad feelings through him, now does he, darlin'?'

This sounded strange to Flora – that a man should think like that.

'I'm from a big family, and me sisters are always 'aving kids. Me ma gets on at them if they don't keep a 'appy disposition; she says as the baby can sense it. She should know: she birthed fourteen.'

Flora felt safe with this man and didn't want him to leave

her. He was right, there would be time enough to live without Harold in her life, and to grieve for Francis. At least the Francis that she remembered as a child. Reaching down to her stomach, she gently massaged her bump. In doing so, she hoped she conveyed that everything was fine.

As they lifted her onto a stretcher, she looked over at Harold once more. Still he stared at her as if she'd gone mad. And although she didn't want to speak to him, she had no choice. 'If you never do anything else for me in your life – and, God knows, I don't ever want you to – will you do one thing for me? Please go to the St Pancras Hotel and tell Cyrus what has happened. Harold, please, I beg of you.'

'Still hankering after him, are you, Sis? Anyway, I wouldn't if I could. But in any case, I'm going to the hospital with Susan – she needs me more than you do.'

'Harold!'

'Don't you worry, love. I'll get the ambulance driver to get a message to Cyrus for you. Is he your man?'

'No! He's not her "man", he's her brother, who—'

'Harold!'

'Oh, as you please. I wouldn't want anyone to know, either.'

Thankfully, the officer didn't respond to this, but inside, Flora wished with all her heart that it had been Harold who'd died in the fire, and vowed never again to have anything to do with him. In coming to this decision, she felt a release, and yet sadness, because in cutting him out of her life, she knew she was cutting Mags out, too.

This left her feeling further bereft, but she was so tired, and the blessed relief of sleep called to her as the vehicle trundled along. Not even the clanging of its bells could keep her from drifting off.

The feeling of hands on her had her opening her eyes. 'I'm the doctor. I'm just checking you over. You've been very lucky, from what I have heard, and very brave, too. Everything seems fine with your baby.'

'Thank you, Doctor. Can you tell me how the girl is; she was brought here, she was in the fire and – and was anyone else . . . ? I – I know about my . . . my brother, but –'

'Yes, I'm sorry about your brother. I understand he didn't get out. But there was no one else injured in the fire, or any other deaths. They found a man and a young girl, on the lawn at the back of the house. The man had carried the girl to safety. Both were fine, if a little shocked. The girl you saved is badly burned and in shock. She faces a long road to recovery, but she will recover. She has her young man with her, and he is helping her. Now, I think you are well enough to go home. There is a man in reception – a Cyrus Harpinham. Is it all right to let him in? He says he is your friend.'

The relief Flora felt, knowing that Cyrus was here, had the effect of breaking down the barrier she had put up to prevent acknowledging the true horror of everything that had happened. She couldn't answer the doctor's question; she could only stare at him, without really seeing him.

'Nurse! She's going into shock: wrap her up, and elevate her legs. She's breathing all right at the moment, but give her oxygen if there is any sign of that deteriorating.'

Knowing what shock can do, Flora tried to keep calm and breathe slowly and deeply to steady herself. Inside, she wanted to scream out and rid herself of the tight knot of emotional pain that clutched at her, but she knew that to do so would leave her out of control, and she needed to fight.

'That's better, love; your temperature's back to normal and you've stopped shaking. I reckon you're all right now. You helped yourself with your breathing technique. Where did you learn that?'

'It's a long story, Nurse, a very long story.'

'Well, I've no time for one of them, but it stood you in good stead. I'll fetch the doctor to check you over, and then we'll let your friend in, eh?'

Her friend . . . My Cyrus, the best friend I'll ever have. With him by my side, I can get through this. I can.

When they got into the car, Cyrus told Flora that from tomorrow he would never leave her side. 'That's if you feel well enough to take the first step of our journey into our new future tomorrow, darling. I have everything ready.'

'I will. Nothing will stop me. Only, can we possibly go? I – I mean . . . oh, I want to, my darling. I want to go now, this very minute, but, well, Francis . . .'

'I'm so sorry, darling. But there is nothing we can do. I know you will grieve for Francis, as you have told me how good your relationship with him was as a child, but, darling, there will be no funeral, as there were no remains. And knowing what I know of Harold, no memorial service, either.'

'If there was, he wouldn't invite me. And neither will he think of the livelihoods of the staff. At least, with a sale, they could have been kept on by the new owners. I worry about them, especially Cook. I've always loved her.'

'Did she live in?'

'No. She used to, but she married. But her husband is a lot older than her, and she is the breadwinner.'

'Well, at least she has a home, which is a blessing. And we can help her. I'll go to the bank and draw out a sum of money and we can drop it in to our solicitor, with instructions to give it to Cook. He can tell her that it is from you, to tide her over till she gets another position.'

'Oh, darling, you're so thoughtful, thank you. With that done, I can go with a clear conscience. Although Cook does need more than money; she needs support, after what she witnessed yesterday, but I will have to hope that her husband can give her that. I think she will understand that I had to leave, as she knows more than anyone what I have suffered.'

'Good girl, thinking of yourself for a change. Sometimes we have to. We and little Freddy – and our unborn child – are the important ones now. It has to be so. No matter what happens, no one is ever going to part us again.'

'Will our sin corrode us in time, Cyrus?'

'We were sinned against, especially you. I won't let guilt at our situation enter me at all. I love you. You are my wife, and nothing else, and yet you are everything . . . everything. I can't live without you, and that living has to be complete – we have to be as one.'

'Oh, Cyrus, I'm so glad you feel like that, because it is the same for me. Finding out about our relationship means nothing to me, because who we are is nothing to do with that. We are husband and wife, and I love you dearly.'

'That's that then. We must make a pact never to speak of this again, ever!'

'But the children: will they have to know?'

'One day it may have to be addressed, but I hope not. I hope they grow up as French citizens and never learn the truth. And as long as no one who would harm us ever finds us, then there is no reason why they should ever know.'

'There is one thing that I worry about, darling. I have read that children born of incest can be defective in some way. Alice wasn't, and nor is Freddy, but our unborn child . . . I am afraid.'

'Don't be, Flora. I think that as our first two were fine, that must show we haven't done any harm by coming together.'

Flora snuggled into Cyrus. It felt so good to be held in his arms. All her worries left her as she thought about how God would view them. What was meant when the words *Let no man put asunder* were spoken at their wedding? Innocent then of the truth of their birth, had they done wrong? At this moment she didn't care. She had a lifetime of being with her Cyrus, and that was all that mattered.

EPILOGUE
France, 1920

~

Flora, Cyrus and Freddy

A New Life Is Forged

Chapter Thirty-Seven

'Freddy, I've brought your nephew, Freddy, to meet you. How I wish you could be here to meet him properly.'

Flora felt Cyrus's arm round her shoulder. Freddy's little hand clasped hers, as she read the inscription on the cross marking her brother's grave: 'Frederic Hatton, Private. Essex Regiment – killed in action 1916.'

'Doesn't the cemetery look lovely? The French people have done our soldiers proud.'

Flora nodded; she knew this was as painful for Cyrus as it was for her, and that he was trying to distract himself from the emotions that threatened to overwhelm them both.

Flora's mind showed her her time with Freddy, from first meeting him on the station all those years ago, to when she held him in her arms as he died. A young man, barely sixteen years old, but a brave soldier.

After a moment they turned away. This was the most difficult thing for Flora to do, because what had just happened was like a final goodbye.

Cyrus didn't speak as they got into the car. But as they

drove away, his chatter was about vineyards, and in particular the *Phylloxera* bug that had all but destroyed the wine industry in France some fifty years previously, and which had left many vineyards deserted. This gradually helped Flora to think of other things than the pain of those she had lost. His enthusiasm was inspiring and gave her hope for their future.

'The agent that I wrote to replied, with a particular vineyard for sale in Languedoc-Roussillon in south-west France. He said that at one time it was the best in the region, but the family never recovered after the *Phylloxera* epidemic. Sadly, the stress killed the father, and the son took his own life. The wife went back to her family in Spain. The vineyard has been run by two tenants since then, but neither really had the funds to restock it properly, and so it is now for sale. I'm very excited to see it, Flora. There is a chateau that is in need of repair, and ten acres of land.'

'Will this *Phyll*-whatever-it-was come back?'

'Very unlikely, as they now graft vines from North America onto the natural French vine. These North American vines are resilient to the bug.'

'How did you learn so much about it all, in such a short time?'

'It isn't a short time, darling. It has been a dream of mine for many years, since we studied the subject in our botany class. I became fascinated by how a little bug can destroy thousands of vines. That led to my interest in the whole process of wine-making. It hasn't been an all-consuming interest, as my music has always been that, but a sort of hobby that I enjoyed reading about. And then, in the prisoner-of-war camp, there were some French officers. With me being able to speak the language, I got along really well with them. One, Monsieur Raynard d'Olivier, was from

Languedoc. We spoke for hours about vine-growing. His family owns a vineyard. Sadly, he died of dysentery. I vowed that one day I would visit his family and tell them of our friendship and how it helped us both.'

Flora put out her hand and laid it on Cyrus's knee. 'The lives of so many have been torn apart.'

'Yes, darling. So many gone. But those of us who are left must build a new world. Remember, they are saying that the war was the war to end all wars, so we have brought peace to the world. Now we have to make it an even better place.'

The French countryside sped by – areas that looked green and peaceful, but that had seen thousands of deaths in their fields.

It was two days later when they arrived in the Languedoc area. The vineyard they were to look at was in the village of Laurens in Hérault. The houses of the village were large and would once, Flora knew, have been painted white, and their windowboxes would have been full of trailing flowers. Now paint peeled from their closed shutters, and bricks showed through, where once plaster had covered them. Every house was in need of a fresh coat of whitewash.

Some children were playing near a three-foot-high wall. The boys were dressed in dark all-in-one suits, with the trousers flaring just below their knee. The girls were mainly in navy-coloured frocks with high necklines and long sleeves. One boy had a hoop and stick and was trying to keep the hoop running along the road, while the others laughed at his antics.

It was a welcoming, if shabbily attired group as the children ran towards them when they pulled up, all of them excited to see such a car in their village. And maybe the first car they had ever seen in their lives, as there was no sign of any other vehicles. A horse and trap were tethered to a fence a short distance ahead, but that was all in the way of transport that Flora could see.

Cyrus got out and answered their questions, making the children laugh and promising them a ride in the car, in return for the many favours he would need as they settled in. 'The first favour is for you to take me to the house of Madame Ferrouk, as we are to lodge in her house.'

The children shouted, 'Let me show you', 'I know Madame Ferrouk' and 'This way – follow me.' One enterprising young boy said, 'Let me sit in your car and take you there. These others will take you along the paths, but I will take you the route of the road.'

This seemed the best offer, and so Juan Felipe started his friendship with them.

'My family is from the other side of the Pyrenees, in Spain. But my father came here looking for work.'

'Did he find work?'

'Not yet, Monsieur. But he is a fine wine-grower. His father – my grandfather – lost our land to gambling. He was not a good man.'

Neither of them commented on this, as the boy looked forlorn.

'Here it is, the house of Madame Ferrouk. I'll help you with your bags.'

'Thank you, Juan. We are staying for a few weeks, so no doubt we will see you often, and I would very much like to meet your father. I may be able to offer him work in the future.'

When Juan left them, he had a shiny coin in his hand and a big grin on his face. 'I will tell my father that you wish to see him. He will be here quicker than a hare can run away from his gun!'

They both laughed at this.

Madame Ferrouk's house was a three-storey building and stood on a corner, with views towards the village, but a backdrop of the magnificent Pyrenees in the distance. Flora caught her breath with the excitement that overcame her, and for the first time in a long while felt a deep happiness and peace enter her. She looked at her Cyrus, his tall, handsome figure climbing the steps to the house, and thought how very much at home he seemed. Eagerness and hope shone from him. How much he deserved them to. They had been through an abyss of misery, separation and loss, but now they had the rest of their lives in front of them. Those lives were shaped by their past, but they were also full of promise. They would work hard to build a better world for their family.

She didn't dwell on how fractured that family was, but thought of all they had to look forward to: being together in a place where no one could hurt them or point the finger at them.

Flora clasped little Freddy's hand and held her ever-increasing stomach with her other hand as she climbed the steps. Hope filled her heart for their new beginning. At last the happiness she had been seeking was firmly within her grasp.

Letter to Readers

Dear Reader,

Thank you for taking this journey with me; I hope very much that you enjoyed Flora's story in the first in The Girls Who Went to War trilogy.

My research for *The Forgotten Daughter*, and the whole trilogy, took many turns. I had previously visited the Somme and Dieppe, where I trod the path of many of the theatres of war. But though this immersed me in a sense of the place, it sadly didn't give me much of the story of the women who went there to nurse. The only evidence that they had been there was a picture hung on the wall of a museum of a nurse being presented to the King on his visit to the area.

I hope there is more of a recognition of the hundreds of young women who valiantly went to France, and many other parts of Europe, to nurse the injured, and that it was just me not finding it. However, I did feel enriched in their history, by taking this trip, as I stood on the same ground that had once run with a river of blood, and was aware of the shadows of tent hospitals where the wounded were tended.

But, for the details of a voluntary nurse's life, I had to rely on searching the internet, where there is a wealth of stories to draw inspiration and information from. One piece in particular gave me the basis for this trilogy, a starting point of the friendship between the girls. It was the diary of Miss Esmee Sartorius, a nurse who took the journey to Brussels that Flora, Mags and Ella take. It can be found at http://www.firstworldwar.com/diaries/august1914.htm and is a story that fills you with admiration.

The next book in the trilogy is *The Abandoned Daughter*. This is Ella's story, from when she and Flora parted, leaving Ella in the thick of the action in France. It sees her become part of a team who provide medical care nearer to the front line, and then takes her journey into her past, following both the harrowing and the uplifting events that take place in her life. This is scheduled for publication in Spring 2019.

At present, I am writing Mags's story, *The Wronged Daughter*, which will conclude the trilogy. That, too, begins from her parting with Flora, and takes us on Mags's journey through changes in her life that have far-reaching consequences. Of all the girls, Mags was the most changed by the Brussels experience. And it is her regrowth that we witness as she takes on life after the war: a life of disappointment, betrayal, sorrow, but ultimate fulfilment. This is due for publication in Winter 2019.

However, the story doesn't end there, as the tragedy of the first half of the twentieth century saw the world flare into another conflict, far greater in its impact on the lives and infrastructure of the home front in Great Britain. This is the time of the sons and daughters of Flora, Mags and Ella, a war that will pit sibling against sibling, break hearts and ruin lives as, brought up in what is to become Vichy, the so-called free France, they take different sides in the conflict. I will be writing this spin-off to the trilogy next. Possible publication will be spring 2020.

If you enjoyed this book, do keep the others in mind for future reading, but also visit my website to learn more about my books and me: www.authormarywood.com

You can also join me on Facebook. My page www.facebook.com/HistoricalNovels is a lively interaction with my readers, with laughter and love in abundance, as well as all the latest book news, competitions and guest authors. I would love to see you there.

Much love to all, Mary x

Acknowledgements

An author is nothing without her editors and I am blessed to have the wonderful Wayne Brookes and his team, and Samantha Sharman and her team, at Pan Macmillan publishers taking care of me and my work. Along with freelance editor Victoria Hughes Williams, they take my creation and make it sing off the page.

To these I can add my son, James Wood, who reads my work before I release it to anyone. James finds the areas where I should have put more drama, or should cut as not needed. He suggests scenes that could be added, and after carrying out his suggestions, I feel confident in sending my manuscript out to my publisher to begin its journey.

And, besides editors, others within the Pan Macmillan team work very hard on my, and my books', behalf: publicist Kate Green and her team tirelessly arrange book signings, press releases and blog tours, and make sure I am taken care of while carrying out these events. And the sales team, who work so hard to get my book shelf-space.

Thank you to you all, from a very grateful author.

And thank you, too, to my agent, Judith Murdoch, who

is always there for me and always encouraging, as her signature words 'Onwards and Upwards' testify. Judith, you are simply The Best.

To my darling husband, Roy, for his love and support. And our children, Christine Martin, Julie Bowling, Rachel Gradwell and James Wood, their partners and the beautiful grandchildren and great-grandchildren, and added family they have given me. And to my Olley and Wood families. All of you give me support, encouragement and above all, love. You all enrich my life. Thank you.

And to those not involved in this book, but who saw me to this point with their editing and book designing skills in my self-publishing days. You are never forgotten; without you I wouldn't have made it this far: Rebecca Keys, Julie Hitchin, the late Stanley Livingstone and Patrick Fox. Thank you.

But no acknowledgement is ever complete without giving my thanks to my very special readers. Especially to those who follow me on Facebook. Each and every one of you brings so much to me. Your eagerness for every book is such an encouragement, seeing me through many hours of writing. Your help with promoting me and my books is invaluable to me, and here I must mention two of you in particular: Beverley Ann Hopper and Anna Saul. Both go above and beyond to recommend my work, by sharing my posts, creating their own for me, and making sure all my news on events and book releases is spread far and wide. But all of you inspire me and bring so much to my life, by sharing yours with me and helping me in so many ways. I wish I could name you all. Without each and every one of you, there would be no 'Author Mary Wood'. You help me to achieve my dream. Thank you.

My love to you all x

If you enjoyed

The Forgotten Daughter

then you'll love

The Street Orphans

by Mary Wood

**Outcast and alone –
can they ever reunite their family?**

Born with a club foot in a remote village in the Pennines, Ruth is feared and ridiculed by the superstitious neighbours who see her affliction as a sign of witchcraft. When her father is killed in an accident and her family evicted from their cottage, she hopes to leave her old life behind, to start afresh in the Blackburn cotton mills. But tragedy strikes once again, setting in motion a chain of events that will unravel her family's lives.

Their fate is in the hands of the Earl of Harrogate, and his betrothed, Lady Katrina. But more sinister is the scheming Marcia, Lady Katrina's jealous sister. Impossible dreams beset Ruth from the moment she meets the Earl. Dreams that lead her to hope that he will save her from the terrible fate that awaits those accused of witchcraft. Dreams that one day her destiny and the Earl's will be entwined . . .

'Wood is a born storyteller'
Lancashire Evening Post

Available now

Brighter Days Ahead

by Mary Wood

War pulled them apart, but can it bring them back together?

Molly lives with her repugnant father, who has betrayed her many times. From a young age, living on the streets of London's East End, she has seen the harsh realities of life. When she's kidnapped by a gang and forced into their underworld, her future seems bleak.

Flo spent her early years in an orphanage and is about to turn her hand to teacher training. When a kindly teacher at her school approaches her about a job at Bletchley Park, it could turn out to be everything she never realized she wanted.

Will the girls' friendship be enough to weather the hard times ahead?

Available now

Tomorrow Brings Sorrow

by Mary Wood

You can't choose your family

Megan and her husband Jack have finally found stability in their lives. But the threat of Megan's troubled son Billy is never far from their minds. Billy's release from the local asylum is imminent and it should be a time for celebration. Sadly, Megan and Jack know all too well what Billy is capable of . . .

Can you choose who you love?

Sarah and Billy were inseparable as children, before Billy committed a devastating crime. While Billy has been shut away from the world, he has fixated on one thing: Sarah. Sarah knows there's only one way she can keep her family safe and it means forsaking true love.

Sometimes love is dangerous

Twins Theresa and Terence Crompton are used to getting their own way. But with the threat of war looming, the tides of fortune are turning. Forces are at work to unearth a secret that will shake the very roots of the tight-knit community . . .

Available now

All I Have to Give

by Mary Wood

When all is lost, can she find the strength to start again?

It is 1916 and Edith Mellor is one of the few female surgeons in Britain. Compelled to use her skills for the war effort, she travels to the Somme, where she is confronted with the horrors at the Front. Yet amongst the bloodshed on the battlefield, there is a ray of light in the form of the working-class Albert, a corporal from the East End of London. Despite being worlds apart, Edith and Albert can't deny their attraction to each other. But as the brutality of war reveals itself to Albert, he makes a drastic decision that will change both Edith and Albert's lives forever.

In the north of England, strong-minded Ada is left heartbroken when her only remaining son Jimmy heads off to fight in the war. Desperate to rebuild her shattered life, Ada takes up a position in the munition factory. But life deals her a further blow when she discovers that her mentally unstable sister Beryl is pregnant with her husband Paddy's child. Soon, even the love of the gentle Joe, a supervisor at the factory, can't erase Ada's pain. An encounter with Edith's cousin, Lady Eloise, brings Edith into her life. Together, they realize, they may be able to turn their lives around . . .

Available now

Proud of You

by Mary Wood

**A heartfelt historical saga with a
compelling mystery at its heart.**

Alice, an upper-class Londoner, is recruited into the Special
Operations Executive and sent to Paris where she meets
Gertrude, an ex-prostitute working for the Resistance Movement. Together they discover that they have a connection to
the same man, Ralph D'Olivier, and vow to unravel the
mystery of his death.

After narrowly escaping capture by the Germans, Alice is
lifted out of France and taken to a hospital for wounded
officers where she meets Lil, a working-class northern girl
employed as a nurse. Though worlds apart, Alice and Lil
form a friendship, and Alice discovers Lil is also linked to
Ralph D'Olivier.

Soon, the war irrevocably changes each of these women
and they are thrust into a world of heartache and strife
beyond anything they have had to endure before. Can they
clear Ralph's name and find lasting love and happiness for
themselves?

Available now